# OVER THE LINE

# PRAISE FOR OFF THE EDGE

**So Tense.** I have just finished *Off The Edge*. What a story, I could hardly bear to read the final chapter. The book has really alive characters who you can imagine, and vivid descriptions so you can really visualize the landscape. I can't wait to read the next. I remembered a lot about the land and wilderness, and I could just feel it as if I was there. So, so Good! *Gayle Comeau*

**Really gripping.** With many novels, you have to read a bit to get into them. With *Off The Edge*, the prologue kind of hits the reader...like a fish biting on a hook... All the action really sustained my interest. I also liked how the subplots intertwined and came together. Very interesting characters. This has to be a series! *Ginny McCuen*

**Wow**! I really got into the complexities of plot and simply couldn't put it down. Read well into the very early morning. It's an edge of your seat suspense thriller with a complex plot that unfolds with seemingly unrelated events in multiple locations. It presents unique challenges for the cast of heroes to discover and solve in order to rescue and save innocent lives that are in mortal danger. The ending appeals to even the romantic female reader, which is unusual for most plots in the thriller genre. *Jeanne Rex*

**This is** one of the most exciting books I have ever read. I couldn't put it down. I had to know what happened next as I got caught up in the search by Jim and his buddy Brush, first to find the Pasayten Killers and then to work out how to stop the spread of the virus. I liked the parts in the wilderness. I'm not a scientist but I found I was gripped by the science. Then when we got to a wild car chase through Seattle followed by a great gun battle and helicopter chase. The end left me wanting to know what happens next. *Doug Dunlop*

## PRAISE FOR OVER THE LINE

**This book had me gripped from page one**. I like the variety of characters & the ways they find of dealing with a whole host of difficulties & experiences. It's nice to meet some old friends from Off The Edge & see them change & develop but this book stands on its own. As always with Randall Perry one of the most intriguing aspects of the novel is the way in which very different worlds are woven together in one exciting narrative. *Jan Good*

**I** really hate that Najma. *Betty Rhodes*

**Having enjoyed Perry's first book** *Over the Edge* in his series about the secret missions of Jim Johnson, Assistant Head of the State Department's Biological Warfare, I looked forward to reading his second *Over the Line,* knowing it would be good entertainment during the 6 hour train ride ahead of me. I was not disappointed. In his inimitable style, Perry hooked me at once with his prologue (just as he had done with his prologue in *Over the Edge*) and I read the book in one sitting, unable to put it down. I was unprepared however for the attachment I would develop to his characters. There is depth and feeling in this second book as Perry carefully develops and crafts his characters further. Throughout this book, Perry lets us almost live in the shoes of his characters, to involve us in his soul-searching study of good and bad and what makes people do what they do. *Catherine Fosnot*

# OVER THE LINE

RS PERRY

*To special people, mountains and countries.*

# Prologue

A brightly colored gecko scurried across a whitewashed adobe wall. Pedro followed it, moving only his eyes, not wanting to make a sound. His brother, three sisters, mother, father, and cousins were crowded around their deep-grained wood dining table. The upper ridges of the barren table were smoothed to satin by years of oil, plates, and hands. Pedro clutched his older sister Maria with both arms as he watched the gecko. His big brown eyes followed the green gecko as it moved slowly across the wall. Neither Pedro nor the gecko knew why the family was gathered; neither cared. Pedro was a child and infinitely more intelligent than the gecko but neither had had a choice. The gecko was there because of some indefinable primal urge to be there rather than somewhere else. Pedro had been told to be there and to be still. He obeyed.

'You are being stupid, Miguel. You have not thought with your head, only your penis,' said his cousin as he slammed his fist on the table.

Pedro jumped, the gecko jumped.

'You will watch what you say while in my house, Roberto. Your language offends the women as it should,' said Don Pablo sternly.

'You talk of civilities when you should be trying to save yourself before it is too late,' said Roberto. 'Madre Dios, you are without brains. I come here to warn you only because you are family. They will kill you. Miguel must get away, disappear, vanish, and then perhaps they will let the rest of you live.'

'You should be ashamed,' said the don. 'You should not work for such men.'

'We should all stay poor or be priests or pretend the world is a good place? It is not so. It has not been so for a long time,' said Roberto, knowing he was getting nowhere with Don Pablo.

The don was a good man and a good father and he believed others were also good. He often said that everyone has some good in them. But he didn't know or understand the people Roberto worked for. He would never understand what Roberto was risking his life and livelihood to try to tell him.

Roberto stood and looked around slowly at his brother's family, his cousins and aunt. 'I have warned you; there is nothing else I can do. Miguel will never be with El Padrino's daughter. The boss will never allow his daughter to be with a Mexican, let alone a lowly Yaqui descendant.'

No one except the don dared to say anything to Roberto. He was their cousin, their family. He was also a feared member of the Siastra drug cartel where he was known as Roberto La Cuchillo, The Blade. His family had never seen the things he had done but they had heard of them.

Pedro continued to watch the gecko. He wondered if he could make the little lizard a pet to keep his old yellow mutt company. He called his dog Rojizo, because he was covered in red, dusty soil much of the time. As the years went by, Rojizo spent more time sleeping, sprawled on the warm earth, than he did playing. Everyone said Rojizo, the rust-colored dog, came from north of their village, just over the border. Pedro couldn't remember. He had been just a baby when Rojizo came to live at his home. But no one really knew how the dog had arrived in Tubutama, their village. It didn't matter, he was here and Pedro loved him.

Najma stood quietly a hundred yards west of the small adobe house. She was content, as there was no danger for her here. Only the scent of brush and warm earth touched her senses. The danger was for those inside the house—Miguel, Don Pablo, and their family. The danger was what would happen to them in the next few hours.

The five cartel men she had brought with her waited silently in a shallow arroyo, fifty yards behind her. Behind them, a ribbon of yellow cottonwood trees snaked away into the darkening night.

The gunmen had no remorse for the pain they had inflicted on others or would inflict tonight. Whether they were natural psychopaths or whether time had blunted their feelings did not matter, they were heartless killers. Men-boys with sterile futures. They belonged to their cartel. Emotion rarely had a place in their thinking. Death was an everyday part of their existence. But then, there was this woman, Najma. If they ever felt anything, it was fear for her. She had the devil in her. *El diablo es temido por todos.* 'The devil is feared by everybody,' they would say. They remained still and silent, as she had ordered.

The small adobe house sat alone outside the village. Close enough to walk the dusty road into town but out of sight and sound from others. Perfect from Najma's point of view. No one would hear the family's screams. She walked back to the men and felt their nervousness, maybe even fear, as she approached. It pleased her. All of them were tougher, harder, and certainly stronger than she was.

Why would such men fear her? She knew the answer: she always found a way to make it personal. She sensed her victims' weaknesses and took not just their lives but their pride, their self-worth, and their humanity. Killing someone was easy. Taking away everything was not. These men killed, it was their job. But Najma killed for the power it gave her. If death came too quickly, she felt deprived of the control she had over others' lives. She wanted to see into the minds of her victims and watch the struggle between their hope and pain. They never seemed to understand that she was not like them. Her victims had compassion and believed, as Don Pablo did, that there was some good in everyone. But Najma knew they were only her puppets, onstage until they had played their parts.

'Take your positions now,' she ordered. Three of the men walked off into the darkness. They would use their cell phones to alert her if anyone approached. Najma speed-dialed the other two men. Their phones stayed silent but lit up as the call was received. She had instructed them to hold their phones in sight. Her phone was set to vibrate. She wanted her hands free. Communication could have been done in many ways but Najma always had her own way. The men didn't question her, they obeyed, just as Pedro did inside his home.

She watched them go and then she walked toward the house, followed by the two remaining men. The old family dog, Pedro's Rojizo, was slow to sense the intruders. He lumbered up on his old joints to defend his territory, to do his duty for his family. But before he managed a warning growl or bark, Najma shot him in his old, dusty, red-yellow head with her small, silenced 22-caliber carbine.

Najma felt as one with the little 22 nestled snuggly into her shoulder. She even liked the little rotary clip that fit flush in front of the trigger. However, the small carbine looked like no other gun, with the breech encased in a bulbous, custom-molded plastic polymer that reached all the way to the end of the silencer. The plastic covering made the breach silent although the low velocity sub-sonic bullets were quiet enough without the addition of the silencer on the barrel. The lightweight gun had everything she wanted. It was quiet and the small bullets injured but without much shock. Carefully placed bullets gave her the control she wanted. A large caliber was not only impossible to silence but also hard not to kill with. She wanted damage without causing shock and death until she was ready.

# Chapter 1

Thousands of yellow aspen leaves floated and swirled to the ground in the November breeze. The warm weather and the rare lack of October wind and rain had left the tiny leaves clinging to their branches where they would normally have fallen much earlier in the season. A few of the yellow leaves drifted to where Jim sat on the six-sided deck he had built five years earlier. Suspended on tall posts in a small grove of quaking aspens, it floated among the tree trunks and leaves like a tree house. He had interrupted building on his house to construct a series of decks and stone planters that descended twenty feet into the grove of trees and wild roses. He then cantilevered the deck with some support posts into the trees.

A hundred yards farther down the canyon, a river of yellow aspens trailed for nearly a mile, following Wolf Creek to the valley below. The yellow of the trees was the same as the yellow in the far south of Arizona where Heather was camped with JT, and farther south still, in the arroyo, where Najma had approached Don Pedro's house.

An artesian well gushed from the ground just below the house watering the trees surrounding the deck before going underground and then rising again on top of a bed of green clay giving life to the ribbon of yellow trees, which snaked down to the valley below.

He sat alone, thinking and remembering. Over the past ten years, the deck had been a favored spot to have coffee and lunch with Duane and Craig. They had often sat here between bucking hay, feeding animals, and building fences. Duane and Craig had been hired to work on the ranch but they quickly became more than employees, they were friends. They were good people, as were their families. The leaves twinkled in the sun, greenish leaves clung to their branches while ripe yellow leaves drifted down. Old leaves, dead brown leaves, rustled and shifted on the ground around the tree trunks.

Jim felt a connection to the aging leaves still clinging to their trees. His friends Duane, Brush, JT, and the general still held fast to life, although they, too, were perhaps not as green as they had once been. But knowing that Craig would not sit with them again added a melancholy note to the rustling sound of brown leaves settling under the wild roses.

Jim looked up and to his right at the house and its large window wall. The house was not big but the sixteen-foot-high windows, made of dozens of three-foot wide by eight-foot tall panes stacked two high, provided a spectacular view west to the North Cascade Mountains. The view from the house and the tree-house deck were the same, except quaking aspens framed the deck's view while the house stood clear with only mountains and sky around it.

It was one of the few times that he had the ranch, and its solitude, to himself. His mind drifted to past times when he had first stayed here in the small homesteader's cabin that was just visible lower down the canyon along the edge of the trees. He had once stayed there in the dead of winter in subzero temperatures with only a small woodstove. The isolation in the canyon crusted over with snow under blue skies had been a wonderfully serene time. The beauty and peace of that stay never left him. Neither had the old planked outhouse behind the cabin. In the freezing temperatures it made for a chilling adventure when he needed to use it.

It was the first winter after he had purchased the 1200-acre ranch. He didn't know it at the time, but the aspen grove he was looking at was one of the largest in eastern Washington State. He heard a soft high-pitched whistle mixed with caws and turned to look back up toward the head of the canyon and Wolf Mountain. The hills a few hundred yards behind the house rose steeply. Soaring high upon the wind was a bald eagle, with several crows flicking in and out, pestering it. The eagle seemed to accept the crows' harassment and paid no more attention than a bear did to honeybees.

He thought about Heather and JT in Arizona on their special project. He wished he could have gone with them. Today he seemed to wish a lot of things. He watched a lone inky-black cloud on the horizon. It was the cloud's singularity that drew his attention. He watched it change shapes as it drifted lazily along in front of a dimming, gray-blue, twilight sky.

Jim thought back to when his friend and old graduate mentor, Simon, had discovered the inky-black fungal clumps that Heather and JT were now collecting. He and Simon had been looking at desert-varnished rocks with a hand lens when they noticed hundreds of small black dots speckling the surface, especially visible on smooth, white quartz rocks when the little bundles of black balls crowded into tiny fractures. Geologists hadn't documented them before. They weren't interested in the outside of rocks: they wanted to break them open and see the fresh inner crystals.

It was some time later that JT's microbiology department at the University of Washington started to show a real interest in the black microcolonial fungus, or 'blackberries' as they had been affectionately nicknamed and which Heather still liked to call them. As part of JT's budding interest in astrobiology they had been irradiating bacteria to see which might survive in space the longest. Most of the bacteria could be killed in a few hours. On a whim one day a graduate student had said, 'Let's see how long the desert fungus, MCF, will last in the radiation chamber.' After two weeks it was still thriving. They couldn't kill it.

Jim allowed his thoughts to roam between the ranch views, old times with Duane and Craig, the Arizona desert, and Heather, now out in the desert collecting MCF with JT. But the pleasant memories stopped abruptly as his mind floated back to Vietnam. To the village where the two little girls had been killed with their mother. Their eyes still haunted him. But the memory dissolved as a coyote sauntered forty feet in front of him, across the knoll in front of the house.

He stretched back, putting his feet up on an empty chair, contented again, sipping a gin and tonic, his and Heather's favorite drink, lulled by the peace and serenity. Duane had taken Betty Lou, his wife and sometime ranch employee, to visit their granddaughter in Bend, Oregon. They had a new thirty-three-foot RV, and had been looking for an excuse to try it out.

With Heather and Duane gone, the ranch felt as lonely as it did peaceful. The fall chores had mostly been finished before they left. It was all the more lonely as Craig had always been here on the rare occasions when Duane was away. Jim thought of one of Heather's favorite places, Horseshoe Basin on the Canadian border. The basin would now be snowed in for the winter. The subalpine firs would be spires of green projecting from the vast fields of glistening snow. They had never been to the basin in the winter but it must be beautiful, he thought. Perhaps sometime they could go.

Memories of the basin brought back the grizzly discovery of Craig's body in the gravesite near its edge. The Pasayten Killers had rolled through the basin and ruthlessly killed Craig, Whitie, and three horse packers. Najma had tortured Craig before killing him. With sudden realization, Jim thought Craig would not be here this winter to plow the roads with his old blue Jeep CJ-5. The ranch would not be the same without him.

Loretta, Craig's wife, had not yet been able to accept Craig's murder. She barely communicated, even with her best friends, Betty Lou and Duane. However, a teenage boy, Ben, the only survivor of the Pasayten killings, had assumed the role of her protector. He did the chores and lived in a small room in the barn. For Ben, it had become his home. He was happy living there, needed and appreciated.

Jim took another sip of his drink as the sun settled behind the top of Oval Mountain, the tallest peak in his view. His pleasure, enhanced by the gin and tonic and the knowledge that Heather was safe and happy, was marred only by his thoughts of the terrorist that had gotten away—Najma. She was out there somewhere, waiting for him. He felt her presence now just as he had at the campfire two months ago in Horseshoe Basin.

The terrorist plot against Seattle had failed. However, it was all too obvious, Jim thought, just how vulnerable people were to attack. Not only in the US but throughout the world. The solutions were not guns and strength but finding ways for people to live in peace. The government's solution—his government and employer—was to make rules, restricting people's freedom. To invade and conquer: it didn't help. He knew his job was essential because there were evil people in the world that needed to be stopped, just as there were good people that needed to be protected.

While he might wish for a peaceful world, one thing would never allow it to happen: the people he and Brush, his friend and partner, faced did not want peace; they wanted power. There were many times when a hazy depression settled over him, as he realized that the adversaries he and Brush went after were no worse than many of the politicians in the so-called civilized governments, including his own. A small plume of dust a half-mile away interrupted his wandering thoughts. It would take several minutes for the approaching vehicle to crest the small rise above the long flat stretch of road they called the speedway. When it finally appeared, the vehicle took Jim by surprise: it was a blue Jeep, Craig's Jeep.

When it got closer, Jim could see two heads through the Jeep's window, but couldn't tell yet who was inside. He waved anyway. Whoever they were, he would know soon enough.

'Jim, hey. How you doing?' shouted Ben as he waved at Jim through the trees.

'Nice to see you, Ben,' Jim called back. No one called him 'young Ben' anymore. He was a grown-up now, first taking responsibility for Loretta and now here he was driving Craig's Jeep. Ben smiled at Jim as he walked up; he liked plain Ben better than he liked young Ben. Even more of a surprise, it was Debbie and not Loretta trailing along behind Ben.

The pair walked between the aspen grove and the house, dropped down three stone steps and a wooden step before reaching the deck. Jim stood and gave Debbie a hug and clasped Ben's shoulder.

'If there were three things I didn't expect today, it was to see a blue Jeep, you, Ben, and you, Debbie. Quite a nice surprise three times over,' said Jim.

'Loretta said I should have Craig's Jeep,' Ben explained proudly. 'I'm going to get the plow on soon and I'll plow out at the house and… if you'll let me, plow the roads here?'

Jim studied Ben for a second. He was proud of the boy and happy to see him in good spirits, especially after what he had witnessed in the basin. Maybe the young were better equipped to get on with life after such harsh events. Maybe Ben just buried it better than many adults he knew.

'The Jeep suits you, Ben, it has character. I'm glad Loretta gave it to you, and I'm sure Craig would have wanted you to have it. You're welcome to plow here. Glad to have you do it. If you have time and would like to work up here with Duane some, I'd be glad to have you do that, too. You know how Duane hates to work alone. It would be good for him.'

A big grin appeared on Ben's face. Not only did he want to, but being asked to work on the ranch was a sign that he was respected and wanted. His parents hadn't had much interest in him. Then he became friends with Craig. Now he had Loretta, who depended on him, a home, and a job. He knew that Jim and Heather were really particular about who they allowed to work around the animals on the ranch. He felt proud.

'I'd like that, Jim, thank you,' said Ben with complete sincerity. 'I'll work hard and try to be as good as Craig.'

'Would you like a Coke, Ben? Debbie, maybe a drink?'

'A Coke would be good,' said Ben.

'If you're having a gin and tonic, I'd love one, too,' said Debbie.

A few minutes later, they were all sitting on the deck.

'Heard anything from Brush?' asked Debbie.

Jim had suspected that Debbie was here to find out about his partner. However, he didn't have anything he could tell her, at least not anything she would want to hear. And he was not about to get involved in Brush's love life, if he could help it. That would be a full-time job.

'He's in Seattle, why don't you call him?'

'I guess I want him to call me, but he hasn't,' said Debbie.

'Wish there was something I could say, Debbie.'

'I don't mean to put you on the spot, Jim; I just wanted to know if you had heard from him.'

'He's fine,' Jim said watching her and feeling more than just a little sorry for her. She was a nice woman and he hated to see her upset. Falling in love with Brush was a sure way to end up hurt. For a few weeks in September Jim thought that maybe Brush had found someone to have a relationship with. They seemed good together and Debbie was certainly as attractive as any of Brush's past girlfriends. She was smart and capable and spunky. A good partner for any man. Maybe he would have stayed with her but after saving the FBI lady in the Space Needle attack, Brush started to visit her in the VA hospital in Seattle and his attentions shifted from Debbie. Jim very much doubted if Brush would ever call her again.

Debbie bit her lip and asked, 'Any more word on the bacteria? Is the general doing OK?'

Jim knew she was changing the subject. Since she had been so involved with the killings in the basin last month and the hunt for Nusmen and his killer bacteria, she had become aware of the secret Bio Warfare Center labs south of Seattle at Fort Lewis.

'The general is at the hospital on the military base now getting some further tests. He is nearly fully recovered. From what I hear from the nurses, he gets more and more demanding by the day. He has staff people in and out and is making them all cringe with his voice.' Jim fondly pitched his own voice louder than normal to imitate the general's booming tone.

Usually Jim would not be able to talk about the laboratories or even the general with Debbie and Ben, but after they had been involved and heard so much, the general had sent two judge-advocate lawyers over to Twisp with a memorandum swearing them to secrecy.

Jim still couldn't let them know any more than they had inadvertently found out a few weeks ago. He really couldn't say much about Nusmen and how the laboratories were coming on finding a cure for the vancomycin resistant bacteria that Nusmen had let loose at the University of Washington hospital.

'They're working round the clock and hopefully will be finding a solution soon,' was all he said, knowing it sounded shallow.

Debbie detected his inability to say more and again changed the subject. 'This really is a special place, Jim. There isn't any other place in the valley where you can see the Cascade Mountains and have this much privacy.'

'I always feel lucky to have found it,' said Jim. 'It was quite a fluke. It was the first property I looked at over here and I immediately knew it was special.'

'Most of the property is like mine down in the valley. This is one of the few pieces of non-government property on the east side of the valley. And you have all the lease land surrounding yours,' said Debbie.

They watched the snow-tipped mountains, the last of the sun igniting them in points of color. Above the mountains, the fall sun was hitting the bottoms of the clouds, making them glow fire-orange like the mountain-top snow.

## Chapter 2

Yousef, I want someone in the US to find out where this American agent Jim Johnson is, and also his habits. Maybe Sharon could hack into his email?' demanded Amir.

'Too dangerous to hack into anything right now. It could jeopardize our plan. It's less than two months away and we have been planning it for over a year. The more focused we stay, the less chance of failure,' replied Yousef.

'All right, so hire someone to investigate,' said Amir irritably.

'I'll find out for you, Amir, but it is a waste of time and money.'

'I'll be the judge of that, he was my brother.'

'OK, but your brother is gone and trying to make a personal vendetta out of finding this guy you *think* killed him is going to distract you from our millennium plan.'

'I won't let it; just find out the information for me, I want him dead.'

Amir opened his computer, signed on to the proxy server, and logged in to his brother's eBay account. He clicked the sell tab and listed a set of January to June 1989 *National Geographic* magazines in a stamped slipcase. The method was simple. Each placement in eBay went to the next six-month set. Previously the contact code was July to December 1988. His brother, Farasie, had a representative in the US with several years' worth of *National Geographic* and he mailed a set if there was a successful bidder.

Amir hoped that Najma would answer if she were alive. But with Farasie dead, why would she even check the eBay site? He hoped she would, he wanted her to avenge his brother's death and if she got in touch, he was willing to pay her a great deal to kill the American agent. Besides, Amir thought someone as ruthless as Najma would be valuable to have around. But Amir was naive. He didn't understand what motivated the people that his brother had worked with, people such as Najma. She didn't like being bested by anyone and so she fully intended to go after Jim, on her own with no encouragement or money from Amir. Just like the old west shoot-outs, one winner one dead.

Amir had barely escaped death himself after his brother's failed attack in Seattle. Their Middle Eastern employers had been less than happy with the money they had lost. Perhaps it was better to say the money they had not made. They had come out almost even. If they had not, Amir probably would not be having thoughts of any kind. He would be dead like his brother, Farasie.

The brothers were a good team: they had expected to make a fortune following the 'terrorist' attack in Seattle. Farasie was the mercenary with some financial skills and Amir was the financial whiz with some computer skills. They had initiated large short positions in the markets, as had Farasie's financial backers at their behest. The market had initially plummeted after the attacks, as they predicted it would, but then it recovered much more quickly than they had anticipated. They were just able to cover the short positions before the market fully rebounded, almost breaking even. 'Almost' meant that after Amir tabulated their trades they had lost several hundred thousand euros rather than millions. It was better than being wiped out completely but losing money made him nauseous.

Worse, Farasie was chased, hounded, by the American agent before he died. The two brothers had been close with no other family. They had trusted no one besides each other. Farasie's death angered Amir and left him feeling empty. He wanted revenge. He would have it.


Pedro's dog, Rojizo, lay dead in the reddish dirt next to the porch. He hadn't died in pain or unhappy. He had had a good life. He lay now where he had dozed contentedly for the last few years in a small depression near his family and Pedro.

The adobe house behind him was clean and well cared for. It belonged to poor people but ones that obviously took pride in their home. There were two slim poles on either side of the stone porch. A very old metal light hung next to one of the poles. It was unlit. The roof was covered with old, dusty, red tiles. The poles supported a metal roof that covered a small porch. There was one window and in contrast to the tan walls, there was a vibrant, shiny, freshly painted, cerulean-blue door. The window was a few feet to the left of the door and shuttered on the inside. Small streams of light passed through cracks in the dry wood. Najma stepped onto the stone porch in the front of the don's family home. She could hear male voices coming from inside.

Najma listened as she silently crept to the window. Through a crack, she could see a slice of Don Pablo's family seated around a large wood table. One of the male voices sounded familiar which puzzled Najma. A chair scraped on the floor and the familiar voice said, '... El Padrino will never allow his daughter to be with a Mexican, let alone a lowly Yaqui descendant.' She silently walked back to her two men.

'Hector, do you recognize the male voice?'

'Sí, señorita, it's the voice of The Blade. I know him well.'

Hector swore he saw a small spark of delight twinkle in her eyes.

She had planned to enjoy the evening's activities with the family but a capable opponent added a new dimension, more entertainment.

Najma walked back to the door and listened for a few seconds, and then just opened it and walked in. Startled faces looked up at her.

'What are you doing here?' asked Roberto already knowing the answer.

'I'm here to have some fun, La Cuchillo,' she taunted him.

Hector Luis walked in and stood behind Najma. The other man stayed in the entrance. Roberto looked at Hector, his fellow cartel member for so many years, but did not receive an acknowledgement, nor even eye contact. Roberto silently cursed his brother for forbidding guns in his house.

Don Pablo started to get up. 'Sit back down, old man,' ordered Najma.

Hector raised his machine pistol and Don Pablo realized he had no choice. It would be better to obey. Surely the woman was here only to talk to them, lecture them about his son's passion for the cartel leader's daughter. After all, nothing had happened between them.

Roberto knew differently, he knew why they were here. He pulled out his knife. Maybe he could take the woman if he moved quickly. He tried to close the eight feet between them. Najma was holding the small 22 carbine at her side, pointed at the ground. She casually raised it 45 degrees, almost in slow motion, and shot Roberto near the top of his left knee.

The low-velocity 22 bullet was ultra-quiet and small. Nevertheless, the damage tearing through Roberto's cartilage forced him to the floor. Najma moved closer to him, watching his face; she raised the rifle, looked down the barrel at his right hand, his knife hand, and pulled the trigger. The knife slipped from his fingers to the floor. Roberto knew he was defeated and now his only hope was that she would finish him fast. The family hardly stirred. The silenced rifle was so quiet that what was happening hardly made sense to them. It certainly didn't make them jump but their cousin was on the floor bleeding. He must have done something wrong and the cartel had come for him.

They would soon be forced to face reality, as would Roberto. The end had come for all of them and it would not be quick, that was not Najma's way. As callous as Hector and the other cartel assassins were, the carnage that followed made them wonder what the woman Najma was made of. She didn't kill people, she stole their minds and souls. Even Hector would come under her control before the night was over. Perhaps she really was the devil.

Najma looked at the small boy, Pedro. 'Is that your dog outside?' she asked in a monotone.

Pedro, wide-eyed, nodded.

Najma turned to the man in the doorway. 'Bring the dog in.'

He hesitated for a fraction of a second before complying.

As Najma looked away Roberto tried to move his uninjured hand to the knife, but Najma saw him and casually shot him in the left shoulder. Then she aimed at his left elbow and shot him there too, then two more shots: one to each foot. Roberto was completely helpless now. Najma looked into his brown eyes and saw what she wanted, what she lived for. She smiled a little.

Then a girl, Don Pablo and Rosita's youngest daughter, Pedro's little sister, screamed. Najma turned toward the sound and unhesitatingly shot her in the head. The gunman reentered and dumped Rojizo on the floor near the girl's lifeless body. Pedro started to cry. Pedro's older sister Maria covered his face and mouth. The green gecko watched but with no more compassion than Najma for what was happening.

Najma knelt over Roberto. She took his razor sharp knife and cut away the buttons. His shirt fell open. His eyes followed the tip of the blade as Najma slowly traced a line from Roberto's shoulder across his chest to his belted pants then momentarily stopped. She watched his eyes as the knife penetrated easily through his skin. Then she retraced along the incision and cut through fat and finally his stomach muscle, exposing his intestines. Another sister screamed. Najma stood and looked into the young girl's eyes and then slowly raised the small gun watching her wild look of fear change to acceptance and then nothingness, death. Roberto watched as his intestines spilled from his stomach. The evening progressed under the uncaring eye of the gecko. The lucky ones were the ones that screamed and died quickly. There were not many. A scream meant death. With silence, there was hope but it was a forlorn hope.

Emboldened by the shooting of his daughters and brother,

Don Pablo tried to grab Najma but she easily knocked him to the ground. His family was dying before his eyes. He could not grasp that a human could do this to other humans; he could not believe this was the end of his family.

Miguel, however, was the reason Najma was here, this six-teen-year-old that had dared to think romantically about the daughter of El Padrino, the second in command of the cartel but its de facto head. El Padrino did not look like the mixed blood mestizo that he was, as lingering Spanish genes had asserted their influence and El Padrino had grown tall with light skin. When he became powerful in the cartel, he had carefully chosen a fair-skinned European to marry. He would choose the same for his daughter, Mary, his only child. His light-skinned grandchildren would have no physical connection to his Mexican roots.

After being informed of Mary's brief encounter with Pablo's son and the boy's subsequent interest, El Padrino had chosen to simply eliminate Miguel and remove any possible hindrance to his plan. He was no more or less important to El Padrino than a gnat was to the green gecko. He ordered Najma to take care of the lovesick boy; an example would serve to highlight to other males that his daughter was off-limits. If she killed the family as well, it was no concern of his.

Najma's evil was rooted in sex, something she had experi-enced only as a girl when she was raped by the man her father had given her to. She had killed that man for his trespass, her first time. And in that moment, as she stood remorseless over his dead body, she had understood the power of both sex and violence and their primal connection. She had felt it coursing through her.

'Come here to me, Miguel,' she commanded. He walked to

her, timid and frightened. 'You want to live, don't you?' she asked. As he nodded she looked into his eyes, searching for a glint of hope surfacing through his fear. Then she looked at Maria, the one remaining daughter of Don Pablo.

'You want to live also, no?' she asked.

The fourteen-year-old girl looked at the floor and managed to say softly, 'Sí.'

Najma reached up and smoothed Miguel's dark hair. She touched his arm and then trailed her fingers down his side to his thigh. She dragged the back of her fingernail down the metal zipper of his jeans, undid his belt and slowly pulled the zipper down. Miguel reached to stop her.

'I thought you wanted your family to live,' said Najma. She turned to the only girl still alive, Maria, Miguel's young sister, and casually walked to her, looked into her large brown eyes, and raised the gun.

'No,' yelled Miguel. 'I will do whatever you want.'

Najma returned to him and smiled. She touched his lips lightly, moved back and looked at him, then caressed his hair and put his hand on her ample breast. She moved forward again and kissed him softly and then deeper and more aggressively. Her open eyes stared into his, willing him to respond.

Miguel was a typical boy with far too many hormones. Najma reached down and felt his penis. He was hard and throbbing as she knew he would be. Were the spasms from fear or excitement or both?

She pulled the top snap on his jeans. His pants fell to the floor. She held him about the waist and turned back to the young girl. He was exposed, erect before his whole stunned family, all shocked but too afraid to speak or cry out.

'Take off your clothes,' she said to the young sister of Miguel. The girl, trembling with fear, complied. 'Now turn around, hands on the table, and bend over. That's it. A little sex is better than dying, isn't it.' She walked Miguel to the table, kissed him, caressed him, and then moved him behind his sister. She reached between the girl's legs and rubbed her slowly while guiding the boy into position. Miguel's mother crossed herself and looked away as her daughter let out a muffled cry of pain.

Miguel was only a young boy, sex dominated over right and wrong, his brain had no place in the equation. He was appalled, he was embarrassed, but his throbbing, sixteen-year-old penis would not behave. It stayed firm. There was no stopping it. He was a virgin, she was a virgin, his mind was swirling; he couldn't help himself. He was overcome with sensations he had never felt before. She, his sister, felt only a deep sickness, both for what was happening to her and for her future. She was paralyzed with fear, self-loathing, and embarrassment. Only jumbled thought-fragments formed in her mind; ruined, worthless now, no man would want her, disgusting to her family, to herself. She wished she had screamed and died.

But Don Pablo had had all he could endure. He leaped at Najma just as his son lost control. Najma turned and shot Don Pablo in the stomach. She watched impassively as he fell to the floor. His wife went to his side, cursing the she-devil. Najma shot her in the back as she held her husband. She then casually replaced the rotary clip in her carbine.

Miguel was standing in a daze. Najma took out her knife. She looked at Miguel and said, 'This is what happens to boys that try to fool around with girls that they shouldn't. A message from El Padrino.' She grasped his limp penis in her left hand. Miraculously it started to get firm again. She kissed him and with a quick flick of her wrist cut off his member and tossed it on the table next to where the naked young girl still stood. Miguel fainted and dropped to the floor. The girl's tears spattered the coarse wood. She was frozen, she couldn't move, moving would expose her more. Being still, she was invisible. Her mind was in turmoil rolling over and over with no connection to her body.

'Hector, take care of Miguel.' Leering, Hector shot the boy twenty times on full automatic. This he was good at. The boy was the one they came to make an example of.

Najma turned to the daughter still frozen at the table and asked her if she wanted to live. The girl said nothing, knowing she was about to die. She was not afraid. She wanted death now. Najma pulled the girl upright by her hair and slowly ran her finger across her cheek. Looking into the vacant eyes of the traumatized young girl, Najma sneered and said, 'You're a woman now, perhaps Hector will enjoy furthering your education. You shall live.'

The Blade, Don Pablo, and his wife Rosita lay in pain, helpless on the floor. They were alive still but hope had faded from their eyes; an end to the pain of life and release from this hell on earth was all they wished for now. The fun and excitement ebbed from Najma, she had tired of this place. She straddled Don Pablo, looked into his eyes, and shot him in the chest, watching as he died. Rosita still clung to her husband's arm and Najma watched the distraught woman's reaction for a few seconds before she shot Rosita in the head. Then she smiled at Roberto, who looked at her blankly. 'Hector, take care of him but make sure the girl has some fun.'

Only Pedro remained untouched.

'Come here, boy.' The boy came to her and looked directly at her with gecko eyes. Najma lowered her gun and took his small hand. She looked at Hector and the other man. 'Stay as long as you like. Make certain they are both dead before you leave,' she said. Still holding Pedro's hand, she walked out into the starlit desert night.

In the days that followed the massacre, the village was in a state of shock. It was more than many could bear. The cartel would stop at nothing. It was rumored that it was a cartel woman who was responsible for the atrocities. In hushed tones, she was referred to as La Serpiente and El Diablo. The villagers were afraid. Some packed their meager belongings and left the village, while others stayed, but the joy of their simple existence here was tarnished. Some blamed the don, as people do. He should have controlled his son.

# Chapter 3

Heather and James Taylor, JT, sipped Starbucks coffee on the crest of a saguaro dotted hill, in the White Tank Mountains, northwest of Phoenix. A soft breeze wafted up from the ravine below their campsite. Pungent air and birdsong filled the evening breeze. The sun had just set. To the west, nearly touching the horizon, there was a small point of light.

'I'm used to seeing Venus at sunset but we don't often get to see the planet Mercury,' said JT.

'Beautiful, isn't it, all the stars and planets,' responded Heather easily.

JT gazed at the distant orb, smaller than Earth but larger than the moon. 'Mercury's an interesting planet. I never really thought much about it until the last couple of years, when we started to consider space settlements on planets.'

'I thought Mercury was too close to the sun, too hot for life?' said Heather. Then in her usual way of asking a second question before the first one could be answered, 'It couldn't have any water either, could it? How could you live on it?'

JT was tired but he knew he had to assuage Heather's curiosity. 'It's incredibly hot and cold but might be tolerable in a twilight zone and there's lots of water ice in craters near both poles. You could always build a settlement belowground, possibly in a lava tube,' said JT.

'I don't get it, JT, water ice? And what do you mean, stay in the twilight zone? There isn't much gravity either, is there?' Heather managed to get three questions asked back-to-back.

'You sure you want to know all this?' asked JT.

'You bet,' said the ever-curious Heather.

'You should come and listen to some of our seminars at the U; but if it's OK with you, let's talk science tomorrow. We'll have all day. It's just nice to sit here with you and relax away from work.'

'I always think about you as just the microbiology professor but now you're into the grand things in the universe, not just small microbes. I'm impressed, JT.'

JT felt a little embarrassed, as he was a humble person by nature. 'Well, I've learned some new science since the university got involved in the astrobiology program and with NASA. And you, Heather, should know just as much or more than I do since Jim has his degree in it.'

'Well, I guess I should, but since we are apart so much, we don't seem to have time to talk a lot about much other than the llamas and the ranch,' said Heather wistfully looking at the twinkling sky.

'Guess the whole reason the two of us are here now is because of Jim and Simon,' said JT. 'But these days I don't get to see enough of either of them. It was great when Jim was still a student at the university and we all first met. It was also my first experience outside of microbiology; working with Simon and Jim in the geology department. Seems like things got too complicated for all of us after that. Simon's planetary exploration lab got busy and he became the department chair. Then Jim graduated and we drifted into our separate lives.'

'JT, you sort of got busy too and became famous after the Legionnaires' deaths.'

'Jim, just as much as me,' said James Taylor. 'That first notoriety brought Jim to the attention of the State Department. They recruited him and I chose to stay in academia. Guess we all just got too busy to spend much time together. Glad at least you and I could come out here to work though, Heather. Maybe all of us can do this sometime. It would be nice to get Jim and Simon out here in the desert.'

'Would be, but our record of getting together is not so good lately. Look at what happened in September with our llama packing trip. But perhaps that's all the more reason to try another one, maybe next summer,' she said. 'Jim might have come with us this time, but he's still caught up in finding the woman terrorist. He doesn't say much but I can tell it's on his mind.'

JT decided it was time for a subject change. 'Besides stars, planets, and sleep, I'm looking forward to collecting some fungus tomorrow.'

'I still like to think of those little fungal balls as blackberries,' she replied.

'Yep, that name stuck for years until Jim called them by their more proper Latin name in his master's thesis. When was it? About 1985, when Simon and I named them microcolonial fungus and that caught on.'

'Think I'm going to crawl into my sleeping bag, JT. We have a lot of those little black fungal balls to pluck off the rocks tomorrow. What fun,' she said, and meant it.

'Good night, Heather. Think I'll just sit here and watch the stars for a while.'

'See you in the morning then. Maybe I'll make us some fry bread.'

That certainly made JT happy. Nobody made fresh fry bread like Heather. *What a treat,* he thought, *but not so good for my midsection.*

JT looked up at the white band of the Milky Way and felt at peace with himself. Having Heather's partner, Jim, as both an undergraduate and graduate student had changed the direction of his life. Before Jim had approached him about being his adviser, JT had spent most of his time looking at culture plates and staring at bacteria in his microscope. He enjoyed every minute but later the whole exobiology topic blossomed when it was renamed astrobiology and embraced as an important area of study by the National Aeronautics and Space Administration. He was now the head of that program at the University of Washington in Seattle. He had moved from being an environmental microbiologist to an astrobiologist but in his heart he was still a microbiologist. A big change, maybe not as big as the big bang made to the universe he was looking at, but a big change to him nevertheless.

*I'm just a tiny speck,* he thought, as he often did. Nearly *every point of light above me is a sun bigger than our sun.* There are billions and billions of suns in our galaxy, as Carl Sagan was famous for saying, and it's just one of billions of galaxies. It kept him humble. It kept him who he was: nothing more than a collection of small bits of evolved chemical compounds on a tiny blue planet in a big universe.

# Chapter 4

Najma felt nothing as she opened her computer. No remorse, it was not something that occurred in her thoughts. Out of habit she opened eBay and was amused to see the correct series of *National Geographic* for sale. A code to contact Farasie. She wasn't concerned about who placed the advertisement. She would acknowledge seeing it on a proxy server. The email she sent would not be traceable to her computer's IP address. Her message was simply, 'Yes?'

It would be up to the person placing the ad on eBay to post a more explicit message. Farasie had probably left instructions with someone on how to contact her. She was curious who it would be but knew she would find out soon enough.

Amir saw the 'Yes?' and followed the next set of instructions left by his brother. He sent an email through a proxy server asking how to contact her. Najma responded that he just had contacted her and to say who he was and why he was doing so.

Amir wrote back that he wanted to discuss rewarding someone connected to his brother's work last September. Najma thought about this. She knew of the existence of Farasie's brother but had never had any contact with him. But he obviously knew how to contact her. She wrote back, 'I am going to be in Mexico City on business in two days. Perhaps we could meet?'

She had no idea where he was located in the world, but assumed that if he was serious he would be able to get to Mexico City. She didn't want him to know where she was at this point, but Mexico City was far enough away and it probably was Farasie's brother. Still she would be careful.

Amir quickly checked the flights and found a direct flight from London Heathrow to Mexico City. He wrote, 'I can be there the day after tomorrow. I will stay at the airport Hilton and we can meet there.'

Najma thought about whether she should take some men with her. She decided that she didn't want anyone to know what she was doing or who she was seeing. She would take care of this herself. She would leave tomorrow, which would give her a day to observe the hotel. If anything was not as it should be, she would notice. She would dictate the exact location and time for the meeting.

Najma sat in the lobby of the hotel. She was wearing a light brown, short-haired wig, a tan suit, and platform sandals. She carried a briefcase and appeared just like so many other busy business travelers. The lobby had a cold austere atmosphere with modern furniture placed in groupings. The air-conditioning was too high, making it colder yet. She watched the concierge and particularly the men at the reception desk. She wanted to get a feel for their mannerisms and what type of personality the hotel hired. She would check on them several times this evening and again in the morning. She would recognize if someone seemed out of place before her meeting. After twenty minutes, she got up and walked to the newsstand, purchased an *International Herald Tribune,* and walked to the elevators. She watched the lobby and saw nothing that did not seem as it should be. She took the elevator to the fourth floor, got out, and then walked down the stairs to the second floor and her room, 216. There was no one in the halls and no one had followed her.

Carelessness was not one of her usual traits, but this time she was watching for the wrong people. She had not noticed Carlos and a woman seated in the bar. Mexicans had not entered her thought process. She was looking for Caucasians or Middle Easterners. Najma had assumed she could come and go as she pleased but the cartel didn't trust her. They survived because they didn't trust anyone. As soon as she said she was leaving for a few days, a group was assembled to find out where she was going and for what reason. In fact, they were more than just a little curious. It was the first time since she had come to them two months ago that she had left the compound without other cartel members.

Najma was not a trustful person. However, she usually worked with Farasie and people she had known for a long time. While she did not trust the cartel, she misjudged how little they trusted her as a newcomer.

The cartel was investing plenty of resources in finding out what she was doing. Six men and two women were now in the hotel. They had rented four rooms on her floor, one on either side of hers, 218 and 220, and also room 217 directly across the hall. The fourth room was next to the stairwell on the first floor. It served as their headquarters, a room where they could come and go without her observing their movements.

While she was in the lobby, they had been busy inserting small audio-visual devices in her room. Directly across the hall they had installed a micro-monitor in the peephole, to observe who was at her door.

When Najma returned to her room, the first thing she noticed was the piece of lint she had placed in the keyhole was missing along with the tiny ribbon of dark colored paper she had secured between the door and the doorjamb. The next thing she saw was a robe and slippers placed on the edge of the bed with a welcome note card signed by the manager.

The cartel's men were experienced and assumed that she might have taken precautions. They had bribed a woman in housekeeping in order to obtain a key and the robes. The woman recognized their manner and assumed they were cartel, or possibly police, it was sometimes hard to tell the difference. She didn't care. She took the money but she would have given them the key and robe without payment. By the time they left her, she was certain they were cartel, Norteños from the north region, next to the United States.

The cartel members expected no less than obedience; even though the money meant nothing to them, it meant everything to the underpaid housekeeper. It was her fate; alive but poor. She and her co-workers shifted between alternate realities. They moved between the wealthy at the hotel, poverty at home, and those with power— the gangs, police, and their bosses. They coped with the hostile world they lived in by never allowing their minds to grasp its realities. They drifted through their days, doing their work—if they were lucky enough to have work—and attending their families. Tomorrow would be just as yesterday, a panorama of sameness. A niche existence separated and sheltered from a big world that was experiencing a kaleidoscope of change, approaching the year 2000.

The cartel members came from much the same background. Their alternating realities were between their families and their chosen path: uncaring killers; loving sons. Both the maid and the cartel members were mestizos. Most Mexicans were mestizo, a mix of Indian and Spanish. Almost eighty percent of Mexicans were from a crossing of that blood. However, they grew up in different regions acquiring different beliefs. The maid instinctively disliked her northern blood-relatives, the Norteños. The cartel from the north and the Pacific regions equally disliked the Mexico City residents, the Chilangos.

Najma was appeased by the robe. It was just housekeeping. Her mind and body had gone on full alert at the door. Now all that lingered was a residual edgy feeling. She inspected her room and saw nothing else out of place. She considered changing rooms immediately, but decided to wait until morning as she had originally planned.

She went out several times, observing and committing to memory the staff that she saw. Nothing raised her suspicions. Her instincts were normally good—and she observed nothing abnormal.

This waiting ritual bored neither her nor the cartel members. They both spent much of their lives doing nothing, the lulls spiked with infrequent episodes of violent action. They slept, waited, and awoke to the same morning light. The sun rose orange, refracted and reflected by billions of particles ejected by engines and factories.

Najma observed no changes in the morning that aroused her suspicions so she proceeded as planned. She walked to the check-in desk. 'I wish to change rooms.'

'Sí, señorita. Hay un problema?'

'No problem. I would prefer to be on the first floor.'

It was a problem for her observers, however. They also needed to shift rooms and set up again, but there was only one room available next to Najma. One would have to be enough. They did not want to become conspicuous by forcing Najma's new neighbor to leave.

She moved rooms; the cartel redeployed. Najma checked her email. At three-fifteen there was a message to meet 'Gabe' in room 514 at five p.m. Najma sent a message back that she would arrive at the bar in the lobby at four o'clock and he should meet her there. She had planned to change the meeting to an outside location but there seemed to be no reason for the extra caution.

Najma walked through the lobby immediately after leaving the message. It was the same bartender as when she last looked. The concierge was the same. The reception staff was the same. She saw no observers. There were men in suits but none seemed to linger. Families and couples moved in and out with bags. No one looked suspicious.

She looked outside the entrance and again saw nothing suspicious. She moved to the opposite side of the street where she had a good view of the lobby and could see the door into the bar.

The cartel team was unhappy about the room move but happy that something seemed about to happen. Najma was acting suspicious. They called the cartel lieutenant, Raul, who had accompanied them to Chilangolandia, as they referred to Mexico City. Raul was not the smartest member of the cartel. He would never be its leader. But, he was ruthless and effective: an enforcer.

It was, however, uncomfortable to have Raul so close, he was demanding and would be critical if anything went wrong. They could pay with their lives; Chilangolandia was as good a place to die as any but they would prefer to die fighting as men, rather than by Raul's capricious hand. Perhaps even worse, if they made a mistake, Raul might let the devil-lady punish them. They saw no good outcome for this particular job. Nevertheless, they had their orders and one way or the other it would be over soon.

Lena and Cheto sat in a taxi at the front of the hotel. They watched Najma leave the building, cross the boulevard, and stand next to an old building in the shadows. It was nearly four p.m. Che, as Cheto was nicknamed, ordered the taxi driver take them around the corner just as two men walked through the door into the bar. One man disappeared inside. The other walked back and stood a few feet inside the lobby. Najma watched them just as she was being watched. Che and Lena had left the taxi and were walking back toward the hotel entrance, wearing different jackets and sunglasses they had extracted from their briefcases.

Najma crossed the street nearly bumping into them and entered the lobby. She sat down on a sofa. Che telephoned the other couple in his crew who were now sitting only a few feet from Najma and asked what she was doing.

'Just sitting,' replied the man.

'Stay there for another two minutes, check your watch, and then go outside as if you are waiting to meet someone,' ordered Che. 'Let me know if she moves.'

Najma waited until 4:10. She saw nothing amiss. The second man, standing outside the bar entrance was obviously a bodyguard. He was not trying to be inconspicuous. She did not like entering the bar and having her exit blocked by that man but she could handle him. They were all the same: big men, confident in their strength over a woman and always unprepared for her. She was well armed but planned to use only pepper spray if nothing stronger was required, so as not to attract undue attention.

She approached the bar door. The bodyguard moved only slightly. He watched her but stayed in his position. Najma stood in the door, searching the room. Seated near the back on the right side was a lone man. Farasie's brother?

He stared at her as she walked directly to the table. She was watching the bodyguard in the bar mirror. He hadn't moved. As she neared the table, Che and Lena walked to the bar and ordered a green tinted drink and a beer. It bothered Najma that they came in at the same time as she did, but they seemed completely engrossed in each other and never once looked her way. They didn't seem connected to the bodyguard or Farasie's brother, if he was the brother. In a few minutes she would have the answer to that question as she continued to approach him.

'I am Gabe; sit, please,' said the man as he held out his hand. Najma took it. It was dry and he didn't seem nervous. She watched his eyes. She looked at his coat for the telltale bulge of a weapon. The coat was tight and tailored—perhaps it was in his belt or ankle.

'Hi, Gabe,' she said with a becoming smile. 'You do look a bit like your brother, a little taller maybe, but I could have sworn Farasie called you by a different name.'

He smiled. 'I am Amir. Almost all of our lives, my brother was the taller one.'

'Why did you want to see me?' asked Najma.

'Were you there when my brother…had his accident?'

'I was there, I was watching.'

Amir felt certain that this was Najma. He had seen a picture of her and the height and facial features were as he remembered, not the same but similar. She was a sexy-looking woman, he thought. Very attractive but a cold aura surrounded her. He couldn't describe it but he could feel it. No warmth. Flat unblinking eyes. She appeared completely unafraid.

Najma also was fairly certain that this was Farasie's brother. He fit the mental description she had. She would let him talk more though and see if he said anything that raised her suspicions.

Amir seemed to know that she needed more verification. He spoke for a few minutes about their childhood, giving Najma facts he hoped she knew, convincing her of his identity.

'Let's walk a little,' she said.

They got up and walked out of the bar. She put her arm through his and they headed toward the lobby door, just as any happy couple would. They walked outside and stood talking but still she did not see anyone suspicious. Najma steered them back through the automatic door and walked to the elevator. Inside, Najma pushed the sixth floor button. Amir didn't say anything.

Amir's bodyguard watched them go into the elevator then walked over and pushed the up button. His plan was to ride to the fourth floor and then walk up one flight and observe from the stairwell to see if anyone followed his boss and the woman to Amir's room where he was certain they were headed.

Raul's white Yukon pulled up outside the hotel. He had two men with him. Che walked from the lobby to the spotless new SUV and got in the backseat with Raul, grimacing to himself as he thought his boss had even more hair growing from his ears and nostrils than just a few days ago. Secretly they called him La Mosca, the fly, but they were very careful never to be overheard; Raul would kill anyone he heard saying it.

Raul said nothing, just looked at Che.

'The woman is cagey,' said Che. 'We were all set up but she switched rooms this morning. But our surveillance is set up again and she just met a man who has one bodyguard with him. Apparently, he has a room here at the hotel. They went up a few minutes ago followed by the bodyguard. Her elevator stopped on floor six but the bodyguard went to floor four,' said Che.

'Fuck this, Che. Too much work, no results. Leave someone monitoring her room in case she goes back to it before we find her. Get over to the desk and find out what room the man is in. Then send someone to find the bodyguard and take care of him.'

The nervous clerk, recognizing Che's manner, didn't hesitate to give Che the room number of the man he thought they were looking for. It was on the fifth floor. He also gave them a key to another room on that floor. Che sent one man up each stairway and another up the elevator, giving him the key. Two minutes later, Lupe called Che. 'I heard a cough on the stairs close to the fifth floor.'

The man Che had sent on the elevator had gone to the fifth-floor room. He stayed, observing, just inside with the door ajar.

Che called him and asked, 'How close is the room to the east stairwell? Can you see anyone or anything?'

'Nada,' whispered the man.

'OK, stay put. Lena and I are going to get off the elevator and walk down the hall. Stay ready by your door. Lupe is going up the stairs. We'll have the bodyguard between us.'

Amir's bodyguard, Musa, watched the couple get off the elevator and walk toward his position at the top of the stairwell. He didn't see anyone else. He was relaxed, there was no one else around. But he hadn't heard Lupe come up the stairs behind him until he turned, hearing 'psst.' Six feet away was a man pointing a large chrome revolver at him. He thought about trying to make a run for Amir's room. The thought evaporated as he sensed someone else now behind him in the hall.

'Tranquila, señor, be very calm,' said Che. 'Move down the stairs.' They walked the man down. Musa saw no opportunity to escape and no chance to warn Amir of the danger. They stayed three meters in front and also too far behind him. Musa tried slowing but the man behind just smiled, maintained his distance, and told him to keep going. The woman made a call on Che's cell phone.

'We'll be there in a few seconds,' she said as they continued their descent to the cartel's room. The door to 114 swung open as they approached it. Musa walked inside with the others. There were six men and the woman in the room. Escape now looked impossible and his captors looked crude and hard.

One man, the man clearly in charge, walked up to him. His breath stank of garlic. His face was pitted and had several small scars. He was not quite as tall as Musa, possibly five feet ten inches, but he was stocky and barrel-chested. He had thick dark hair covering his bare arms. The matted growth extended onto the back of his hands and fingers.

Raul silently stared at the man and then said, 'Tell me who you and your boss are and what you are doing here.'

Musa knew there was no escape but he hesitated before answering. The hesitation cost him. He was hit with a vicious blow from behind to his kidney. He arched back in pain and Raul slammed his hairy fist into his stomach.

'When I ask you something, you will answer right away,' commanded Raul. 'What is your answer?'

Musa answered slowly as the pain clouded his mind. Another mistake. He was almost paralyzed by a blow to his right kidney.

He managed to gasp out, 'We're from London and friends of the woman.'

'Keep going and fast. Names and what you do, who you are associated with, and why you are here to see her,' commanded Raul.

Musa's head was spinning and he didn't know that much. 'Amir is my boss's name. He is a businessman from London and he came to visit the woman.'

'What does he want with the woman?'

'I don't know,' answered Musa. He wasn't holding back, he really didn't know.

'What is his room number?'

'Five fourteen,' grunted Musa immediately.

'Bring him,' ordered Raul.

They walked out of the room and down the corridor. There were pictures hung along the hall and next to the elevator a framed portrait of President Ernesto Zedillo. Raul spat on the carpet in front of Zedillo and said, 'Fucking punta.' He hated the man in charge of the country and just like his underlings he hated Mexico City, it was full of chilangas and pochos, Americanized Mexicans, just like upper-class Zedillo.

When they reached the fifth floor, he ordered three men to room 514. The first man quietly inserted the passkey they had gotten from the maid. The door made a tiny click.

Amir was getting a scotch from the small bar and Najma was standing near him, away from the door. The click was enough for Najma to jump behind Amir and pull out her nine-millimeter Beretta.

Three men rushed in, guns drawn, only to face La Serpiente pointing a gun at them from behind the Middle Eastern man. Najma recognized a man called Lupe. If she hadn't recognized him, he would have been dead along with the other two.

'What do you buttheads want?' she asked calmly.

The men lowered their guns, they didn't know what else to do. From behind them, Che looked in the room.

'Put your gun down, Najma. Raul wants to talk to you.'

'Let him talk then,' she said to Che.

'When you lower your gun and put it on the bar,' said Che.

The four cartel members had spread apart a little. Che raised his gun slowly and pointed it squarely at Amir. He motioned the others to keep their weapons down. Najma lowered her gun and set it down within reach.

'All right, Raul,' said Che.

Musa was pushed in first, prodded by Carlos, and followed by Raul.

Najma looked at Raul and thought what an ugly man he was. It only took a fraction of a second for her to realize the cartel had followed her. *I should have thought of that. Why would they trust a newcomer, even one that does their dirty work?*

Raul walked straight up to Amir. With a hairy fist, he grabbed Amir's custom-tailored shirt and crumpled it. The foulness of Raul's breath momentarily distracted Amir from thoughts of his fine shirt and then Raul's breath disappeared behind a wave of total pain. His testicles felt as though they were in a vise.

'Now, Mr. Biz Man, tell me who you are and what you are doing...' but the rest of the sentence trailed off as Raul felt a cold metal barrel pointed against his head. Najma had dropped her Beretta onto the bar but she always carried backup weapons. She held a small-sized 45-caliber gun to Raul's left temple.

'I guess you don't trust me, Raul. I do your dirty work for you and you should trust me, but I can understand why you don't. Move to the side, Amir.'

Everyone stood still. Che knew Raul would kill this woman for doing what she just did. Raul, in his mind, was already watching her die a long, lingering death. No one pulled a gun on him—especially not some foreign-devil punta.

'I know this will upset you, Raul, but Mr. Amir here is a friend of mine and I don't like the way you are asking him questions. Just ask him nicely and he will tell you,' said Najma as if she were in charge.

Najma wasn't worried about what Amir would say as the story was not only plausible but would be the truth. 'I just did. I don't like to repeat myself,' spat Raul. 'Take your gun away and we'll start over.'

Amir felt sickened with the pain. He knew he had better start talking. If this Raul thought he was not telling the truth he was certain he would be in a lot more pain regardless of Najma's help. 'She worked for years with my brother. He was hired out to do tasks for people, mostly in the Middle East and Russia.'

'Fucken' asshole, pinche culero,' Raul said under his breath. 'Tasks don't mean shit to me. What does that mean? Spit it out or I'm done asking nice.' Raul glared at Najma as she moved the gun away but still pointed it at him.

'My brother was a killer, a mercenary, a terrorist for hire. One of the best. We were close, even for brothers. He was killed a couple of months ago in north America.'

'Pendejo, stupid ass,' hissed Raul. 'Where do you think you are? Mexico is North America.'

'It was way north, near Seattle, where he was killed.'

Najma cut in, 'Everyone was killed.'

'Except you, eh?' said Raul.

Najma knew she would kill this hairball sooner rather than later. *I will not give him the chance to kill me.*

Amir continued, 'I contacted Najma using my brother's method. I want to avenge Farasie's death and Najma is the one who can do it. There's an American agent responsible.'

'Two American agents,' added Najma.

'What business are you in?' asked Raul with a little less aggression.

'I take care of money for wealthy clients.'

'You launder money, amigo?'

'Sometimes, yes,' said Amir reluctantly.

'Che, call the airfield and tell them we'll be ready in thirty minutes.'

Che nodded at Lena, who made the call.


The King Air twin-engine stood on the tarmac. The steps were down. Raul told his two men to go in first, followed by Che and another man. He wanted the two men and Najma separated from the pilots. He sensed that what he had heard was the truth: he would check it out with his FBI source in the US.

Raul glanced at his captives. He had few worries about the two men causing him any trouble. Musa could barely walk and looked near death, and the other, Amir, was inept physically. Perhaps he was, as he said, a businessperson. Najma was the danger. He didn't like her, maybe because she scared him a little. Was everything as she said it was? They hardly ever had a woman in any other capacity than for sex or housework. He thought about her body. *Yes, perhaps I will fuck her before killing her.* She had been useful so far but there was a never-ending supply of warm bodies to fill their ranks. She was of no account to him and now she had insulted him in front of his men.

The King Air C90-B, had been cleared to taxi without any hesitation by the tower, and rapidly proceeded toward the runway. Raul had left the two women and the rest of the men to drive the vehicles back. The plane was full but still under its load capacity. The twin-turbo engines had been modified to just over 600 horsepower each, and it could cruise at better than 350 miles per hour. It would still take at least three hours, depending on wind, to return to the hacienda.

Raul was sitting behind Najma. He had his gun pointed directly at the back of her seat. Lupe sat across from Raul and also kept his gun pointed toward Najma.

She wasn't concerned about them. Raul would wait to try to kill her under different circumstances. It would not be gratifying to him to kill her fast in the plane, he would choose a later time and a more drawn-out method.

Even with the quiet four-blade props, the light twin was better suited to sleeping or thinking than talking. By the end of the flight, Raul had concluded that the English Arab was who he said he was. While contemplation and reflection were not his strong suits, experience told him that what the man said added up. They started their descent from 18,000 feet into Nogales. Musa died moments before they touched down.

# Chapter 5

Sheilla was happy with her new job, working for the general and Jim at the Bio Warfare Center. She had even started to like living an hour south of Seattle near Fort Lewis, Washington. She respected her boss and liked the staff just as she appreciated the respect they showed for her. Money was less important, all the same she was happy with the substantial boost in her pay level.

Sheilla had had mixed emotions when working for the FBI. She had liked the excitement of being a technical analyst, however, she found the male-dominated FBI moribund in outdated traditions and bigotry. Worst of all, her last boss, Stiles, was not the most intelligent guy around, which made it difficult for her. It was hard to respect a boss who seemed mentally inferior. It felt like he was always one step behind her and he often made wrong decisions.

The general, two months ago, had recognized her abilities and asked her to work at the Bio Warfare Center laboratories. He was a good man with a huge voice. She had liked him from when they first met at the University of Washington operations center during the terrorist attack on Seattle. Everyone at her new workplace was like a breath of fresh air. They were fun, kind, effective, and best of all smart—very smart. She had a lot of responsibility and at times it was very hard work, but it was worth it.

One of her assigned tasks was to locate the terrorist that had gotten away in the Pasayten Wilderness. The woman and her group had nearly killed thousands of people, including Jim and the general, who had been in critical condition for several weeks after being shot. If it had not been for the two partners, Jim and Brush, the terrorists would probably have succeeded. The FBI had been no match for the well-planned attack. It was the general's group—with some important analytical help, especially from Sheilla—that had won the day. The general recognized her ability. As was his habit, he would go to great lengths to get the best people but he didn't have to work hard to convince her, she wanted to work with them.

When the FBI operations center was first set up, its purpose was to try to stop an untreatable microbial terrorist threat to Seattle. The general was called in to run the operation, much to the consternation of Sheilla's FBI boss. The bio-threat turned out to be minor compared to what they had accidentally stumbled onto—a plan for a massive terrorist attack on US soil. Initially her job during the threat was to track the bio-terrorists. As it turned out it was not a group, but one lone man, William Edgar Nusmen. He had been jilted, had temporarily lost his mind, and was getting even with his girlfriend for dumping him. There was no terrorist threat, just one upset ex-boyfriend with special scientific knowledge and a massive lack of judgment.

He did get even. He released an antibiotic-resistant bacteria and the BWL were still working, full-time, to find an effective treatment. The most amazing part was that Nusmen was now working right here in the lab, too. Even more amazing was her surprising attraction to him. She detected in Nusmen an underlying humanity and sincerity that lacked any pretentiousness. He was clearly brilliant and that attracted her too but she was surprised by her physical attraction to him. He was tall and geeky but she just found him exciting. Men had never been of that much interest to her and she had little time for a relationship now, but maybe one day they could have coffee and she could learn more about him.

Barbara Milton, the overall lab supervisor, was also softening toward Nusmen, a man she had loathed at first but she had come to respect his intelligence and skills in the lab. At first everyone had shunned him and given him a hard time. Against Barbara's wishes, the general had saved him from prosecution for releasing the bacteria and had convinced the attorney-general that their best chance of finding a solution to the untreatable bacteria was to keep Nusmen working in the BWL under house arrest.

'Barbara, I think I might have found a trail left by Najma,' said Sheilla to Dr. Barbara Milton.

Barbara knew that the general had brought in Sheilla because of her great instincts. She could absorb copious amounts of material and filter the important components.

'Worth bumping up to the general?' asked Dr. Milton.

'Without a doubt. It has Najma written all over it. Her modus operandi.'

Barbara was not really involved in the fieldwork. The laboratory was her environment. The way things were, however, they all crossed lines. Jim was a trained microbiologist and the general an MD, but they both worked best in the field. Barbara, however, rarely ventured out of the secret underground laboratories at Fort Lewis. It was her domain and she liked being there.

'The general is back in the hospital undergoing some tests. Better call Jim with what you've found,' said Barbara.

After Sheilla called, Jim wasted no time in getting the few miles from the ranch to the Winthrop airport and preparing his twin-engine Seneca. If Sheilla thought she had found something, it was worth his immediate attention. Najma had become his focus since she got away in September. He knew she would eventually come for him but he worried that she could just as easily go after Brush, the general, or maybe even Heather. As long as she was alive, none of them could relax.

There were no local air traffic controllers or radio contact in the Methow Valley. The mountains blocked the signal at lower elevations. As he climbed above eight thousand feet, he called Seattle Radio and asked for a flight plan to Gray Army Airfield.

It was only a sixty-minute flight if he pushed the speed and skimmed the mountains. By the time Jim climbed to ten thousand feet, he was cleared to descend. Most of the short flight crossed jutting snow-capped peaks. The views never stopped amazing him, however this trip he hardly noticed them, as his thoughts were focused on Najma and wondering what Sheilla had found. Before he knew it, he was taxiing under the guidance of ground control to the BWL hangar. The large hangar sat off by itself away from the other military facilities. It was attached to an office structure that had underground parking for the BWL employees. The laboratories were entered from guarded elevators near the back of the hangar. The BWL was a massive underground structure housed all on one floor but more than six stories belowground.

Jim walked briskly through the lab directly to Sheilla's office, which was next door to his own. He rarely worked from the office and sometimes wondered why he even maintained one, but occasionally, as the assistant director, he held meetings with other State Department employees, or government and military personnel.

'Hey, Sheilla, what's up?'

'Nice to see you, Jim. You got here fast. Haven't seen you since Seattle. I still want to thank you and the general for asking me to be part of BWL. It's the best thing that has happened to me since I got my degree. And I think I might have something on Najma.'

Jim smiled at the auburn-haired Sheilla. He was just as glad as the general that she worked here now as their head analyst. If anyone could track down Najma it would be her. Jim waited while she pulled up a news story on one of her computer screens.

'A truck driver was found dead in a truck stop near the Mexico border, south of San Diego. He had his throat slit and his genitals cut off. Sounds like something our nice lady would do. But here's where it gets interesting. The truck driver had a brother. I contacted him and he said that his brother had been writing him emails from truck stops down the West Coast. Here's the best part, the night before he was killed his brother said that the truck driver called him. He said and I quote, "I struck gold, little brother. I have found the sexiest woman I have ever met. She's been riding with me all the way from Mount Vernon, Washington. She's a looker, brown hair and big black eyes. She's so good-looking, and smart too, that sometimes she scares me. I don't know why she likes me. I never thought someone like her ever would." '

'So she managed to get over the North Cascade Highway, hook up with a truck driver, get all the way down the coast to the Mexico border, and then killed him,' said Jim. 'Good work, Sheilla, but I knew you would track her down.'

'Really think it's her, Jim?'

'I do. She's slipped into Mexico probably. Let's locate her. It's your first priority. Do you need anything? Have enough people to work on this?' asked Jim.

'Thought you would say that so I've passed everything else I was working on to other staff. Bridget and Mark are going to help me full-time with finding Najma.'

It was one of the great things about Sheilla. She was always a step ahead and the step she took always seemed to be the correct one.

'I'll be in the lab, or my office. Let me know as soon as you find anything,' said Jim as he smiled at the shy, medium height, auburn-haired prize the general had stolen from the unappreciative FBI.

# Chapter 6

Heather and JT were drinking lemon and ginger tea in Professor Herman Ritter's laboratory at Arizona State University.

'Doesn't look a lot different than your labs, JT,' said Heather.

'Actually, they have more sophisticated throughput DNA analysis than we do. His culture plates and bacterial separations work automatically. Fascinating to select the microbes by color, texture, and whatever other parameters they use. Seems to work well and it is fast compared to our manual methods,' said JT.

'Bacterial remote sensing using a camera lens or micro-array, just like satellites. Since Simon told me about his work at the University of Washington on a llama-packing trip, remote sensing has started to interest me.'

'Like how, Heather?' asked JT.

'Simon and Jim were originally studying the moon and its mineralogy using mostly visible light and some infrared and UV gathered with telescopes.'

'Oh yeah, that was back when Jim first worked in Simon's lab, before I met either of them.'

'Anyway, it impressed on me that we actually don't perceive

reality the way we think. We look at things with our eyes and then call that reality but it is all just filtered through our eyes and then processed in our brain whether we look at it directly or see it through a lens or on a computer screen. In the case here, we have visible light reflected from bacteria, viewed through a camera.'

Before she could finish a small, animated group burst into the DNA laboratory. Herman was the first through the door. He was a fast-moving, and fast-thinking, microbiologist and JT's counterpart at Arizona State University's astrobiology program.

'And through infrared and UV detectors, not just visible light,' added Professor Herman Ritter. 'JT, great to see you. You should have let me know you were going to be down this way and we could have had dinner, but I don't have time now as I'm leaving for a conference in Vienna this evening and have to get my talk ready before I go.'

'Sorry, Herman,' apologized JT. 'I didn't think we were going to actually come to the university. By the way, this is Heather. She's a botanist and we're working on a desert fungus together.'

'Pleasure to meet you, Heather. This is Ralphy, one of my best Ph.D. students,' said Professor Ritter.

Heather and JT shook hands with Ralphy. 'Behind him is Kristina,' continued Herman. 'She's visiting from Woods Hole and she is going to be interested to hear what you're working on, since she's a fungus expert. And this lady is Dr. Adrijana Ljotic. She's visiting from Madison and is working with my wife on an amino-acid organic chemistry project.'

They shook hands all around. Adrijana pulled some muffins and donuts out of a bag. 'We were just about to take a break,' she said.

They gathered around a table and within seconds, questions and answers were flying. JT gave a detailed description of microcolonial fungi. Kristina was fascinated and wanted to get some samples to work with.

'Woods Hole is sending me to the Cologne Biological Radiation Hazard Center in December. It would be really cool to check out your fungi and see what their limits to radiation exposure are,' she said.

'The facilities both here and in Cologne are certainly a lot better than we have in Seattle. Let's get you some samples,' said JT.

'Would you mind if I went back up to the Tank Mountains with you and collected some? I would like to see them in the field,' said Kristina.

'Sure you can, we'd be happy to have you,' said Heather.

'If Herman will let me out of the lab, I'd like to come along, too,' said Ralphy.

'I don't mind letting you go into the field with JT; you won't be able to help learning something from him. Perhaps you could collect some samples and see if there are any bacteria associated with the fungus,' said Herman.

The group was getting excited and Adrijana started talking about the petroglyph she had heard about in the Tank Mountains. It supposedly represented a supernova in the constellation Scorpius, and had been incised in the rock in A.D. 1006.

JT and Heather both chimed in that the petroglyphs were carved into desert varnish. 'And the MC fungi always seem to be associated with the black desert varnish,' said JT.

'Wish I could go and see it,' said Adrijana wistfully in her strong Yugoslavian accent. 'But I have some lab experiments that can't be left.'

'Could we go for just a day?' asked Kristina. 'I really want to go too, but my boyfriend, his colleague Misa and I are planning on going camping south of the Huachuca Mountains in Mexico. None of us has been into Mexico. We are leaving the day after tomorrow.'

'We can easily go to the Tank Mountains in a day but I have always wanted to see the Sonoran Desert south of the Huachuca Mountains,' said Heather. 'Maybe we could all go there instead. There is bound to be MCF and desert varnish there.'

'Actually, I would find that interesting, too,' said JT. 'But are you sure it would be alright with your friends, Kristina?'

'Absolutely! It would be great. My boyfriend won't mind at all. He and Misa are consumed by a computer project. And Misa is an interesting person, she trained as a computer engineer at Oxford. They'll just be talking about computers all the time, so I could use some company. Are you sure this desert varnish and the MCF will be in that area, too?'

The question was answered by a man who walked into the room with another woman just at that moment. 'No question, desert varnish will definitely be there!' said Richard.

'Hey, Richard!' said JT. 'What are you doing here? Have you had enough of the planetary science department at U Dub?'

'They have a great imaging center here. Really state-of-the-art scanning electron microscopes. This is Nicola, by the way. She came up here to meet me from Auckland. Her special interest is silica in hot springs and she is really great with the microscopes,' added Richard. Nicola nodded to everyone as they quickly introduced themselves.

'Silica is what I'm working on with Herman's wife,' said Adrijana. 'I'm an organic chemist and we're working on amino acids bonding with silica.'

'Cool,' said Nicola. 'I'd love to talk to you about it because that probably happens in hot springs, too.'

'So what did we interrupt? Are you planning to go look at desert varnish in Mexico?' asked Richard. 'I'm interested in the stuff because it's possible it's on Mars and it is no doubt in the Sonoran south of the Huachucas that I overheard you talking about. Plenty of basalt rocks, which desert varnish seems to like as a substrate but sandstone and granite works, too.'

'We were going to go to the Tank Mountains and look at DV and MCF but we started talking about going south to Mexico to look at it instead,' said JT.

'Look, why don't you all go,' said Herman. 'Ralphy needs some field experience and he can get a department van and camping gear ready tomorrow.'

'Geologists love field trips,' said Richard. 'Do you have room for more?'

'Sure, the van can easily hold eight and gear,' said Ralphy.

'Nicola, you want to go?' asked Richard.

'Sounds like a plan. I'd really like that,' said Nicola.

'All right then, I'll call my boyfriend, Vidya, and ask him,' said Kristina. 'If Misa wants to go that makes a proper international party.' Then she looked at Heather and mouthed 'Oh Mexico.' Heather nodded and the two leaped into 'Oh Mexico, it sounds so sweet with the sun sinking low.' Then everyone but Adrijana and JT joined in.

'Come on, Adrijana,' encouraged Herman.

'But I don't know the words,' she objected. She had no idea what they were singing or why. She had been a star student in Belgrade but didn't learn English until she came to the United States on a Ph.D. scholarship. US culture and history were still foreign to her, especially pop culture.

'You too, JT, this is your song,' said Heather. 'Oh Mexico, it sounds so sweet, with the sun sinking low...'

JT looked sheepish. 'I can't sing at all,' he said. 'What do you mean it's my song?'

'JT, the artist that made the song famous is named JT,' said Heather.

JT looked perplexed.

'James Taylor, JT!' exclaimed Heather and Kristina almost in unison.

'OK, everyone, I'm out of here. Got work to do in the lab,' said Ralphy.

After Ralphy had gone, Heather said, 'He seems like a nice, soft-spoken guy.'

'He is, and very smart too, one of the best grad students I've ever had,' said Herman. 'He'll make you good company and he does need a break. He works seven days a week on his Ph.D. research and has teaching duties on top of that. See you all when you're back from "Oh Mexico"!' Herman went out the door humming and waved good-bye over his shoulder.

# Chapter 7

'Getting shot has turned out to be a lot of fun,' laughed Glenda Rose.

Jim watched Brush. His best friend was clearly enamored with Glenda. He had never seen Brush look at a woman with that sort of tenderness before.

'I can't say it has ever been that much fun for me,' said Jim.

Glenda did look great. He could understand why Brush was attracted to her. There was obviously chemistry, but it went a lot deeper than that, a synchronicity. Jim decided that Brush just plain liked this woman. Maybe he respected her abilities, too. She was well trained and possibly an equal match for him. She was a good FBI agent and they had both seen that she was brave. She had not been shot out of carelessness but rather by putting others first. Jim, Brush, and the divorcée, Sandra Fisk, had been lucky in the confrontation with Najma in the Seattle Space Needle restaurant. Glenda had risked her life to protect the innocent tourists but she had not been so lucky herself and was one of the few casualties in what might have been a true catastrophe.

Brush was the first one at her side after she was shot. He did all he could to stop her bleeding. The medics and doctors said she would not have made it even to the hospital without his care. Jim wondered if Brush somehow felt responsible for her now, as Jim had felt when he saved a small fawn from dying on the ranch. It had always treated him as her mother and Jim liked taking special care of the now adult deer. Glenda and Brush might feel something similar, a belonging. Call it what you want: serendipity had pushed them together. Would they stay together? That was long odds with Brush.

Glenda was going to be released in two days after nearly two months in the hospital. She would have some fairly large physical scars marring her exceptional body, but mentally she seemed unaffected by her experience. In fact, quite the opposite. She had a very positive attitude, the same as Brush's would have been if the circumstances were reversed.

'Did you come over to Seattle just to see me or Glenda, Jim?'

'I've seen you enough, most of my life in fact, to keep me happy, Brush. Glenda, it's really nice to see you smiling, not to mention alive.'

'Nice to see you, too, Jim. Guess we're sort of the Space Needle's version of the Three Musketeers.'

'What's on your mind, Jim?' asked Brush. 'Don't keep me in suspense.' He knew Jim wasn't on the west side of the mountains just for a chat.

'Sheilla has a possible line on Najma. Seems like it fits pretty well,' said Jim.

'That is some worthwhile news!' said Brush. 'I'd like to find that lady just as much as you and I'm sure that Glenda feels the same way.'

'A woman that fits her description hitched a ride with a truck driver who told his brother that he was one lucky guy. Said he had "struck gold." The truck driver was killed just north of the Mexico border and the woman disappeared. Timeline fits with her leaving the Pasayten Wilderness and getting to Seattle. The killing had some sexual overtones,' said Jim.

'I think you need to track her down sooner rather than later, Jim,' said Glenda. 'She's a psycho and I wouldn't put it past her to come after you.'

'She knows that we will be looking for her. The best option she has is to get rid of us and hope that everyone else lets her fade into history,' said Brush. 'What's the next step?'

'Nothing we can do right now. Sheilla is on it full-time with two other analysts. She'll find her,' said Jim. 'Think I'll leave you two alone. Take it easy, Brush, and especially you, Glenda.' He bent over and gave Glenda a careful hug and a kiss on the forehead.

'I don't think I mentioned that we are going to take a cruise to Alaska when Glenda leaves the hospital. That sort of activity, or inactivity, will be good for her for a week,' said Brush.

Jim ran his hand through his hair, turned his blue-gray eyes on Glenda and then Brush, smiled, and walked out the door. 'Keep in touch, you two.'


'This is good, better than good!' said Sheilla. 'That is, as far as finding our psycho, but tragic for the family in Mexico. I can feel it's her. She's got to be stopped.'

Jim was standing with the general at Sheilla's desk looking at a news story about the gruesome slaying of a large Mexican family in the small village of Tubutama, not far from the border town of Nogales, Mexico.

'Let's move into the conference room. Bring your other ana-lysts, Sheilla, and get Barbara in as well,' said the general in an uncharacteristically subdued voice.

The analysts presented increasing data supporting the hypothesis that Najma had left the Pasayten and made her way to Mexico. A car stolen from Hart's Pass had been found abandoned at a truck stop near Arlington, Washington. It seemed Najma had walked from Horseshoe Basin to Hart's Pass. They had not previously assumed she would hike that far. The FBI had concentrated their search in the Horseshoe Basin area, centered on the same route the terrorists had ridden on horseback a few days earlier. It was not surprising she had eluded them; the wilderness area of north Washington State is one of the largest in the US.

'The next connection,' continued Sheilla, 'is the dead trucker south of San Diego. We have not been able to find a trail from there to the Nogales area. We don't know if she crossed into Mexico at Tijuana or managed to get east to Nogales. My guess, and it's just a guess, is she slipped across the border a little farther east of Tijuana. A border patrol guard was shot on the US side, at about the time she would have been there but nothing concrete connects her to his death other than he was shot with a 38 caliber. The truck driver's brother said he thought that his brother kept one in his truck but it wasn't found. We are looking for bullet purchases and making inquiries of shooting ranges or other friends that might know if his gun was a 38.'

'Let's make it as certain as we can,' said General Crystal. 'The important part is these unfortunate deaths in—what's the village?'

'Tubutama,' said Sheilla. 'Fred has been working on that.'

Everyone looked at Fred, who wasn't used to talking to anyone. He was most comfortable communicating with his computer.

'OK, ah, it was a large family and one cartel member that were killed. It was more of a slaughter and the word is that it was the local drug cartel that carried out the murders. They are part of the larger west Mexico cartel. It's perhaps interesting that the Mexican authorities think that the cartel leader may be holed up in that area,' said Fred. 'Oh yeah, the cartel member that was killed was the brother of the father of the family, a Roberto Pablo.'

'From all the information you've gathered, Sheilla, it points to Najma. How do we find her?' asked Jim.

'That's what we're focusing on now. It's difficult as the Mexican authorities have too many ties to the cartel. I don't want to alert them we are looking for Najma. I suspect that the cartel even has ties to our own law enforcement agencies. What I've done is route our inquiries through the AP news agency. Our interest should appear to be nothing more than reporters tracking a story. I think the best way to find her is to build a scenario based on what we know and fill in the gaps with logic. It will be part fiction and part reality. Fred, pass out the sheets that Mark printed,' said Sheilla.

There was not one person sitting at the table who was unimpressed with what Sheilla had constructed. There were maps of the area and she had looked for motives for the slaying of the family and their implications.

'Even if this turns out to be a false lead, Sheilla, I'm impressed. Excellent job,' said Will Crystal. Every day that Sheilla had worked at the BWL confirmed his decision in recruiting her.

'My best guess,' said Sheilla, 'is that this is a personal act by the cartel leader. It might have gone unnoticed except for the exceptional brutality, which we attribute to Najma. The locals claim it was a she-devil that did it and they are frightened. We are using Landsat to look at all the possible residences or compounds that could house the cartel leader. I think he is close by and we should have it narrowed down in a couple of hours.'

'This doesn't sound like the smartest thing for the cartel to do,' said Dr. Milton. 'Why draw this much attention to yourself?'

Sheilla nodded to Katarina. She was the closest person they had to a profiler. She was a computer expert who spoke Spanish, French, and Dutch. She had majored in psychology but her first love had always been computers.

'The best answer appears to be that the leaders live a dichotomous existence. On the one hand, they need to stay secluded from the public and government and on the other, they need to have everyone know who they are and fear them. The killings support this concept. Brutality that brings fear followed by obedience and, in the cartel's eyes, respect. The downside is the risk of exposure,' said Katarina.

'Well done all, let's find them and the she-devil,' said the general as he got up. 'Jim, let's talk in my office.'

The general looked at Jim. He was his second in command and would one day be his replacement. That is if Jim wanted to be, as he would have to take on the political issues that went with running a government facility. The Biological Warfare Laboratory was a large, important operation with a big budget, especially for a secret agency. Little was known about it outside the State Department's inner circles, the administration, and of course the finance committees that approved their budget. The government did not want the public to know how dangerous the viral and bacterial threats were. Beyond that, Jim and Brush had become legend within various government agencies and were often requested to head missions far outside their mandated job descriptions.

The general momentarily cut short his reflection on Jim's ability or desire to move from field operations to administration. At this moment, it wasn't a worry; Najma was. Jim had survived some extraordinary missions. He and Brush were as capable, intuitive, and effective as any of the current Special Forces personnel. They had fought endless battles together, starting when the three of them had first met in Vietnam. He would put them up against anyone and the duo would prevail by strength of will and intelligence. At least he had always thought they would. Najma, however, was not normal. She might be Jim's toughest opponent yet. Just one lone female but maybe now with the support of a drug gang. He was sure that Jim was assessing Najma's character and considering her abilities. Brush, on the other hand, wouldn't give her a second's thought. Jim was reflective; Brush was instinctive. Najma was ruthless and reminded him of Dr. Hannibal Lecter in *The Silence of the Lambs*. The general, for one of the first times in his life, was worried about Jim.

'Not used to this silence from you, Will.'

The general smiled at Jim. 'What do you expect to do when we find her?'

'Depends on where, but we might need Nielly and his Special Forces team at least as backup. I haven't worked with anyone better.'

'I liked them, too. Makes me wish I could trade places with you.' He meant that more than was apparent on the surface. The general did wish he could go after Najma himself. 'I'll get Nielly and his group ready to go, as long as they're not occupied with something else.'

'Let's assume that Sheilla is right and Najma and company are located near Nogales. We are going to be interfering in the Drug Enforcement Agency's business. Do we take out the cartel leaders, bring them back, or include the DEA? We won't be able to control it precisely but we can try to slant the outcome,' said Jim.

'I'm not going to ask the DEA. Don't trust them. The cartel may have more inroads into them than we think. We'll keep this as our operation. I trust Jasper Nielly. We'll handle the DEA after,' said the general.

'What if DEA has someone in the cartel?'

'Possible. Maybe I need to contact Mike, my old school buddy at Yale. He's at the DEA, but I trust him.'

'Like we used to say, nothing for it but to do it,' said Jim. 'I'm going to call Heather.'

'I'll get Nielly on board and see what I can find out about any DEA moles from Mike,' said the general.

Jim got up to leave but the general stopped him. 'Forgot to tell you. When I was in Washington I had a discussion with the attorney-general. The psychiatrist we brought in to evaluate Nusmen confirmed what we thought. She said Nusmen was brilliant, as we have found out from his work. In her words, Nusmen went temporarily insane, a crime of passion, a form of reactive depression. In short, she says he just flipped out over being dumped. A one-off event in her opinion. Not his true nature. The AG agreed to set aside any prosecution and leave him here with us.' They exchanged looks and shook their heads.

'Hope she's right,' said Jim as he moved toward the door.

# Chapter 8

Get rid of the Arab puke's body, Che,' snarled Raul, while looking first at Najma and then Amir with a sneer.

Actually, neither Najma nor Amir really cared about Musa. Najma was indifferent to Musa's existence and Amir's first thought was that he wouldn't have to pay him his salary. Musa had been useless as a bodyguard anyway. There was always an upside to everything, he thought. Musa had told the Mexicans where his room was. Couldn't be trusted. He would be easy to replace and he would look for better security next time. In truth, Musa had been a loyal servant and bodyguard. He had endured lots of pain and died for his employer. Amir, from the world of finance, was blind to the realities of the world he was entering.

They loaded into four black Yukons and raced off south from the airport on Highway 15. The string of speeding four-wheel drives turned right on Highway 43, which eventually angled southwest. Along the way, they passed several police cars. Many of the local police were paid more by the cartel than by the government. The police were there not as a show of force, rather a show of support. The cartel wanted them to show anyone who dared concern themselves with the matter, who really controlled things. Not one local even glanced at the caravan. They knew cartel members were inside. The residents turned away and let them pass, ghosts blowing by in the wind.

Just south of the village of Reforma and north of Tubutama, they turned east on a small dirt road. Dust billowed in their headlights as the bouncing lights illuminated cactus and scrub brush. Eventually they reached a walled compound. The hacienda appeared peaceful but, as they neared a gate, several guards emerged from the shadows.

Inside the compound Najma went to her rooms in a long, one-story building where the guards and cartel members stayed. Amir was taken to a different guest facility and locked in a room. The room was orange and blue with dark wood furniture, fresh flowers, and an old stone fireplace. It had character.

'Be ready for breakfast at seven. You do not want to make El Padrino unhappy,' said Che.

Raul placed calls to contacts to find out more about the Seattle attack. He also called his sources in London and said he wanted a history of Amir by the next morning, no later than nine o'clock Pacific time. The cartel's aging leader was not in Mexico and would not return for a week. Raul was a lieutenant but Guillermo was the lieutenant in charge. Guillermo, El Padrino, recognized as the future leader, was in fact, the defacto leader, something Raul was unhappy about and planned to change if the opportunity presented itself. But Raul's style and expertise, although still valuable, belonged to the past.

'Raul, sit,' said Guillermo. 'Want some refreshment?'

'I'd like a Negra Modelo,' said Raul.

Guillermo nodded to his manservant. He never consumed alcohol. He was not typical in many ways. He was tall, six foot two, slender and light skinned with a slightly hooked nose. He looked and acted more like a Spanish aristocrat than the second in command of one of the most powerful cartels in Mexico. His manner had fooled many who were now dead. He was as ruthless and capable as he was smart, intelligent, and educated. El Padrino was the future of the cartel.

'Tell me what you found out, compadre,' said Guillermo.

'Najma met a businessman, the brother of a terrorist who was killed in Seattle a couple of months ago. He says he wants her to avenge his brother's death. The woman worked with the brother before coming to us. But I don't like her and the man is a pussy,' answered Raul.

'You have evidence yet of this story?'

'I will have a background on the man and the activities in Seattle tomorrow morning.'

'Nothing else then tonight,' said El Padrino dismissively.

Raul finished his beer and left Guillermo in the main house. Raul was jealous of Guillermo on the one hand, and on the other hand, he had learned to respect him. He was cagey and dangerous. For the time being, Raul was content with his position.

There was a knock on Amir's door at seven o'clock sharp.

'Yes,' said Amir. The door was unlocked and Amir opened it. An average looking but not unattractive small woman stood outside.

'Breakfast will be in the main house at eight o'clock. I will return to escort you, señor.' She turned immediately and walked away with her hips swinging as she had been told to do. Amir felt relieved that it was not Raul but also slightly confused by the courtesy and the now unlocked door.

Raul had received both his reports earlier than requested. Reports never came later than requested. Everything supported the story that Najma had told, that Amir was a businessman with questionable contacts, who lived in an exclusive area of Kensington, London.

The cartel did not trust Najma but she had come to them with an extraordinary recommendation from one of Guillermo's business partners in Malta. He had been personally acquainted with her mentor. Guillermo knew that she had worked with a man called Farasie since her teenage years and was a skilled mercenary. He did not know very much about her but had found no evidence that she was anything other than a violent but skilled assassin. She was invited into the cartel primarily as a courtesy to his business associate but partly because Guillermo could see that there might be advantages to having a woman with a man's skills in his organization. Still, she would have to prove her loyalty.

Amir was escorted into the house through big wooden doors. The house was magnificent and tastefully decorated. It was not what he expected; nothing this morning was expected. His female escort led him through a large sitting area and out of a door into a small walled garden where a table was set covered with white linen, expensive-looking china, and polished silverware. A tall, elegant man sat at the table reading the London *Financial Times*. Amir felt even more confused.

'Good morning, Mr. Saidani,' said the man, rising and extending his hand. 'Please be seated.'

'Thank you, Mr....'

'Forgive me, my name is Guillermo Vasquez. Please call me Guillermo and, if you don't mind, I shall address you as Amir.'

'Certainly. I would prefer Amir.'

'Would you like coffee or something else to drink?' asked Guillermo solicitously.

'Coffee would be very nice.'

'Would you prefer it any special way? Cappuccino, Americano, or perhaps espresso?' offered Guillermo.

'Perhaps a double shot of espresso.' Amir was now completely unsure of where he was and who he was talking to, much less why he was being offered a selection of coffee. Just a little over two hours ago, his bodyguard had been killed and if not for Najma, he might have suffered the same fate. A little over twenty-four hours ago, his driver had taken him to Heathrow from his elegant Regency house located between South Kensington Station and Knightsbridge and then an airline representative had escorted him to the departure gate for the flight to Mexico City and seated him in first class. He didn't know where he was now, only that he had been confronted with some serious thugs, driven to an airport and then flown somewhere for several hours. He had no idea who this man seated across from him was, other than his name.

A well-dressed male servant brought their coffee within a minute.

'I understand you work in the financial arena, Amir?' said Guillermo pleasantly.

Amir was feeling more relaxed but he also remembered a similar question from the hairy, foul-mouthed Mexican yesterday afternoon. He didn't know what to say. As close to the truth as possible might be best, he reasoned.

'Yes, that's true. I handle money and investments for several wealthy clients,' said Amir.

'For a Mr. Shadi?' inquired Guillermo casually.

Amir was dumbfounded. Shadi was one of his largest and most secretive clients. He wasn't known to anyone as far as Amir knew. He hid behind layers of international business corporations located around the world, from the Cayman Islands to Hong Kong and then further hidden behind New Zealand trusts and Panamanian foundations. Amir did not know where his money came from but there was a lot of it. Amir was careful to protect the money and the confidence of Shadi.

'You know Mr. Shadi?' Amir asked.

'Until this morning, I had never heard of him, Amir. But now I know a great deal about him and also your dealings with him.'

Amir felt as though he had moved from the jaws of a crocodile to the jaws of a leopard. How could this man know anything about his dealings with Shadi? His expression must have betrayed his bewilderment.

'Come now, Amir, let's be friends. We shouldn't have secrets between us.'

'What do you want to know then?'

'I would like to know who you are and what is your connection to Najma. It is possible we might be able to do some mutually beneficial business together,' said Guillermo with a friendly smile.

Amir now knew that the teeth were smiling and white but just like the leopard, they were sharp and potentially lethal. He started to have the feeling that cooperating would benefit him and if he did not, the alternative would be joining Musa. He was unaware just how right his feeling was.

'Start from the beginning with Najma and your relationship,' said Guillermo, still smiling.

The story then poured out from Amir. He kept it as short as he could but held back nothing.

'If I wanted to avenge the death of my brother, Najma might be my choice as well. However, I am not sure that I want her to go to the United States. Perhaps I can assist you in finding something out about this agent you mentioned.'

'As I said, I am looking into it,' Amir began.

Guillermo interrupted him. 'Please allow me. My contacts are quite good in our neighbor to the north, I assure you. Good, that's settled. Now tell me; what is your best recommendation for investing, as we approach the twenty-first century?'

Once again, Amir looked at this man and decided that crossing him would be a fatal mistake. He was under his control now but possibly, if he was careful, he could turn it to his advantage.

'You've no doubt heard of the millennium bug?' asked Amir.

'Of course,' said Guillermo. 'My technical experts tell me there is nothing to it. Our computers have been adapted for the change; it was a minor correction and it is nothing more than another news event for the press. Baseless worries.'

'I believe you are correct and more knowledgeable than most,' said Amir more and more impressed as each minute passed. He then proceeded to explain his plan and how they could both benefit financially from it.

Guillermo stopped him after a few sentences. 'Let's have our breakfast and talk of other things. You can explain it in more detail to my computer experts. We shall talk of it later, perhaps after dinner this evening.'

The conversation shifted to literature and from there to opera and Shakespeare. Guillermo wanted to know all about Amir's London social set and the clubs to which Amir belonged. Amir mentioned that he belonged to The Queen's Club in London and Guillermo suggested that they should play a set or two of tennis when it would be cooler later this afternoon. Amir was not surprised. Guillermo was obviously well educated and he was probably quite good at tennis. Amir thought, however, that he would not try too hard to win, as he was a very accomplished player. He was now on more familiar ground; the thought bolstered his confidence.

'If you will excuse me, Amir, I have business to attend to. Please feel free to have more coffee or explore the hacienda today.' Guillermo smiled suavely once more and left Amir to his own thoughts.

Amir asked for some more coffee, cappuccino this time. If he was being held here, this would be the sort of prison he could get used to. He concluded that Guillermo possessed so much power, the kingly kind, that he could act the gentleman. Raul, on the other hand, had raw, primal, animal power, the kind that needed constant attention in order continually to generate fear. The power that Bertrand Russell called 'naked power.' He would have to be very careful.

A man and a woman walked into Amir's room shortly after lunch and asked if they could talk to him. They were Guillermo's computer experts and he spent the next two and a half hours going over the specifics, as much as he knew them, of his millennium plan. He didn't understand many of the details they asked him. He provided them with the name of his head computer person, Yousef. They thanked him for his time and walked out, leaving him feeling mentally exhausted. They obviously knew that business and computer types were never his sort of people. Amir liked money.

'El Padrino wishes to invite you to play tennis at six o'clock,' said the same saucy woman that had knocked on his door that morning. She handed Amir a stack of neatly folded white clothes. 'If you wish, I shall come to your room at 5:45 and take you to the courts.' Amir nodded. She smiled and walked off in the same alluring way she had earlier this morning.

'P or d,' said Guillermo, spinning his Prince racquet, after they had hit a few balls and practiced their serves.

'P,' said Amir.

'You win.' Amir glanced at the vestiges of the sun and said he would serve.

'Let's just stay as we are,' said Guillermo, not choosing to switch ends, as was now his choice.

The court lights were starting to glow just as they began their first game. Amir had a very fast and accurate serve. He was planning to hold back a little but his host seemed to have no trouble returning his serve. They exchanged shots, getting a feel for one another. Amir sensed that as good as he was, Guillermo was nearly his equal. The first set advanced to six wins each and they played a tie breaker. Amir made a bad shot on the first point, thinking that he would keep it close and then let the game proceed in a natural way with the best man winning. He didn't get another point. Guillermo won nine to love. Amir was a little taken aback and decided to up the level of his game in their second set. He did; he played his best but he lost all six games. In fact, he only got a couple of points. He had never been so soundly defeated before. The confidence he had started to feel evaporated.

Guillermo smiled and said, 'Well played, Amir. I must tend to some business and we can talk more over dinner.'

Guillermo had been born in a poor village next to a tennis club. At an early age, he started to shag balls to make tips. When he had just turned eleven and was growing tall and slim, one of the instructors thought it would be a lark to teach the ragamuffin kid some tennis. The instructor was surprised; the boy seemed to have natural ability and he allowed Guillermo to practice with a young teenage group. When he was thirteen years old, the instructor entered him in a junior tournament. Guillermo won and it changed his life. He made friends in a class to which he would never otherwise have had access. The father of one of his new friends sponsored his education in a private school. He excelled in his studies and eventually received a sports scholarship to UCLA.

Midway through his undergraduate degree, his sister was found dead: she had been brutally raped. He returned to Mexico, cutting his studies short, found her murderer, and killed him. The man he killed was a police officer. A friend sent Guillermo to the Tijuana drug cartel who protected him. He quickly rose through their ranks as he was intelligent and even though he had only a partial college education, he was leagues ahead of the other members. His poor background, understanding of men, ruthlessness, and native intelligence served him well. Through the deaths and imprisonment of his superiors, he rose to be the second in command of the largest and most powerful drug cartel in Mexico. He was determined he would eventually lead that cartel, not Raul.

His underlings called him El Padrino, the godfather, but only when he was not in earshot. It was a form of respect, as they knew where his destiny lay.

The dinner was magnificent: prairie chicken, an endless selection of traditional Mexican dishes, and the best mole that Amir had ever tasted. Amir was as full as he was anxious.

'Would you be so kind as to join me?' asked Guillermo. They moved to a cozy study adjoining the dining room. Amir was served an exquisite liquor based on a cactus flower. To the strange events of the last twenty-four hours he could now add being held captive in a splendid villa by a man who had soundly defeated him at tennis, being treated to exquisitely prepared food and first-class wine, and liquors. And most unfortunately, divulging the details of his grand money-making scheme for the year 2000.

Guillermo studied Amir for a few seconds. 'I would like to offer you a small business proposition. You spoke to two of my technical staff this afternoon. They have since conferred with your computer group and another within my organization. They think that your plan is intriguing, but has several probable fatal flaws. I would like to suggest we become partners.'

Was there a choice? No, he did not have one. They could clearly use his plan without him. So why did Guillermo want to be partners? Amir decided to be straightforward.

'You now know the plan; why not just execute it yourself? I sense you do not really need me.'

Guillermo gained a small measure of respect for Amir with this forthright question. 'It is always better to work with friends than to steal their ideas. You are a good tennis player and from what I hear a good businessman. A liaison serves me better. What do you say?'

Amir said the only thing possible, 'Yes, of course I agree.'

'Then a toast, my new friend. To a successful enterprise!'

Guillermo only needed Amir as a convenience in London but his computer people might prove temporarily useful. The original concept would stay essentially the same. Guillermo planned, however, to expand the original plan to stealing billions of sterling from one of the largest British banks. The bank would be led to believe that their systems had crashed due to the millennium bug and that would cover the movement of the money to Cuba and then on to various accounts throughout the world.

Guillermo's new plan was far more involved than Amir's original one. It had to be, since banks in the real world didn't actually keep billions just laying around. In fact, it was all paper trails at the Bank of England. To extract billions, his main computer expert, Ramirez, had devised a way to intercept the money flows at several points and divert them. It was a complex plan but Ramirez assured him it would work flawlessly.

Amir clearly was acting deferentially to him but that was not good enough. He needed to understand the terms of their agreement. 'I will also help you with your reason for being here. The men you seek are a team of agents. Unique agents, I might add. My sources say that they are quite extraordinary. Your brother was not killed by an average US policeman. If they were not American government agents, I might even be encouraged to employ them myself.'

'What do you know about them, Guillermo?'

'They work for a biological warfare facility, very secret I am told. Other agencies often request them for special projects. It appears that your brother stumbled into their backyard with his plan. Unfortunate and unlucky.'

Amir opened his mouth to speak but Guillermo held up his hand. 'I know what you want and I cannot allow Najma to enter the US. I will help you, however. It is the least I can do for our new partnership. Tomorrow I will know more about the two agents. You mentioned you were seeking information about them. Please call tonight and cancel whatever inquiries you have started. My people will be more discreet than anyone you might hire. Tomorrow,' continued Guillermo, 'my counsellor will work out the details of our new business arrangement with you.' He rose from his seat and said, 'Enjoy the rest of your evening, I have some matters to attend to.'

They shook hands and a servant escorted Amir out into the night air. He had never seen so many stars. He had never felt so helpless. Still, this might serve him well. He might profit and he certainly had a new and powerful partner. He had always thought of himself as intelligent. The reality was, he was useful to Guillermo for reasons he did not understand. He would have to endure, and perhaps he might emerge richer.

He passed the night trying not to think about his situation. There were no decisions he could make, they were being made for him. Possibly, he thought, that made life simpler—not being in charge. He searched through several DVDs and chose to watch *The Terrorists,* a Sean Connery movie, because of his brother. It was not a very good movie and it left him even more deflated than the tennis match.

They left his door unlocked. The Mexican woman, however, knocked at seven the next morning and came into his room. 'Buenos dias, señor, did you sleep well?'

'What is your name?' asked a weary Amir. He hadn't slept well.

'Lola,' she said with a demure smile that she did not feel. 'You don't look so good, Mr. Saidani.'

'Call me Amir.'

'You have an hour before breakfast with El Padrino. Perhaps I can assist you in getting ready?' She smiled coquettishly at Amir as she had been ordered to and closed the door behind her.

Close to eight, Lola escorted him to the house. On the way, she said she thought she might have dropped an earring in the room. She wanted to make a thorough search of the room and his belongings while he was at breakfast.

'How was your night, Amir?' Of course, Guillermo knew all about his morning as he had ordered Lola to entertain him.

'Restful enough,' said Amir.

Coffee the same as yesterday arrived. 'I took the liberty of ordering for you. Would you like something different this morning?'

'No, no, the espresso is just right, very kind of you.'

'Without seeming to be rude, I would like to get right down to business, today. I have thought about your plan and your plan for Najma and have acquired a great deal of information about your agents since yesterday. Their names are Dr. Jim Johnson and Mr. Brush McGuire. They work for a General William Crystal at a secret biological warfare laboratory, as we already discussed. The man Jim is the leader of the two. He is second in command of the laboratory but is primarily a field agent.

'Agent Johnson lives with his girlfriend on a remote ranch in northern Washington State. But fortune is smiling on us, Amir. As of today, his girlfriend, or partner, if you will, is in Arizona. My sources have found out that she is leaving with a group to go camping about sixty miles from where we are now. They plan to cross the border into Mexico at Naco and proceed to just south of the Coronado National Memorial. It is also just south of a remote area, called the Huachuca Mountains. It is also where the warrior Geronimo lived and it is now home to a military base.'

Amir wondered how Guillermo found this out overnight. Impossible, he thought, unless he had been able to hack into email, which is exactly what Guillermo's computer techs had done as soon as they found out who Heather was. Her emails told them all they needed to know.

'Are you telling me that the American agent will be in Mexico, too?'

'I didn't say that. He is apparently in Washington State but we had more difficulty gaining access to his email there. We do not want to be detected in this search. The universities' and personal emails, however, have very little protection.'

Amir's mind was racing with what this would mean and what Guillermo had in mind. Guillermo knew this would be the case.

'The plan is simple. As I said, I will not let Najma go to the US but this group crossing into Mexico makes things different. Najma will take the agent's girlfriend hostage. He will come to rescue her and we will kill him for you.'

'He will bring others with him, though, will he not?' suggested Amir.

'I don't think so. The government will not want to send people over the border. They will try to get information from their informants and negotiate. From what we know about the American I predict that he will not wait and will come alone or, even better, with his co-agent.'

'I want to be there. I want him to know why he is dying!' said Amir with his voice rising above its natural smooth baritone. He was so overcome with thoughts of blood vengeance for his brother that he had not yet thought about why Guillermo would go to all this trouble for him. And Guillermo never did anything without a reason.

'I will discuss this with Najma and Raul today, and perhaps tomorrow we can put the plan into action,' said Guillermo. 'And now you must excuse me. Perhaps once again we can talk during dinner.'

# Chapter 9

Be careful, precious,' said Jim into his cell phone. He was worried about Heather going to Mexico with Najma likely to be there. Jim opened his mouth to warn her that Najma might be in the area but then he closed it again. Najma would have no way of knowing anything about Heather's whereabouts, she'd only briefly glimpsed her on the day Farasie was killed. It was Jim that Najma wanted but she would probably wait for things to die down before making her move. Anyway, he planned to find her first. This was Heather's first camping trip since they had found the mass grave. She had never shown any fear of being in the wilderness since then, but Jim didn't want to worry or scare Heather when she was so happy about her adventure. His job had caused her enough pain already; she'd be fine. It was not often that Jim underestimated his enemy, especially one as dangerous as Najma.

'Oh Mexico!' sang the group as they headed south of Phoenix, past saguaro cacti glowing in the morning light. They turned on Highway 10 and drove toward Bisbee. Richard had suggested they drive there for lunch.

'I can't get that song out of my head,' said Kristina.

'Me either,' said Misa.

'Hey, how did you get the name Misa? Is it a nickname? Or is it your proper name? Wait, maybe it is an Americanized name that you use here?' asked Heather turning from the front seat. Heather liked riding shotgun and had called it as soon as the group headed for the van, making them all laugh. Nicola, or Nic as they were all now calling her, sat behind Ralphy, who was driving. She had maps all over her lap. She loved them and was the self-appointed navigator.

'The short version is my mother liked the sound of Misha but didn't know it stood for Mikhail, or Michael, and obviously didn't know how to spell it either. Actually I am happy the "h" got left out, otherwise I might have taken a lot of teasing,' she added, brushing back her full-bodied wavy blond hair. It was long and if she could figure out how, she would thin it.

'I call her Mike,' said Vidya. Misa hit him with an elbow and he laughed.

If Misa had a problem, it was not her name. She often had a hard time relating to people although she was reasonably attractive, very smart, a well-thought-of Ph.D. and a brilliant computer engineer and programmer. But she was more comfortable with her computer than people. Vidya adored her intelligence, and liked her as well. He always explained her personality quirks as simply 'interesting.'

Richard was busy staring out the window at the landforms of the southern desert. It was beautiful and one of the reasons he had gone into sedimentary geology. He just liked looking at them. JT was in his own space, too. Sitting on the opposite side from

Richard, separated by Kristina, he was staring out the window but not really seeing anything. His revised microbiology textbook occupied his thoughts. Would it sell better with the revisions that he had just made? Should he have rewritten more of it?

It was a happy and contented group; a compatible, fun-loving, intelligent group and, as was typical of universities, a mixed group, from all parts of the world.

Jim was restless. He wanted information and wanted to finish this business with Najma. More than a day had passed. He had slept in his office; many of them did overnights at the labs. The general had found out from his old school friend that the DEA had a mole but was still trying to find out who it was. Sheilla was becoming irritated; she couldn't understand why things were moving so slowly and why there was so little useful information about the cartel.

Meanwhile, Heather and her new friends were approaching the old west town of Tombstone.

'Looks like a tourist trap,' said Kristina.

'It is, but it's sort of fun,' explained Ralphy. 'We could watch the shoot-out at the OK Corral.'

'Go on,' said Misa. 'Get a life!'

'We could stop here for lunch,' said Heather. 'Might be interesting to get a little of the old Wild West history and I am hungry already.'

'Me, too,' said Ralphy. He was always eating, nibbling on something, but never seemed to put on any weight.

'I wouldn't mind stretching my legs,' added JT. Ralphy pulled into a side street and parked in front of a wood-planked old west house.

'Not like Europe at all,' said Kristina. 'This is as old as it gets here and in Europe this is post modern. Don't know about the rest of you, but I want to look around. Did you guys see that sign for a re-enactment of the OK Corral gunfight? Yeah, yeah, OK, so I'm a tourist in a tourist trap.'

'I'm up for that,' said Nicola. 'I like this kind of stuff. I'm dying to go to the Star Trek museum in Seattle sometime. The old west, the final frontier.'

Everyone rolled their eyes or arched their eyebrows except JT who was the first to say something. 'Think I'll pass,' he said. 'Think I'll get some lunch and maybe look for a gift for my grandson.'

'Lunch,' said Ralphy. 'I'm in.'

Kristina and Nicola shrugged their shoulders. 'If you guys aren't in for an adventure, what time should we meet back here?'

'Twelve-thirty,' said Ralphy, 'if we're going to stop in Bisbee. We have to get across the border and then you might want to stop at the open-air market in Agua Prieta and get some food. They sell some weird stuff, white cheese and fruit at a place called Fruteria Chihuahua. I would like to get the tents pitched before dark and it's going to be close, time-wise.'

'What if they don't camp where they planned?' asked Amir nervously.

'No problem,' said Che. 'We have people following them to the border and someone on this side as soon as they cross.'

Che did not like working with Najma but Raul told him he had to keep a close eye on the 'Puta.' They loaded into three GMC Yukons. All black with dark tinted windows. Che had brought four men with him. With Najma, Raul, and Amir they numbered eight in total.

'Do we need this many?' asked Lupe.

'No, but Raul doesn't want anything to go wrong. Wants all gringos to disappear. This is straight from El Padrino.'

Kristina and Nicola were standing in front of a small audience with six-guns strapped to their waists and big smiles on their faces.

'Ladies and gentlemen, it looks easy but to men that carried six-shooters, it was life or death. The guns strapped on these cowgirls are equipped with a laser that will light up a spot on Tex's or Sam's vest if the little ladies' shots are true to their mark. The guns sound and feel real but no actual bullets are fired. The gals are wearing the same laser-detecting vest. You ready there, lil' ladies?'

Kristina and Nicola exchanged glances and nodded at the M.C. Nic, who was a bit of a tomboy, said to Kristina, 'After all that "little lady" business, let's shoot to kill!'

'Ready, everyone? All right, you're at the OK Corral and it's October 26, 1881.'

Tex and Sam both held their hands out to their sides not far from the holstered guns. They started to move apart. The Ph.D. and the master's student watched the cowboys and put their hands in the same position.

'Watch their eyes,' said Nic.

'I can't see that far,' said Kristina.

Nicola drew her gun, cocked it as she had been shown, pointed at Tex who was the biggest target, and pulled the trigger. The gun jumped in her hand and her ears hurt from the report. There were no red spots on Tex. He walked slowly toward her. She fired twice more. Tex drew his gun, and in fast motion, cocked and let off a shot at Nic. A bright red light appeared on her chest. Dead.

The commentator said, 'It's not always the fastest that won the shootout. One of the little ladies is left to take care of two gunslingers.' Kristina thought to herself, *What the heck, let's get this over with*. She pulled out her gun, cocked it, closed her eyes, and squeezed the trigger. Boom. No red spots. Tex was getting closer, she could see his eyes now. She cocked the gun again. Tex raised his. She pulled the trigger and a red glow appeared in the center of Tex's vest. The audience yelled. Nicola jumped in the air and yelled, 'Yeah. Way to go!'

Kristina looked pleased but then of course, the other gun-slinger 'killed' her. The show went on with Doc Holiday, Wyatt Earp, smoke and noise, and dead bodies lying on the ground.

'Let's get back,' said Nicola when it was over. 'I'm glad you got one. Woman triumphs over macho man. I got a couple of pictures of you.'

The group drove south and stopped at Bisbee. Ralphy grabbed a cupcake and a Coke. The others peered into an enormous hole in the ground, left from years of copper mining. They continued toward the border. Just as Ralphy had said, there was an open market across the border from Douglas in Agua Prieta. They looked around the colorful stalls, bought some food, then drove southwest toward Cananea, Mexico. None of the group paid any attention to the old, dusty-green pickup or the older, yellow-gold-colored Mercedes. The followers were careful, though they need not have been. There was no one in the group that would have even given a thought to someone following them. It was out of their area of understanding. That happened in the movies but not in real life, and certainly not to a group of academics on the hunt for fungus. But their lives were about to change forever. Real life in Mexico was about to eviscerate their sheltered views of life.

'The tail says they are nearing El Sauz. Our information is that they are going to turn just past El Sauz on a dirt road and head north toward the border and the mountains.'

'How far are we from them?' asked Amir.

'Only a few miles. There is an old mining camp and workers' building in the hills. We are going to use it after we capture them.'

Amir looked at Che. 'You want to tell me the plan now? I want to know. My brother's killer isn't with them, is he?'

'No, but his girlfriend is. He will come for her.'

'So we hold the scientists and then kill the agent when he shows up. They'll be witnesses won't they?'

Che looked at this unscarred businessman. 'There won't be any witnesses, compadre.' Amir looked at Najma, alarmed. She smiled at him. Amir wanted revenge but he was starting to feel rather sick.

El Padrino, Raul, and Che knew what he was going to see. It was meant to be an object lesson. It was a pledge; this would happen to Amir if he did not keep the best interests of the cartel in mind.

'How many are in the group?' asked Amir.

'There are eight, señor, four women and four men.'

The sick feeling in Amir's stomach increased. Was this what

he wanted? Fantasy and reality were not the same. For the happy academics, the electronic games filled with killing that Vidya played, the action films that Kristina watched in order to distract her mind from research, and the kung fu movies that Professor Richard Graves secretly loved, were a different reality from the world of the drug cartels.

One hour before sunset, the Arizona State University van turned north on a small gravel road. Mesquite and cactus grew on the flat ground to their left and right. Ahead they could see the mountains rising. From their vantage point, the mountains looked as if covered in a blanket of the same desert they were driving through.

'I always think of the mountains here as islands. Instead of in the sea, they are in the desert,' said Richard. 'Low down they have desert flora. On their tops they are pine covered, green, and even have flowing streams. Everyone! Look on the right. A stone playa—a black stone playa! Desert varnish and we'll find out tomorrow if your black fungus is around here, too.'

'I want to stop now, if only for a minute,' said Kristina excitedly.

'Me, too,' agreed Heather.

'I think we had better wait until tomorrow,' said JT. 'It's too close to dark and we need to find a campsite and get set up for the night. There will likely be lots of desert varnish around and you might even be able to check for the blackberries with a flashlight tonight if you really want to.'

'Probably right, JT. I'm just anxious to see them in the field,' said Kristina.

'Glad to see you so interested, Kristina. It will be fun to work with you. I'm up for blackberry-searching by flashlight if you are,' said Heather. The women smiled at each other in silent agreement.

Two miles back, the three Yukons followed along. They watched a plume of dust from the researchers' van. There was no need to be any closer.

Jim had not slept very long or very well. He was sitting at his desk. His head nodded, overcome with a feeling of hot, wet fog descending over his thoughts. A buzzing barely penetrated the electric static between his consciousness and dreams. He shook his head, rubbed his eyes, and answered his phone.

'Hey, boss, finally we got something good. I know where she is!' exclaimed a jubilant Sheilla.

Jim was instantly alert. 'Should we meet in the conference room or your office?' he asked and before she could answer—he must be getting this from Heather—he asked another question. 'Do you want anyone else present?'

'I called the general. Let's meet in the conference room in five minutes. I'll bring Mark along, too.'

Jim went to the small bathroom attached to his office and splashed water on his face. His mind was wide-awake but his eyes felt dry and unfocused.

Sheilla was smiling as Jim and the general walked in.

'I bumped into Barbara on the way,' said the general. 'She'll be here in a minute. Let's get started. What did you find, Sheilla?'

'We have a large hacienda near Reforma and not far from Tubutama. It's the only structure that could house something like a cartel organization. There is nothing else in the vicinity that would work or is big enough. There is no ranching or agriculture surrounding the compound. It has to be someone with a lot of money, like the cartel. Mark found several small articles in local papers that suggest no one goes near the hacienda. It's off-limits. A mayor of the closest village said she wanted to clean up the drug dealers so it would be safe for her children. The article quoted her, "We need to burn down that compound and take back our land." She was killed two days later.'

'Anything from your DEA friend, General? Their agent could confirm what Sheilla just said,' said Jim.

'No, but I'll call him as soon as we are finished.'

'What else, Sheilla?' asked Jim.

'Miss anything?' said Barbara as she walked in.

'Sheilla's found a likely cartel house and some backup information. Go ahead, Sheilla,' said Jim.

'Nothing else, other than news articles with small supporting bits and pieces, all pointing to this location and a few suggesting the existence of a she-devil. It's where she is, I can feel it.'

'Jim, give me a few minutes and then let's talk about a strategy. Thanks, both of you, good work.' The general nodded at Sheilla and then Mark before continuing.

'Nielly and his team get back to Fort Bragg from South America late tonight. They'll get re-equipped tomorrow and leave the next day for Fort Huachucha. ETA late afternoon. I talked to Mike. He says the DEA has a woman in deep cover with the cartel. She is a maid and they get limited information from her. Latest communication from her said there is an Arab-looking male and a woman that everyone stays away from. The man just arrived but the woman has been there for several weeks. The mole searched the man's room and found nothing. She can't find out anything about the woman. It's our terrorist. Sheilla is right. It all fits.'

'Can we contact this woman?' asked Jim.

'Michael said the DEA was pretty gun-shy, since they had never had anyone stay alive long, working undercover with the cartel.'

'Looks like I should meet up with Nielly and get reconnaissance of the compound. What sort of intel do you think they might have at Fort Huachuca?'

'Might be that they can help us. It still is the Strategic Air Command headquarters for the army, so I know a few people there. It is not widely known that it's still a StratCom facility. What might be helpful to us is they are testing new unmanned reconnaissance aircraft. Possible that I could get you some help with the crustiest old general I know.'

'Drones would be useful; an unmanned flight sending images sounds just the ticket. No use sitting around here,' said Jim. 'I'll coordinate with Sheilla and find out if any planes are flying south. Hopefully you can get me set up with the base commander. We need to know who the DEA plant is and how to contact her. At a minimum, we need a description of her or a code name. I'll think about possible scenarios if the compound turns out to be the right place,' said Jim. He felt his chest tighten just knowing Heather was anywhere near the compound.

'Careful on this one, Jim,' said the general.


'Turn left here,' said Nicola. She had been studying the topographical maps. 'There should be a good camping spot a few hundred yards in.'

'Boy oh boy,' said Ralphy. 'This is one pretty spot. The

whole place is turning to red-gold as the sun sets. I've seen lots of birds, too. Migrating south, I guess.'

They stopped the van on a small flat plateau just above an arroyo. It was a perfect spot at the base of a hill. They had gained a little over two hundred meters in elevation. The land sloped off south, east, and west. To the west the cottonwoods, willows, and sycamores disappeared in ribbons of gold into the sun-saturated desert landscape.

'Must not be the only ones here,' said Ralphy, as he pointed back toward the road. 'Looks like more than one car from the dust plumes. But they need to find their own camping spot. I'll start getting the gear out.'

Kristina looked around for Vidya to see where he wanted to put up their tent. A small green gecko scurried up on a rock at her feet and held its head motionless as if studying her. It was so tiny and cute but an involuntary shiver rippled up her body. She shook her head and looked back at the rock but it was gone.

'Come on, you two, we could use some help,' she shouted over to where Misa and Vidya sat deep in conversation with arms flailing. *He notices nothing but computers,* she thought. *He probably wouldn't even miss me if I disappeared.*

# Chapter 10

It was a glorious day for Glenda Rose's hospital release. Nearly two months in the hospital was just about all she could bear. Brush had purchased some new clothes for her and moved her happily from the hospital to a cruise ship docked alongside Seattle's waterfront. He was taking his caregiver duties seriously and had Glenda tucked under a blanket on the deck of a huge Princess Cruise ship. Next stop was Juneau. Brush had traveled most of the world but he had never been to Alaska. He had wanted to go since he was a teenager but he hadn't quite managed to get there, even though it was not far north of where he and Jim worked at the Bio Warfare Center. He remembered the magazines in the library back in his hometown of Smith Falls, Ontario, about Kodiak Island and the giant brown bears. The images from those magazines had fueled his imagination hour after hour. Going north to Alaska was a childhood dream.

Glenda was enjoying his attention and letting him fuss over her. No one had taken care of her before and she found she liked the idea. She was capable of taking care of herself and Brush knew this. In the past, she would have resented someone coddling her but Brush was different. They seemed to have an understanding and both enjoyed their new roles and accepted them willingly. It was likely that there would be a time when he would need the same from her. It was all new ground for both of them; a happy place they never knew existed.

Sheilla located a military transport that was leaving McChord Air Force Base and would get Jim to Davis-Monthan AFB in Arizona in just over five hours. Another old friend of General Crystal's arranged to have Jim brought to Fort Huachuca using his personal Huey helicopter. Jim had left in a hurry but was not traveling light. He had arranged it all the day before and had a substantial amount of gear with him, all requisitioned from the BWL armory and packed by his supply sergeant. He had everything from night vision to his favorite black square parachute, and a wide assortment of weapons. He did not know what to expect or what items he could procure at Fort Huachuca so he traveled prepared.

Jim always felt good as he traveled closer to Heather. He thought of it as the right direction. She would be less than a hundred miles away when he got to Fort Huachuca. He liked that part of the world, just as Heather did and remembered it fondly from when he had been stationed there as a young lieutenant before shipping to Vietnam. He wondered if Sierra Vista and the fort would be the same. Tombstone was close and if he had been eight hours earlier, he might have been able to surprise Heather and JT with a quick visit but Heather would call him tonight with the satellite phone he had given her for the original trip to the desert in Arizona. When they spoke, he wouldn't tell her where he was, she was used to secrecy around his job, but it made him smile to think of her so close and happy.

The military transport flight to Tucson had been uneventful. As his Huey approached Fort Huachuca, the mountains towering above the desert floor in the early evening moonlight looked mysterious. If he believed in such things, he could easily imagine that the ancestral spirits of the Apache or Geronimo himself roamed below. From the air, the terrain appeared silver-blue. The mountains were high above the desert floor despite Fort Huachuca's nearly mile-high elevation.

Heather was thinking of Jim, far away to the north, at the same time as he was thinking of her, and getting closer and closer to her. A confluence of events always seems more than coincidence after it happens. Is it fate or is it simply that those things happen just as they do? Najma was thinking of Heather being almost in her grasp. Sheilla felt anxious about how Jim would fare with the information she had given him. Nielly and his Special Forces team were settled in for the night after an arduous mission in South America. The day after tomorrow they planned to join the convergence in the southwest desert. Only Brush and Glenda headed away from the lingering warm days of the Sonoran Desert as their ship churned past Vancouver Island northward toward the cold days and long nights of Brush's childhood dreams.

# Chapter 11

I love this,' said Heather, 'the smoky aroma of the cholla cactus-wood skeletons in the fire and it's so clear out, too. Zillions of stars over us, just like my wilderness up north. There's a different smell in the desert than in the mountains though. I like them both.'

'Those zillions of stars,' said Richard, 'make me realize that the fight to keep light pollution out of the sky is worth it. Just look what people in populated areas miss, and it would be so easy to change. We're careless as a culture. Hey, everybody,' he continued, 'one thing we did that was fun on a Grand Canyon rafting trip was to have a rock band. We made music with rocks and anything else we could find. Mostly rhythm, obviously. It was a blast. Anyone interested? We couldn't get the stuff together in the dark but maybe tomorrow we could practice and then play tomorrow night.'

'I'm in,' said Ralphy.

'Us, too,' said Kristina nodding as Vidya nodded.

'OK, I'll try,' added Misa.

'That's five. We've got a rock band!' said Richard clapping his hands.

'I'm going to call Jim soon,' said Heather. 'If any of you have anyone important to call, you are welcome to use the sat phone.'

'I am quite enjoying not having any connections to the outside world, but I might take you up on that and call home,' said JT.

'Well, I don't need to make any calls,' said Vidya, 'but I'm on edge without my computer. I don't know if I am cut out for this wilderness stuff.'

'I can do without it for a day or maybe two but I do miss working on our project. We need connected computers everywhere,' added Misa.

'What's your project?' asked Nicola.

'We're trying to find a way to overcome the speed barrier that is caused by silica-based computing. I've been interested in quantum computing and Misa is interested in biological and molecular computing. Right now, we are trying to figure out how to use light instead of electrical processing,' said Vidya.

'Better stop him, guys, or this could turn into an all-nighter!' said Kristina only half-jokingly.

'Did you hear that?' Heather asked no one in particular.

'I didn't hear anything,' said JT.

'I thought maybe I heard footsteps,' said Nicola. 'Is that what you heard?'

'Probably a lone deer or maybe a family of javelin out for a night stroll,' said Ralphy.

'You guys seem to love it out here, but it seems spooky to me. I'll be glad when the sun is up,' said Misa with her arms wrapped around her coat.

'Footsteps, I think. Sounds like they are on both sides of us now. It's more than one. If it's deer, they're not moving like any deer in my north woods,' said Heather.

Jim's helicopter put him right in front of headquarters. The old general and a small staff were standing there to greet him with two open-topped jeeps. Jim snapped a salute. General Will Crystal had informed two-star General Whitcuff that Jim was a colonel in the army and his second in command. Jim did not look it, however, dressed in civilian clothes and without a standard military haircut; still the old general returned his salute.

'Nice to see a jeep,' said Jim with a big smile, holding out his hand.

'M151-A jeep, military utility tactical truck. Last of its kind, I'm afraid. Decided a while ago that me and the old jeep would go at the same time. Never liked the HMV replacement.'

'It's nice to meet you and to be both at one of my old bases and in a jeep,' said Jim sincerely.

The general introduced his staff and they set out for his quarters, which were just across the parade ground. Despite his scruffy appearance, General Whitcuff liked Colonel Jim Johnson. He respected Will Crystal too and his old friend had told him to treat Jim right.

'We'll put you up in an empty house instead of the BOQ. The sergeant will drop off your gear. We'll have a snack and drink at my quarters and discuss what you need from us,' said General Whitcuff. 'When we get there, drop the general and call me Sam. I'm trying to get used to it before I retire.'

'I hope you don't mind, General... Sam, I'm expecting a call on my sat phone. If it comes in, I would like to excuse myself for a couple of minutes.'

The call never came that night.

# Chapter 12

Where are the Superstition Mountains?' asked Kristina.

'They're not far from us in Phoenix,' said Ralphy. 'What do you want to know about them?'

'Nothing. I thought they might be close to where we are. I was wondering if there were spirits lurking around out here. This silvery moonlight makes things look eerie.'

'Don't start with the ghost stories,' said Nicola. 'I want to sleep well tonight.'

'Footsteps are getting closer,' said Heather. 'This is a bit scary.'

Nic rolled her eyes at the thought of ghostly apparitions as she looked behind her into the dark. Then a shudder went through her body. A ghostly face appeared out of the darkness.

'What the hell is that!' Everyone looked around as the ghostly faces now surrounded them and moved closer.

Ralphy jumped to his feet.

A voice said, 'Sit back down, don't move, don't talk, put your hands in front of you.'

'Oh Christ, banditos,' said Richard.

There was a little poof noise and a stream of blood erupted from Associate Professor Richard Graves's head as he slumped over.

The voice said, 'I said no talking. Comprende?'

The apparitions moved closer. They were people not ghosts, several of them. The same voice said, 'Silence and do as I say. Don't move or you will also die like the one there that disobeyed my orders.'

Kristina was visibly trembling. She would have yelled but she didn't seem to have a voice.

'Better,' said the woman in the same calm, steely voice. 'You are being kidnapped and we are holding you for ransom. Any sounds or trouble and you will die like your friend. As I point to you, get up and walk to the gentleman with the baseball cap,' commanded Najma, pointing to Lupe.

Lupe carefully frisked them and was thorough, too thorough as he felt Heather's and Kristina's ample breasts. He didn't seem as interested in the less well endowed Misa. Each person, one by one, was frisked and tied up. They stood in a line.

Then their gear was thoroughly searched. They took everyone's cell phones and Heather's satellite phone. The Mexicans were surprised that they found no weapons other than three small knives.

'Lupe, since you did such a thorough job searching the women you can take care of the gringo's body, but first get our vehicles up here,' said Raul. 'Che, make sure that the camp is clean and you get everything in that big long van of theirs. The body too. He walked over with a sneer to Kristina and moved up close. She almost gagged as his breath blew across her face.

'I think, señorita, that you will keep me company tonight. I could see you watching me. I'm most handsome and sexy, yes? I can tell you want to fuck me, eh.'

The group was in a state of shock. Their starlit night in 'Oh Mexico' had turned into a horror story, and it was soon going to get worse, much worse.

Najma said, 'Heather,' while looking at the three women. Heather couldn't help it, she turned and opened her mouth then quickly closed it again but that was enough. Najma walked to her. 'I thought I recognized you from the north mountains but I wanted to be sure. I remember you, too, old man,' she said to JT. She moved close to Heather just like Raul had done to Kristina. 'I think perhaps you will keep me company this evening and then perhaps Lupe. He seemed to like the feel of you. Maybe even Raul if he can still get it up after the blond-haired girl.'

Heather felt acid burning in her throat and she started to shake. She had never experienced a sexual threat before, or even a physical threat. She was getting nauseous and thought she would rather die than be touched by any of them.

*Jim*—the thought of him gave her a moment's happiness. Jim would come for her and save them.

Najma motioned with her small bulbous carbine toward one of the three dust-covered black Yukons that were now idling nearby. 'Walk, you two!' she commanded JT and Heather. Najma knew what Heather's hope was. It was hers, too. 'Soon maybe your Jim will be here. Keep moving. Maybe I can entertain him, too.'

Heather turned at the mention of Jim. It came to her. She should have known. She would have, if she was thinking straight or thinking at all. It was the woman terrorist. 'Jim would never touch you or give you the time of day but he will find you,' said Heather.

Najma raised the small 22 rifle and put the barrel close to Heather's face. Heather felt faint. If it had been anyone other than Heather, she would have been dead for disobeying Najma's instructions to keep moving. Instead, Najma said, 'Yes, I hope he does and then I will touch you both and as long as you both live, maybe only days, you will wish you were dead.' Heather's head spun and she fell, fainted, falling flat-out. JT grimaced as her head made a loud crack hitting a rock. He bent to help her and received a vicious kick to his ribs. There was a small cracking noise as if a tiny echo of Heather's head hitting the black varnished stone.

# Chapter 13

S hit!' Sheilla uncharacteristically exclaimed. She jumped up and sprinted the few feet to the general's office. Her eyes were wide and she hesitated before blurting out, 'They got Heather and her whole science crew in Mexico. An Associated Press reporter said they had a tip and was given my name. What were they even doing there? The AP are sending a fax through. I'll go get it.'

The general immediately called Nielly at Fort Bragg. 'We have a problem. I want you at Fort Huachuca immediately. My clerk will get you transportation. When can you be ready?'

'Give me two hours. We were just working on our gear and some rest,' said Nielly.

The general called Jim at Fort Huachuca. He was not looking forward to telling him what Sheilla had just heard. *Nothing for it but to do it*—the old officers' motto. If it's unpleasant, best to just get it over with.

'Jim, can you get to a secure phone and call me back right away?'

Jim recognized the urgency in Will's voice. He immediately excused himself and left for the Strategic Air Command headquarters. General Whitcuff had lent him a driver and jeep and said he would clear his entry into the facility by the time he got there. General Whitcuff, as Will Crystal had requested, ordered his staff and the StratCom headquarters to give Jim every courtesy.

An MP gave Jim a swipe card at the entrance, told him where the communication center was, and then called ahead. A sergeant was waiting at the door and asked him what he needed.

'Secure phone line.'

'Go through that door and use the first office on the right,' said the staff sergeant.

Jim thanked him over his shoulder as he headed into the office and dialed General Crystal. The general had been glad to have a couple of minutes to think before talking to Jim. He immediately concluded he would not be able to hold Jim back and the best thing he could do was get him all the support he could and as fast as he could. His chief clerk arranged Nielly's transportation on a C-17 Globemaster. It was the only thing he could get that could transport the Special Forces team immediately. The general had given his assistant a list of instructions. One of them was to get Brush to Fort Huachuca as fast as he could.

'Your line secure, Sam?' the general asked Major General Whitcuff.

'Scrambled, Will, but not completely secure like our crypto com center is.'

'We have a situation developing and Jim is going to need some help.'

'I have already greased all the wheels for your colonel. I'm short-time and it is more gratifying to help old buddies than worry about protocol. If I've got it or can get it, he'll have it, whatever he needs.'

'Thanks, Sam, this one is important. Jim will be going after the one surviving Seattle terrorist and it just turned personal. It appears they have kidnapped his girlfriend and a science group from ASU. Jim will push with or without support and I won't be able to slow him down.'

'Call me if you need me and I'll look out for your boy,' said Sam as he hung up. At least something interesting was happening for his last few days in the army, he thought, but he felt badly for Jim and his girlfriend.

'Will, what's up?' asked Jim.

'Bad news. I don't know the details yet, or even if it's true for sure, but we just got a message routed through the Associated Press that Heather and the rest of the ASU scientists have been kidnapped in Mexico.'

The general didn't wait for Jim to say anything. He filled him in with what they knew so far and told him that he was getting Nielly and Brush to Fort Huachuca as soon as possible. Jim's mind was racing and again, acid crept up into his throat. He heard himself say, 'Heather was supposed to call me last night on the sat phone but she never did. I was hoping that she would call this morning.' He regained his control a little. 'Do everything you can from your end, Will. I got a lesson last night on the latest drones they're working on here. They might be useful for recon. I'm going to assemble a support team. I'll need MPs and whoever they have here with criminal division and as much intel as I can get about the area and the cartel.'

'I've talked to Sam Whitcuff and he will get you what you need. But remember, Jim, I didn't say it was the cartel or Najma that was involved; we don't know any details yet.'

'It's Najma and she's tied to the cartel now. I'm going to see what kind of an encrypted portable phone they can give me. Call you back,' said Jim as he replaced the handset in the cradle.

His mind was reeling. He moved to efficiency mode. It was the only safe place for him to be. He was used to doing this in difficult situations but Heather's involvement added a completely new dimension. He wondered if he could live without her; he cursed himself for not warning her. He shook those personal worries from his mind for now; he needed to concentrate on getting her back. This was what he did. He didn't lose people, he would get her back. The image of two young faces formed, the two little girls he hadn't gotten back; he'd thought he could protect them, too. He forced them from his mind. That wouldn't happen this time. Not with Heather. *Don't dwell on things past,* he told himself, *just react to the situation. That's what you do best. Get a plan and get her back.*


'Do you think we could do this all the time, just sit around and enjoy the scenery?' asked Glenda.

'I like it with you now, and can't think of anywhere else I would rather be, but neither of us is ready to put our feet up just yet. Our golden years are still a few years away,' Brush laughed.

'Brush, I don't want to push things and maybe we shouldn't even talk about "us"—it's just that right now, I like being with you. You're the guy for me in the here and now. If I go back to my old job at the FBI and you do yours, we won't be able to see much of each other. After these past two months, that doesn't sound very attractive to me.'

Brush never planned for the future. If he had a motto it was *Carpe Diem.* He always lived in the present; he had learned that in Vietnam just as Jim had. Maybe they all had. There might not be a next moment. It allowed you to relax in the present with no agitations or worries about tomorrow and Brush had always hung on to this concept. But Jim hadn't; once out of Vietnam he reverted to being a planner. Brush gave Glenda a kiss. They were good together and he wanted to be with her, too, in the here and now. Tomorrow would take care of itself. Their kiss was interrupted by a PA system announcement.

'Brush McGuire, please report to any cruise ship staff or come to the bridge.'

'Sounds like our home away from home Alaska idea is probably in trouble,' said Glenda. 'I'll wait for you in the cabin.'

Glenda had no intention of staying on board without Brush. She made her way to the cabin and packed their few belongings. She still hoped they could stay but had been an agent long enough to know that sort of announcement meant an emergency.

'Got to go, beautiful,' said Brush when he returned.

'Wrong, sweetie, we've got to go. You're not going anywhere without me!' she said in a way that told Brush she meant it.

Brush looked at Glenda Rose. He didn't want to leave her either and had told the captain 'they' would both be going. 'The ship's captain said he would tell his home office to give us a rain check on a future voyage. Sure you're up to a helicopter flight?'

'I'm not whole yet, but I'm not going to bleed to death. Let's hit it. But we are going to come back and do this trip. I hope you thanked the captain,' said Glenda with appreciation for his offer.

Nielly and his fifteen-member team had an ETA of 16:30. Brush and Glenda would not get to Fort Huachuca until after 22:00. The BWL, Sheilla and her analysts, and the general were all focused, working as diligently as they ever had in their lives. Outside events rarely touched their office staff personally. The rule was, they chased the bad guys but the bad guys never chased them or their families. Having this rule broken was an eye-opener.

'We've had a fax,' announced Sheilla. 'They are holding Heather, JT, and their friends and they want a five million dollar ransom.'

'Damn it to hell... I'll call Jim immediately,' said the general.

'Maybe this isn't connected to Najma,' said Mark.

'It is but something doesn't fit,' responded Sheilla.

'Come on, think,' she whispered aloud to herself. 'What's going on here? It's Najma, so why the ransom? Why notify BWL? They must know Heather is connected to Jim and Jim to BWL. Heather wouldn't tell them unless she was forced. How did they find out—think, think.'

At the base, Jim was getting all the cooperation he needed. General Whitcuff was assembling a technical staff for Jim as fast as he could, but there were limits on their efficiency while they got organized and they could not answer Jim's main question: where was Heather being held?

The general also helped Jim set up both an operations team and what would eventually become his center of operations. At first it was more a liaison team than a true tactical operations team and its first responsibility was to help him access the base's resources.

'They must have captured them in this area'—Jim pointed at a map—'just south of the Huachuca Mountains and the US border. It's approximately where she said they would be camping. Are they still close to this area? How did they know where to find them or was it a local gang that just bumped into them or saw them driving up a remote road? Anyone have any ideas on how to check any of this out?'

A soft-spoken soldier said, 'Possibly we should monitor all cell calls and look to see if we can get into the cartel's computers. Maybe there is information there, if it is the cartel.'

'Can you do that from here?' asked Jim.

'I could get their cell calls, not sure about penetrating their computers… but I wouldn't be allowed to,' said Specialist Gordon.

Jim didn't want to put General Whitcuff at too much risk but he needed information.

'Could you advise someone else how something like that might theoretically be done?' asked Jim.

'Sure, leaves the army out of messing with the Mex nationals. No problem.'

'Call this number now and get started. You will be working with Sheilla. Did the base have any surveillance aircraft along the border last night?' asked Jim.

'We were testing the cameras on an unmanned aerial vehicle, a drone. It might have covered a little of Mexico, maybe thirty miles south of the border. We also had a piston-popper prop plane up, tracking behind the UAV with its own cameras. We already assumed you would want that aerial footage. It's on its way here now with a technician,' said the master sergeant assigned to the group, just as there was a knock on the door and the technician walked in.

'Our recon mission last night was testing our cameras one hour before sunset to one hour after. I've put the images into moderately fast sequence. It's like a jumping movie. Not smooth but we can see the changes. One frame every five seconds. The chase-plane footage won't help us much, since it was mostly monitoring the drone.'

*Good news at last,* thought Jim, *as long as the film covers the right time.*

'Before we start looking at the footage, I want someone to get some detailed topo maps of this area.' He pointed again on the large-scale map to where Heather had told him they were headed. 'Now show me where the drone started filming.'

'Here, sir, just east of Yuma and stopped here, just west of Douglas.'

'Skip ahead to this longitude.' Jim pointed a short distance to the west of where Heather had said they were headed.

'Yes, sir. Start time of the footage is 17:32. We'll start then at 18:45.'

# Chapter 14

There, slow the film. That looks like a fire and head-lights, three vehicles close together moving north and another without headlights on, pointing southeast, close to the fire,' said Jim. 'The cars are converging near the fire.'

The picture frames flicked across the screen for another minute and the lights faded from their view. The specialist walked in with the high-resolution topo map for the area that Jim had asked for.

'What're the exact coordinates where we saw the lights?' asked Jim.

'Here, sir.'

Jim traced his finger along the roads. Down a spur road three miles south of the cars' lights, there was an abandoned mine with several buildings.

'Sir, I have your analyst, Sheilla, on the phone.'

'Sheilla.'

'Jim, I'm so sorry about Heather. The army guy you had call helped us and we have several cell calls in this area in the time frame you asked for, but no luck with penetrating the cartel's computers.' As Sheilla spoke, Jim wrote down the coordinates where the cell calls had originated.

'Thanks, Sheilla.' He found the coordinates on the map. The abandoned mine was there, right where the cell calls had emanated. He double-tapped his finger. 'I need to get here fast,' he said. 'Here's what I want to do. I'm going to make a High Altitude High Opening jump on this side of the border and glide across to the mine. Can you get a drone launched, that can send live video, and can you fix me up with two-way communication? I want the drone doing surveillance and you verbally keeping me posted after the HAHO. Constant ground and air surveillance. Any problems with that?'

The group got busy, made calls, and got Jim what he wanted. He then explained his plan to the captain who would be in charge of the operation from what would become the tactical operations center for his planned penetration into Mexico.

The master sergeant walked to Jim and the captain. 'Excuse me, sir. We have everything set; the com, a plane for the drop, and we can muster a drone and crew. It will take about an hour to outfit the drone and get it up. We should be an all-go at 15:00. Main problem is we don't have any good daylight camouflage parachutes, just round, steerable ones in light colors. The other problem is the weather is turning bad in that area. Thunderstorms are predicted.'

'I brought a black, night-jump Ram with me. It'll have to do. The weather, though, is good news; it will help. Captain, Sergeant, you have any questions?'

'No, sir,' responded the captain and sergeant together.

'I'll get my gear together. Have the chopper standing by where I originally landed, near my quarters,' said Jim.

'Roger that, and we'll watch your backside,' assured Captain Fuller.

The master sergeant just looked at Jim. He was old school and airborne. This brought back memories of what the army was supposed to be like. He nodded and said, 'Good luck, sir.' The sergeant had weighed the risks and didn't like Jim's odds. *Black chute, as black as me,* he thought, *in a white sky.* A bad combination. Not to mention the communication might fail or the video might not work right. Something would fail. One man up against however many those cars could hold.

Fifteen hundred miles north in the bio lab, Will Crystal was having similar thoughts. *What if they are trained and not just a rabble group? Jim seems to believe they might be cartel. The odds aren't good.* He trusted Jim's abilities more than anyone else's and was not accustomed to worrying about him. The unrelenting concern made him wish he had never been promoted and exacerbated his dislike for desk-time. He hated sitting behind a desk. He picked up the phone.

'Jim, you know it would be better to wait for Nielly, but I'm not going to ask you to. We have set up continuous communication between us and your tactical operations center. We'll have two-way with you and with Nielly when he gets there. Brush is headed your way, dragging his convalescing FBI lady along. They won't arrive until 22:00. You done any HAHO jumps lately?'

'I haven't made any jumps lately. But we used a lot of them in Africa. It never leaves you.'

'Be careful, I'm not planning on running this place alone,' said Will as he hung up.

Jim's driver pulled the jeep up to the Huey as Jim twirled his fingers at the pilot. They unloaded all his gear into the chopper as the blades spun up to speed. Jim checked his watch. Twenty minutes until the drone was flying. He put his headset on, looked at the sergeant riding in the back, and gave a thumbs-up. The RPMs increased and the chopper lifted off. The pilot knew where the drop was.

'General, Glenda and I are in a Canadian Coast Guard helicopter on a military secure line,' said Brush. The general knew he was telling him he was on a secure line but the Canadians would probably be monitoring. 'Can you give me the current situation?'

'Not good. They have JT, Heather, and six others. Jim thinks he knows where and has headed off on his own. Sheilla thinks something doesn't fit and is talking to herself and scratching her head a lot trying to figure out why she is bothered,' said the general.

'He should have waited for me. I don't think he has ever done a HAHO without me before. What's Sheilla worried about?'

'She thinks it's too easy. Either the group is not skilled or they are very skilled. In which case it was too easy for us to find them.'

'A trap,' said Brush, 'and he's headed right into it. It's our nasty lady.' Brush followed with a string of expletives that would make the Canadian eavesdroppers' ears burn.

The general had never heard Brush upset before. He usually accepted things as they came with a certain nonchalance.

'I'll call as soon as this bird lands and we get on the State Department plane in Nanaimo, General. It's apparently the closest airport on Vancouver Island.'

'It is the closest airport and the fastest plane I could get you on. A chopper will be waiting to pick you up in Tucson,' said Will. But he had no idea he would be flying that helicopter.

# Chapter 15

It was a turbulent glide. Building cumulus clouds, a few turning elephant gray with white tips and black-slung bottoms. Better than a white-blue sky to conceal his black, night-jump parachute. The flight, and his exit from the comforting thump of the green helicopter, had come off without a hitch. He was gliding, suspended from his Ram Air at 17,000 feet, about 12,000 feet above the ground just south of the Mexico border. It was 15:45. Hanging below his feet was a heavy pack with his gear. The tactical operations center was in contact with him and the drone had been launched successfully. The video feed from the drone was acting as a lookout for Jim. It was flying on the US side of the border but scouting for aircraft or anything it could see on the ground to the south into Mexico. It was also monitoring Jim's glide toward the old mining camp.

Jim's face was set. He concentrated on terrain and wind. He had committed the topographical features to memory. He wanted to glide up to the back side of a hill just west of the mine buildings. He did not think they would have a lookout that far away. He would have the afternoon sun at his back coming in, and when on the ground; he needed to time his descent just right.

Dark clouds were looming larger and closer. Harder for gliding but better cover for his approach. As the dark clouds grew, the moving black speck in the sky blended perfectly with the hodgepodge of gray, black, and white billowing mounds of moisture.

He kept his mind off the fact that Heather, JT, and their friends had been captured last night, nineteen long hours ago. He should have been there earlier, checked into the call from her that never came. *Damn it to hell, I should have told her to stay in Arizona.* He received a continuous feed from his hastily arranged TOC back at the base. There had been neither aircraft nor anything else moving on the ground. The desert seemed devoid of human life. The TOC team gathered information about the mining buildings and relayed a description of the layout to him. They were made of concrete and adobe.

He bounced on the gusting wind, happy to see the target hillside, doing his best to keep thoughts of what had happened to the researchers and Heather from his mind. He didn't expect that it would be good, but he would keep hope alive and not let alternatives enter his thoughts. They would only make him less effective.

A soft landing onto the hard scrabble of the hillside. He was just below the crest of the hill. He took the minutes necessary to fold the parachute and carefully weight it with some large smooth rocks. Then he grabbed the fifty-five-pound pack and started for the west side of the hill's crest.

He crept to the top, positioned himself between a barrel cactus and a rock, and took his first look at the mine through a high-powered spotting scope. It had to be the right place. It was. Men were stationed outside and there were four vehicles—one with an

ASU emblem on the front door. Relief coursed through him but he drew a curtain in front of any thoughts about Heather's fate.

He didn't have a plan, just get in and play it by ear. He didn't think they would be expecting anyone to find them this fast. That was his only advantage—going now. Originally, he had thought, as a minimum, he would be able to recon the facility and wait for help. He knew now what he had known all along, he wouldn't wait. He couldn't wait. The kidnappers were likely an experienced group of hardened men but they were not professional soldiers. But then Najma's image crossed his mind. Was it her? He could only hope the others were not professionals, she would be enough to contend with. Poor odds. Was he doing the right thing, was he good enough on his own? Were they waiting for him? The answer to the last question of course was, yes, but not today. He had reacted faster than they had thought. They didn't expect him to come now and come alone.

His radio crackled. Someone was calling but the hills must be obscuring the transmission.

'Damn it,' said Will Crystal when Jim didn't answer, 'he's walking right into the hands of Najma.' He wished he had tried harder to persuade Jim to wait for Nielly. 'Let me know the instant you get through to him, Captain. Thanks for trying to patch me through.'

He yelled for his adjutant. 'Get me a ride to Fort Huachuca now. I want to be there ten minutes ago. Then call General Whitcuff and tell him I'm arriving. Call me on my cell and tell me where the departure will be, McChord or our airport. I'm headed up top now, so get me something fast,' he boomed. 'I don't want to stand around up there waiting.'

Jim counted the men. Two standing in front of the building

and one on the roof. The building was L-shaped with a small square room jutting from the long side. Jim picked a route to approach. He hid a 9mm Beretta just under the edge of a large boulder. He took the rest with him. His plan now was to leave the weapons he didn't think he would need at two places along his approach. If he failed to kill the kidnappers, he wanted a way for himself and the others, Heather, to fight back along an escape route.

The three women, all except Misa, were put in a concrete room and told to sit against the wall on the floor. The old bunkroom had several old, dirty mattresses. The stuffing was protruding from holes. The room smelled stale, old, unused. Thousands of black mouse droppings covered the floor. Insects with a hundred legs scurried back and forth, spiders sat waiting on their webs.

'What's that squeaking?' asked Nicola.

'Mice,' said Heather. 'They're having babies in the mattresses. From the looks of this room, probably dozens of babies.'

Kristina started shaking. 'What's going to happen to us? I'm scared and I hate mice!'

Heather was scared too, but she was trying not to show it. She didn't like the way the man Lupe was looking at them or had touched them at their camp. And she wasn't quite sure why Misa had been separated from the other women but she was certain the explanation wouldn't be pleasant. Jim would get here, he would save her life, just as he had saved her before—but this wasn't the same. What would she have to endure while she waited for him? What had she brought down on her new friends? Why hadn't they just gone to the White Tank Mountains? She shook her head and tried to force hope into her thinking.

There was loud laughing outside—men coming closer. The door flew open. Raul, Lupe, and Najma walked in. Kristina started to sob. Nicola's jaw was set. She looked defiant. She wasn't, she was petrified. Her mind was deserting her, fleeing to a better place, a safer place. 'Three little chicks lined up against the wall,' spat Raul. 'How pretty.' He looked at Kristina. 'I think you want me the most, heh, little lady.'

Najma leaned casually against the wall and watched Heather. She pulled her small double-sided knife from its leather sheath.

'Stand up,' she said to Heather. 'Take off your clothes.'

Heather didn't move. Najma turned to Kristina and kicked her in the head.

'Quiet, blondie, you don't have anything to be sobbing about yet. Up,' she repeated to Heather.

Heather stood this time.

'Now take them off.'

'No, screw you. I'm not doing anything you say.'

Najma turned from Kristina, who was barely conscious, to Heather. She moved so quickly that Heather didn't see the knife flick down her face. Blood dripped from her smooth cheek. Najma left her with a six-inch-long razor-slice from just below her right eye to her jaw. Heather almost fainted but Najma grabbed her by her throat, pinned her to the wall. 'Do as I say, or Lupe over there will take them off for you.'

Raul walked over to Kristina, picked her up, and threw her on one of the old mattresses. Stale beer and garlic would be the last memory she had of North America. Her addled mind drifted to her home in Poland, Vidya, and black fungus.

If Najma's massacre had left impressions on the people of

Tubutama, the events that followed would change Heather forever. She was forced to watch their suffering for what seemed like hours before Kristina and Nicola finally died. Najma sat next to Heather the entire time, refusing to allow her to escape into unconsciousness or even look away. Heather had never wished for someone to die before. But she wished it for Kristina and Nicola fervently; it would be their only escape. The sheer terror of seeing what these people were capable of made her truly hate, for the first time in her life. She was demeaned and exposed and she knew that she was witnessing the prelude to what would happen to her.

A mouse sat on top of the once beautiful Kristina. She was crusted in black blood and lay naked and discarded on the mattress. The mouse cleaned its face with its quick-moving front feet. It stood up and looked about. It had a snug home and babies to take care of. The events had no more meaning for the mouse than the events witnessed by the green gecko a few days earlier.

Heather was numb. She had learned, in the span of a few short hours, to hate and loathe people. She had cried for hours in the night, with her two new friends dead and defiled only feet away. Soft moonlight passed through the small open squares in the building. Light and then dark as clouds passed by. Heather had fallen asleep out of pure exhaustion at some point in the night. She had no idea what time it was, only that the sun was up and the left side of her face was throbbing and crusted with dried blood. Her hands and feet were tied. She was naked and shivering against the cold concrete. She didn't understand why she wasn't dead with the others.

The desert warmed as the day passed. Najma walked around,

looking at the buildings and her prisoners. She had wanted to taunt Heather more but had been satisfied with touching her body, reading her mind as she watched Raul and Lupe use and torture the other two women. Heather's turn would come when her agent-man arrived. He would watch as Heather had watched, before she killed them both.

Najma scanned the hills above the mine. If he came today it would probably be out of the west but more likely it would be at night. She didn't expect him today, it would be too early for them to figure out where they were holding the captives. Tomorrow or the next day would be most likely. The middle of the night was when they would need to be most alert. Nevertheless, she checked the men and ordered them to be watchful. Toward evening, she would place one of the men on a rise to watch. Raul was not pleased with Najma telling his men what to do, taking charge.

Amir was literally sick and lying in the backseat of the Yukon. He had heard the sounds of the women last night and had eventually covered his ears and hidden in the four-wheel drive vehicle. This was his doing and he was ashamed. He was mortified to hear in the morning that two of the women had been raped and beaten to death. It was beyond comprehension. They had had nothing to do with his brother. He didn't even wish for the American agent to die anymore.

Jim followed a small dry streambed around the hill from where he had landed. He was not as concealed as he would have liked but there was no other choice. He pushed on. His approach would have to be from the west. Just where Najma would expect him if she knew he was here.

The storm was getting worse and small distant thunderclaps were moving closer to the mine, helping to conceal his approach. He was dressed in standard army-issue, desert-camouflaged fatigues and blended in with the desert browns. He moved slowly, trying to use what little cover there was. He could creep to about one hundred and fifty yards from the building. There was no way to move closer without the man on the roof seeing him. *Where are the prisoners being kept?* he wondered. Men stood outside two different doors of the long cement building. They must be inside one of those doors.

Among the weapons that Jim had brought were three silenced guns. Two were pistols; he quietly pulled the third from the rucksack and extended its stock. It was a Heckler & Koch MP5SD. He had used it many times over the years and trusted it. He had subsonic ammunition to keep the bullet below the sound barrier. It was not silent, however, as many people assumed silenced guns were, listening to the *fwip* in movies. Only Najma's specially made twenty-two was truly silenced. He willed the thunderclaps closer. He would try to conceal his shot at the roof guard with the thunder. Once he had calculated the time between lighting and thunder, he would take the shot.

If he were lucky, the man would die without making any noise and the thunder would cover both his shot and perhaps the man falling on the roof. Only one man would be down, he thought, but he would be out of sight on the roof. He watched as the lightning flashed nearly twelve seconds before the long, low rumble reached his hearing. He needed to get the timing right but he was feeling impatient. He restrained himself, knowing that effectiveness would get the captives out alive and Heather into his arms. Impatience would hamper the rescue and perhaps all eight would die. Unknown to him, he only had five to rescue.

Minutes passed; Najma walked around the building and into his sight. He thought for a second, *I can take her out and all will be fine.* He willed her to move to a position where he could eliminate her without instigating an open fight and putting Heather in danger but instead she stayed by the door. He let out a long breath, counted the seconds. Only nine seconds between flash and boom. Move back inside, he willed her. She did and he waited several more minutes. It was time.

He slowed his breathing. It was not a long shot but the wind was starting to gust unpredictably. He focused on the wind, watching dust near the building. Eight seconds. He took the tension out of the trigger and squeezed, just as the thunder rumbled. The Mexican doubled over and fell. The door guards didn't move. He saw nothing change. He put a silenced 9mm Glock in his front belt holster, slung the heavy rucksack, and with the HK MP5 pointing to the front, crept toward the buildings.

'Lupe, I think you need some fresh air. I want you up on the ridge near those rocks,' ordered Najma. 'You stay quiet, sound-less, and motionless until I tell you otherwise. You see anyone, you call me on my cell. Don't start shooting.'

Lupe started to say something and then thought better of it. Najma looked carefully at him with barren, black eyes. Lupe thought, the farther away from her the better. He went to the car to get a coat, night-vision goggles, and a rifle.

Jim looked carefully into the first small opening in the build-ing that he came to. There was no glass covering. His eyes blazed with fury as he saw two young women, probably once beautiful and intelligent, now naked and twisted in death. Anger filled him. Where was Heather? He heard someone walking to his right at the other end of the building. He moved cautiously back around the corner to stay out of sight. He peered back where he had heard the footsteps and saw a man carrying a rifle and a gym bag walking up the hill.

Jim moved to the opposite corner. The two door guards were still in the same place, out in front. He looked behind him and could hear but not see the man climbing the hill. Only four seconds now separated the thunder from the light flashes. The speed of light made the lightning flashes appear nearly instantaneous. Light could travel around the Earth nearly eight times in one second. The thunder travelled nearly as slowly as his silenced subsonic bullets.

He watched. He couldn't go back to the south side, the man on the hill cut off that route. He couldn't go forward, there were two men and Najma and he didn't know how many more. He waited as the thunder got nearer and louder. He couldn't have wished for anything better. If there was a god and one that cared what Jim was doing, he had created the best of all possible worlds, as Pangloss might have said in *Candide*. It wasn't the best of all possible worlds for the two women scientists lying still, only a few feet on the other side of the wall but then it hadn't been that good in Voltaire's book either, Jim thought absently, as his mind calculated what he should do next.

He relaxed, waiting for something to change. Something he could take advantage of. He waited. A gust of wind formed a small swirling cone of dust: a miniature dust devil. The guard stationed at the farthest door looked at the sky. He turned and said something to someone inside the building. One man on the hill, at least three more in the camp, and Najma. *Is that all of them?* Jim wondered. Then the farthest man turned and disappeared into the building. Jim moved toward the closest man taking long but quiet steps. The man turned, Jim shot him twice, just as more thunder sounded loudly in the sky. Luck: he had always had it—he would need it more now than ever. But his luck was about to run out as the sky turned black as coal.

Nielly's transport jet touched down at Davis-Monthan. The Special Forces team hustled off carrying bags of gear. Two-and-a-half-ton trucks and a pair of high mobility, multipurpose, wheeled vehicles, better known as Humvees, stopped next to the plane. Six soldiers helped load the team and their gear into the open-backed trucks. A minute later, they headed across the airfield.

A Chinook helicopter waited with the rear-loading ramp down. The Special Forces formed a line as a soldier in the back of each truck tossed gear bags. The bags traveled down the line and ended carefully placed inside the oversized Boeing helicopter. Then the team loaded, seven soldiers on each side. Nielly waved at the ground troops and jumped onto the raising ramp. He walked straight to the two sergeants waiting inside the helicopter.

'You have current weather in the drop zone?'

'Cumulus tops to 35,000 feet, thunder and lightning, scattered heavy rain. A great night for parachuting in,' he said with wry smile. 'Weather predicted to last through the night. What's our departure time from Huachuca?'

Nielly, however, was pleased. His team either ignored weather or did just as Jim was now doing; used it to their advantage.

'Zero two thirty,' said Nielly. 'I want a briefing on the ground there before we go. Two of my men will stay with the chopper and check our gear. The others will get some shut-eye. I want you and the pilot to stand by after we land and be ready to fly at a moment's notice if we have to go earlier.'

Brush and Glenda were sitting next to each other on a Gulfstream 550.

'Just about as cozy as our cabin, eh,' said Brush.

'The only way I can tell you're Canadian is when you use the "eh" at the end of a sentence,' said Glenda looking at him with smiling puppy dog eyes. 'I think I'm feeling really serious about you, Brush. I don't know what to think about that.'

These were the words that had always sent him running for cover—'serious' and 'I love you.' For the first time in his life, he looked at a woman who uttered one of those fateful words, and didn't want to run. He wanted to stay.

'How much longer to our touchdown, do you think?' asked Glenda.

'Best guess is ninety minutes. Probably another hour to the army base after we land.'

'You worried about him?'

'So far Najma has shot you, shot Jim. I'm worried.'

# Chapter 16

Jim carefully looked into the room. He was stunned to see Heather sitting on the floor naked with arms and hands tied. Crusted blood covered the right side of her face. Tears instantly started to wash across the crusted blood as soon as she saw him. He grabbed the dead man in the entrance and dragged him inside.

All he wanted was to hold her and set her free but he couldn't, not yet. 'I'll be back,' he said softly. 'You're safe now.' He turned to go, he knew it was the right choice, the one that he should make to save them both, but he couldn't do it. He ran to her, cut her loose, and pulled her to him. 'We'll leave in a few minutes,' he whispered. 'We'll go home, we'll be together and safe. Stay where you are until I get back.'

He quickly grabbed a blanket from the bed and wrapped her in it.

Heather could only nod as a torrent of tears streamed across her face in a mixture of relief that he was here and terror for what might still happen.

Jim moved to the other door. He heard no one. He had been lucky so far. Relief flooded through him. Heather was alive. He forced the feelings away for the moment and focused with renewed energy. He had to get the other two men and Najma. Just as he got to the door, Che and another tough-looking Mexican walked out only feet from him. Jim shot them both and moved to the second door. Inside were three men and a woman, all bound and gagged, but no Najma. He moved inside, cut JT loose, and gave him the knife.

'Cut the others loose, JT. You OK?'

'Nothing serious. They killed Richard though and last night we heard awful screams.'

'Yes,' said Jim as he squeezed his friend's arm.

'Any of you know how to use a gun?' asked Jim.

'No,' said Vidya. 'I don't like them.'

'I've done some shooting,' said Ralphy.

Jim looked at Ralphy. 'Drag these two inside and take their guns. All of you listen, no talking. Ralphy, watch to the east, to your right and the others, move as fast and quietly as you can to the first door on your left. Heather is inside.'

Jim looked outside and ran back to Heather. He pulled his old Vietnam MAC-SOG knife from its sheath and carefully cut the remaining soft metal wrapped around her wrists and ankles. He put his arm around her and moved to the front wall near the door, watching the small window at the back. Najma was somewhere close by. They looked at each other and tears started to slide down her cheeks again gushing as she bawled just like young Ben had in the mountains not so long ago.

'You're OK now, sweetest. No one is going to hurt you.'

'I don't think I'll ever be OK. They're monsters. Inhuman. I didn't know people like them existed,' she blurted out between sobs.

'I'll make sure you are OK. We have each other and friends like

Duane and JT.'

'Thank God he's alive.'

Just then, Ralphy, JT, Vidya, and Misa ran into the room and stopped as if they had hit a wall. They stood there staring open-mouthed at what only a night before had been their happy campmates and Vidya's girlfriend. JT had to grab Vidya to keep him from falling.

'My baby,' he whimpered.

'Ralphy, guard the door.' Jim looked at Misa and the pile of clothes on the floor. 'Please, get Heather some clothes and help her get them on as fast as you can. Use the other clothes to cover your two friends.'

Jim walked to Vidya and looked him in the eye. 'I'm very sorry. We have to go but we'll come back for her. Nothing more can hurt her now. I know how hard this must be, but we have to move.'

Jim peeked out the door past Ralphy. Still no sign of anyone. *Are Najma and the guard on the hill the only ones left?* he wondered.

He looked at Misa. 'Can you help Heather walk? I want you right behind me. Move out the door to your left and follow close behind me. Ralphy, watch to your right and shoot the second you see anyone.'

Heather struggled to move her legs. JT grabbed an arm and helped Misa walk her behind Jim. Heather was numb from multiple doses of adrenaline, cortisol, constant fear, and huddling naked against the concrete all night. She hardly gave a thought to her face and its large gash or the bump on her head.

General Will Crystal was always happy when he got to fly a helicopter. General Whitcuff was proving to be better help than could be expected. The only chopper available was a Bell Long Ranger reserved for the use of the Air Force general at Davis-Monthan air base. Whitcuff had convinced him to loan it to General Crystal.

A driver took Will Crystal to the helicopter. It was pretty and almost new. He quickly checked it over, started it up, and hovered. The general taxied, hovering precisely ten feet over the concrete. He turned the moving helicopter sideways ninety degrees, left and then right, getting a feel for it. Much to the consternation and amazement of the tower, he did a full three-sixty-degree loop, maintaining exactly ten feet ground clearance and moving forward at the same speed. He thoroughly enjoyed himself. He hovered and held it without any movement for almost one minute, and then settled onto the tarmac as Brush and Glenda's plane taxied toward him. He kept the blades turning.

'Doesn't look all that military,' said Brush, as Glenda climbed into the front seat, leaving him to sit in the back alone. Will Crystal ignored Brush. 'You look good, Glenda. Glad to see you out of the hospital.'

'I haven't had much chance to ride up front in one of these,' said Glenda.

'And I thought you were making a smart move, trading that Canadian in the back for me. Now I find out you just want the best view.'

'You'd be a good catch, General, but I think I'll hang on to him a while longer.' Will wondered if Brush, the quintessential playboy, would be a good match for her. Maybe this was different, maybe. *She certainly was a good one,* he thought, *capable, attractive, worth keeping for anyone in his right mind.*

The general lifted straight up, tipped the nose down, and then headed south.

Jim looked behind him, didn't see anyone. Around the corner, it was clear, too. He scanned the hill searching for the lookout. He didn't see him.

Someone was watching Jim and the kidnapped group, though. Amir had heard the sounds and looked out the window. He surprised himself. He was glad to see the cartel members killed and the prisoners getting away. He knew he didn't belong to the world that Raul and Najma did. All he wanted was to get home to South Kensington and try to pretend he had never come to Mexico. That was not to be his future.

There was a movement to Amir's left. Najma and Raul walked around the far corner. He wanted to warn the prisoners that Raul and Najma were there. But he couldn't find the courage to yell out and hated himself for it.

Ralphy saw them a second later, just as Raul saw him. Raul pulled out a chrome-plated Army Colt 45 from his shoulder holster, pointed it at Ralphy and, before Ralphy could react, walked straight toward the inexperienced grad student firing steadily as he walked. It was a big gun and loud.

'Chinga tu madre, gringo,' spat out Raul. He would kill this white-faced boy. He had no fear of him.

His first shots blew small bits of concrete, hitting Ralphy in the neck and arms. Ralphy fired two shots. There was no evidence of them hitting anything, no dust kicked up or flying concrete fragments. Najma ducked back into the room. She wanted an automatic weapon, not the small 22-caliber pistol she was carrying. Then she raced out and around the south side of the building, carefully peered around the corner, looked up to her left, and saw

Lupe. She pointed at her eyes and then to the west. Lupe waved his hand sideways. He hadn't seen anyone. Najma moved to a small cluster of rocks fifteen feet from the building on the edge of the same hill where Lupe was positioned higher up.

Jim looked at Misa and Heather and said, 'Don't move.' He quickly stepped to the corner and peered around. He was right-handed and moving around a right corner was awkward. He never liked doing it. He had never been good leading with his left. A pugnacious-looking Mexican was walking directly at Ralphy and still firing. Ralphy lay slumped and bleeding in the doorframe.

Raul's attention was on his prey and the blur in his peripheral vision registered too late for him to respond. Jim stepped out and shot him several times in two-round bursts. Jim didn't know this was revenge on the perpetrator of the sadistic rapes of the two women. He scanned the area, focused on the overall picture. *Where is Najma? Somewhere unexpected,* he reasoned.

There was blood dripping from Ralphy's face and neck but otherwise he looked OK. He had been lucky.

'Follow me, stay close,' yelled Jim as he ran back to the west side of the building. He peered around to the south and looked up the hill for the other man. Bullets hit the side of the building and kicked up dust at the corner. Najma waited. She had hoped they would run along the base of the hill behind the building but there was little chance of that now that Lupe had told them where he was. She had not seen the man well enough to know if it was the agent, her enemy. She sprinted, pointing her Russian KPB assault carbine back along the east side of the building. Now, with their escape cut off to the south, she expected them to make for the vehicles or run for it to the west.

Jim loaded a new thirty-round clip. He peeked around the corner again. He guessed that the man had shot ten rounds the first time and would not reload. Jim thought the sound was from an M16. He stepped around the corner and immediately stepped back. The man fired again on automatic. Jim exposed himself again. The man fired again. Jim figured that was close to thirty rounds and his gun would be empty, or at least close to it. He hoped he would reload now. Jim crouched low and ran obliquely along the base of the hill. There were no shots. He stopped behind a small pancake cactus that sprouted next to a rock, and peered around the opposite side from where he had run. He could see Lupe pointing his rifle at the corner of the building. He had not seen Jim move, too focused on replacing his spent clip.

Jim had been lucky once again. More than he could have hoped for. More than he knew. If Najma had stayed where she originally positioned herself, he would have been dead. Luck and skill, neither more nor less important than the other. The man, Lupe, was exposed in his new position. Jim took careful aim and squeezed off a single round. He hit Lupe in the neck and a red fountain of blood washed over the rock as he fell forward.

*The agent.* He was here sooner than she had thought possible. She now knew she had guessed wrong. She hated the American agent for that. He had bested her again. She assumed Raul was dead. If Lupe was dead, she was the only one left. She moved cautiously back to the southeast corner of the building.

Jim took a chance. He was leaving the group exposed on the west side of the building and Ralphy would not be much help to them now. But he thought his best position would be staying where he was and watching the building. He wanted the group where he could see them. Jim whistled. Heather heard and whispered to Misa to look around the corner. Jim motioned with his hand to come toward him and mouthed, 'All of you,' and pointed at the building. Jim allowed a small smile as Heather came around the back with Misa's and JT's help. She was alive, he would keep her that way.

Jim was watching Heather and watching the building when he saw Najma at the corner, looking up the hill. Jim had twenty-nine rounds left. He lifted the MP5. Najma caught the movement and fired on full automatic in his general direction, walking the rounds toward him as she moved the barrel up to where he kneeled. As bullets from her assault rifle landed closer and closer, he squeezed the trigger. She was in his sight and he couldn't miss from this distance. He aimed mid torso and that was a mistake. The bullet hit the KPBs magazine and ricocheted, ripping a deep gash along her right forearm. Even wounded she kept her gun moving in his direction. A fraction of a second later her remaining rounds showered his rock. The firing stopped; her clip was empty. He pointed the HK nine millimeter at the corner where she had been standing. She was gone.

He moved to his left traversing the hill. He wanted to change positions. The group was huddled directly in front of him along the back side of the building. There was nowhere for them to go without being exposed. It was a triangle. He was at the top point and the two corners of the building were the other tips. Heather and the others were along the triangle's base between the two corners.

Najma ran back to where she and Raul had started from, in the corner building. She grabbed a satchel containing several grenades and moved into the room where the two dead women still lay, now covered in polar fleece and Gore-Tex. She would kill the captives with a grenade that she could easily drop out the open window, killing Jim's woman and maybe him, too. She smiled to herself.

She walked to the window staying low and was nearly there

when the forlorn face of Vidya looked in at her. He still couldn't believe that Kristina was dead. He had to look back into the room to see if it were true. As soon as he saw Najma, he yelled, 'Woman! It's the killer woman.'

Just moments before he had had no use for guns but after seeing Kristina he wanted to shoot. He had taken the gun from the injured Ralphy and now he pointed it through the window, pulled the trigger, and kept it depressed. It was on full automatic. Thirty rounds danced inside the concrete building. Najma ran for the door. She tripped and almost fell, dropping the satchel with the grenades. Miraculously the bullets ricocheted around her, never touching her as she scrambled through the door.

Najma, just as she had done two months earlier in September, decided to cut her losses. She was wounded and outnumbered. Jim had won again but she would find him another day. He wouldn't defeat her a third time. She ran to one of the Yukons, grabbed the key from under the mat, started it, and pressed the accelerator to the floor, then went swerving down the road spewing rocks and dust. It was the Yukon that Amir was hiding in.

Jim heard the car leave. He motioned for the group to stay where they were. He watched the windows, the building corners, the roof, the desert. Birds were chirping as the sun began to set low over Oh Mexico.

# Chapter 17

Eventually Jim moved, peered through the unglazed windows, checked the vehicles and the bodies to see if any of the Mexican cartel were still alive. He quickly retraced the way he had approached the old mine and collected all of the gear. They might need it and he didn't want to leave evidence of US military involvement. He had no plan when he glided in for getting back to Fort Huachuca. His only thought had been to rescue them. Heather was not in shape to walk and neither was the wounded Ph.D. student. He knew he couldn't take the vehicles over the border. There were no good choices.

The best seemed to be to go back north to their original campsite. He wanted all of them to be away from the mine.

'JT,' said Jim quietly so as not to upset the others, 'can you help me move Kristina and Nicola into the van with Richard?'

'No,' said Vidya. 'I'll help you.'

It was a poignant reminder for all of them to have the bodies so near. They watched sadly as Jim and Vidya gently placed Kristina and Nicola into the van next to Richard Graves's body. A hard moment for everyone that stirred memories for Jim of the bodies of friends he had helped load into choppers in Vietnam.

It was nearing 22:30 when Jim got the van and one of the GMC Yukons ready to leave. They retraced the road to where the happy group had camped just over twenty-four hours ago.

The general settled the Bell helicopter onto the grassy expanse of the parade grounds in front of the officers' houses and a few yards away from the green hulking Chinook. Its two giant front and back rotor blades drooped toward the grass. It was just after 21:00 and the lights in several of the houses blazed. It was only a few hundred feet to General Sam Whitcuff's quarters, but the old general had two jeeps waiting and was there himself to greet his old friend.

'General, this is Major Brush McGuire and Agent Glenda Rose Stuart.'

'Pleased to meet you, General. We're anxious to hear everything you know,' said Brush as they set off across the grass to General Whitcuff's house.

General Crystal said to his old friend, 'I've known Brush and Jim since Vietnam. Brush is Jim's partner. Glenda is an FBI agent, also very capable. She was shot several times last Labor Day and was just released from the hospital the day before yesterday. I pulled them both off a cruise ship headed for Alaska.'

'Here's the situation. Your colonel insisted on HAHOing in alone though he took some high-end equipment and firepower with him. Not sure if he remembers his military training. He set off in a rush with no plans for how to get back over the border. Maybe we should see if the DEA or Border Patrol will help,' General Whitcuff suggested.

'We can't get either of them involved, too many possibilities of leaks. Cartel has too much money and there're too many people willing to take it. I don't trust them,' replied General Crystal.

'We lost contact with the colonel just about the time he should have landed. We have no idea what his status is,' Sam Whitcuff told him bluntly.

Will Crystal sat thinking, then he nodded his head as though he had come to some resolve. 'My boy is good, maybe as good as they get. He and Brush have survived where no one else would have. There's no reason that this should turn out differently.'

'OK then, what do you have in mind? You were thinking pretty deep a minute ago, Will.'

'First, send someone to get Captain Nielly. I have an idea but you probably won't like it and we need to get Nielly involved. If you'll go along with it, we need to get up and running pronto.'

General Crystal outlined his plan. Nielly would make a HAHO with his Special Forces team, just as Jim had.

'Not without me,' said Brush.

'Thought you would say that.'

'I'm not going to sit around here twiddling my thumbs,' added Glenda.

'You're not recovered enough for fieldwork, especially jumping,' said Brush. 'I think you should sit this one out.'

'No way, mister, and I don't want any argument. I won't jump but I'm flying with you.'

At that moment Nielly walked in, snapped a salute, 'Great to see you, General Crystal, General Whitcuff,' said Nielly. 'Brush, thought you were cruising for Alaska.' Nielly was pleased to see Brush, they had hit it off in Seattle. 'Hardly recognize you, Glenda. You look a bit better than you did leaking blood at the Space Needle. We were never really introduced but Brush here has mentioned you a few dozen times so I feel like I know you. You're a brave lady. It's nice to meet you.'

'Here's the plan,' said Will Crystal. 'We go at 23:30. That's about forty minutes from now. Your full team and Brush HAHO just like Jim did this afternoon. I'll fly the big bird. Now for the fun part. After the jump, I'm parking it here.' He pointed to the same detailed topographical map Jim had used. 'It's a canyon. Continues on into Mexico for about three miles. The general here tells me that the Border Patrol watches that area pretty close and they also have listening devices and a radar plane they use in the area. However, he has a way to neutralize them temporarily. When you are ready, I'm going to cactus-top fly that Chinook in and pick all of you up,' finished Will.

'What about our friendly border guards?' asked Nielly.

'I understand there is going to be a lot of activity twenty miles west that should keep them busy long enough to get in and out. Enough said about that,' he stated as he looked meaningfully at the battle-worn base commander.

'Nielly, you ready? Can you get Brush set up with gear?'

'Pleasure, General, we have extra gear and my men are standing by. See you at the chopper.'

Brush and Nielly walked out. General Whitcuff turned to Will Crystal.

'You get caught on this and you're going to be retiring with me, old friend.'

'With your help and a little luck, we'll be OK. It's the way Jim, Brush, and I first got acquainted in Vietnam. I picked them up on the wrong side of the border in Cambodia. This will be déjà vu. Even if we get found out the army won't want to say anything unless the Border Patrol or the Mexicans make a big stink.'

'Uh-huh, well they won't cause me any grief, as short-time as I am,' said Whitcuff. 'Don't worry about me because I want to thank you, Will. You made my last few days here a real pleasure. I'm tempted to fly over with you but I'd better stay and make sure things don't get all gummed up here.'

'Wind her up, General,' said Nielly. 'We're loaded and ready.' The big Chinook lumbered off south and climbed, just skirting east of the Huachuca Mountains' tallest peaks.

'Be careful all of you, see you later,' said Glenda over the internal com. The Special Forces smiled, including the two women on the team. No one had ever told them to be careful before. The message wasn't meant for them but for Brush. He keyed his mic and said, 'Thanks, we'll take care, beautiful, and see you soon,' receiving several amused looks from the Special Forces.

They jumped. If there had been anyone below to look up, they would have assumed they were either dreaming or in a science fiction movie. Fifteen black wraiths streaming across the night sky, visible only between dark clouds. Then they joined up and headed south to the abandoned mine.

The old mine was in sight. Two of the commandos veered off and headed to hilltops south and east of the mine. Nielly always placed snipers, known as guardian angels, as lookouts for his team. The other thirteen including Brush dispersed along a line and glided onto the same hillside that Jim had landed on six hours earlier.

Nielly scanned the mine from the hilltop. 'Nothing observed from alpha,' he said. Both lookouts called in negative movement. 'Approach target,' ordered Nielly. He turned to Gaston, put two fingers facing his own eyes and then pointed at the ground. Gaston would stay on the crest observing. The others split as they had been directed; one group following Jim's approach, the other circling left around the hill and approaching the mine from the north.

The eleven men and two women approached the buildings below. They were nearly invisible, differing from the cartel, who had appeared as light-faced ghosts in the firelight the night before. The Special Forces faces were as dark and as invisible as their bodies. Black raiders on a stormy night.

'Body, Mexican,' reported Sergeant Grant who nearly stumbled over Lupe on the hillside.

They secured the area and buildings and found six bloodied bodies and shell casings scattered everywhere. 'Looks like we missed the war, Gaston,' said Nielly. 'The bodies are all Mexicans. The one-man army didn't need any help from us.'

Mac and Marilyn walked up to Nielly. Marilyn screwed up her face and said, 'Did you see that one ugly mother, sir, Gaston? The guy had hair sprouting from hands and ears, just about everywhere except for the pockmarks on his face.'

'Yeah, I saw him,' said Gaston. 'You think one guy took out all these Mexes? Seems hard to believe. They were well equipped and from the looks of them a pretty ugly crowd.'

'Seems so. Guess the colonel didn't need us. He's like a tornado, leaving death and destruction behind him. Looks like all he needs is a clean-up crew. So hop to it. Let's get the rabble moved and out of sight,' ordered Nielly.

'Somebody else move the hair ball. I'm not touching him. Gives me the heebie-jeebies just to look at the guy,' said Marilyn.

'Raider one, over,' said Nielly, contacting Jim.

'Raider one, hear you loud and clear,' replied Jim immediately.

'Location, One?' responded Nielly.

'Moving in two vehicles approximately three klicks north of mine.'

''Reverse your course, Raider One. We'll call for a ride. Proceed approx 100 meters west of the mine and along the approach road. You'll see the landing zone. Rendezvous, ten minutes. What's your status?' asked Nielly.

'Two in need of care, three others OK, and three that aren't,' responded Jim.

They were being purposefully ambiguous on the off chance that someone was eavesdropping, even though they were talking on 'secure' radios. Jasper Nielly would find out the details about the killings soon enough.

Nielly ordered his team to move the six bodies away from the mine buildings and bury them. He wanted the cartel members hidden.

Brush was the first to the meeting point. 'Nice to see you, and you brought some transportation too, or so I hear,' said Jim. 'Guess your trip to Alaska got shortened. Maybe you aren't meant to get there!'

'That trip is going to happen. The ship's captain got us a rain check.' Brush studied his buddy's face. 'You look unscathed but what's the status of the others—Heather?'

'Pretty rough. Heather's got a nasty gash, a present from our lady friend. Physically she'll be OK. One of the grad students is wounded but not seriously. Two of the women raped and tortured and dead and my old friend from the U Dub, Richard Graves, was killed but not tortured,' said Jim.

'Heather's OK physically?'

'She's going to need some TLC. They stripped her and made her watch while the two women were raped and beaten to death. Najma cut her face and was there taunting her the whole time.' Brush grimaced.

They both knew that what she had watched was a living nightmare, one not easily dissipated. The images would stay with her for the rest of her life. She might never be the same. 'Given time, she can put it behind her,' said Brush trying to be optimistic. Neither of them needed to say more. They both knew the task that lay ahead for Heather. Brush was further convinced that Glenda was not only the right person for him but would be a great help to Heather in the future, too. The two old friends and Glenda had witnessed the mayhem that existed in the world and had learned to deal with it. Maybe the three of them could help Heather to do the same.

Jim took Heather by the hand and walked a few paces into the desert. They sat down on a rock and looked at the stars. Jim put his arm around her.

'We'll be back up north soon. A helicopter is on the way to pick us up. First thing we'll get the cut worked on.'

Heather nodded.

'I'll debrief later. I have no intention of leaving you. I'm going to take some vacation time as soon as we get back.' Jim kept talking, trying to reassure her. He ran his fingers through her hair, knowing she liked it. She let her eyes close for a moment and relaxed a little. The moonlight penetrated between less boisterous clouds in the cool night air, illuminating their faces. Her eyes glistened with a mixture of relief, love, and fear. Heather, for the first time, had personally experienced an alien world, one that Jim regularly stepped in and out of. She had known he lived dangerously but the reality of it made her afraid for their future, afraid for him. Would their life ever be the same? Would she be the same person? She had been baptized by Najma. Could she ever see the world in the same way again? Would she ever feel safe?

Jim sensed her thoughts. The cure would be time. He would love her, hold her, and be there for her. Nothing else in this world was more important to him. He took her hand and said, 'Let's walk back to the others and make sure they are alright.'

Jim looked at Ralphy's wounds. He looked like he had been slapped with a cactus. They were not deep but it would take a doctor a while to pick out the bits of stone and concrete. He looked at Heather's face again in the light from the headlights. There was redness. He had earlier applied an antibiotic ointment and pulled the cut together with butterfly bandages. He would make sure that whoever sutured it used plastic-surgery-style stitches. It was not because he wanted her to remain beautiful but because he wanted her to see less of a reminder of Najma when she looked in the mirror. Heather was lucky to be alive. Najma had planned much worse for her, for them both.

They joined the others, who were sitting a few feet from the Yukon. They were giving the ASU van with the bodies plenty of distance.

'Yeow, what the heck was that?' yelled Vidya.

'Lechuguilla,' said Heather quietly.

Jim smiled a little; it was the first thing Heather had said that sounded like her old self, even if she didn't say it with much enthusiasm.

'What's a letchiguya?' asked Vidya.

'You sat down next to a plant that looks a bit like a scrawny agave. It has needle tips that are very sharp. They just poke you though, no back barbs or anything,' replied Heather in a monotone.

'The wilderness is full of surprises. I don't think I want to see or feel it again for a long time. I take that back, never.' *It would only remind me of Kristina,* he thought. 'I'm staying inside where it's safe. My new motto will be, what's wrong with the great indoors,' he added bitterly, while concentrating on holding back tears.

'I agree with that,' added Misa. 'My biggest risk from now on is going to be a bad back from sitting at my computer,' and she gave Vidya a sympathetic look and patted his arm.

Dark figures started filtering toward the group, the Special Forces team looked like futuristic robots. Nielly smiled, white teeth appearing in a dark-smudged face as he said, 'Dan, our medic, will take a look at your wounds while we wait for our ride. Should be here in a minute.'

Just then, a faint sound of beating blades rose and lowered on the dying winds of the storm.

'Chinook,' said Jim.

'It is, and guess who the copilot is?'

'I give,' said Jim. 'Who?'

'None other than Glenda. She seems to have taken a liking to riding shotgun with the general,' said Brush with more than a little bit of pride. 'Just like old times, eh? The general coming to our rescue.'

'That's one general that I like,' said Nielly. 'Tree-topping a Chinook over the border to pick us up, or as he called it, cactus-topping.'

'If Washington finds out, he'll probably be busted back to captain,' added Marilyn, one of Nielly's best small arms experts and the team's helicopter pilot when they needed one.

The helicopter looked like a prehistoric bug as it settled onto the desert, 100 feet away from where they were waiting.

'How did he know where to land?' asked JT.

'We marked the landing zone with some long wave infrared lights. Can't see them with your naked eyes,' said Nielly.

The Special Forces soldiers walked to the Chinook with the scientists. Jim had his arm around Heather. Brush was waving at the cockpit. One of Nielly's men drove the van up the ramp into the Chinook.

'Twenty minutes on the timer,' said Nielly to one of his men. The dark figure walked to the Yukon and tossed a small packet into the car. 'Sort of a shame, I'd like to have one of these and here I am melting it instead.'

A merry group of eight had driven into Mexico and a subdued but relieved group of five boarded the chopper to leave. Vidya had not known he liked Kristina so much. Now that she was gone, all he could think about was how wonderful she was. He hadn't treated her right lately, too consumed by his own project. Just a few hours ago, Vidya would have said he was a pacifist, normally a peace-loving, kind person. Now he felt an anger bordering on rage for what had happened. He felt guilty and wished he could have a chance to tell her something, anything nice.

'Hi,' said a smiling Brush, as Glenda walked up. 'Thought you were getting serious about the general.'

'I'd rather be back here with you, Brush, and you know it.'

'Just checking, I want you with me wherever I am.'

*A beautiful woman with a great attitude,* he thought. One that almost matched his devil-may-care take on life, but she could be serious and focused when the situation called for it. A woman that could match his abilities and understood the way the world was. It was a new experience for him, an exotically sensuous woman who was his equal.

'Base One, loaded and bringing in the delivery, some damage to two of the packages,' said General Crystal.

'Roger, Crusader, ready for your arrival and will have an inspector to look at the damaged goods.'

# Chapter 18

Ambulances were standing by and Heather and Ralphy were quickly en route to the base hospital. Jim sat by Heather's side holding her hand. He smiled at her and she made a small attempt to smile back. He didn't know what to say; Heather's happy words had always filled the silences. All the normal platitudes seemed trivial after what she had been through. She would never understand how any human could do what they had done to the two women, or how Najma could encourage it.

Jim knew she would need him in the weeks to come but he wouldn't patronize her. He just wanted to be there for her. It was what she had always wanted from him, just to be there with her. Now he hoped it would be enough.

The hospital emergency team injected a local anaesthetic and then carefully removed the field dressing and butterfly bandages. The Special Forces medic had decided to leave the bandages Jim had put on, since she would be getting care in a hospital soon.

'Not bad fieldwork,' said the doctor in charge. 'Some inflammation but that shouldn't be a problem. An excellent plastic surgeon will arrive in a few minutes. General Whitcuff ordered us to get the best available and luckily Dr. Morrel was on duty at Davis-Monthan. He could have made a fortune in private practice.'

A small slight man moved rapidly into the emergency room. He immediately moved Heather's head to the side and examined the cut.

'Yes, OK, looks fairly clean.'

He patted Heather on the shoulder and opened a large medical bag.

'What did you numb it with and did you clean it with anything?'

'We did exactly what you said, ropivacaine local and only sterile water to flush the wound.'

'What was used in the field?'

'A triple antibiotic ointment,' replied Jim.

'No harm done then, nice butterflies. Next time though, better to leave it open if you're not too far from a hospital. Heather, we'll have you stitched up in no time.'

He turned to the other doctor. 'Let's get her a room for the night. Heather, I'd like to give you a propofol injection that will put you to sleep.'

She shook her head side to side in short movements with her eyes closed; more of a tremor. 'No more shots and I'm afraid to sleep in the hospital.' She knew she would be safer at the house with Jim.

Dr. Morrel looked carefully at her. He had been briefed that she had been through a lot. 'OK, young lady, but I am going to give you a midazolam. It's a benzodiazepine and you'll stay awake. I want you to look just as pretty as you did before. This will take a while and I need you to be relaxed and to keep very still.'

Heather nodded.

'Inject some more ropivacaine here and here.' He pointed between her jaw and ear. 'After we're finished, we'll take a look at the other patient.'

When the surgeon had finished with her, Jim's driver picked them up in a Chevrolet staff car.

'Thought this might be better than the jeep.'

Heather couldn't feel anything, her cheek was still numb. She sat on Jim's right side, keeping the new bandages away as she snuggled into his shoulder, not disturbing the new dressing and ice packs that covered most of the right side of her face. The doctor had reassured her many times that she would look just fine and there would be little scarring. He wanted her to come to the air base in two days so he could see how she was healing.

It was as if the local anaesthetic went straight to her brain. Combined with the stress of the last two days it was a potent sleeping pill and moments later she was sound asleep. She barely remembered Jim getting her inside the house and into bed. He should have reported in but he didn't want to leave her. The army had its turn with him and now it was hers and he wanted to be there if she woke up. He called Will Crystal after he had her settled and looking peacefully asleep in bed. Two houses down the street, Brush was happily holding Glenda when he received a call from the general.

General Crystal told them to be at Whitcuff's house at 07:30 and to get some sleep in the meantime. Unlike Heather, sleep wasn't on either Brush's or Glenda's mind.

Brush carefully traced his finger around Glenda's still red scars.

'I think these make you much more attractive. I like them, adds character.'

'You'd better like them, they're part of the package.'

Brush stopped tracing the scars and moved to Glenda's breasts, kissing her softly and they made love with a slow passion befitting both their growing love for each other and her still healing wounds.

Nielly was animatedly giving the general a report of the mission. 'Next time I suggest you just let us sleep at home, save some money, and send in the one-man army. Couple of the Mexicans looked mean and well equipped: submachine guns, automatic rifles, grenades. They were scattered in good defensive positions and Colonel Johnson took six of them out and didn't even get a scratch.'

General Crystal sat amused. This wasn't the first time Jim had gone up against some bad odds and come out unscathed. They used to kid him and say that he had used up his nine lives but he always managed to pull off the impossible.

'Nothing new in that,' he said. 'He's good and he's always been lucky.'

'Luck and skill. I wouldn't mind if you let him come back to Bragg and work with us. I'd take Brush as well,' said Nielly getting out of his chair. 'But if that's it, sir, I'd like to see to my men.'

'We meet here for breakfast 07:30,' said General Whitcuff, 'and bring along your second in command.'

'Roger that, sir.'

'Nice work, Nielly, thank your team for me,' said General Whitcuff as the Special Forces team leader left.

'Pretty nice job flying that big bird in without getting spotted, too, Will.'

'You cleared the way, Sam, or we would never have gotten this done at all.'

'Most fun I've had in a long time but I'm really sorry about the three that were lost and your boy's girlfriend as well. I admit I'm anxious to hear what else you have in mind but guess I can wait until morning.'

'See you in the morning, Sam. I'm going to head over to the TOC. Couple of things I still want to look into.'

# Chapter 19

Guillermo Vasquez was neither pleased nor displeased after hearing Najma and Amir recite the details of their encounter with the scientists and Jim. Failure never impressed him but he wasn't bothered about this. It wasn't a failure for him as he had accomplished what he wanted. He didn't care about the American agent or Amir's or Najma's vendetta. Amir owed him now and had been given a firsthand object lesson in what would happen if he didn't honor that obligation.

'Najma, you lost me one of my more valuable lieutenants. I'm not used to failure and won't tolerate it again,' he said sternly but was secretly pleased with this development. Raul was gone. At some point, he would have become a threat. He had not been smart, nor particularly ambitious. However, Guillermo was certain that Raul was dumb enough to think that he could replace him as El Padrino. His replacement would need to possess more finesse than Raul had.

Najma was never likely to be a threat to him. She was an outsider and a woman who had no ambitions. She only had her primal instincts to assuage and then she would be content. He was convinced of that. She would only be a danger to him if he could not channel her cruelty to suit his purposes. A person like her would always be a challenge to control. She would be his replacement for Raul as an enforcer but nothing else. A she-devil was something he could use. The weakness with her was that he would probably never have her loyalty, if she even had any. She would be a useful employee but for only as long as she wanted to stay. He would use her until that day came and then decide her fate.

'I have a job for you in Cabo San Lucas. Two brothers who have overstepped their bounds.' Najma was pleased and Guillermo noticed that she was. The key to this woman was providing her with people he wanted eliminated and made examples of.

'Ortega will give you all the information you need. I will be away for a few days.'

After Najma left the living room, Guillermo turned toward Amir. 'We are departing for England tomorrow morning.'

Lola sat with Pedro in the kitchen at the hacienda. Her mind vacillated between anger and sympathy. The cartel had killed her son when he was fourteen. Pedro, she guessed, was close to six years old. He had not said a word since the woman without a soul brought him to the hacienda late last night and ordered her to look after him. Pedro was in a state of fright and that made her sad. Being traumatized and alive, however, was better than her son, Ramon. She had agreed to spy for the DEA because she was angry at what the cartel had done to the light of her life, her baby boy. Pedro's presence renewed that anger. She could only imagine why this little boy was here.

'Cuál es tu nombre, poco uno? Please speak to me, tell me your name. Are you hungry, little one?' she asked.

Najma appeared suddenly like a ghost, walked to the boy, and slapped him. 'Answer her. You are my niño now; do not disobey me, ever.'

'He is frightened, señorita.'

Najma walked close to Lola and captured her eyes. A shiver ran down to Lola's toes and repeated itself wave after wave, up and down, down and up. Lola looked at the floor, fear replacing her anger. Najma released her and looked at Pedro.

'Pedro.'

'Sí, señora, tengo mucho hambre.'

'Bring him to my room after you have fed and washed him.'

Najma walked out, much to the relief of Lola but now a new worry supplanted her personal fear of the woman. Why did she want Pedro brought to her room?

Brush woke up and for just a moment did not have the faintest clue where he was in the world. A second later, his mind pinpointed that location as Fort Huachuca, Arizona, in an officer's house with Glenda. He opened his eyes and looked into Glenda's golden-brown smiling eyes. Contentment and happiness permeated them both.

Brush reached over to Glenda and held her side in the wonderful soft curving place between her hips and rib cage. He moved closer and kissed her.

'I couldn't imagine anything I would rather watch in the morning than you peaceful and asleep. Now I'm even happier with you awake. We still have forty minutes before the breakfast with the generals,' whispered Glenda as she pressed every inch that she could close to him. They both wanted to make love, each as much as the other and so they did. Neither talked but there was no need, their bodies were in perfect communion.

Brush and Glenda walked to General Whitcuff's white, wood-sided house.

A staff sergeant opened the door as if by magic, just as they stepped onto the porch.

'Sir, ma'am,' said the sergeant. 'Please go right into the dining room to your right.'

'Morning, General,' said Brush.

'I see you both look...' General Crystal couldn't find the right words as he had never seen Brush—or Glenda, for that matter—looking quite so happy with the world. Finally he just said, 'Wide awake and ready for breakfast. I'm glad you are a little early and that must be Glenda's influence since it isn't normal for you.' He held up a hand as Brush started to say something. 'Glenda, I want to ask you a favor. Could I persuade you to go send Jim here and stay with Heather while he's gone? Since he and Brush know more about our little female tyrant than anyone else, it would be very useful to have Jim here too when I lay out my plan. It might be a good time for you to get to know Heather as well.'

'Can do, General, but you're not excommunicating me from the action, right?'

'No, understood. The sergeant at the door will point you to his quarters. Need him in about five minutes if you can get him here that fast.'

Glenda walked as fast as she was able, to where the sergeant had directed. She was feeling better all the time but still did not have any endurance even for simple things. Well maybe she had some endurance for some things, she thought happily. She tapped on their door and Jim opened it before she had finished knocking.

'Glenda, glad to see you looking so good. What's up?'

'General Crystal would appreciate it if you could pop over for breakfast and a meeting in about three minutes. Thought I might keep Heather company if she doesn't mind.'

Jim understood. The general would not ask if it wasn't important and Glenda was being courteous. Then again, it might be good for the two women to get acquainted, perhaps Heather would find it easier to open up about her experience to another woman. He walked her in to where he and Heather had been eating breakfast. 'The general would like to speak to me for a minute and Glenda would like to chat, if it is OK with you?'

'Sure, it will be nice to talk to Glenda,' Heather replied as she looked at Glenda Rose.

Jim walked briskly down to Whitcuff's and the sergeant let him in. Will Crystal was seated at the head of a big rectangular table. He was the junior general but clearly in charge. Jim realized it wasn't going to be a brief meeting and hoped Heather would be OK. It was probably a good idea for her to see someone different and since Brush and Glenda were quickly becoming an item, maybe they should get to know each other better.

General Crystal pointed Jim to the corner chair just to his left, along the side of the table and next to Nielly and Marilyn. Brush took the seat on the opposite side, kitty-corner from Jim, next to the Special Forces second in command, Master Sergeant Gaston. To Gaston's left was Captain Fuller and General Whitcuff on the corner next to General Crystal, directly across from Jim. Everyone had breakfast in front of them.

Jim looked at the orderly and said, 'Toast and coffee.'

'Pancakes, two eggs over easy, sausage, orange juice, and black coffee,' said Brush.

'While we're eating, I'm going to brief you on the general

situation. We're going to go after the woman terrorist at the drug cartel's compound about 50 klicks south of the border. The State Department convinced President Zedillo to allow our trespass into Mexico with the guarantee that it won't make any news headlines, "American Troops Invade Mexico," that sort of thing. An impossible thing to guarantee, of course. Zedillo is not communicating with anyone in his government. This is a solo event. The few people in the State Department that are turning their heads now will disown us if we screw up.

'But if we pull this off, Zedillo will be rid of the biggest cartel in Mexico and he will take full credit. He will look like a hero and it will be suggested that it was his special military forces that raided the cartel's headquarters. If we're found out, then there is going to be a lot of trouble. So we're going to do this right.'

Glenda and Heather smiled at each other. Heather was idly comparing her to Debbie and Glenda was wondering how tough a lady Jim's girlfriend was.

Heather broke the silence first. 'Glenda, what's the general want Jim for?'

Glenda decided that she should not try to hide anything. In Heather's place she would want it straight. 'Basic planning meeting. I suspect we're going to go after the cartel and the general wants Jim to advise on the plan.'

'Thought as much,' said Heather. 'You want to get involved, too, Glenda? Are you recovered enough?'

Glenda understood Heather was asking these questions about herself as well. 'Answer to the first question is hell yes; the answer to the second is that I'm not recovered enough for any rough stuff, but I'm ready to help. I want to go after the woman responsible for shooting me and killing your friends and hurting you in whatever capacity I can. Observer or operations center, wherever they'll let me be and wherever I can know what Brush is doing. I'll bring coffee if it helps. It's not even about vengeance because I'm not angry; it's just that Najma has hurt enough people and she needs to be stopped.'

Heather instinctively liked and wholeheartedly agreed with Glenda. She looked a little like that FBI lady from *The X-Files,* they were both good-looking with nice figures. But Glenda didn't talk like an FBI agent, she was honest and had a nice smile that made Heather feel like maybe things would be OK. She had all of Debbie's attributes and just like Jim and Brush she was probably very good at her job and made of tough stuff, not letting a few bullet holes hold her back for long. No wonder Brush was smitten. Heather was a little smitten herself.

'I'm with you, Glenda. You want to be there and I want to see that woman caught, too.' Even as Heather found her voice, she couldn't quite bring herself to say the name Najma out loud. 'Let's crash this meeting. I want to know what Jim is up to just as much as you want to know about Brush. Maybe I can even help.'

Glenda was about to say, *Not a good idea.* But then, Heather had been through a lot, and maybe she had useful information about Najma's plans. The general wouldn't throw her out and Glenda wanted to hear what the plan was herself.

Heather hadn't waited for an answer but was already at the door. Glenda realized that Heather wasn't giving her any choice and had to hustle to catch up. She decided that Heather was going to be worth getting to know.

'Heather, wait up, I can't move that fast!'

Glenda caught up with Heather standing on the sidewalk in

front of the jeep. Since Jim was not there, the driver saw no harm in asking if he could give the two women a lift.

'Sure,' said Heather, 'but we are only going to General Whitcuff's,' and she jumped in the back as Glenda climbed into the front seat.

When seconds later they reached the general's porch, the door opened, again as if by magic. The sergeant recognized Glenda and stood aside as they walked to the dining room and straight in to the meeting.

General Crystal was saying, '...So we're going to do this right.'

'I have no doubt of that, General,' said Heather. 'On a personal note, I would like to see you get'—she had to concentrate to say the name out loud— 'Najma. So do you mind if we join you? Maybe I can help.'

Brush smiled at Glenda, his girl must have a magic touch. Jim, at that moment, loved Heather more than ever, something he would not have thought possible yesterday. He had always loved her completely and cherished every moment of their time together on the ranch, but now, seeing her calmly standing there bruised and bandaged and ready to fight, his respect for her reached a new level.

General Crystal smiled, too. 'Please sit down, ladies,' he said as if he had a choice. Inwardly he was happy and a little proud to see Heather showing this strength of character. Heather sat at the end of the table and Glenda sat on her right, opposite Brush, so she could look at him.

'Heather, on the other side of Glenda is Chief Warrant Officer Four Marilyn Cutter and sitting next to Brush is Master Sergeant Gaston Reese, the SF XO, in case you didn't meet them formally in Mexico. The only person you haven't met is Captain Jeff Fuller. Captain Fuller was in charge of the TOC, the tactical operations center, when Jim and the SF team went into Mexico. Tell the orderly what you two want for breakfast and I'll get on with a general briefing, no pun intended.

'The cartel's compound has as many as fifty people. Best information is about thirty-five cartel members and fifteen staff workers. The staff are mostly women and the cartel are mostly men except for Najma.' Will looked at Heather as he said 'Najma' and didn't see any reaction from her but he knew it was there, raw and just below the surface. 'They have plenty of weapons, machine pistols, machine guns, including at least two fifty calibers. We don't know the exact nature of what else they have, but if they have surface-to-air missiles we have to assume they have the latest and newest weapons. Nielly, your team will have to keep in mind that these are not conscript military opponents but cartel soldiers who have been trained in the field of battle. Don't expect limited return fire, every man there will be willing to fight to the last, which brings up two problems. What do we do if there are wounded and captives and what do we do with the staff?' The general nodded at Nielly.

'Wounded are coming back with us. We'll have two choppers to extract and another helicopter for security and backup.' Heather wanted to ask why they needed backup but decided this wasn't meant to be an educational meeting for her. 'Through the general's DEA contact we have identified four cartel staff as possible friendlies. We want to try to get them out safe and keep them away from the other cartel.'

'Our game plan,' said the general, 'is to take the compound, leave no evidence that it is American forces, bring materials and weapons out along with the wounded and selected staff. Everyone finished eating? Let's get the table cleared and Captain Fuller will bring in maps and an attack plan.'

Vidya, Misa, and JT had quarters near the hospital where Ralphy was recovering. 'I feel lucky to be alive,' said Misa, 'in fact, I don't quite understand why I am.' The explanation would eventually come to her, in fact it would seem startlingly obvious, as explanations often are: Najma had planned the same fate for Misa and Heather the next night when they sprang their trap on Jim. She had kept Misa separate to keep Heather feeling isolated. But the two would die the same way with Jim replacing Heather as the naked observer.

'I can't stand this sitting around doing nothing. I need my computer and internet access.' Vidya agreed. He couldn't get Kristina out of his mind and desperately wanted a distraction from his thoughts.

The phone interrupted their musings. Misa answered it, then turned to the others. 'We've been asked to come to the hospital and have a debriefing.'

'I want to do something, so yeah, let's go see Ralphy,' said Vidya. JT nodded his assent.

'OK, we're ready.' Misa listened again and then hung up the phone. 'We're being picked up at ten-thirty. Then after that we get to be grilled by some military guys about what happened in Mexico.'

The general, Captain Fuller, and several other staff had spent the night going over aerial photos of the compound, working out communication and contingency plans. Specialist Gordon and three other computer technicians worked through the night with

Sheilla and her staff trying to hack into the cartel's computer systems. So far, they had only been hitting walls. At first, they were surprised that the cartel had such a sophisticated computer system, however, it soon dawned on them that of course it made sense. Millions and millions of currencies changed hands and they had to have secure communications. In fact, they were even good enough to hack into law enforcement agencies' computers. Guillermo had quickly realized that technology would change the world's playing field and decided several years ago that he needed the best people and equipment, not only to do his business, but to survive. He had even gone further and invested a considerable amount of money through shell companies in a corporation that wrote programs for the Department of Defense. The US government would be more than surprised to find that some of their most secure software had back doors controlled by Guillermo. He was right where he intended to be, light-years ahead of governments and businesses around the world.

But with all his expertise and access, he had not yet found direct ways to profit. Amir's scheme would be his entree into the fuzzy world of cyber-crime and consequently was much more important to him than just the scheme itself. How fitting that his first crime of the millennium would be a wave of cyber attacks on banks.


Heather liked maps and so did the military personnel. It had always surprised her that many of her friends loathed them. The general had an overhead projector displaying a hazy image of the hacienda. He was busy drawing on the screen with a felt pen and pointing with a red laser at the projected image.

'The main road off the highway is here.' He traced it with the red laser light. 'There are several other rough roads but none are normally used to approach the compound. We have to assume that they have sentries posted along that road, maybe even farther along the highway, here. It makes sense for them to watch the rough roads from the compound but probably not to have sentries posted. We can see only one gate and it is closed and guarded twenty-four hours. Above the gate, on top of the wall, are some closed structures. We have to assume heavy weapons, likely machine guns. Everything we see suggests that nearly all their focus is on an assault from the road but they are bound to have some sort of plan for an over-ground attack by a military-type unit. Anyone have any bright ideas what that might be?'

'Listening devices, probably night vision, and perhaps patrols. I would put at least two people out. Toss me your pointer, General,' said Nielly. 'Here and here.'

'Yes, all things we talked about and it makes sense except there is nothing to suggest any activity from the south, east, or north sides. If they are smart operators, it doesn't make sense. An informer, now missing, told the DEA that there was an active center with a lot of electronics.'

'Video surveillance?' said Whitcuff.

'Seems like a real possibility,' said General Crystal. 'Makes it tough to devise an assault plan without knowing any more than we do, and no real recon. They have lots of money, lots of people, and the government and other cartels as enemies. They wouldn't leave themselves as exposed as it looks and that worries me. Too risky to fly a drone low and satellite just isn't clear enough.'

'Only one solution then,' said Brush. 'We've got to send someone in for a little ground recon.'

'Seems like the only way,' added Nielly. 'One of my guys is the regular invisible man. He could work his way in but it would take a few days for him to approach without taking too many chances.'

'It's one idea we talked about last night. Master Sergeant Smith, who was in your TOC, Jim, is old school and spent much of his time in Vietnam, Grenada, and Iraq leading Long Range Recon Patrols. He's still around so must be pretty smart about it. I've picked a few of those LRRP guys out of hot-zones, in times past, when they screwed up and were spotted.'

'The general saved Jim's and my bacon more than once,' added Brush.

'Here's the idea. Sergeant Smith is dark skinned and has an old Mexican LRRP pal. Smith has a Mexican girlfriend just over the border from Douglas. I want to send them in and have them approach the hacienda from the east pretending to be locals. No stealth, just acting like Mexicans walking through the desert. They'll have communication with us and if they are caught they will ditch the com equipment. All we'll need is a plausible reason for them to be strolling along near the cartel's headquarters.'

'Have them collect palohierro,' said Heather.

'Explain for us, Heather,' requested General Crystal.

'*Olneya tesota*—ironwood. It's becoming quite rare and expensive. Used for carvings by the Indians in the Sonora. Seri Indians, I think. They could be collecting it to sell or make carvings. They could also collect *Peniocereus striatus*. It's a medicinal plant and becoming rare since it grows under ironwood trees. Probably lots of both of them around the hacienda if the local people are afraid to go there.'

'Captain Fuller, work on Heather's idea and see if Sergeant

Smith or his LRRP buddy are comfortable with it as a cover story. Thanks, Heather.'

'If something like that works, they're probably going to get themselves killed as the cartel guards won't care about what they're doing. We could send one of my sniper-watchers in to observe from a distance to see how the cartel detects them. He might find out something useful that will help us, but if he can't shoot, those two are just going to be sacrifices. You willing to do that, General?' said Nielly.

'Let's see if we can come up with anything else and make that choice if we have to. Any other suggestions?'

'We can HAHO in and land close to the hacienda at night. Maybe bypass any outer security. We'd have surprise on our side and that might be a way. They would be expecting an assault, but without recon I don't like it. We could be spotted and caught outside the wall,' said Nielly.

'We could be up and over the wall in minutes,' suggested Sergeant Gaston.

'That was the only other plan we came up with last night. Don't see how we could take a chance landing in the compound. That only leaves landing outside,' said General Crystal.

'Conclusions are the same as ours last night then. We need recon and the only good way is getting someone there on the ground. It's a risk, but one we have to take. In the event that the recon team is caught, we need to move fast before they give up what we really intend to do. That is unless MSG Smith and his partner are told the assault is just in the planning stage. If we're all agreed, then we go in tomorrow night. The recon team goes in tonight, has tomorrow to look around. They keep live com with us through the day or as long as they can. We use Nielly's watcher to monitor them but not to support. We HAHO in and land close to the east wall, hopefully with some better recon. Nielly, I want you to get with your group and come up with a detailed assault plan plus alternatives depending on what the recon shows. Anything else?'

'One question, General, will I be flying armed support or just evac?' asked Marilyn. Heather's mouth dropped a little. She had seen two SF women in Mexico at the mine but it had not occurred to her what they actually did.

'For those of you who don't know, Marilyn is a light weapons specialist, fluent in Spanish and the SF unit's primary pilot. To answer your question, your bird will be armed but your primary mission is evac. Second, is to support the primary attack helicopter if they need some backup. Meet me at my quarters at 14:30. We'll talk about the flight plan and get in some flying time.'

'We will meet here again at 18:00 and go over the details.' The general stood and motioned to Heather, Jim, Brush, and Glenda to stay. Then he turned to General Whitcuff. 'General, again I want to express how much we appreciate your support and allowing us to literally take over your quarters.'

'Will, as I said before this is giving a spark to my last days. Best fun I've had in years. But our deal stands.'

'You know what the Pentagon is going to say if they hear that two generals went on an op together!'

'Not a hell of a lot more than they will say for one going. Going out with a bang, Will, and for that it's me that should be thanking you.'

'Deal's a deal then. You ride in the troop commander's seat in my bird. Plenty of room for Nielly's men, plus the other cartel we bring back. Marilyn's Huey can bring back another ten to eleven people, if need be.

'Heather, glad to see you on your feet and I appreciate your suggestion. Jim, I want you and Brush to supervise things back here. I won't have my XO in the field at the same time as me.'

Brush just looked quizzically at General Crystal and then Jim. They were going and the general knew it.

'Jim, I'll be OK, I just want to be informed as much as possible,' said Heather. 'I've learned a few things and I have a feeling, from what I've seen, that you can help and I want you to.' She stood a little taller and held her head up and said, 'Get Najma.'

The general had known he was spitting in the wind saying Jim and Brush would not go. They would most likely make the difference in a successful or a failed mission. 'Glenda, I can't have you fly, as I promised General Whitcuff shotgun in the bird. TOC is the place for you to help this time.'

'I'd rather be in the field with you and Brush but truthfully the FBI never trained us in the exotic stuff you guys do, like HAHO and flying helicopters, even if I was fit. Heather and I will keep each other company and that means both of us in the TOC. I'm guessing that is what you want, Heather?'

'You've got that right; this is a new world for me. I have always thought that women are mentally equal to men...or better,' she said with a mischievous smile. 'But after my recent encounters with Najma and then meeting Marilyn and Glenda, I have a better understanding that women can be everything that a man can be, tough, skilled, accomplished, cruel, perceptive, or kind.'

Heather was beautiful, even with half her face covered with white gauze. More importantly, the determined smile told Jim that she was going to be OK.

'I've had a firsthand lesson in your abilities, Jim. I'll be just fine with Glenda; actually I have some questions she can answer for me. So I want you to help. I want you to rid the world of this psychopath.'

Brush couldn't keep his eyes off Glenda. He was proud to be with her and she was so damn sexy that his mind started to wander. Then he looked at Chief Warrant Officer Marilyn Cutter. She had a lot of skills, as Heather pointed out, but no shape, tallish with an overlong face. *Great to have along in a fight, but not my style off duty,* thought Brush.

# Chapter 20

Lola gave Pedro a big plate of reheated rice and beans with a few slices of bread. She stood behind him and rested her hands on his shoulders as he shoved big forkfuls of food into his mouth. She liked little Pedro. He seemed a nice, shy little boy. The hacienda was no place him or for her any longer, she thought. She had to get away from this place and take him with her. She was terrified here. She hadn't cared about herself after the death of her son. Now things were different. But could they escape? As he continued to eat, she became more worried for him. Where had he come from? What did the crazy woman want him for? She couldn't disobey, it would be certain death. She would have to believe that no harm would come to him.

'Pedro, take off your shirt and wash yourself in the sink. Let me see your hands, your fingernails need a good cleaning.'

After he had washed, she took a deep breath, clasped his hand, pushed her lips together, and walked him out of the kitchen across the courtyard to Najma's room. She told him to knock on the door and then in tears, moved out of sight into the shadows.

'Are you tired, little boy?'

He looked at the floor and said, 'Sí.'

'Time for bed.' She held his freshly scrubbed hand and walked him to her bed. 'Take off those rags,' she ordered. Najma took off her own oversized shirt and climbed into the bed, moved over to the far side, and patted the space nearest Pedro. 'Here, little one.' Pedro crawled in and Najma arranged the sheets and blankets around him in a maternal way, rubbed his hair and arms. Pedro fell immediately to sleep. Najma put her arm over the sleeping boy and whispered, 'My little niño.'

Sheilla swiveled back and forth in her chair in deep thought. Long, mid-back auburn hair swished side to side against her black leather chair. She had been right about the kidnapping. It was only a ruse for Najma to get Jim. But why would the cartel want to get involved in going after an American agent who had no dealings with them? They'd have a lot to lose and nothing to gain. It just didn't make sense and nonsensical things bothered her. She had been swiveling and thinking about this for over two hours with no new answers. When she couldn't figure out a problem, she could dwell on it for hours or days searching for an answer. Eventually she had to accept that she didn't have enough information. She needed to know and understand more about the motivations of the people involved. She rolled the chair to her desk and dialled Katarina.

'Hi, take a seat,' she said when Katarina arrived. I'd like you to work up some profiles for me. I know you are not officially trained as a profiler but I think you're as good as the ones I worked with in the FBI. So do the best you can. Let's start at the beginning, then maybe we can understand what is going on and try to make some predictions that will help our guys down south.

'First, what do we know about Najma and her dead boss, Farasie? Can you work up a profile on them and also one on the cartel honcho, Guillermo, and maybe the hairy dead guy, Raul?' asked Sheilla.

Katarina was still blushing from the faith Sheilla expressed in her ability. Sheilla was a very nice person and a good boss but one with high standards. She would not accept anyone who harbored illogical thoughts. Sheilla could zero in on a problem, work it from all sides and angles, penetrate to its core, and emerge with a clear understanding. Praise from her acknowledged that she thought a person was indeed high caliber.

The two women's thoughts progressed independently but along similar paths. Sheilla had no time for anyone who played politics, had petty grievances or problems, and above all, she did not suffer men who had the temerity to think they were better than women. She had had enough of that in the FBI and now realized how pleasant and productive it was to be here with her carefully assembled staff.

The general, with faith in her ability and enough respect to let her do her job in her own way, made being in the BWL feel more like a family than just a job. She felt at home and thought the world of Dr. Milton, Jim, and the others. She even respected Nusmen for his intelligence. The few super intelligent people she had encoun-tered all seemed to be close to the edge of reality but Nusmen had crossed that line when he lost control and released the deadly bacteria.

Katarina interrupted Sheilla's thoughts and said, 'I've been studying the pictures and reports that Nielly faxed. I can hardly look at the ones of the two women, especially the photos of Kristina, whose name is so close to mine. I keep thinking that it could be me in those pictures. I like being down here in the lab. We're safer and less vulnerable than out there in the open air.' She took a deep breath. 'The ugly, hairy guy isn't hard to profile. A typical macho brute, none too intelligent, more than likely a psychopath. I'll need more data on this Guillermo and Farasie though.'

'We don't have much on Farasie. Get Bridget to help you re-search him. I want this as quickly as you can, so give me details and thoughts but don't go overboard writing it up. There is probably plenty of information available about the cartel leader. Fred could help you faster on the computer but he's all bogged down, working with his new army computer friends at Fort Huachuca. I don't want to take him off that at the moment. Unfortunately, they're having zero success penetrating the cartel's firewalls. That's another thing, why do they have such seemingly sophisticated software protection? How do they have it? None of this is making sense,' she said as she waved Katarina off and went back to swiveling and turning an occasional full three-sixty. If the general could see her, he would be amused. He did three-sixties in helicopters, Sheilla did them in chairs.

# Chapter 21

Low clouds scurried across a lumpy gray sky. The people were dressed mostly in black with an occasional red, pink, or yellow fabric bobbing among the moving crowds. Black cabs made U-turns in front of an endless stream of dark Mercedes, Porches, BMWs, and Range Rovers. Just like the pedestrians, an occasional red or yellow Italian sports car or a white Bentley punctuated the streams of shiny black automobiles. Most of them were driven fast and efficiently with little distance maintained between cars. As fast as possible that was. There were no wide roads, and drivers by necessity inserted their cars into every possible space, otherwise it would be faster to walk, and it often was.

Amir felt relief at being back in London. He was home. This is where he belonged. The events of the past few days were quickly disappearing into obscure brain cells. Less than twelve hours earlier, Guillermo and his daughter Mary, her governess, a computer specialist, five bodyguards, and Amir had boarded the glistening white Cessna Citation X. Amir had stood mesmerized by the plane. Its backswept wings and downward pointed nose and oversized bulge below the main cabin made it look like a pregnant predator.

'Muy bonita, isn't she?' said a young man dressed in white with gold swirls on his shoulders.

'It doesn't look like any jet I have ever seen before,' said Amir.

'It's only two years old and the fastest private trans-ocean small jet in the world. Cruises over 600 miles per hour. Sir, I am Copilot Rodriguez,' he said standing straight.

Rodriguez was ecstatic that he was allowed to fly this plane. It was a job made in heaven for a young pilot. He was a skilled pilot and extremely proud of his status as copilot. He tried to forget that a pilot employed by the cartel had once disappeared after a rough landing. It was only a rumor. Rodriguez chose to ignore silly rumors and live his dream.

'Please board, señor,' said Rodriguez as he waved his arm in a flourish toward the descended steps. 'We can seat twelve but today we have only ten passengers, including yourself.'

Amir was rich by most standards but this was out of his league. The plane was not large inside but it was sumptuous with cream leather seats and swirling grains in polished wood. It had a European elegance; there was nothing to suggest that its owner was from Mexico, not even the food.

The flight was smoother than his British Air flight only a few days earlier. It was faster too, partly since they wasted no time at the airport and were steeply catapulted into the sky like a rocket.

Amir felt better every moment that he was on familiar ground. There had been the flight taking him to Heathrow, and then the drive into the city. As fast and plush as the jet flight had been, he was relieved when Guillermo and the rest of his entourage were rapidly escorted to a waiting helicopter at the Heathrow FBO. He was amazed that they did not have to clear customs and immigration. A pretty woman at the Fixed Based Operators door checked the stack of passports handed to her by the pilot and they were through. He hadn't known that private jet passengers were pre-cleared by the UK Border Agency and did not have to endure the long lines at immigration and customs. Neither did he have any idea that the passport provided for him was false. Guillermo would arrange for Amir to officially re-enter the UK on a diplomatic plane from Cuba, which would tie Amir to the Cubans after the cyber-heist.

Amir remembered letting out a sigh as he sank into the dark gray leather seat of the private car that took him into London. The past few days in Mexico had felt like a lifetime. The death and dying he witnessed in Mexico seemed worlds apart from where he was now walking on the familiar stone squares of Knightsbridge. Maybe he could control this situation and even come out with a profit, he thought to himself. It made him feel good to claim that illusion but he knew the truth. His life would never be the same again. He belonged to Guillermo. His childish need for revenge had meant selling his soul. If his brother were still here, he would know what to do. Without him, Amir felt helpless, impotently vacillating between grand notions that he could do something and the realization that he could do nothing.

He could have had the driver take him directly to his house but he had little to carry and he wanted to breathe the air and rub shoulders in his city. The excitement of walking the familiar streets from Knightsbridge to his house quickly became tainted with thoughts of the new world that he belonged to. He must banish these thoughts and not bring them into his home, he thought.

Guillermo and his daughter, Mary, followed by their body-guards, the computer technician and Mary's governess, had their passports checked by the FBO staff and walked to a helicopter that would take them to Mary's school. The Eurocopter EC155 looked as new as it was. This was only its third flight since delivery to the air charter company. The seats were white, decorated with dark red piping and without any signs of previous use.

The helicopter lifted off and headed into the westerly wind toward Maidsbury Ladies' College. The school was for girls to age eighteen and it pursued an excellent education regime, however, as its name implied, its focus was on ensuring that girls from wealthy families became ladies.

Mary and the computer technician were the only two aboard that looked happy as the quiet helicopter rushed west. Alejandro, the computer specialist, had never been to England and he was enthralled by the patchwork, irregular green fields passing below. Mary was excited at the thought of seeing her friends at school. She was Mexican by birth but this was her home.

Gabrielle, her governess of fourteen years, however, hated the cold and damp here and liked it less every year. *Two more years to go,* she thought, *and then Guillermo will let me return to my family in France.* She longed for the scent of lavender and clear skies that were only a lingering memory of her treasured Provence. Mexico was warm and less dreary but she didn't like it any better than England. And the hacienda was a fortress not a home. She had freedom, at least, to go in and out at Maidsbury Ladies' College, which was better than at the hacienda but it still felt like a damp prison.

Gabrielle and Mary were friendly but they both knew that the governess's duty was to Guillermo. By arrangement with the Ladies' College, Gabrielle was allowed to stay close to Mary but kept a low profile. A narrow stairway led down to a private exit on the ground floor that she used when she needed something from the town. Her room was next to Mary's, separated by an adjoining door. She could enter to assist Mary, take care of her clothes, and clean her room but most of all, her duty was to make sure Guillermo's daughter had no communication with boys or anyone else that might prove to be a bad influence while on the school grounds However, whenever Mary left the school's property, a young-looking twenty-two-year-old woman named Fiona secretly shadowed her. Guillermo had enticed Fiona away from a special assault-training unit at New Scotland Yard by offering her an extravagant salary to be Mary's incognito bodyguard. Fiona also supervised the added security Guillermo required at the school.

Mary was ebullient as only teenagers can be. Her half-term break from school had been wonderful. It was Saturday and classes didn't start until Monday. Telling her friends about the Day of Dead Festival in Mexico and the boys she had met, made her quiver with excitement. Some of the boys seemed to be completely taken with her, and several were cute, but none were that interesting and she remembered none of them in particular. Miguel, the don's son, had been one of those infatuated boys. An observer wanting to prove his worth reported to the don that Mary and the don's son had been exchanging flirtatious looks and there might be something more going on between them. If Don Pablo was in heaven and could see into El Padrino's daughter's teenage mind, the absurdity of his family's death would have made him mourn all the more. Mary, Miguel's love interest, didn't even remember him. The irregular fields with scattered groves of trees bearing English country names—Hollow Wood, Lemmonhill Grove, Spoonley Stone, and Billis's Coppice—gave way to rows of houses penetrating the fields of the old market town. The helicopter smoothly banked left, turning southwest into the wind as it approached Maidsbury Ladies'

College. It passed over one large rectangle of lawn and a building separating it from another green expanse. It settled lightly onto the ground as if not wishing to harm the fragile blades of grass.

Three bodyguards immediately jumped out and moved away from the helicopter followed by Mary, who rushed to the headmistress and her assistant with a smile. The staff of the school sincerely liked Mary. She was a bright flower among their students; a proper young girl that they were fashioning into a confident and glamorous woman. The extravagant amount of funds provided by Guillermo was something they never discussed.

'I must be on my way, niña. Study hard and continue to make me proud.'

'Bye bye, Papa,' said Mary as she hugged her father. She stood waving as the Eurocopter lifted straight into the sky and then slowly eased west over the school's stone wall before picking up speed and circling back toward London. She waved until they were out of sight and then jumped, clapping her hands. She loved her father but what she really wanted was to find her girlfriends.


Guillermo switched seamlessly from the loving father to El Padrino as they headed back across the countryside toward the London Heliport on the edge of the Thames. Two black Mercedes were waiting. They followed a curving road along the Thames, made a left turn, and crossed over the wide gray river on Battersea Bridge. Then the driver turned right onto the famed Kings Road. Alejandro became enthralled by the women in tall spiked heels supporting slim legs and bodies, walking along the street and past boutique shops. Their clothes all looked expensive and there was a set look on their faces—eyes straight ahead, lips closed, looking and walking as if they were the center of the universe. They were models on a concrete ramp, certain they understood the way of the world and their place in it. Ahead there was a large bright neon sign saying 'Royal Court' above a small playhouse, where—unknown to Alejandro—Olivier made his first big impression on the acting world. The shops changed as they turned left driving up Sloane Street. Tiffany & Co. first on the corner and then designer shops, dozens of them, Vidal Sassoon, Hermes, Calvin Klein, Armani, Fendi, and Christian Dior. Huge trees towered over squares with funny names like Cadogan Square. They passed by the Peruvian embassy and then Jimmy Choo and Ferragamo. Men in dark suits and earpieces stood at the doors. The crystal-clear windows reflected dozens of double-decker buses, blurred red images mixed with indistinct black cars, including their own. He saw no customers inside any of the shops. He wondered if they would allow just anyone to enter.

They turned right onto a much busier street. He looked to his left and saw Harrods behind crowds of people. Alejandro was happy to be in the front seat. The car moved faster, past a corner of Hyde Park, through a large roundabout, and immediately drove into a little crescent. The two cars stopped and an attendant in a fancy outfit and top hat opened their doors. The few cars positioned in front of the hotel were probably worth more than he would ever make in his lifetime. He was told to stay in the car. One of the bodyguards stood beside his Mercedes and watched Guillermo followed by four other bodyguards, as they disappeared through the revolving door and into The Lanesborough Hotel. He then got into the car and they drove away from the hotel.

Ox, the stocky Mexican bodyguard, was dressed in a quality but ill-fitting suit, barely stretching over his oversized shoulders and fat neck. The driver stopped and accelerated and moved around cars with far less finesse than he had used on his way to the hotel. His charges now were not important and he let them know it. Then he glanced at Ox and quickly decided to drive more respectfully. They reversed course and this time drove past Harrods with elegant window displays barely visible behind the throngs of sightseers and shoppers. Two more blocks and they turned left, leaving the bumper-to-bumper buses and entering a small side street. Then right onto what the sign said was Edgerton Gardens followed by a quick left into a small curved lane called Edgerton Crescent. The driver stopped in front of a polished brass number plate on a black glossy door.

A long-faced Amir opened the door. The bulky bodyguard roughly pushed past him and walked in. They turned into a sitting room on the right where seven other people were already assembled, including two of Alejandro's computer coworkers from Mexico. Another cartel man lounged in a chair with his feet up and a more business-looking type, Yousef, who was clearly uncomfortable, sat upright next to a lounging, slight, pinched-faced, mean-looking Mexican male.

# Chapter 22

You want to walk around a little, Heather?' asked Glenda.

'Let's, I need to be outside. The weather's great and I haven't seen much of Fort Huachuca, only the inside of this house and General Whitcuff's.'

'OK then, as long as we take it easy. I haven't done a lot of walking in the last couple of months.'

'I see that you and our two guys have one thing in common, the ability to understate things! From what I know, you haven't done any walking,' laughed Heather as they headed out the door.

'I suppose once upon a time, I understated things or made flippant remarks to show my bravado, but now it's become a way of thinking for me, probably the same for both of our guys.' After a moment's pause Glenda continued, 'We've learned to put events and feelings into a different perspective. A non-fatal injury is just an injury. We go on living and try to keep it that way, no fatalities allowed.'

'Yeah, I can see it. Jim used to tell me that one of the most important lessons he learned in Vietnam was to cherish the moment. But he's a planner, thinks in the future a lot of the time, though he still believes in the "live in the moment" philosophy even if he can't always do it.

'You know, Glenda, I never thought I would see what I have in the last few days. Things I guess everyone knows exist, I'm sure you do, but for me they always existed somewhere else, somewhere I would never be and I managed to ignore them. It's a real shock—a reality check—for me to be face-to-face with people like Najma and those men. Like the difference between knowing a plane can crash and being on one while it is crashing.' Heather's voice trailed off as she looked away, uncertain if she should continue.

Glenda put her arm over Heather's shoulders. 'Talk all you want. You're giving me some new thoughts to consider. I like your style and pace but you have to slow down, I can't keep walking this fast.'

'Sorry, Glenda. I'm so wrapped up in my thoughts I just forgot to move slower. To look at you, it's hard for me to imagine you've just got out of the hospital. Where were you shot? I hope you don't mind me asking, it's just a scientist's curiosity.'

Glenda stopped and pulled up her blouse and showed Heather three red, angry-looking scars spaced across her stomach.

'Jeez, Glenda. It's amazing you survived. I'm glad you did but how the heck did you?'

'Just lucky, I guess. The bullets all missed things I couldn't live without. This one went through my left kidney and I lost it, and another through here,' she said pointing at a red, bumpy ridge. 'Lost a piece of my liver with that one. Where I was lucky, I guess, is that they missed my spine. Most of the time in the hospital, I was fighting infections where my intestines were punctured. Lost a lot of blood and if a little more had leaked out, probably wouldn't have made it to the hospital.' She smiled and added, 'That's thanks to

Brush and the doctor that was there.'

'I'm glad you're here now and that Brush was there then!' They walked along in the mile-high sunshine, past large old wooden buildings, some with a few misshapen cacti along their walls. 'Hum, the army doesn't seem to be much on gardening or aesthetics.'

'Not their way. I think I'm about ready to walk back,' said Glenda.

Heather took Glenda's arm and looked into her brown eyes glinting with gold, *Cats' eyes,* she thought. She really liked this woman and wondered if her relationship with Brush would last. She hoped so. It was nice to find a sympathetic woman with experience from Jim's side of life. 'I'm glad you're here, Glenda,' she told her. 'It's nice to be able to be friends with a woman who lives in Jim's world. It'll help me understand better, I hope. It already has.'

'I'm glad we met too, Heather. In some ways, getting shot was the best thing that ever happened to me, as it meant meeting Brush and you. I hope we have a chance to get to know each other better. Maybe someday you'll take me llama packing.'

'Say the word, anytime. I miss those furry guys. It seems like a month since I've seen them and it's only been a little over a week.'

*Heather will make it past her experience,* thought Glenda, as they started to walk back. *She has a good attitude and given a little time, her nightmare memories will fade along with the scar on her cheek.* Glenda knew very well, though, that although Heather was taking it well now, there would be some bad times, nightmares and maybe bouts of depression or worse after what she had been forced to watch.

A sergeant pulled up beside them in a cloud of dust. 'Hey, la-dies,' he called. 'I'm here to drive you wherever you want to go, no need to walk.'

'Glenda, think you can handle a little bouncing around in the sergeant's jeep?'

'I'm up for it. Drive us around this old fort but don't get too enthusiastic about being a tour guide, just tell us the really interesting stuff,' added Glenda.

They spent over an hour hearing stories about Geronimo, traveling past the Old Buffalo Parade Grounds, along the edge of the Huachuca Mountains, the Army Intelligence Training Center, and Libby Army Airfield from where the drones were launched.

'How come we didn't land here? Looks like a big airfield,' asked Glenda.

'Off-limits sometimes,' said Sergeant Murphy.

'Hum, wonder what that means but doubt he is going to be able to tell us,' said Heather.

'Sorry, ma'am. Not sure I know myself.'

Heather looked around at the mountains that rose to the south and toward Mexico. 'I'd like to go hiking in those mountains sometime. I hear there is an old ranch up in them someplace that it is run by the Nature Conservancy as a bird sanctuary.'

'Heard mention of it, ma'am, but that's all,' said their driver.

'Stop!' yelled Glenda and Murphy slammed on the brakes looking perplexed. Glenda got out as fast as she could, walked to the other side of the road, and picked up a tortoise the size of a big pancake. She turned back and smiled as Heather ran over to her.

'It was heading out onto the road and I was afraid someone would come along and run over it,' said Glenda. They walked for several minutes in the direction it was headed and Glenda set it down in the sand pointing in the same direction it had been walking on the other side of the road. It had a mark about three inches long on its shell, a small crevasse cutting across its patterned armor.

'Maybe the mark is from a previous encounter with a car,' said Heather, adding, 'They're getting rare with all the off-road vehicles and cities expanding into the desert. I wonder if an army base is a safe haven for a tortoise?'

'I just hope it stays off the road and out from under tires,' said Glenda. The tortoise's head poked out and then got longer. It slowly craned its long neck back toward the two women before continuing its ambling journey to an unknown destination.

Heather looked at Glenda as they got back into the jeep. Glenda had probably had enough but wouldn't say so. 'I think it's getting to be lunchtime,' said Heather. 'Take us back to the house, Sergeant, please.'


'Ralphy, I think we should head back to ASU. You look pretty good now, not that I would actually take you out in public or anything,' said Misa.

'Do I really look that bad?'

'Just giving you the business—kidding.' She raised her hand in a sign of surrender.

'They said I had to stay another day,' said Ralphy.

'I'm not going to leave,' said Vidya. 'I want to be here when they take care of that woman. Is there anything we can bring you, Ralphy?'

'Yeah, some good food! I'm sick of mashed potatoes and vege- tables.'

'We'll do that next time,' said JT. 'We're off to get some lunch and then I am going to go out to an old Clovis Indian site and see if there are any microcolonial fungi on the desert rocks nearby. Seems these two don't want to go with me.'

'You got that right. Neither of us wants to see any wide–open sky, dirt, or desert for a long time. They've given us access to a couple of computers at the operations center and that's where I'll stay,' answered Vidya emphatically.

Misa looked at Vidya feeling exactly the same. She had always liked talking computers with him. She wondered if he was going to be able to get over Kristina. Or would she, by her presence, only remind him of Kristina and Mexico? She had never said anything to him because of Kristina but she liked him a lot and had felt something special when they first met.

'Later, Ralphy,' said Vidya giving him a high five.

'Yep, see ya,' said Misa.

'And "good" food next visit,' added JT as they walked out the door.


'General Whitcuff has borrowed some extra people for us,' said Will Crystal.

'What sort?' asked Brush.

'Support types, but pretty high end, I think. He put together a good backup group for your excursion into Mexico but there were some weaknesses. After seeing what happened there and hearing about how frustrated the computer tech and Sheilla's group are, trying to break into the cartel's systems, he has been busy finding some experts. He's grabbed a couple of teenage ex-hackers, one in the Strategic Communications Command and another from the Intelligence Center. They've got some pretty high-tech outfits here between Drones, Communications, and Intelligence. Sheilla has been bending my ear about the cartel's impenetrable computer systems and asking why they were interested in abducting scientists to help Najma get to you. Why would the cartel care about Najma? Sheilla said it didn't make sense and I'm inclined to think she's right,' said Jim.

'I don't feel like we understand enough about the cartel or their setup yet. They're not just a bunch of hooligans with a few guns. The old mine was one thing but their home base is the hacienda. I don't want too many surprises when we go in tomorrow night. I hope these new guys can get into their computers and find out more about what we are up against.'

'The planned recon is risky,' added Brush. 'I don't hold out much hope for the master sergeant and his Mexican buddy. Nielly's guardian angel isn't going to be able to help them and from what we've seen there aren't many good Samaritans in the cartel.'

'Meet me back here at 17:30. We'll talk about it before the others get here for dinner,' said Will.

'I'm going to go see how Heather is doing,' said Jim.

'I just want to see Glenda Rose,' said Brush.

# Chapter 23

'A ny ideas, Fred, as to why their computers are so damned hard to hack?' asked Sheilla.

'No, I just don't. I always thought I was good and so is Marcus Gordon, the army guy that I'm working with. All of us thought we were cool kid hackers. But the cartel computers have a firewall we can't get through and so we're nowhere. The other two with Gordon aren't any help either. He says we're getting two more guys but he doesn't know anything about them, other than they're supposed to be special, whatever that means.'

'Stay with it and let me know the instant you get anywhere.'

'Nobody's home yet and I'm hungry,' said Glenda. 'OK if I look in the fridge? Maybe there's a Coke or something.' She disappeared through the door to the kitchen.

The front door opened startling Heather. A shiver ran down her spine before her face lit up with a beaming smile. 'Hey, guys, we were hoping you would show up. We're ready to eat. Glenda's starved.'

A big grin appeared on Brush's face as Glenda walked back into the room. *Incredible,* he thought, *she always looks better in person than my mental image.* He wasn't sure how that was possible. Just minutes earlier, he was thinking about lunch, but seeing Glenda, all his food desires disappeared.

Glenda gave him a lingering kiss, recognizing the look he was giving her. 'Let's all get some food,' she said as she grabbed Brush by the arm and tugged him toward the door.

Heather smiled up at Jim, put her arm around his waist and they followed Glenda and Brush out the door.

'What's a good place for lunch?' Jim asked the driver as he, Heather, Jim, and Brush climbed in the back, giving Glenda the front seat.

'O' Club's decent, I hear, sir.'

'Officers' Club it is then. Move it,' said Glenda, 'I'm ravenous.'

'Me, too,' said Brush, as he reached around the seat and caressed Glenda's arm.

The lunch was good by military standards. No one wanted a long lunch though. Brush's reason was obvious to everyone and Glenda didn't seem to be eating slowly either.

'Not bad for an O' Club,' said Brush. 'Drop us off at our quarters, Sergeant.'

The driver dropped Brush and Glenda off first and a few seconds later, Jim and Heather stood in front of the house that General Whitcuff had provided.

'Thoughtful of the general to give all of us a house,' remarked Jim.

'You are a full-bird-colonel now and Brush is a major and these are, as the sergeant told me, field grade officers' housing.'

'True but still we're just here temporarily and there are no doubt visiting and less comfortable hotel-type rooms somewhere on the post.'

As soon as they got into the house, Heather turned to Jim and put her head on his shoulder. 'I don't think we are quite as obvious as Brush and Glenda. But, Jim, I feel just as passionate about you as I always have. I need you to hold me,' she whispered.

Jim kissed her softly and held her head in his hands. She wrapped her arms around him and the passion that they had always felt for each other enveloped them. A flickering thought penetrated his mental haze: Perhaps he should treat her delicately after what she had seen in Mexico. Maybe she would associate sex with what she had seen. But what Heather had seen was brutality and had no associations for her with what she felt for Jim and seconds later, all conscious thoughts evaporated and they reveled in the feelings that, for them, never dissipated with time.

For the first time in two days, Heather let the recent memories drain completely from her mind. Only brief images of llamas, flowers, and mountains crept through her thoughts as she floated ahead of a trail of clothes. *How is it possible that after all these years he still makes me feel this way?* she wondered. *How can we make each other feel this way? Maybe we truly are just meant for each other.* He had told her once that they could never really touch as their skins' electrons repelled each other and maybe that was true as far as science goes but their minds touched. Sometimes the world of the senses knew things science could not explain.

He laid his head on her chest, both of them in their own thoughts. He was starting to think about the mission while Heather was only aware of the feelings coursing through her body. She could lie happily like this for hours.

He stretched and moved on his back and put his arm behind her head. She snuggled her head onto his shoulder and put her arm over his stomach. She was satisfied and content and thoughts of the Mexicans and Najma, though still present, were subdued by her senses.

Jim, from long experience, knew that Heather would have to work hard to dispel the memories. He also knew that first she would have to talk and try to understand what happened. He would let her take her time and do it in her own way, he didn't expect her to broach the subject for a while though. And that was fine. *The important thing is that she's OK,* he thought with a sense of relief.

Heather propped herself up on her right elbow and Jim turned to face her as she surprised him by saying, 'It's like a line, the number line. People are good on the positive side and I have always rated them one to ten on just how good they are. I've always ignored the other side, the zero to minus ten. Reciprocity, as you are always saying about things. Najma was the first minus ten I've ever met. Those Mexican men were the next. Now, I realize that you interact with people on the negative side of the line all the time. You know and understand things that I didn't, couldn't. Brush and Glenda have been there and understand, too. The general understands. They're all our friends but you've shared something with them I never have. My crowd is the JTs and Kristinas and Nicolas of the world.'

A small tear formed in the corner of her eye as she looked down and then raised her head. 'What I still don't seem to comprehend is how you and the others remain nice people after constant exposure to the evil people you encounter. I just saw you kill people. I don't understand. How can you be the kind man that I love?'

After a long pause Jim answered. 'Perhaps the difference is that neither I, nor Brush, take any pleasure in killing or hurting people. The ones you put on the other side of the line, Najma and the cartel types, either take pleasure in inflicting pain or feel nothing. They lose respect for life of any kind. I don't know the answers but I know that Brush and I care about people and Glenda showed us just how much she does too, when she was nearly killed protecting people she didn't even know.'

'Maybe it's saving desert tortoises that makes all of you different.'

Jim looked at her quizzically, not knowing exactly what she meant and at the same time feeling he understood what she was saying.

'Let's give Duane a quick call and see how the llamas are,' said Jim.

'Good idea, lover.' She gave him a kiss and held both of his arms. 'Let me talk to him. I'm feeling OK right now.'

'Hey, Duane, how's everything? Good... yeah... snowing... wow! Yep... OK, Jim says hi and give our best to Betty Lou, Loretta, and Ben, too. Yes, we're fine down here but miss the animals. Call if you need anything. See ya, bye.' She looked at Jim. 'Snowing already just above the ranch. Down here in the desert, I almost forgot what time of year it was.' She was silent for a moment then said, 'Dichotomies: snow, sunshine; hot, cold; mountains, desert; good, evil; pleasure, pain; you and Najma.'

# Chapter 24

Vidya and Misa were issued visitor badges and escorted into a room close to the TOC. There were several computers in the low-lit room and three uniformed soldiers were typing away furiously. They didn't look up as the civilians sat down in front of two computers. The escort walked out without saying anything.

'You're going to need a password,' said a young man with an upside-down chevron on his shoulder. 'Give me a minute.' He continued to stare at his screen.

'What's that on his shoulder?' Misa whispered to Vidya.

'No idea, looks like a chevron; so far we've only seen stripes on their sleeves. But there is one thing for sure, my mood is rapidly improving looking at these computers.'

'Here's your password,' said Specialist Gordon.

'Thanks. I'm Vidya and this is Misa,' Vidya said holding out his hand. 'I see your name stitched over your pocket is Gordon but are you an officer or what?'

Specialist Gordon and the other two, a corporal and a private first class chuckled at that. 'I'm just about as low as it gets on the pecking order around here. The only thing lower is that PFC sitting there, Peter.' Peter nodded his head. 'And maybe a fraction of an inch higher on the pecking order is Bob over there.' He pointed at Corporal Bob Preston. 'I'm Marcus Gordon. Have at the computers. I've got to get back to work. I hope you all are doing better being back in the USA after Mexico. We're all real sorry that things worked out like they did but at least some of you are safe.'

Vidya couldn't say anything. Misa asked, 'How do you know about that?'

'Not sure how much I can tell you, but I was monitoring and taking care of communications. That's my specialty, computers are secondary.'

'Sounds like all three of you are pretty fast on your keyboards,' said Misa.

'The three of us don't normally work together but there's a problem we're trying to solve,' said Gordon. 'If you need any help operating them just let us know.'

From outside the office the word 'attention' reverberated and in walked Generals Crystal and Whitcuff. Specialist Gordon jumped to attention, as did Corporal Preston and PFC Jones, who knocked his chair over as he jumped up. Misa was amused as the three enlisted men stood ramrod straight and still.

'At ease, gentlemen,' said Whitcuff. 'Any progress?'

'No sir,' said Gordon.

'You have two computer experts arriving in a few minutes. They're supposed to be about the two best in the army, so they tell me. One is an officer and the other a senior NCO. Who are you two?' asked Whitcuff.

'Well, sir, I'm Misa and this is Vidya. We were in Mexico.'

Whitcuff looked at the enlisted men. 'You three ignore us and get back to work.' The general studied them for a few seconds but was not one to dwell on the past. 'I seem to remember hearing that you two do something with computers?'

'I guess you could say that. I'm a Ph.D. from Singapore and Misa is a Ph.D. computer engineer from Oxford. I'm working on the new computation technologies that might allow us to overcome the slow speeds of conventional silicon based...'

The general held up his hand. 'You're over my head, son, doctors from foreign lands will do. Pretty good too, I imagine? The truth, no need to be shy.'

The three soldiers stared at their computers but were all ears. These two Ph.D.'s were probably light-years ahead of them in ability but they were old, maybe in their thirties.

'We're considered to be at the top of our field,' answered Misa softly.

'Don't suppose you've had security clearances before?' asked General Crystal.

'I do,' said Misa. 'UK government work and Vidya has worked on some Aussie government projects.'

'Yeah,' said Vidya, 'but I don't have any idea about whether I've ever had a security clearance. They just said they had vetted me, whatever that means.'

Whitcuff looked at Will Crystal and raised an eyebrow as if to say, *How much more trouble can I get into*?

'You two want to see if you can help us out here with a little problem?'

'If this has anything to do with Mexico, General, you bet your ass I do,' said Vidya, as the enlisted men raised their eyebrows at his choice of words to a general.

'OK, I'm in,' added Misa, happy to be doing anything with computers. 'Whatever we're in for, that is.'

'Gordon, fill them in and give them whatever they need. Tell the lieutenant when he gets here to work with them.'

'Yes, sir,' said Gordon almost shaking, as the generals vanished through the door. PFC Peter Jones said, 'Man oh man, two freaking generals, I just about shit a cow. Oops, sorry, Professors.'

'Jesus, me, too,' said Bob. 'Makes me feel inferior only being a corporal. That was a lot of brass all squeezed into such a small place.'

'Forget the "professor" bit, Gordon. Show us what you're working on and give us a quick rundown of your computer systems,' said Misa.

Gordon had just finished briefing them when the two new recruits walked in. Preston, Gordon, and Jones all stood at attention but not with the same enthusiasm that they had when the generals came in. The lieutenant looked about fourteen years old. He was nineteen. The master sergeant first class also looked like a teenager. Vidya couldn't help asking why someone so young should have so many yellow stripes on his sleeve.

'This here high ranking non-com,' said the lieutenant, 'is only in the army as an alternative to jail, after he was arrested for breaking into the State Department's computers. He was given the E-7 pay grade when the army figured out just how valuable he is. He's sort of my favorite all-time hero.'

'Non-com?' asked Misa.

'Non-commissioned officer,' said the lieutenant. 'Sit, everyone. I already looked at what you're doing.'

'How'd you do that?' asked Gordon.

'Never mind. Gordon, you've tried a couple of interesting things but you're obviously outclassed, so my hero and me will try to educate you some. What about you two? Who are you?' he asked as he looked at Misa and Vidya.

Gordon told him and filled him in on what the general had said.

'Let's see what the "professionals" have in their heads,' said the lieutenant.

Misa laughed. She was used to hearing arrogant upstarts think they knew more than she did.

'What's so funny?'

'Lieutenant...'

'Just call me LT or Jake and the sergeant here is just Jas or Jason.'

'All right, Jake and Jason. What's so funny is that you two are going to lose a little of that juvenile alpha-dog attitude when you start to find out what you always wanted to know about computers but were too self-educated to learn.'

'Looks like we got us some competition here, Jas,' said Jake. 'This might just turn out to be a blast.'

'Cool,' said Jason, which didn't sound like anything Marcus Gordon, Bob, or Peter had ever heard from a master sergeant first class before.

'Fill us in on the problem,' said Misa.

'Go ahead, Gordon, tell us the problem as you see it,' said Jake.

Gordon didn't have much to say since they hadn't found out much or been able to get through the firewall but he did explain more about the hacienda, the Mexican cartel, and their location .

'First task then is penetrate their firewall and/or find out how they're getting data in and out without triggering any traps.'

'Seems pretty obvious and also just what Gordon has been trying to do. Is that the best you've got, LT?' asked Vidya.

'I'm just starting at the beginning so we can get somewhere on this from here on. Linear development you know. First we need to find out what firewall they're using and after we figure out the configuration we'll build a customized tunnel to get in.'

'Whatever firewall they'll be using will be a SYN/ACK, packet filtering firewall starting with a SYN handshake,' said Gordon. 'That's what I've been working on.'

'Not true,' said Vidya. 'Could be a lot of things that are safer than packet filtering. Like, Raptor maybe.'

'What is that and why is it safer?' asked Gordon a little taken back.

'You tell him, LT, I'm going to mash some keys,' said Jason.

'Driven by proxies: safer because a proxy acts as a more intelligent agent on behalf of the user,' said Jake.

'Hey, before I get started, too, either of you two college grads up on the fine points of SSH or Virtual Private Networks?'

Misa smiled a little and shook her head before saying, 'I helped design SSH in Helsinki. That good enough for you?'

Jake laughed. 'Let's hit some keys then. Which one of you three has been liaising with this Sheilla up north?'

'Me,' said Gordon.

Jake turned to the other two enlisted guys. 'You two can take a break but I want you back here at twenty hundred hours.' He didn't think they were going to be any help but he might use them for making food runs. 'Gordon, I want you to make sure voice communications between us and Sheilla at Fort Lewis are completely secure and then see if they can help you check the whereabouts of all the crackers listed on this disk. One of them is in Mexico or spent time there. My guess is that one of the keyboard cowboys on this list designed their system and if we can find out who, we'll have a pretty good idea how it was designed. Then I want you to find out how they send their data out, phone line, satellite, cable, or a combination?'

He then turned to Vidya, Misa, and Jason. 'We're the Wolf Pack then.' *And I'm the Alpha Dog,* he said to himself. 'I suggest the four of us jump in separately, do our own thing, and see if we can break into their system. Any other ideas before we start?'

'An obvious one,' said Vidya. 'If it's SSH 1.5 it will be easy to break in.'

'Maybe,' said Jake. 'But I have a feeling that if they're any good they've already added compensation detectors.'

A rapid-fire discussion ensued about Secure Shell, data protection from CRC-32, deep magic, integer overflow vulnerabilities, and how they might execute some arbitrary code with SSH privileges of the SSH root daemon.

To anyone listening, they might as well have been aliens, but after a few minutes of discussion, the group sat down at the computers. Jake cracked his knuckles. 'Raster burn time,' he said with a smile.

'This might be fun. Let's teach these two upstarts a lesson,' said Misa. 'You ready?'

'I'm ready, but they're not the ones I care about teaching a lesson to. The cartel and that woman are the ones I want to get,' said Vidya with a venomous look.

# Chapter 25

Jesus criminy. Never seen anything like that,' said Brush. 'You, Jim?'

Nielly beamed, looking at his latest piece of equipment.

'Not since being a kid and looking at comic books,' answered Jim.

'Looks like a Batman outfit,' added Brush.

Nielly pulled a tarp off another crate and they all looked in.

'You're full of surprises,' said Jim.

'Boy that one beats me. Is it underwater or for flying to the moon?' asked Brush.

'Come on, Nielly, quit smirking and give us a rundown,' said Jim.

'Brush had the first one right. We call it the Batman suit. Two movable mini-turbo jets, carbon fiber wing, full life support, thermal suit, and steering in each hand. Almost undetectable with radar and wind independent for long-range insertions.'

Brush was smiling now. 'I got to try this, Nielly.'

'OK, you're on, pal, as long as we don't use it and lose it in Mexico, you can test fly it.'

Jim was looking in the other crate and Brush could tell his mind was racing. 'How many of these do you have, Nielly?'

'Just these two. We brought them along just in case, but they're experimental.'

'You tried it yet?' asked Jim.

'Sure and it worked great. Eleven to one glide ratio. Pretty easy to control. The experimental part is landing; messed up the last one pretty good, otherwise it's a piece of cake.'

Jim was rubbing his chin while admiring the six-foot long, open-topped-winged glider and thinking, *The wingspan isn't much, maybe about the same as the length and they're more like blades than wings.* 'How much does it weigh?' he asked.

'Thirty kilos.'

'You said you don't land it?'

'Not yet. Right now you use your own parachute and a static-type line deploys the glider's chute. That's how we messed up the last one, trying to glide in. All manual controls, and with the wind deflector it's just like being in a ninja-racer motorcycle but absolutely quiet. Only one problem. When it hits its own air cushion about six feet off the ground, it starts buffeting and becomes unstable.'

'Damn cute little thing, a bobsled with wings,' added Brush.

'Let's check out the rest of the gear and then we can talk about the insertion plan,' said Jim as they set off toward the other side of the hangar and three of Nielly's men.


Guillermo sat in an elegant gray suit with his legs crossed, as he looked out the window at the green trees of Hyde Park and its famous lake, the Serpentine, glistening in the late afternoon sun.

'Tell me, Rameriz, this scheme of Amir's. Will it work?'

'With the modifications we've been making, yes, jefe, it will work.'

Rameriz was usually a cool customer but he could feel a slight dampness on his forehead. He was well aware that he had just staked his life on having that successful outcome. Fortunately he was certain now that they could make it work and with the percent El Padrino had promised him, he would be set for life.

Sheilla had her feet on the desk reading the short profiles that Katarina had just given her. She stared up unblinking, mouth slightly parted. Her mind was almost a blank but a part ticked along logically assimilating the information she had just read. The missing information was there she knew, but what was it? She moved away from her desk and started swiveling.

'Got it! Has to be the connection!' she shouted as her phone chirped, interrupting her thoughts. 'Sheilla. Hey, Specialist Gordon. Yeah, I understand... We never use Advance Encryption System for anything in our lab. We'll only communicate using a special high-level encryption and now using the encryption you set up for us with Fred.'

'Sorry, I just wanted to make sure that no one sent an un-encrypted fax or email by accident,' said Marcus Gordon.

'That's all right, Marcus. So, anything happening with the cartel?'

'Actually lots. Your general and the base commander were here and gave two of the Mexico veterans, the ones that Jim rescued, Misa and Vidya, permission to work on the problem. They are both computer scientists. Then two hotshot teenage ex-hackers were brought in and they seem to be having a competition with the two older scientists to see who's best. Doesn't seem to be much doubt about that now. Vidya and Misa identified the cartel's firewall in a couple of minutes and now they're working on something to do with a proxy server. I think the two hackers are just a little surprised that they may not be the best around. Otherwise, we're trying to find out who the cartel used to set up their network.'

'Thanks, Gordon. Gotta run.' Sheilla immediately dialed Jim's cell phone.

'Jim, I think I have an idea about Najma. Farasie had a brother who is a financial guy in London. I'm going to have Fred try to find a connection between him and the cartel. I'm willing to wager that this Amir, Farasie's brother, has a financial connection with them. It all makes sense. That's how Najma hooked up with the cartel and why they helped her come after you using Heather. Makes sense don't you think? How is she doing?'

'She seems to be coping right now. Let me know anything else you think is useful. Don't worry about the time, just call me.'

'I'm going to fax Gordon the profile on Guillermo. It might help. He seems very unusual and consequently I suspect he could be very dangerous.'

'Well, boss,' said Yousef. 'I don't know what you were thinking getting involved with this lot. I think I would sooner go to Transylvania and sleep with Dracula.'

'You were right, wish I had listened to what you said in the first place,' Amir said ruefully. 'It wasn't worth getting even for what happened to my brother and the attempt failed anyway. After watching how barbaric these people are, I was actually rooting for the American to get away. What a mess. These creeps are in my house. It's all turned to rubbish. I don't know what we should do.'

'One thing for sure is that their computer guys are light-years ahead of us. I thought I was competent and Sharon is brilliant but they just know more than we do. I thought our scheme was big, pilfering five million pounds sterling. And I thought we could get away with it. Their new scheme is so much bigger; I'm not so sure we can get away with this one. Where are we going to hide if we bankrupt one of the largest UK banks?'

'With this Guillermo character, I don't think we can do anything. He is capable of things I never knew people could do and he has so much money and power. We can't hide from him, so maybe all we can do is go along and make him trust us. Maybe that way we'll survive this and have a life afterwards,' said Amir without much conviction.

'We're not going anywhere and we're not getting away—he's going to kill us. He can't afford to have the three of us out there as a loose end. Bloody Hell. No, Amir, if we just go along we're dead. I'm sure of it. We have to figure out something. I'm going to the loo and then let's get something to eat.'

'I can't eat. This whole thing is making me sick, they are all over my house for Christ's sake,' said Amir.

'I eat when I'm nervous and that's what we're going to do. Go and get Sharon and let's discuss this. Do you think they will let us leave the house?'

Yousef and Sharon both had Middle Eastern parents but were raised in England and didn't really know anything about their Arabic roots. They were British through and through. Yousef even had a slight upper class accent he had acquired at Winchester College before studying computer sciences at Bristol University. His parents had spent their life's savings to pay the steep fees at Winchester. They wanted the best for their son but still couldn't understand why a private school for boys was called a public school and why it should cost so much. It further confounded them that it was called a college.

Sharon's education was far removed from the rarified campuses of public schools. She went to a state school in south London and then received a scholarship to Bristol to study computer science; there she and Yousef had become friends. Her parents still lived in a small council flat and all she wanted in life was to get them a house where they would be safe and happy. Far better than Yousef with computers, her logical mind allowed her to write brilliant yet simple code and intuitively understand how to penetrate what she considered to be ill protected corporate systems. She had been critical of Amir and Yousef's plan but was she even necessary to the cartel's? Her only interests in life had been computers and her parents. Now to her narrow interests she added a third: survival.

'Where the fuck you think you're going?' said Ox as they started down the hall to the front door of Amir's house.

'We're going to get something to eat,' said Yousef, foolishly trying to push by Oxochitl. As a fog cleared from his brain, he mumbled, 'What happened?'

'I don't think we're going to be able to leave,' said Amir. 'The big guy slapped you when you tried to push by him. Knocked you out for a few seconds.'

Yousef shook his head. 'I'm feeling whacked all right. Jesus.'

'Bloody Hell, Bloody Hell! What are we going to do?' exclaimed Amir.

The two men had always felt in charge but now they felt helpless as they saw their futures ebbing away. They were confused; the world that they knew, one they had controlled, was a distant memory.

Sharon, on the other hand, was gaining resolve and her strength was giving her the determination to fight. It wasn't just honor or pride, it was simply that when pushed she had learned to push back.

It was a way of life on the streets in her neighborhood.

Her parents had changed the spelling of her name for some unknown reason, from Shareefa, meaning noble and honored one, to Sharon. Growing up in some hard state schools left her more resilient to the rough Mexican bodyguards. The big brute, Ox, didn't scare her but the little weasel, Felix, did. She could see the intelligence and cruelty in his darting eyes.

They helped Yousef up. 'You all right?' Yousef nodded. 'Let's go to the kitchen,' said Sharon.

'I don't think I'm hungry anymore,' said Yousef.

'Let's go to the kitchen and talk,' she whispered. 'Eat if you like or not.'

The two men didn't yet comprehend; they had relinquished control over their futures not only to Guillermo but in a matter of seconds to Sharon. Their spirits improved a little as Sharon took charge of their hushed conversation in the kitchen.

# Chapter 26

The knock on the door did not startle Heather as much as it had when Jim had walked in earlier. She was starting to feel more secure, a little less edgy. She walked toward the door, thinking it was crazy to be nervous with a part of the US Army to protect her, along with Jim, Brush, and Glenda, not to mention Nielly and his Special Forces. Off base, she might feel vulnerable but being here was as safe as it got, though she had one overriding wish, to get as far away from Mexico as she could. But she fought the urge to go north, to the ranch, and place distance between herself and Mexico, and what it now represented. She knew she needed to see this through no matter what her fears, or there would be no peace for her anywhere.

Heather peeked through the peephole in the door and saw Sergeant Murphy, the jeep driver, standing on the porch.

'You've been requested at the TOC,' he told her.

'The what? Oh yeah, the tactical operations center. All right, Sergeant, can you give me a minute, please.'

'Sure thing, ma'am, just come out when you are ready.'

After a short drive, Heather was escorted into the building the same way that Jim, Misa, and Vidya had been and issued a building pass hanging from a chain. Her escort stopped at a door and knocked before walking into a small conference room.

Master Sergeant Smith smiled and held out his hand. 'I'm Glen Smith and this is my long-term friend and army buddy, Jay Hernandez.'

'Pleased to meet you,' said Heather. 'I guess you two are the ones that will need to learn a little botany.' She looked a little sheepish and added, 'I didn't mean to sound presumptuous, maybe you know more about plants in this area than I do.'

'I assure you, Doctor, that is not the case,' said MS Smith with Sergeant First Class Hernandez shaking his head in concurrence. 'We know a bit about what to eat in the desert and the jungle, too, for that matter, but we don't have a clue what you call most of them.'

'OK then.' She walked to a blackboard and wrote the names of the plants they would have to know.

The two sergeants asked several questions before starting a slide show with pictures of the plants in their natural habitat and what they were used for.

'Where did you get this PowerPoint presentation from?' asked Heather.

'The captain said the Arizona-Sonora Desert Museum sent it.'

'I don't think I've given you much extra information. Are you sure it will be enough? I understand this could be dangerous for you.'

Sergeant Smith smiled. 'With the background you've given us and now seeing what these plants look like in real life, it seems like it will make a good cover story.'

'But why do you want to do this?' asked Heather. 'It will be very dangerous and I can tell you from firsthand experience that the cartel members are despicable psychopaths. They will not be interested in your plant cover story but just that you are there trespassing, so why do it?'

'We know the odds aren't good but we signed up to do this sort of thing a long time ago and in the past couple of years things have been sort of, well, boring. Missions are always like this—why have we ever gone on them? But if we didn't do this, then we wouldn't think much of ourselves. The need is there, we've been asked and we'll go.'

Tears welled up in Heather's eyes.

Everything made her cry lately. The two men in front of her would look just like Kristina and Nicola by tomorrow. 'Sorry, sorry,' she said. 'Let's go through the slides again.'

The two sergeants were touched by her reaction but it gave them even more determination to go. They didn't intend to be harmed; sure it would be dangerous but just like the base commander, General Whitcuff, they wanted to leave the army with a growl not a whimper. It was who they were and always wanted to be.

Captain Fuller arrived just as they were finishing up. He found his orders distasteful even if necessary. He was ordered to give the two sergeants false information. They would be walking onto the cartel land at sunrise tomorrow and the main mission would commence tomorrow night. If they were captured as everyone thought they would be, and if they were tortured, also as everyone suspected they would be, then eventually, even though both were hard men, they would break. They would tell what they thought to be the truth, that the Mexican government planned an attack in a week's time with the assistance of the US authorities.

Heather was convinced that the two sergeants knew as much as possible about how to harvest the plants, their uses, and the prices they would receive. Captain Fuller had found out what the going rates were, and where they could be sold. They all knew that the story was convincing, but would the cartel care about their story? Why should they? The only hope was that it would sound plausible and if the two were very lucky, they would be detained and later released or held alive until they were rescued.

'Nice stuff, eh?' said Brush. 'The gizmos get more exotic all the time.'

'Useful too though, especially in our line of work.'

'Any ideas about the mission? You're the planner but right now it seems sort of half-baked to me. I don't mind so much when it's just you and me, we can adapt, but with this many people involved too many things can go wrong.'

'It's the recon that's missing and no matter what the two sergeants find out, there are still going to be too many things we don't know,' said Jim.

'Our main reason for going is to get Najma,' said Brush. 'But we don't even know if she is there. In any event I'll leave the thinking to you and the general. Going to go pay Glenda a visit before our dinner meeting.'

Heather felt edgy. She was putting up a good front but inside she was filled with conflict. The realities were seeping into her mind. She felt depressed, listless, worried, and anxious. She opened her diary and started to scan. It was her best escape; private notes, thoughts, and words about her life and feelings that had at one time seemed important to her to preserve.

At first she tried to remember the short poem that she had made

up in Mexico only two nights ago. The words would not come to
her so she read random musings as she turned the pages that held
clues to her past:

*All I am ever thinking about is you and being together and hav-
ing a life and looking at movies, making love, seeing beautiful
things, and smiling at the good things...*

She smiled for a moment and then asked herself, *What beautiful
things?* They were spoiled by the ugly products of humans. And
what good was anything?

Then something caught her eye. A trip they had taken to Nepal
several years ago. She had loved Kathmandu, its frenetic buzz,
prayer flags, the golden robes, and ancient monasteries, and then
there were the mountains so tall and jagged they appeared to sit on
top of the clouds.

*Horoscope from Kathmandu paper, the* Kathmandu Post—
Pisces... 'Do you know who's really on your side? Now is the time to
find out, or at least to speculate. Things are likely to get weird
before they make sense, but you can figure it all out.'

What a lot of gibberish, she had thought then, but now she wondered who could you ever really trust? Would she look at people the
same now as she had before? What about Rwanda? Neighbors
hacked up friends with machetes. Why? How could they do it? She
had pondered this when they had visited the gorillas in Rwanda's
north mountains. The people walking the streets who looked so
friendly and normal might have been the ones that killed women
and children just a few years ago. What did they say to the children?
How did they explain why they had done such things?

How could men and women in the cartel be like they were, cruel
with no empathy? She would never be able to understand them.
How would she ever make sense of her new world? She thought

about how lucky she was to have Jim. He had been able to find her and rescue the ones left alive. Then she turned the page and found the one thing that did make sense to her still, when she had first found Jim, how they had found each other:

*I was searching but you found me,*
*Running, and you stopped me*
*Dead in my tracks.*
*Falling for you, you caught me,*
*Looking, and you saw me...*

She couldn't finish reading it. It was the first poem she had written after they met, long ago; every time Heather started a new notebook, she opened it to a random page and copied the poem on it. All she wanted to do was have things be the same as they had been, the same as when they had met. Then a knock on the door, a key inserted; her breath caught, and instantly she realized it could only be Jim. He knocked his familiar two longs, one short, and one long so as not to scare her when he walked in.

She ran to him, holding him as tight as she was able, tears freely rolling down her cheeks, soaking the white gauze.

'I'm scared, Jim, I feel weak and nauseous. The two women were nice and special, intelligent, and they were hurt and killed for no good reason just like your old geology friend. For a while, I thought I understood how I could deal with it, but I don't—I can't. Let's just leave, go back to the ranch with Rosie, Skipper, the llamas, and just be. You could be killed or tortured. The sergeants are good men, brave men, and they probably will be hurt or killed. Nielly, the general, or Brush, they could all be killed.'

Jim had known this was coming. It was inevitable. Deep down

he still felt certain she would be all right. She was a fighter and a scientist—logic and understanding would eventually allow her to reconcile with a world that was not always the best of all possible worlds.

'Sweetie, you know we have to go. My hope is that it allows people in the middle of your number line to live without ever encountering the Najmas that exist. I don't know what it is that makes people so different but we seem to be a flawed species. There have always been people spanning the length of your number line. Sometimes the plus tens have to take up the battle with the minuses to keep things balanced so more people can live in peace.'

'I don't know, Jim. Will you really make a difference? Or is it just an illusion you live with?'

Looking deep into her eyes, he said, 'I want you to stay close to Glenda tonight. Brush and I will take care of ourselves and I want you and Glenda to take care of each other. She will benefit from your ideas and so will the rest of us. Do you want to go to General Whitcuff's with me now?'

'You go ahead. I will just stay here and think. See you when you are finished,' she said not able to smile but feeling the strength of will in his eyes and face; it gave her some solace.

# Chapter 27

If anyone was nervous, you couldn't tell from their appetites. Good food was not something in short supply at General Whitcuff's. As a group they were used to eating for nourishment in the field or the office: they were not used to eating finely cooked meals. Everyone sat at the same places as last night with one exception, MSG Glen Smith sat in Heather's chair.

'How do you feel about your cover story, Sergeant?' asked General Crystal.

'It's as good as it can be, sir. She did her best to teach a couple of old duffers something useful.'

'I can't emphasize enough how important your recon is. I don't know what you will find but since we know little, anything will help. Anyone have anything to add?'

No one said anything until Nielly added, 'Good luck, Sergeant, both of you. Hope to see you back here in a few days.'

'Thanks for the meal and the company. We leave at 20:00. Sort of feel naked without weapons other than pruning shears and collecting bags. Generals, Captain Fuller—nice meeting the rest of you. Adios then.'

'How are they getting to the site?' asked Glenda when they had gone out.

'Driving across like they often do, to visit Sergeant Hernandez's girlfriend. They'll spend the night and head out in an old pickup with Mexican registration that belongs to her. They'll park it about eight klicks east of the hacienda and start collecting plants and moving toward the hacienda,' said Captain Fuller.

'My watcher is going in at 01:00, HAHO just like Jim did the other night: same procedure. He'll work his way in and position on a small ridge about 4,000 feet away from the hacienda. He should be in position well before sunup and he will be hard to spot with the sun at his back,' said Nielly.

'I thought you called them Guardian Angels?' asked Glenda.

'Most times I do but they won't be protecting the sergeants, just observing.'

'Any chance the cartel will have people out on similar ridges or listening devices that far out?' asked Jim.

'He goes in both quiet and invisible and he has scanners to detect radio and cell frequencies. Like I said before, he's the regular invisible man. We've also got some extra help as your specialist Gordon has been able to start accessing their cell phone conversations. I'm assuming if they post sentries that far out that they will communicate with cell phones or radios. We might get as much recon from listening in as we do from the sergeants on the ground.'

'Might get some info from snooping their computers, too. I don't know what their latest is,' added Captain Fuller, 'since the computer whizzes seem to be charging ahead a mile a minute. Last I heard, they had broken the cartel's firewall and had a short list of possible ex-hackers that might have designed their system. They were mumbling something about traps and landmines and wanted to know who the designer was for sure before they penetrated more deeply. When I left them, they were all arguing about things that made no sense to me.'

General Whitcuff looked at General Crystal and said, 'I'm thinking maybe I should retire. Occurs to me that all this mumble-jumble computer stuff might actually be more valuable than good old snooping using our five senses. Soldiers look more like a cross between humans and robots nowadays, all connected to satellites, and drones rather than pilots doing the flying. All great advances but lets me know what a dinosaur I am at the old age of fifty-four.'

'Just what the army always wanted isn't it? Robots always obey orders,' added General Crystal.

'This BS'ing is fun,' said General Whitcuff. 'And I mean that—but let's get to work on the assault plan, subject to change of course after we get some ground intel and whatever the computer techs can give us. It will be an early day tomorrow and then a long night, so let's get this nailed down and get some shut-eye.'

# Chapter 28

Guillermo sat cool and confident in his suite studying Rameriz who had just arrived by commercial jet. His problem with computer types in general and Rameriz in particular was that they were motivated by their computer interests first, then greed and the fear that the cartel instilled. They were not like his men; paid employees with little or no loyalty. Rameriz was tall with intelligent brown eyes that gave away little. He was a good manager but not ruthless and Guillermo needed that now.

'You keep tight control here, Rameriz,' said Guillermo. 'I'll take care of negotiating with the Cubans. With this sum of money, I will feel safer having it go through them before it ends up in our Panama accounts. Following your plan it will go through a Cuban government account and then to the multiple Cayman Island accounts and end up in our Panama accounts, except for Amir's money that is.

'I am counting on the idea that the Cubans will actually take pleasure in being the brunt of western governments' wrath, and will enjoy taking part of the blame for the bank's demise. It is a lot of money and they will be well compensated for their trouble.

The British economy will survive. The governments will do a lot of blustering and threatening but in the end they will do nothing except blame the banks for their poor security and pass some new meaningless regulations.'

'What do you plan to do with Amir and his group?'

'They will swap their money for gold in the Bahamas. That is all you need to know for now. I want them traced by the authorities to the Bahamas. Their money takes the same route as ours through Cuba, then goes on to the Bahamian accounts you set up for them, where we will have them withdraw it.

'Tomorrow you move to the new London location not far from here. Amir will be found eventually as the new owner of the internet café. It will be closed for renovation starting tomorrow. Set up a way that the UK government will be able to trace them. Keep it subtle. No overt clues that they are involved. I want the authorities to have to work hard enough to find them to be convinced that their investigations paid off and they have the "real" culprits.'

Rameriz puffed out his cheeks as he left the hotel for Amir's house. He was setting them up to be killed. El Padrino had not said as much but that was exactly what would happen. They could not afford to have them caught alive. They would certainly talk if they were. 'And why the gold?' he mumbled aloud. *Of course,* he thought. *Gold is untraceable; it would be in Guillermo's hands with no links to Amir and his group. The authorities would trace them, find them dead, and the trail would end there.*

'You can go out but you have to take one of the bodyguards with you. Sorry about their behavior,' said Rameriz when he met the new members of the London computer team. 'I'll talk to them. They're just doing what they think is their job and mainly that is to protect Guillermo. They're different from us; being tough and looking tough is what boosts their egos. They're not as smart or civilized as we are. I'll do what I can but we have to concentrate on how we are going to do this job and at least for me, how I am going to spend all the money after.'

'Simple question,' asked Yousef. 'What happens to us when this is over?'

'You'll be part of our organization,' Rameriz lied. 'Guillermo will want to use Amir's and your skills to move and protect money and after this operation, there will be trust. We can always use computer specialists like you and Sharon. We are still working on how to shift the billions we steal from the banks here in London to offshore banks, including yours. Guillermo is negotiating with the Cubans for the money to go through Cuba and then on to tax havens for us.'

Rameriz didn't like deceiving them but then it was only partly deceptive; their money would go through Cuba to the Caribbean where they would be killed. *An important difference,* he thought. And a sad difference as in most ways they were more his type of people than the cartel. Especially when he was starting to question his fate. Would Guillermo sacrifice him, too? Why wouldn't he? The only one that would win in the end would be El Padrino. *I need to get back to work now,* he thought, *but later tonight I will think and see if there isn't a way to protect myself.*

'Are you crazy? There is no way they are going to let us go after this,' said Sharon while she listened for steps approaching the kitchen. 'They can't think we would actually believe they would let us go, can they?'

'We will be very rich,' said Amir.

'Sharon is right, Amir, we will be very dead. We have to talk about this and find a way to survive.'

'Quiet,' said Sharon. 'Someone is coming.'

'I talked to Ox and Felix,' said Rameriz. 'You can go out whenever you want but one of them needs to go with you. Felix is ready if you want to go out now. He won't actually be with you but will stay close. Believe me, it is just as much for your protection. They are both tough but also very skilled in looking for people who might be watching or tailing you. We don't know how careful you have been before we combined forces so we just want to protect the project for all of us.' *And I need to get the three of you together on surveillance cameras,* he thought. 'Leave when you want I've got work to do.' When he was sure they had gone, he added, 'Alejandro, you get to work on the computer, you know what to do. Lazio, make sure that we have microphones in all the rooms. Are the microphones working that you planted on them?'

'Sí.'

'No Spanish, only English and don't forget.'

'Yes, they are working fine and Felix is carrying a digital recorder.'

'After you have double-checked all the listening devices, I want you to get on your computer and find out where all the government Closed Circuit TV cameras are installed along our route. We are going to have to find a way to dismantle them or erase them. I want no record of any of us appearing with the three English or even of being in this neighborhood or the old internet café we are moving to.'

'There are cameras everywhere in this city, I've never seen

people so monitored,' said Lazio.

'Let's just find a way to fix it. It is very important,' said Rameriz. 'The rest of our group arrives tomorrow and we move to the new location. I want no surveillance record of us left for the police, only of the three of them.'

# Chapter 29

Will I see you later today, Jim?'

'Of course, sweetest. I didn't mean to wake you but I want to hear what the watcher and the two sergeants report in person. We should start hearing something useful just after sunrise. After we hear what they and the computer experts say, we'll finalize our plans around seventeen hundred. I hope we can spend most of the rest of the evening together before we set off for the mission.'

'You didn't wake me—I didn't sleep well last night. I'm worried, really worried. Even if I wanted to, which I don't, I can never go to Mexico again. You won't get all of the cartel, will you? And what if they come after us just like Najma did?'

'No need to worry. They will all have better things to do when this is over. The government is always trying to get them and if this goes according to plan, the cartel will think it is the Mexican government who's responsible.'

Brush and Glenda were waiting in the jeep when Jim came out.

'Sleep well, buddy?'

'I slept fine but Heather didn't. She's worried about other

cartel members coming after us when this is over.'

'She might have a point. We are attacking them in their home, so what's to stop them from coming after us in ours?' said Glenda. 'Sorry to hear she is worried though. I'd say we slept pretty well, wouldn't you, Brush?'

'Yep, sheer exhaustion,' he whispered in her ear and then so Jim could hear, 'I slept like a baby,' as he took her hand. 'If they come, they come but not very likely.'

The eastern sky had a soft glow hovering just above the horizon as they entered the building containing the now expanded TOC. Inside there was no night or day and it buzzed with activity. The computer group, the Wolf Pack, looked red-eyed but focused. Glenda noted that they were actually smiling at their computer screens. She had noticed this once before in a large internet café in Holland: most of the people looked at their computer screens with affection. Was it like the feelings some people get from pets? Could an inanimate glass screen actually bring pleasure? She thought the answer might be that they were a different type of person who liked computers more than they liked people; but more likely it was the opposite and computers connected them with people. 'The computer nerds seem happy looking at their screens,' she whispered.

'Just like some people like their dogs better than people,' Brush replied.

'I was just thinking that.' Glenda liked being on the same wavelength as Brush. This really was different, wasn't it? And it still didn't scare her. *Wow,* she thought.

'Our watcher's in position,' said Nielly as he pointed at the map. 'He's seen little activity at the hacienda. Nothing interesting or useful.'

'Negatives are useful. Means they are not patrolling the perimeter: maybe they have video monitors or listening devices out,' added Jim.

'Watcher to base. Just enough light now to spot several cameras on the wall, lots of light reflecting off glass in the wall itself, too.'

'Surprise one,' said Nielly. 'Windows in the perimeter wall. Describe size and exact locations.'

'Half meter high and one long. Will send an image shortly and it should be light enough for you to see the satellite uplink in a few minutes.'

'Receiving. Scan the building and then pan so we can get images of the land around the hacienda.'

Outside the TOC, the images were up on screens and being manipulated, enhanced, and interpreted by remote sensing specialists. Data started to flow. Small things at first that would eventually add up to create their overall understanding.

'Sir, we have some interesting features two hundred meters out from the wall but unknown what they are yet,' said the officer in charge of the analysis.

'I want a report minimum every thirty minutes with a quick brief on what you see or don't understand and possible questions,' ordered Nielly.

'What's the expected arrival time for our sergeants?' asked Glenda.

'They are zigzagging collecting plants so expect they average about two miles per hour; ETA about 8:30 before they are close enough to be spotted. They will have to be over this escarpment before the guardian can see them. GPS shows them to be back at this point now,' said Nielly. He swung a portable computer around with a blinking light moving over topographical lines on the screen.

'Seems weird; they're used to being incognito, blending in, not standing targets, but in a couple of hours they are going to be getting their asses busted,' said Brush. 'Great old guys, hope they make it.'

Heather was too anxious to try to sleep. She went for a walk. It didn't help. She couldn't dispel the agitated feelings. Propped up in bed she pulled her diary out again. She couldn't concentrate or write. Images of the two happy women, one with fuzzy black hair and that cute kiwi accent and Nicola's opposite in some ways, Kristina, with her thick, wavy blond hair and Polish accent. She glanced at the diary and saw 'watermelon snow' and thought to herself, pink, cool, safe. Mexico didn't have any pink snow, only 'vermillion sand' she thought and wrote that down. Hot, red, and unsafe. She didn't want to think about her two new dead friends but she couldn't help it. They were worth the entire cartel put together: smart, funny, intelligent women that could contribute to the world. She threw the book down, stormed out the door, and looked around for the driver. He wasn't there. She set off walking, looking almost like a speed walker but without the exaggerated movements.

'They are nearing the escarpment,' said Niclly. 'We'll see them in a few minutes.'

They watched two red dots move west, perpendicular to narrowing topo lines on their screen as they approached the ridge.

The analyst walked in. 'Two manmade structures, here and here,' he said pointing at the map. 'We have no idea what they are, possibly bunkers, but no sign of any movement outside of them. Also, repeating small mounds and small straw-sized posts scattered along the wall.'

'Base, the two IVs just crested a rise about one and half klicks behind me. They are walking along the ridge line to the south toward a brushy area.' The team had given the sergeants a nickname, 'Itinerant Vagrants.'

'Nice move,' said Nielly. 'They will be clearly silhouetted on the ridge. Anyone watching should think that they don't care about being spotted, which is exactly the plan. Next they will take a break and sit down about one-half klick southwest of the watcher. Then they are going to move northwest and then to this area that has ironwood trees.'

'I thought they were going to have communication with us?' inquired Glenda.

'The com is not as secure as my watcher, he has satcom. It's too bulky for the IVs so they will only switch on if they see something important. Both of their transmitting devices are hidden in pieces of old wood. If they are busted, hopefully they can drop them and no one will care. We don't want the cartel finding anything on them or bringing their stuff into the hacienda and they are sure to have radio frequency detectors just like we have. They might scan them before bringing them into the compound, or if our two sergeants are lucky, just question them, search them, and let them go.'

'Or they will just start using them for target practice,' added Fuller.

Jim looked up from the GPS tracker into two green eyes
standing at the door. He smiled, seeing her framed in the door
opening, and then nodded his head for her to come over as the
desk sergeant brought her a chair.

'What's happening?'

'Satellite is tracking the two sergeants' position on this
screen. We have video of the hacienda over here but the sergeants
are out of sight right now. In the outer room, analysts are going
over the images. Brush is in with them now. The watcher is on
this ridge with the video camera uplinked to us.' He squeezed her
hand.

Heather turned her head back to see who had just placed two
hands on her shoulders. Glenda smiled.

'How'd you get here? We asked the driver to wait outside. I
didn't think you wanted to come this early.'

'I needed the exercise and the walk did me some good. I think
I need to see this. I just hope nothing bad happens to Glen and
Jay. They seemed like really nice men when I talked to them
yesterday.'

'Nice to see you up so early, Heather,' said Nielly and
laughed as Jake walked in. 'I could use someone like you, LT.
You look like you just passed puberty and I've never seen a more
wrinkled set of clothes. Don't get me wrong, I like that in a
military officer. Do us a favor and drop any and all jargon. I just
want to know how you can help us with info about what is going
on in the cartel and their security systems.'

Jake looked around and was happy but confused. This didn't
look anything like a military group. Two good-looking but older,
civilian-clothed women. Only a couple of people in uniform and
the major who he was talking to didn't look anything like the

majors he was used to.

He thought for a second, not sure if he could talk without the jargon. 'We've hacked through their firewall and are in their computer, snooping around. It's really magic, super neat. We found the guy who designed it, Ramsey Mann. He was a super-cool dude hacker in the US until he disappeared. A real legend. He was nicknamed Zorro; maybe never would have been caught if his woman hadn't turned him in. State Department had him and then he just vanished.

'We used what we knew about him, or rather those two Mex refugees did, to figure out how he would have designed a system.'

'What do you mean, "Mex refugees"?' asked Heather.

'They were there, the two computer profs, kidnapped but not fucked up...'

'Go a little easy there, Jake. The woman that just asked you that, Heather, was there too and this elegant-looking colonel is the one that rescued them. Just about everyone else here was south of the border or monitoring.'

Most of the color had drained from Heather's face.

'Really, really sorry, ma'am,' said Jake. 'We've been up all night and I need to watch what I say... Sorry.'

'Continue, Lieutenant, but skip your breaking and entering and tell us what is going to help us when we knock on their door tonight.'

'They have a sophisticated system, much of it we can't see as they keep it segregated and off-line unless they are using it. Perfect protection. We are tuned in live, however, to their security and monitoring systems.'

Nielly, Fuller, Glenda, and Jim all looked interested now.

'General Whitcuff was right,' said Nielly. This was going to provide more than they expected and much more than they hoped for from the two sergeants on the ground. 'I've got to monitor things here; our IVs are getting closer. Jim, do you think you could find Brush and get all the details from the lieutenant? You can fill my team in later and then we'll pull the LT in if we have more questions.'

'Let's head back to your room, Lieutenant,' said Jim.

'Me, too,' said Glenda, 'I want to hear this.'

Heather had regained her color. 'You're going to pull Glen Smith and Jay Hernandez out now? Aren't you?' She looked at Captain Fuller and then Nielly.

'No, Heather, I can't, we need to find out everything we can. They might see something that will save our lives later.'

Heather's head dropped and she said softly, 'I'll go with you three, if it's OK?'

# Chapter 30

Vidya, Misa—Hi!' exclaimed Heather as she walked into the computer room and regained a little of her usual cheerful self. Misa jumped up and gave Heather a long emotional hug while Vidya shook hands with Jim.

'Nice to see you again, Colonel,' said Vidya, then nodded to Brush and Glenda.

There was a close familiarity that they all felt for each other now. It was the first time Heather had these feelings for anyone other than Jim outside of her own family. They were now the survivors of the happy band who went to Mexico. Her thoughts were still troubled but she felt a camaraderie she had never experienced before: a deep understanding and trust of who these people were. It gave her newfound strength and surprisingly, a feeling of contentment.

Heather looked at Jim, then she studied them all, especially Glenda, not listening to the computer talk. She liked these people. They were strong and able, knowledgeable and smart, kind and solid.

The next lines of the poem she had written long ago drifted through her mind: 'Falling for you, you caught me, Looking, and you saw me, Between the cracks.'

She tuned in to the conversation just in time to hear the lieutenant say that without Misa and Vidya they never would have been able to break into the cartel's computers this fast.

'Coming from you, I take that as a real compliment,' said Vidya.

'Same goes for me,' added Misa. 'I've seen a lot of bright computer nuts, but none as good as you two, Jason and Jake, and I'm especially surprised to find you in the army.'

Jason rolled his eyes. 'I'm just a little surprised to be here myself.'

'Guess we're all a little surprised to be where we are,' replied Misa, as she reached out and touched Vidya's arm. She felt the same chemical surge that Heather did when she touched Jim.

'You've all done a great job. It's far more than we could have hoped for. We have, seemingly, their complete security plan. Brush, go tell Nielly, let's get the sergeants out.'

'Thinking exactly the same thing,' said Brush as he moved quickly through the door. Unfortunately, what he saw were faces staring at monitors and the sounds of gunfire. He knew it was too late.


'Thank you, Rameriz,' said Yousef but he was not sure why he was thanking him for 'allowing' them to go out guarded.

'Let's walk for a while and talk on the way,' said Sharon.

They crossed Brompton Road and turned right on the footpath between the Brompton Oratory Chapel and Cottage Place. As they approached the small park at the end of the path, Yousef glanced behind them but Felix was nowhere in sight.

'I don't see our beady-eyed chaperon,' said Yousef.

'I wasn't going to give him the pleasure of looking back at him.

I wonder where he is?' asked Sharon.

'This is all a nightmare,' said Amir.

'Just drop it, Amir, lamenting the past won't help us now. I want to look at our options,' said Sharon somewhat sternly. Amir didn't have the heart to say anything back. 'What do you think, Yousef?'

Yousef just shook his head. 'I thought about trying to run for it but even if we got away now they would find us eventually, so that would be just stupid.'

'I think we should turn ourselves in to the authorities and take our chances with them. Perhaps they can give us a new identity if we expose the plan,' said Amir.

Sharon just glowered at Amir. 'This is the last thing I am going to say about the past, Amir, but your harebrained scheme of going to Mexico got us into this mess and there is no way that anyone is going to be able to protect us against these guys—too much money and power. The only way we can survive this is to find a way to destroy them.'

'Jesus, Sharon, you're smart but you're a computer geek. I know my way around a little but how are the three of us going to do anything to them?'

'I don't know, but we will or I will if I have to do it by myself. I want some ideas from you. Let's start with the weaknesses in our original plan. Maybe we can turn the plan against them.'

Yousef brightened a little. Sharon was smart. Then he looked at Amir and hope completely slipped away. Amir was nothing more than a less than honest, scared businessman. He would be no help at all. If anything, he would get them into more trouble with the cartel. He needed to talk to Sharon alone.

They walked along without saying anything, on a small, brick-paved mews with colorful painted house fronts and flower boxes.

Then they turned left onto Princess Gardens and angled across Exhibition Road to Prince Consort Way.

'Let's go to the café at the Albert Hall. It has windows along the south side and we can watch for Felix,' said Sharon. They walked up Prince Consort Way past Imperial College's Royal School of Mines, then the Royal School of Music. As they crossed the street, Sharon looked back toward the corner and there was no sign of their guard.

'Where is that little weasel? Why isn't he right behind us? Doesn't make sense,' she said just above a whisper. However, she was pleased with her idea of the Albert Hall café. It was private and they could see him approach.

Felix was staying well back and out of sight, nevertheless he monitored and recorded every word they said. He heard Sharon whisper 'little weasel.'

Jim, Glenda, and Heather were listening intently to Jake as he explained what he thought about the segregated computers. What he wanted was the hard drives from all the cartel's computers. The information they had found so far came from the computers that were online, controlling the security for the compound and their communication. Up until now, they had put their effort into figuring out how the cartel defended the hacienda. He wanted more.

'Best come in, Jim,' said Brush as he poked his head through the door. 'Maybe Glenda could take Heather out for some coffee.'

'Not a chance, buster,' said Heather as she sprinted back into the control room.

On the screen, they could see the two sergeants walking in front of two men holding automatic rifles.

'Those two just appeared from one of those man-made structures. Now we know what they are—a forward lookout, probably connected back to the hacienda with tunnels otherwise we would have seen them come and go,' said Nielly.

Jim had not yet had time to study all of the diagrams that the Wolf Pack had given him, but this information confirmed the tunnels in the diagrams. 'They are tunnels, we have diagrams now.'

A camouflaged door opened and their captors herded the sergeants through. The desert became still. Everyone stared at the structures on their screens wondering what the cartel would do to the two old-time infantrymen.

Suddenly, the door flew open and the two sergeants burst out. They dodged right and dove into a small dry streambed. No one followed. Heather watched openmouthed. Transfixed. She had feared the worst for them and now here they were outside again.

Gordon yelled, 'Yeah, run for it!'

They could just see, from the watcher's video, the two sergeants crawling east in the small depression. Soon they were up and running when the streambed deepened as it approached the ridge where Nielly's watcher lay. The two quickly moved around the south end of the ridge and behind some rocks. There was still no sign of anyone at the bunker. No activity at all. And no communication since the two men had dutifully dropped their communication devices as instructed.

Heather started to smile but Jim stood perplexed. Why weren't they being chased?

'They got away!' said Heather.

'Appears they have,' said Brush sympathetically but not convinced.

Nielly stood next to Jim staring at the monitors wondering what would come next. Master Sergeant Glen Smith and Sergeant First Class Jay Hernandez had seemingly done the impossible.

'Two 4x4s coming around both sides of the hacienda and men coming out both bunkers. They will be surrounded in minutes,' reported the watcher.

'Shit,' said Heather as she wrung her hands and sat staring at a screen.

The watcher didn't need to ask if he could protect them. He had his orders and wouldn't question them. He would like to take out the two 4x4s and the cartel men on foot. It would be easy to give the IVs time to disappear in the desert. He didn't know the two men but it was still hard to sit and watch while they were killed.

# Chapter 31

Wow, cool, you guys,' said a happy Ralphy. 'Burgers, fries, Coke, candy bars—six of them!'

JT patted Ralphy on the shoulder. 'Misa and Vidya said they would be here to wish us off at noon and the snacks are from them, too.'

'Makes me wish I could just stay here and have you guys bring me good food. It's better than being in a resort.'

'Ralphy, I was thinking. Starting next summer I have a post-doc position open for two years. Do you think you would be interested in coming up to the University of Washington? And if it's OK with Professor Ritter maybe you could come up sooner. I have plenty of lab space and you could finish your thesis work there and come back down for your final exam.'

Ralphy's eyes glazed over. 'I think I would like that very much, JT. It's time for a change and I would like to work with you. What's the post doc doing?'

'The grant is 16S rRNA sequencing of the microbes in desert varnish, with an eye to seeing if any are manganese-iron oxidizers or reducers; and, if there are bacteria trapped in the varnish, how they might change with depth within the coating. But, if you didn't want to work on that we could submit another grant for a project you would like and get someone else for the desert varnish sequencing.'

Ralphy understood that JT was inviting him because they had developed a special friendship in the short time they had known each other but also because he knew Professor Ritter would not have a second-rate graduate student. JT's lab and microbiology department were in the top ten in the country. Ralphy did not need to think about it. He liked Arizona State University but it was maybe time to move on.

'I really appreciate the offer, JT, and I can't think of anywhere I would rather be. Maybe Heather will even take me llama packing someday.'

'I'm sure she would be delighted to do that. Let's get you up and dressed since you're finished with those burgers.'

During their short conversation, Ralphy had devoured the burgers and fries; all that was left was a wrapper and an air-filled french-fry pouch sitting on the hospital bed stand.

JT walked out to the nurses' station to ask if there was anything Ralphy needed to do before leaving. Much to his surprise, Heather was standing there, with her hands on an empty wheelchair, in a subdued conversation with Vidya and Misa. She had tears in her eyes and JT overheard a snippet as he walked up '…I'm sure they'll be OK.'

'They might already be dead,' said Heather.

Heather smiled when she saw JT and gave him a big hug.

'Who might be dead already?' asked JT.

'It's a long story but two very nice old sergeants that for some reason I just don't understand, volunteered to spy on the cartel's hacienda. Let's get Ralphy and you on the road; I want to get back, I have to know what happened but I didn't want to see it live on the monitor.'

The five Mexico veterans chatted in Ralphy's room like age-old friends.

'JT invited me to go to the University of Washington for a post doc and said I could go up now if Herman will be OK with it.'

'Great, we can all go llama packing!' exclaimed Heather. 'Maybe you two can find an excuse to come up next summer and we can all go out.'

'I wouldn't miss it for anything,' said Vidya. 'As long as I don't have to go out into the wilderness.'

'It's a plan then,' added Misa, knowing she wanted to be there with all of them but also wondering how they could go llama packing and avoid being out overnight.

It was still months away but somehow they all knew deep in their minds that they would meet up next summer, no matter what.

A jeep and a Chevrolet sedan stood outside the hospital.

'Take care, stay in touch. We're going to be here until this thing ends.' A gauze-covered Heather gave Ralphy a kiss on his cheek then she gave JT a long hug. She released him. 'Come on, get going, you two. I'm glad you'll be at JT's lab, Ralphy. See you both up there soon, I hope.'

They all waved as JT and Ralphy set off in the olive-drab sedan for Phoenix and Arizona State.

Heather's face looked rigid, she was numb with worry, and as they climbed into their jeep she said, 'Get me back fast, Murph.' They drove back in silence to discover the fate of MSG Glen Smith and SFC Jay Hernadez.


Guillermo sat thinking in his jet with only two of his bodyguards and a male steward. Three hours and he would land in the Cayman

Islands. A helicopter would then transport him to Cuba. He wanted no record of his visit to Cuba. He sat pleased: he had power and wealth and soon wealth even beyond his expectations.

'Their computer guys don't seem so bad to me,' said Sharon. 'Rameriz is perhaps harder but nothing like Felix and Ox. They're the ones that are going to kill us.'

*That's right, little computer-girl. I will be the one to kill you,* said Felix to himself as he listened to their conversation.

'We need a plan,' said Yousef.

'I think we need to start working with the computer people and see what we can find out,' said Sharon.

'Maybe you should get friendly with one of them, Sharon,' said Amir. 'Lazio and Alejandro are not bad looking, you could do worse.'

'That's disgusting, the way you say it, Amir, but unfortunately exactly what I think I will have to do. Neither of you are going to get anything out of them unless they're distracted. Yousef, I think you and I should start thinking about how we can get into their computers. We'll all be friendly, play dumb, and pretend to think about the money that will never come, and distract them. Maybe we can plant a keystroke grabber on one of their computers and get their passwords.'

'Maybe you could just get really cozy and bring one of them to our side,' said Amir.

Sharon just looked at him wondering how she ever got involved with such a lowlife. Eventually she would have to work with Yousef and not tell Amir more than he needed to know. But for the time being they would have to trust him. At least until they had a plan.

They searched out the windows for Felix, wondering what had

happened to him. Why was he not watching them more closely than he seemed to be?

Sharon picked up a pencil and wrote a note. *You two play along when we leave. Don't say anything!!* She held her finger to her lips.

'Let's walk through Hyde Park on our way back,' said Sharon.

'Why would you want to do that?' asked Amir.

Sharon glared at him, thinking what a stupid fool he was.

'What's the matter?' he asked.

She wanted to hit him but just mouthed, 'Shut up!'

Soon they were walking beside the ornate Albert Memorial. 'I want to walk toward the center of the park; if we don't see anyone, let's make a run for it to Paddington Station,' whispered Sharon.

Amir almost said something but a venomous look from Sharon kept him quiet this time.

Sharon walked briskly toward the center of the park, which, if they continued, would take them to the north side and within a few blocks of Paddington Station. She quickly led them around some bushes next to the bridle trail.

She put her finger to her lips and moved into the bushes so that she could see back toward the Albert Memorial.

'Shit,' she mouthed as the weasel appeared running past the memorial. 'Let him pass,' she whispered into Yousef's ear.

She held her fingers to her lips and motioned for the two men to follow as she ran along the bridle path. After a few hundred feet she said breathlessly, 'I can't run any farther. Let's give this up. It's a stupid idea anyway. We'll double back toward the Serpentine and walk home. I'm ready to do whatever they say and maybe we'll get rich like they are saying. I don't really think we can get away like this if we wanted to.'

Yousef had caught on when Felix ran by going toward the center of the park but Amir still wasn't sure what was going on.

Sharon stopped and wrote a note. *They bugged us, just play along with me.*

Amir's mouth hung slightly open and a perplexed look in his eyes changed to astonishment. He started to pat his pockets. Sharon softly put her hand on his arm and shook her head. She couldn't make up her mind about him. They had known each other for some time but the ineptness he now displayed was a new side to him. In some ways, it was endearing, almost childlike.

# Chapter 32

Najma walked on the warm white sand. There were no people in sight. The pristine beach sloped down into the sea only sullied by signs on posts that read: 'Warning, no swimming or walking in surf.'

She was starting to feel at home here in Mexico. Could she have found her place in the world? Guillermo would send her an endless supply of human toys and with the suddenness in which lives are changed she had become a mother.

She strolled to the far end of the beach, occasionally walking in the surf. She didn't want to attract attention to herself but there were no people to be seen anywhere. She looked back at her hotel tucked along the side of a hill as it disappeared behind a rocky outcrop. She walked to the end of the beach where currents swirled and frothed around a rocky point jutting out in the sea. She sat with her back to the stone cliff facing back down the beach, still empty except for wind, surf, sand, and the now tiny warning signs.

This evening she would pay a visit to the restaurant that the two brothers, her targets, owned and used as a headquarters. Guillermo wanted them dead. She would decide tonight where and when she would fulfil his orders.

She smiled wide-eyed, not at the thought of what the evening might bring but of the new and startling turn in her life. She was a mother. She would make her new son, Pedro, into her loyal assistant. She would buy him things and teach him to defend himself, teach him to shoot and use a knife. He would be her caretaker when she aged. Her smile broadened as she thought of her future. Her little Pedro. No, he must have a new name. She would make sure he had plenty of healthy food and exercise: he would grow strong. She would teach him how to think and how to deal with the world.

Would he grow to be big like her old accomplice The Sheik, or smart like Farasie? She would not let him be weak like the Amirs of the world. He might be just a little brown boy now but he would learn to speak other languages and learn manners from Guillermo. She would make him into the right kind of man. He would be sophisticated, smart, and strong and he would belong to her.


Jim looked around the table at his friends and colleagues. 'We found out far more today than I ever expected, thanks mostly to the computer group. We now have the full plan for the hacienda. We know their security systems and the layout of the compound. The sergeants' sacrifice has helped as well, now we know how the cartel responds to trespassers and escapees. Our men were taken to the hacienda alive after being captured, then made a grand escape but they were far outnumbered and eventually recaptured with vehicles after hot-footing about a mile from the compound. As far as we know they are still alive but we have nothing to confirm that they are.'

Jim looked at the lieutenant. 'Go ahead and recap the Wolf Pack's work for us, Jake.'

'First of all, I think we did find out a lot and got lucky, but that luck had a lot to do with the two civilians, Misa and Vidya, and we might have fallen into a trap if it hadn't been for Sheilla's team up north. They pinned down the mastermind of the cartel's systems— Ramsey Mann, a top hacker that the US has several arrest warrants out for. I bring this up since we were only able to get into a small part of their systems. I have a feeling that finding out what else is in their computers would be of high value. We need to recover their hard drives. If they have made the security and design effort that they appear to have, then I think there will be one hell of a lot of interesting data there. I've gone over what we need to bring back with Colonel Johnson and Nielly's technician.'

Nielly turned to the sergeant at the door, 'Lights out, Sergeant. On the screen you see the overall plan of the building. Gun emplacements, tunnels extending in two directions. The vehicles that chased our two recon sergeants exited the front gate. Other than the two tunnels, it is the only way in and out.'

He continued for twenty minutes explaining the layout and security of the hacienda. 'All of our earlier ideas were completely wrong. What we intend to do now is a diversionary attack near where our two boys were taken. If we keep it very small, they will respond as they did with Smith and Hernandez, sending vehicles out the front and putting flankers at the rear of our diversionary attack; the tunnels will allow more men to flank from the front. They have heavy machine guns here and here.' He continued laying out the plan of attack.

Heather was still grappling with why the sergeants had volunteered for a mission that meant certain death. Was there something missing in her understanding of male machismo, or was it a military code? Marilyn Cutter, the pilot and small arms expert, and Glenda Rose seemed to understand it, even though Glenda was FBI, not military. There must be something that she had not yet grasped. Was this breed of person altruistic? They exhibited nothing like the selfish gene of Dawkins or the objectivism of Ayn Rand. Was it cultural or genetic? Or were they just foolish? She shook her head and stared at the wall.

After a moment, she thought of Jim coming for her and the others he rescued. That was selfless and possibly foolhardy but there was more to it. Maybe the answer was that they lived by a code. One where they knew they could die but just never expected to. Was this like being a teenager feeling invincible? Jim would say he took calculated risks. Brush had said the same and denied that he was a gambler. They knew there were risks but they were certain they could beat the odds. They wanted to prove they were better than their opponents: a game then? *Would I do the same thing?* she wondered.

The answer came to her in a flash. Of course she would. It wouldn't be pride or machismo—it was just the right thing to do. The code of the warrior who did what he had to do. But would they do it if there was no one to see what they did? If there were no reward? *OK, OK,* she thought, *maybe I'm making some progress but I still don't understand. My problem now is that I'm not the same person I was just days ago. I feel I'm lost in the middle ground. I don't quite understand but I understand that I would probably have done what Vidya did and shoot that psycho.* Then she laughed to herself. *I would do exactly the same thing–fire into the room a whole bunch and not hit anything.* Then bile bit her throat and the laughter stopped as she remembered what happened in that room.

'That plan is a go then,' said Will Crystal. 'Marilyn and I took the choppers for a spin and they're standing ready now. General Whitcuff has greased everything for us and seems to have a knack for taking out our own government's surveillance on the border. I was also able to find out something about their insider. She is a woman named Lola and you all have a picture of her in front of you. There are others that may be friendly as well. Let's bring them back safe.'

General Crystal looked at General Whitcuff. 'Are you satisfied? I am. Seems all this tech business has some value. I might have to learn something about computers in my retirement. OK, gentlemen, ladies, do whatever you have to do. Rendezvous at the field in six hours.'

'Sam, let's talk for a minute. State Department knows what we plan and are secretly sanctioning it for two reasons. One, to capture Najma. Shows that the US will go to any length to punish an attack on US soil but also apparently some connections with the cartel and Cuba that they seem to be taking exception to. But we are fairly warned if we screw this up our asses will be hanging out there. As the senior officer you could have your hands full and likely it will play havoc with your retirement. So, you sure about this?'

'Thanks for thinking about me, Will. But I got some things to do, I still run a base here. See you at the field later.'

# Chapter 33

It was nearly midnight. Glenda, Misa, Vidya, Josh, and Jake sat huddled over their computer screens. They didn't expect to find anything more, since there was no way to access the segregated computers. It was an effective deterrent. Their only hope was if the computers came alive and a link to the outside world was established. It was a slim chance that it would happen in the next couple of hours—still they watched and waited.

Heather was moving back and forth between there and the control room where Captain Fuller had his hands full coordinating multiple people who were preparing to silence the DEA's listening devices and surveillance cameras. When the attack team secured the hacienda, they would repeat a procedure similar to when General Crystal had flown into Mexico just three days ago: a squad of rangers would fire some shots near the Border Patrol one hundred miles west, drawing the US agents away from where the helicopters would fly over the US-Mexican border. Satellite coverage would be interrupted and listening devices shut down. A second smaller diversion to the east, near the town of Douglas, would draw border agents in that direction leaving a completely unguarded fifty-kilometer swath where they would cross over the line into Mexico.

Captain Fuller let out an audible breath.

'Worried about something, Captain?' asked Heather.

'I'm always worried. There's a lot to coordinate and a hundred things that could go wrong.'

'First problem starts now,' said Brad. 'My drone can't fly.'

'Status?' asked Fuller.

'They're bringing another online but it will take approximately two hours to be fully functional.'

'Two hours will work, but tell them it has to be in the air at zero two hundred, not one second later! This is one of the first real mission tests for the drones. They can't let us down. We need constant surveillance from when the assault team leaves the helicopter and then over the hacienda when they get there.'

'Yes, sir, will do.'


'You all know the plan,' said Nielly. 'I just want to go over the highlights. Chirp in if you have any problems or questions. Remember that our primary mission is to get Najma, one of the surviving terrorists from the Seattle attack last Labor Day. Second is to bring in the cartel's de facto leader, Guillermo, and we now have a third. They have built a sophisticated computer system and we want the information from them. We'll go over the plan again and then Colonel Johnson will give you the details about the primary targets and computers.

'First our watcher stays in place. We will use four other guardian angels, two to the east and two just south of the entrance road. Here and here look like the best positions for GAs one and three,' said Jasper Nielly as he pointed at two locations northeast and southeast of the hacienda. 'Again our watcher will stay where he is. Three, you won't have much high ground but there is a little rise right here. Two will have a direct line to the east wall and their fifty-caliber. The four members of the diversion team will be below the ridge where the watcher is.

'If it goes down as expected, the vehicles will come out the front and head toward the diversionary team. GAs will engage them and anyone coming out the tunnels. If they don't do what they did before with the two trucks we'll improvise. After the trucks and any cartel coming out the tunnels are neutralized, the two GAs and the watcher protect the diversion team as they move to both tunnels. The hacienda defenders will be watching with night vision and I want you to try and take out anyone you see on that wall. All clear?'

No one said anything so Nielly continued, 'As soon as the vehicles move out the gate, we secure the gate and the west wall, move inside, and land the choppers when it's clear. We know they have people along the entry road so we have a small group of three, Tom, Mitch, and Gary, who will set up an ambush at this point in case they make a move toward the hacienda.'

'What about local police, do we take them out?' asked Marilyn.

'Tom's team will have to make that choice if they show up.'

'I don't like the idea of landing inside the compound. Too much opportunity for someone we missed taking out our choppers,' added Marilyn.

'That's worth considering. It was a close call whether we landed inside or outside. But we can get loaded and out faster from inside. Opinions?'

'I agree with Marilyn,' said Mac. 'If we stay just outside the main entrance, we can control the wall above the choppers. The diversion team and our guardian angels can move on the outer flank and protect us. Inside they can't do anything and we're exposed on all sides.'

Jasper Nielly looked at his team; they all nodded their agreement. 'Good change, I'll alert the general. If we're using the wall for cover, then we should stay close. Looks clear enough here about twenty meters out and on the south side of the entry gate for the landing zone. Everything else is standard operating procedure—we're not safe and out until we land back here.' It was an old variation of their mantra, *Not safe until we're done and back and maybe not then.*

'What if there are more people than we can take or if we lose a bird?' asked Joe.

Nielly shook his head. 'The army might not be too happy if we lose two generals,' he said, thinking about the repercussions from Washington. 'The answer is we don't lose that Chinook with them in it! We have two back-up choppers that will be in the air just north of the border, a Chinook and another Huey. Mac, explain the contingency plan.'

'If we lose the big chopper we load Marilyn's Huey up with whoever is most important and then we move survivors and captives to here, about a klick north, set up a perimeter, and the backup Chinook will fly in to extract us.'

Everyone looked at the topo maps and could not find any fault with the route or the plan.

'Inside, we deal with people,' continued Nielly. 'The perimeter defenses that could be turned against us inside should be out of commission and we'll have control of the perimeter walls and the tunnels. Lots of civilians, some friendly and some less than friendly. You've all seen the pic of the DEA informant. Speak

Spanish or say nothing in front of anyone, even the DEA lady, we don't want them to know we are American army. This officially is a Mexican military raid… we bring back all traces of us having been there, everything.' Someone started to say something and Nielly said, 'Don't ask, none of our business what happens to them in the long term and we will probably never know. When we are back here, we put them inside containers in the hangar and we'll be relieved by a small group of interrogators of Mexican descent.'

They looked at a detailed mock-up of the hacienda and Nielly went into specifics about how they would secure each building and move the people out, fingerprinting and photographing bodies for later identification. 'We employ the same tactic we did in Uganda. Questions? None? OK, Jim, give us a quick heads-up on Najma and Guillermo, then an explanation of the computer situation.'

'Take a good look at the two pictures in front of you. The woman is a skilled and very dangerous psychopath. Five foot four, medium length dark hair, and dark eyes. She has a red birthmark, five centimeters across, shaped like starfish on her neck just behind her right ear. Don't be fooled by her looks and don't take any chances with her. The cartel is run by its second in command, Guillermo, aka El Padrino. We want them both alive if possible but no one is going to fault you if you have to take them out.

'Tom and I met with the computer group and they told us what and how to recover what they need. It is a priority. Having the information might have a major impact on the cartel and the drug war and is probably more important than Guillermo.'

Jim looked at Tom, the Special Forces technician, and asked

if he wanted to add anything.

'Time is going to be the biggest problem. Jim, Brush, and I have to get to their computers, run some programs, add some hardware, and then pull their hard drives out. If we run out of time we may need some help carrying larger pieces out,' said Tom.

'Give me a heads-up if you need help then. No more questions? Final gear check time,' said Nielly.

# Chapter 34

Lola stood wringing her hands. Her mind was swirling, trying to think but her thoughts kept moving in circles and never getting anywhere. *I have to get away and save little Pedro.* She stood frozen, paralyzed by her inability to find a solution. *We have to get away. I have to find a way.* She tried but no solutions entered her thoughts, only the mantra, over and over: *We must, we must, but how?*

Pedro turned over in his bed. Lola sat beside him and placed her hand on his head. She would find a way—a way to be safe but not in Mexico. *A better life up north,* she thought, *but the Americans are mean and unforgiving.* Was there a difference between the brutality of the cartel and that of the US government police? The police said the Mexicans were breaking laws. They hid behind a self-righteous snobbery and caused the people they caught misery and anguish. And she was helping them and they probably would not help her. The cartel acted without thought and stole the lifeblood from her people. They had the same power to cause misery as the American police. *But the cartel killed my son.*

No one cared for the people, they were just another low-living entity to be ruled and controlled. They worked and they gained nothing. They lived but what was their life for? It could only be for one thing—hope for a better life for the children. A small measure of determination began to take hold in her thoughts. She could no longer help her son but she would help little Pedro to a better life.

La Fiesta restaurant was on the second story of a corner building a half-mile behind her hotel. It separated the end of the beach area from the tourist restaurants that lined the streets on the other side of the rocky outcrop, where Najma had sat thinking of her son and the future. She would finish this job and tonight the pilot would fly her back so she could greet the sunrise with her new son. She paid no attention to the tourists walking by or the occasional Mexican in mariachi costume going to entertain those looking for the 'authentic' Mexico. Bright reds, greens, yellows, and wide sombreros moved below her vantage point.

The two brothers, her assignment, lived and worked for their drug enterprise in the back rooms of the restaurant. They never went out without several guards and their exits were unpredictable. Guillermo had provided Najma with detailed maps and infor-mation—information that was mostly useless other than convincing her that she would have to execute them inside their domain.

Guillermo could have easily blown up the building, hoping to kill them in the process. However, he wanted both a stark example made of those that dared defy his authority and certainty that they were dead. It was all the same to her. She would enjoy her work but for the first time in her life, she felt impatient. *I want to go home. I have a responsibility and he needs my strong control if he is to be a man,* she said to herself.

She would kill a cleaner that arrived at the same time each morning, take her clothes and supplies, then kill the guard at the door. Her information showed the brothers had a lax attitude to intruders. They thought no one would be foolish enough to attack them at home but were always fearful when outside. Her biggest problem would be a video camera, which monitored the outside doors. From the diagrams, she knew where a lone man monitored the cameras. Foolishly, however, the camera cable ran outside the building. She would cut the cable, kill the door guard, and quickly move to the monitor room. If the other guard came to inspect the blank camera, she could easily kill him, as he would ignore a lowly cleaner.

'I'm going to the airfield,' said Heather as she marched out of the computer room with all the determination she could muster— through the halls, past the door guard, and out to the jeep. Nothing was going to get in her way of seeing Jim. 'Get a move on it, Murphy,' she said as she jumped in the front seat.

'Where t—'

'Airport, as fast as you can.'

'Yes, ma'am.'

'Call me Heather and put your foot on that pedal, I want to get there like right now.'

'Yes, ma'am!'

Heather was already thinking about what she would say to Jim when she found him. Sergeant Murphy decided he liked this woman. *For sure, she is an assertive lady but it is far better to be ordered about by a pretty lady than some upstart officer,* he thought.

Sharon had spent the night drifting from thought to sleep. She wasn't sure how much she had slept. She still had no firm plan. How could she counter what Felix had obviously heard them say through the monitoring equipment? Well, he would kill her anyway, no matter what she said about him. She went sleepily downstairs to meet Amir and Yousef.

'I want you three to go to South Kensington station right now and wait until Felix meets you,' said Ramirez.

'What are we going to do at the station?' asked Amir.

'Just wait there, leave in fifteen minutes.'

'Good,' said Sharon. 'We can talk about some of the computer problems I was thinking about last night.'

Ramirez looked at her with a hint of a smile in his eyes. Information was power; they were giving it to him easily and cutting their own throats.

The three walked out of Amir's house and headed west toward the station.

'What do you think they have planned? Why are we supposed to meet them at the station?' asked Amir.

Sharon handed them both a sheet of paper; she had written, *Play along with the conversation and only communicate our plans in writing, making sure that we destroy it afterwards by flushing it down the toilet or shredding it. Make sure!*

'I've been thinking all night,' said Sharon. 'We can't fight these guys. Our best hope is just to throw in with them and hope they don't kill us. But I think the two goons are going to kill all of us. We're just a means to an end for the cartel guys and I don't think any of us computer types can be left as a loose end. They will probably shift the blame for the bank scam on all of us and we will disappear.'

'I still think you should get friendly with them,' said Amir.

'Shut up, Amir. Is that all you think women are good for?'

As they neared the station, Sharon said, 'Amir, go get me an almond croissant. I want to get a newspaper and some Diet Coke for later.'

Amir scowled at the long line at the pastry shop but walked over anyway.

'Yousef, I wanted to talk to you alone. Amir bothers me and won't be much help to us. I didn't want to say this in front of him but I think he is right, I am going to have to try to get friendly with them. I think Alejandro is the nicest person so I will try to flirt a little with him. Truthfully, I wouldn't have to try that hard with Rameriz, he is just one attractive guy but he is probably pretty loyal to the cartel. Lazio and Alejandro—I don't think they are, they're just employees. As soon as we start working on computers again, let's do what we can to find some weaknesses. In the end, I hope they come to the same conclusion we have, that the cartel is just going to use us and make us disappear. Use them just the same. We're never going to see any of that money, any of us.'

'I agree with you. They are going to get rid of all of us and I was counting on having that money and a nice life for a change, too. Really a bother. What do you think they are going to do with us now?'

'You got any extra change?' she asked him as she handed the clerk four pound fifty for a *Financial Times, Guardian,* and a Diet Coke but was short eight pence. Yousef tossed over a ten pence coin and they walked out. The weasel, Felix, was walking toward them from the south end of the station and an unhappy Amir from the other end.

Felix sneered at them with slightly crooked, gray-tinged teeth and said, 'Follow me.'

'His beady eyes give me the creeps,' said Amir, 'but I think he is the one you should get cozy with.'

'Amir, if they kill us my only hope is that they kill you first so I can watch. I never knew you were this disgusting. Why don't you flirt with him, maybe he likes men.'

Sharon was happy how things were going with the conversation. She knew that no one would believe she would like Felix or Ox. But she wanted whoever got the recordings to believe that they were looking for a way out but did in fact like the computer guys. In truth, even though she hated to admit it, she was strangely attracted to Ramirez. She pursed her lips and let out an audible breath. Amir looked at her as they crossed Fulham Road and walked toward the French area. She flipped her hand at him and wondered where they were headed and what was in store for them when they got there.

Sergeant Murphy stopped as Military Police blocked his path into the airfield. There was no activity to be seen anywhere, which was not what Heather had expected. The MP toggled a radio while looking at them carefully and after a short conversation, motioned them past and pointed toward a large hangar.

Another MP dressed in fatigues waved them over to the edge of the hangar and then said to Murphy, 'Take the jeep back and wait at the entrance. The gate MP will tell you when to come back.'

Murphy drove the old style jeep over to the entrance and parked. Heather was directed through a door. The MP closed it and then opened a second door. Light blazed, almost hurting her eyes. The expansive hangar had four helicopters with piles of neatly arranged equipment near each helicopter. A feeling of peace and excitement coursed through her body as Jim walked toward her. The MP left and Heather wrapped her arms around Jim.

'Let's go outside. I can't take this brightness much longer,' said Jim.

'Won't you need your night vision for the mission?' asked Heather.

'We'll go low light as soon as the equipment is loaded and red light only inside the choppers when we fly. There will be lots of time to adjust.'

'Jim, maybe for the first time I understand what you are doing and why you are going. A week ago I would have just wanted to get back to the llamas, but now I understand that you need to take care of Najma.' She hesitated for just a fraction of a second saying the name, just barely noticeable to Jim.

'I always knew you were capable but the other day at the mine I found out things I didn't know about you. You need to get that woman. She is an ice-cold killer, wasn't that a movie?'

'It was *Natural Born Killers*,' responded Jim.

'Anyway, I want you to take care of this so we can go home,' continued Heather. 'I won't tell you to be careful, I know you will be, but please don't underestimate her. Psychopaths think differently than you and I. I never thought about it until the last couple of days but they're different and not predictable.'

Jim thought back to chasing Najma and the other terrorists through Seattle and in the helicopter. He had always known that Najma survived after the others died. He had gotten used to the idea that she was more predictable than he thought since she did the opposite of what most people expected she would do. *She is a predictable contrarian,* he thought, but it would be foolish to think she would always react that way. 'We'll find her and we'll all be careful. This is a difficult mission that has become more controlled with all the intelligence that the computer group provided. Najma is the wild card. We don't know where she will be exactly but I expect first she will try to ambush us and if she can't control the fight then she will disappear when she sees what is happening. She's too much of a survivor.'

'You sound pretty confident.'

'We are, but we never underestimate. It's a rule of survival. Nielly is something special in this world. He will concentrate on covering every contingency, checking everything, looking for any flaws.'

*But no one can control an ambush,* he thought.

'Take care of Brush, too.'

Jim chuckled. 'Over the years I never know who is taking care of whom but we seem to do pretty well by each other.'

'Glenda and he seem special to me. At first, I felt bad about Debbie but now I really like Glenda and I think she is totally smitten with Brush.'

'Maybe, just maybe, for the first time since I've known him, I think he is interested in keeping someone in his life.'

She put her arms around Jim and squeezed for long time, then pulled back and leaned in to touch his forehead with hers. His eyes were indistinct in the moonless night but she could feel his gaze. They had done this so many times but it never failed to send a cocktail of feel-good chemicals racing through her body. She let go and turned toward the entry gate then stopped after ten steps and turned. He was standing watching her, he hadn't moved. She walked around the corner of the hangar knowing how strong he was but how fragile life could be. You could be full of life and then dead. A wave of nausea slapped her insides.

*Najma and those men really don't deserve to be on the same Earth with gentle people,* she thought as another shiver ran through her body. *If Najma hadn't gotten away we would be on the ranch and Brush and Glenda would be happily cruising toward Alaska. I thought it was always a joke that he had wanted to go and hadn't and now it seems an omen for him to go with Glenda.* She wanted Brush to get to Alaska and now with Glenda Rose.

Najma killed the thirty-three-year-old mother of five who cleaned the restaurant. Marisa worked days as well as this night job to help feed her family. Unconcerned Najma dumped her in the alley and then cut the video camera cable. She knocked on the door just as she had observed Marisa doing the night before. The guard opened the door. He was over six feet and very stocky; he had bully written all over him. He paid her no attention as she walked by with Marisa's meager cleaning supplies. Najma turned, reached up and casually drove her double-edged knife into the back of his neck. He dropped first to his knees, looking stunned, then fell facedown. She retrieved her knife, wiped it off on his shirt, took his Glock pistol, checked to make sure there was a round in the chamber, and then stood still listening for any noise. She quickly walked to the security video room, opened the door, and walked toward the guard with her broom in her left hand and the knife hanging casually by her side in her right hand. She thought, *How stupid people are to just watch death approaching.*

She listened at the brothers' office door, trying to determine how many were inside. There were three. She gave two quick knocks and walked into the room, pushing her mop bucket in front of her, the Glock in her left hand and a razor-sharp machete in her right. One man, not a brother, was standing to her right. Her main weapon would be the long machete. She swung it right at the man's throat and blood gushed from his severed jugular. Two quick steps and she brought the machete down cutting through the top of the younger brother's right shoulder, then lashed out at the older brother behind the desk. He was neither slow nor stupid and reacted faster than she anticipated. He got off a shot, missing her head by millimeters. She was not accustomed to being lucky but this time she was. Not needing to be quiet any longer, she fired two quick shots into his chest just before he fired a last wild shot, hitting only the wall. His hands were supporting him on the edge of the desk and he looked at her with a blank expression as she raised her machete and sliced through his neck severing his head from his body.

The younger brother's limp right arm hung toward the floor. He was on his knees trying to stand, using a chair for support. She raised the machete and struck downward severing his head, which thudded to the floor and rolled toward Najma. With the unexpected noise she wanted to make a quick exit but she could not help herself. She picked up both heads and stood them upright side by side on the desk facing the door.

There was a noise in the hall. She stood to the side as a man burst through the door then stopped, stunned at the sight of the heads. She gave him a vicious blow to the side of his neck, pumping yet more blood onto the red-pooled floor.

She was surprised as she carefully made her way toward the door. No sound, no other people. She first took off the blood-covered cotton jumpsuit she had worn and carefully put it into a small plastic bag. She closed the door, casually walked out into the midst of the tourists returning from late night celebrations, and walked several hundred yards into town. There she got a taxi to the airport. The Cessna 206 that had brought her to Cabo San Lucas was standing by to depart as soon as she arrived. She should be home just before sunrise and would wake her little boy. Perhaps the next time she would take him along so he could observe how to handle himself. *Yes,* she thought, *it was a good idea. They would do things together so he could learn.*

# Chapter 35

Captain Fuller walked into the drone control room and nodded.

'Launch Spy Boy One,' the controller said into his microphone as he held the drone's controls.

Nielly had demanded two drones. He wasn't accustomed to having unnecessary risks affect his missions. The drones were another layer of insurance, giving them real-time air and ground surveillance. SB One was leaving the runway thirty minutes before his team departed.

Nielly listened to the small reconnaissance plane leave the runway then walked back into the dimly lit hangar, contemplated the choppers for a few seconds and, satisfied, made a twirling motion with his right hand. The huge hangar doors began to part and Nielly walked briskly to the Chinook and up the rear ramp. It started to close immediately when he was inside and then the big chopper imperceptibly moved toward the parting hangar doors and then lumbered along in slow motion behind a tow truck onto the tarmac.

His team sat quietly in the faint red lights. Three guardian angels and seventeen others including himself. He wasn't accustomed to having outsiders on his team but Jim and Brush were now as close as anyone had ever been to being accepted into his special fold. The Seattle terrorist fight had given his guys a respect for the two agents they rarely accorded anyone outside their group.

Two generals sat at the controls; possibly a first in military history and one not likely to be repeated when the Pentagon was informed, which it hopefully never would be. 'Here we go,' Will Crystal said to Sam Whitcuff as he started the engines. Sam gave him a thumbs up and was as happy as he had been in several years. This was what it was all about, not sitting around behind a desk and remembering the early years in Vietnam and later Yugoslavia, Iraq, and Afghanistan. The US government had kept him busy fighting in foreign wars as he ascended the ranks but it had been years since he was directly involved in a field operation.

The blades wound up and a satisfied Will Crystal rolled forward and lifted the big bird up into the star-filled sky. He was just as happy as Whitcuff to be flying a mission. 'ETA forty-five minutes,' he said into the com that connected with Nielly and his second in command, Mac. He received two sets of double clicks back as he steadily climbed the chopper toward twenty-seven thousand feet directly above the border.

'Com check,' said Nielly as each team member checked in. It was second nature, checking, double-checking. He had learned a new phrase from Jim in September—*Spit Happens*, which he now used to replace his old phrase, *Shit Happens*. Heather had told him in no uncertain terms, that llamas rarely spit but just like unforeseen events in his missions, sometimes llamas did spit and sometimes they regurgitated and sent a big green slime at whoever was unfortunate enough to be in the way. *Check and double-check*, he said to himself, no slime or shit would endanger his men or the mission.

'Fifteen minutes…ten minutes.' Double clicks in response.

The general said, 'Five minutes.' Mac started to lower the rear ramp.

'Target elevation,' said Will Crystal. 'Good luck and see you as soon as you request us.'

'Roger that. See you in a few hours. Let's go flying,' he said into his microphone as the team shuffled onto the ramp and then two by two disappeared in the night sky.

Within minutes, the swarm of nearly invisible team members, wraith-like, glided south toward the hacienda hanging below their black nylon wings. They concentrated on keeping their descent to a minimum and catching updrafts in the warm air rising from the desert surface. 'Alpha team, go.' The four members forming the diversionary group along with two GAs veered east of the hacienda and spilled air to get to their destination faster as did the third GA as she headed outside of the main gate. The rest of the assault team made a slow curving descent, first to the west and then directly back toward the main gate. They spread into their assigned positions.

The two new GAs and the diversionary team would be on the ground first below the watcher's ridge. The watcher carefully observed the hacienda for any sign that the Special Forces' insertion had been noticed. Nielly, along with his group, watched straight ahead as they approached the hacienda's main gate. Three men headed in the opposite direction up the road, watching the rear for any activity along with the third guardian angel from her position near the front gate. It was just after two a.m. Nielly's group were now low as they headed in a staggered line directly toward the hacienda's west-facing gate. Two on the flanks would land first and immediately cover the others' landing. One man split off west and moved toward his position to cover the road one klick back. Their woman GA touched down twenty feet from her intended position and set up with her fifty-caliber sniper rifle within two minutes. She carefully watched the main team's descent as they glided toward the gate. The eastern diversionary team moved into place as did the two GAs to their right and left.

*Good plan,* Jim thought. Three snipers covering the east side, where they assumed the cartel would send their men when the four-man diversionary started shooting at the hacienda; one GA to cover their approach toward the gate and the ambush team farther out along the entrance road.

Jim, Brush, and the Special Forces computer tech, Tom, or 'Teckie' as the team referred to him, landed thirty meters behind the main force of Nielly and the five men that would enter the compound first.

It was a peaceful starlit night. The teams in their night camouflage had swooped in like oversized ravens, unseen. Suddenly, floodlights illuminated the outer walls and the surrounding ground.

'Gordon, any cell activity? You're ready to block any communications from the hacienda?'

'Yes, sir.'

'All coms checked between Nielly's assault team, the drone team, the tactical operations center, and the Wolf Pack?'

'Everyone has checked in, sir.'

Captain Fuller was in an agitated state. He had his hands full with the drones, knocking out the DEA listening systems and the ground diversions, and trying to supervise the support teams.

The radio made a rustling noise and then Nielly's voice said softly, 'Nighthawks down.'

Specialist Gordon responded, 'Commence shutdown,' and disabled the hacienda's outgoing telephones but not their cell phones, that would come later. Captain Fuller moved into the drone room. The drone had made a sweep ahead of the ground team without seeing any activity and was now flying along the border, monitoring the DEA's movements, making sure they were away from the border where the generals would cross into Mexico.

'Report base,' said General Crystal.

'No activity spotted from the drones, sir,' said Fuller. 'The DEA agents are moving east and west leaving us our corridor into Mexico. Ten minutes to shutdown of their listening devices.'

'The Aerostat still on the ground?'

'It is, sir.'

Disabling the plane had not been a problem since the mechanics that maintained the DEA's radar-equipped, low-flying aircraft detection plane, named the Aerostat, were army. Word had passed down that it was not going airborne tonight. No questions were asked.

'Get me if you see anything unusual, anything!' ordered Will Crystal and then he switched back to Gordon who was poised staring at his mic waiting for the signal to quiet the listening devices. 'Go,' said Fuller. Gordon typed a message to Jake then looked up at the captain. 'They should be silent, sir.'

Fuller then moved into the computer room that now had a sign on the door proclaiming 'Wolf Pack.'

As he walked in, Jake and Jason looked pleased. Misa and Vidya did not look up from their monitors.

'Piece of cake, Fuller. We're in the DEA's computers and with their listening devices silenced they're stone deaf and we can bugger up their communication systems if for any reason they start back toward the helicopter route over the border.'

Captain Fuller laughed in spite of himself. Were these people really in the same army as he was? A lieutenant and a sergeant who called him 'Fuller' instead of Captain Fuller or sir. He shook his head and said, 'Let me know if you have any trouble,' and headed back to Specialist Marcus Gordon who was talking to Glenda and Heather.

'Just giving them a quick sit rep, sir,' said Gordon. He wasn't completely sure that he should be talking to them but everyone else seemed to. His uncertainty was eased when Captain Fuller said, 'Make sure you keep them fully up to date. Anything they need, get it for them. General's orders. Make sure the backup helicopters are ready to get airborne when we signal.'

General Crystal had descended to the desert floor, sitting motionless with engines idling, just north of the border. Marilyn's smaller chopper sat on his right. Both were waiting for word from Nielly.

Captain Fuller was pleased in one sense and extremely nervous in another. Things were going exactly according to plan. Something would go wrong, and not knowing what it was, left him anxious and sweating. 'Good God,' he mumbled, 'I should get promoted to major if this holds together and if it doesn't I'll probably be court-martialed.' He touched his right eyelid as it twitched. The tick would not stop.

Heather and Glenda couldn't sit down but hovered near Gordon. They were both, however, unexpectedly calm. Heather didn't know if she wanted Najma dead or brought back in cuffs. She was consumed with trying to understand what made her so vile.

Gordon handed them headsets so they could hear the communications when the attack started. The silence would soon disappear. He wanted them to quit hovering around him and sit. It worked.

Heather looked at Glenda. 'Can you hear me?'

'Just like you were right next to me talking.'

'Perfect,' said Gordon. 'Except don't forget to keep the toggle pushed to the right otherwise everyone will be able to hear.'

Heather blushed and mouthed, 'Sorry.'

Gordon reached over and twisted a dial on Heather's console. 'I just switched you to Sheilla up north. We have been getting to know each other pretty well and she is also monitoring.'

'Heather, hi, you are going to have to stop in one of these days. I feel like I know you but we've never met.'

'I'd like that, Sheilla.'

'Talk later, Sheilla, things about to happen,' Gordon cut in as he watched his computer clock. There was a list with times along the left edge of their screens. Each action was timed to the second.

# Chapter 36

Diversionary, one minute,' said Nielly.
'Here we go,' said Gordon with an edge of excitement.

One minute passed. Then the diversionary twosome started firing at the hacienda with spaced out single shots.

'Someone is shooting at us,' yelled the east hacienda guard, Perez. He looked through his night vision scope toward the rifle flashes and laughed. 'It is a man wearing a sombrero and a woman next to a big rock below Raphael Ridge.'

Carlos, who was in charge of security, was looking out the main entrance, following his surprise floodlight check. Purposely, Nielly's team was just outside the brightly lit area. The Wolf Pack's information had shown the location and strength of the lights and Nielly had positioned his team just beyond their range.

After a few seconds, seeing nothing more, Carlos said, 'Must be friends of that mestizo and his compadre we captured.' He spoke into his radio, 'Two mestizos, near that big rock below Raphael Ridge. I want three men in the gun truck and four in the Bronco. Same thing as earlier today, flank them and bring them in.

Vamanos. Tunnel A, work your way out toward the shooters, cover the two trucks that will be coming past you. Tunnel B, keep out of sight. Perez, put some flares over them when I tell you.'

They were probably just a couple of local friends of the two plant collectors and likely drunk, he thought. *A sombrero and a woman attacking us,* he thought, *'Abrazo,'* the spirit of Mexico; he admired their courage.

'Who are these idiots anyway, don't they know who we are?' said Perez. Carlos was not stupid and didn't feel quite right about this, probably because no one had ever started shooting at the compound before. The two Mexicans weren't going to do any damage, maybe he should watch and wait for a while before sending anyone out. He put his finger on the talk switch of his radio thinking he would first send someone out, on foot, to investigate and not send the trucks. He pushed the button, changed his mind, and instead called the guard down near the main road.

'Anyone come by you?

'No, señor, only the police on the main road, nothing going past toward the gate.'

'Keep a sharp eye out,' he told him and then called the main gate.

'Open the gates. Send out the vehicles.' Then as an afterthought. 'Send out a three man patrol after the vehicles leave.'

Captain Fuller was standing next to Specialist Gordon who had been monitoring the cartel's radio using two repeaters that the GAs had set up as soon as they were in position. 'Gates opening,' said Josh as he looked at the cartel's security system on his computer. 'Cool man, I like this.'

'Leave off the comments,' said Fuller. Though he thought that what the computer nerd had said was right and this was *cool*. Eyes in the sky, eyes on the ground, eyes everywhere including inside their computers.

Nielly's full group, the Wolf Pack, Sheilla, Fuller, Gordon, Heather, Glenda, and several others were listening and all started to tense. Video was arriving from the miniature cameras mounted on the Special Forces' headsets.

'Ready,' said Fuller.

'Vehicles are out of the gate and moving fast around the southwest corner,' said Nielly.

'Vehicles heading our way. Four hundred… three hundred… two hundred meters.'

'Shut down communications,' commanded Fuller.

'What the fuck,' said Carlos as he tried to call Perez. 'Get me a radio that works,' he shouted, throwing his on the ground.

Carlos, however, would realize too late that all the communications were out and cell phones and radios were jammed. Their computer systems were dysfunctional. Then the lights went out and he tripped, nearly knocking himself unconscious.

'Execute,' said Nielly just as three men walked outside the hacienda gate. The men made it a few feet before they were killed.

The DEA and the border agencies were out of the picture. The general's and Marilyn's Hueys started their engines as they waited to cross the border. Nielly's team launched concussion shells from grenade launchers, which looked like little shotguns with oversized barrels.

'I still love those little pop guns,' said Brush thinking back to Vietnam.

Each man had predetermined targets. The team rushed forward to the gate and moved inside the hacienda compound. The guardian angels, Brush, Jim, and Teckie covered their approach and then moved to the gate.

Simultaneously, the diversionary team and two flanking GAs engaged the trucks and their occupants. The watcher on the ridge first neutralized Perez, and within seconds killed two men leaving the south tunnel. With the GAs covering them, the diversionary team sprinted toward the tunnels. Shots kicked up desert soil as the two men started toward the north tunnel. Immediately the GA closest returned fire as the two SF men made it to the tunnel and threw in a concussion grenade, jumped to the side, and then disappeared into the tunnel after the explosion.

The two GAs started their cautious circuit around opposite sides of the hacienda. The watcher on the ridge covered their movements and continued to watch the tunnel exits. Killing Perez and the two tunnel 'rats' would be the last shots he fired.

Within seconds of Nielly's command to 'execute,' the seven men in the vehicles, the two at each tunnel and the three man patrol leaving the front gate had been eliminated along with Perez and three other men on the wall. Several lay immobilized from the concussion grenades just inside the gate and on the wall. The team couldn't spare anyone to guard them so they were quickly terminated.

The more experienced cartel men had immediately recognized that they were overwhelmed and instead of wildly rushing outside, they moved to defensive positions inside the buildings.

The Special Forces swiftly scrambled up onto the wall, covering their approach as they had done hundreds of times before, both in practice and in real life. Seconds later, shots were fired from buildings near the center of the compound. A brief and lopsided battle ensued with the highly trained Special Forces carefully but quickly choosing their shots while the cartel soldiers fired randomly. Twenty-one members of the most feared cartel in Mexico were dead within seconds. Twenty-one to zero.

Taking control had been easy—all too easy—up to this point but now the more delicate task began, searching the buildings to find Najma.

'You be careful, Brush, we have a cruise ship to catch,' Glenda Rose said softly to no one, then she said louder to Heather. 'No casualties so far, they will be fine and back soon.' Heather was overcome by shaking and she just could not stop. Najma was going to kill Jim while she was listening. She couldn't breathe. Glenda pulled her close and hugged her. She didn't say anything but she understood her reaction. Years of experience allowed her to appear calm but inside, adrenaline ran hot through her veins. Heather faced the reality that Najma was in close proximity to her Jim. *The woman is not normal, what if she is better than he is?* she thought.

Everyone at the operations center watched mesmerized except the SF team controller who never talked but monitored conversations, volume levels, and passed vital information to the team members. The ops group had never seen this sort of action outside the movies. It was lightning fast and surreal, silence and then background noises when the team members talked to each other. The calm voices added a sense of drama to the explosive situation. Fuller was so engrossed that he forgot to be nervous. Everything was working, so far, exactly as planned.

Lola's mind turned circles throughout the day, arriving at no conclusions. The devil-lady would be back soon, maybe even tonight. Suddenly her thoughts stopped at the end of the mantra. They had to get away, it was the only way, and she knew they would leave as soon as she could.

Not all the cartel soldiers were evil. Some had drifted into the organization simply because they had nowhere else to go. It had become their family. Lola had become friends with one man. She had fixed him special meals and they talked when he was not on duty in the tunnel. At first, she had been amazed to hear that the tunnels existed. Over the months, her friend had proudly told her about them, they were his second home. He gave Lola details her mind now grabbed onto with a vise-like grip.

She would take Pedro out through the tunnels tonight. She knew their layout, knew where the guards stayed, and knew that the doors could be opened from inside without keys. The only direction she wanted to go was out and away. Her friend had told her that at the end of the tunnel there was nothing but desert but that cartel guards stationed on the back wall monitored the area. She did not know what she would do when she got outside but her mind was firmly fixed. They would leave tonight; they would find a way to live and be safe after they got through the tunnel to their new world.

Four of Nielly's team stayed on the front wall and searched the area with night vision scopes. Nielly, along with Sergeants Mac Smith and Gaston Reese, moved to the main house. It was empty. The old cartel leader had been partying with his women, which was how he normally spent his time, while Guillermo attended to business. But they had disappeared. However, Nielly's men discovered that the house contained an underground bunker, a safe room buried just below the bedroom. In her haste to get to safety, the last woman out had failed to close the secret door that led to the safe room entrance, otherwise it might have been overlooked by the searchers. One door in, leaving no way out after Nielly fused the steel entrance with a thermite grenade. They did not have enough time to try to open it and did not know who, if anyone, was inside the safe room, whether they were armed, or if there were other protections in place. Leaving it unsealed would risk his men to possible attack if someone came out. Perhaps there was no one and he hoped it was not their two targets, Najma and Guillermo.

Jim, Brush, Nielly, and the three others moved from one building to the other, quickly engaging the remaining cartel in short but intense exchanges. They found startled staff who they moved, along with the captured cartel, to the open courtyard, placed hoods over their heads, and told them to sit, after separating them into two groups: suspected cartel and staff.

Mac Smith, using fluent Spanish, asked both groups where Najma was. Several staff raised their hands and one said, 'The she-devil lives on the corner where the vines grow on the house with the violet door, but she is away.' Mac asked about Guillermo and received no answer. He roughly placed the barrel of his gun under the chin of one of the staff and asked again. 'Tell me now.' The man said nothing. Mac fired a shot into the air and then moved to the next hooded person and repeated the same question. 'He is away, señor,' he answered immediately in a raspy nervous whisper.

The two guardian angels approached the front gate from opposite directions and replaced the men on the wall. The four members of the diversionary team worked their way toward the hacienda through the two tunnels, meeting only slight resistance. Staff Sergeant Grant started moving from his ambush location down the road to the hacienda. Now the only men outside were the original watcher and the SF's one female GA, Roberta. She watched the road and the main gate and would protect the helicopters when they landed.

The cartel guard at the end of the dirt entry road didn't know what to do. Neither his radio nor cell phone worked. Hearing the explosions and shooting, he decided to stay where he was as his responsibility was to guard the entry road. He could still do his duty, he reasoned as he edged backward, from a little farther off the road. Deserting his station would mean death but it wouldn't do any harm to move a little farther away.

Just inside the south tunnel, the diversionary team encountered a door with a video camera above it and an electronic opening device. The door was not strong and they simply kicked it in. There was nothing on the other side, other than a long tunnel. The sergeant in charge of the diversionary team motioned to his teammate who immediately proceeded down the tunnel. He moved quickly almost a hundred meters before coming to another door similar to the first. He kicked it and dropped to the floor as it flew open. Bullets immediately ricocheted down the tunnel fired by a lone guard standing just on the other side of the door. Before the guard could adjust his aim down, Oliver fired a short burst from the floor killing him.

'Tunnel clear, move up, rooms both sides,' reported Oliver.

'Moving up.'

One after another, they opened doors until the fourth door down on the right yielded a surprise. Sitting inside were the two old recon sergeants, still dressed as peasant plant gatherers. Apart from bruises and a small amount of crusted blood, they looked to be OK.

''Bout time you got here. We spent the whole day in here and our host was not the most gracious sort,' said Sergeant Smith through split puffy lips.

'Nice to meet you two. We weren't in a hurry, thought both of you would be fertilizing one of those rare plants you were digging up on the cartel's desert. Come on then, if you're still in the army. There are a couple of guns free for the taking out in the hall if you feel like evening things up with your hosts. Nos vamonos. Let's see if we can find something more useful than you two old bums.'

Heather beamed when they found the two sergeants. Najma was apparently not there, the sergeants were safe, and no one had been killed. Her sense of relief was immediately tempered by the thought that Najma would still be in their lives. She wanted her out of her thoughts, punished and forever gone. Jim was safe for the moment but there was no resolution.

'Señora, take the boy and hide in here. You will be seen leaving the tunnel.'

'But we must go, we have to get away from here. Please help,' she pleaded.

'Even if you get to the other end you will be killed outside.' Lola's friend, Manuel, argued. He was terrified she would be shot if she got out of the tunnel and afraid he would be killed if the cartel found out he had helped her.

Earlier Lola had wrapped some food and clothes in a sheet. With her small bundle ready, she dressed Pedro and told him to come with her. They set off cautiously into the guardroom and then into the tunnel and had walked for several minutes before opening a door and finding her friend, Manuel.

He was angry that she was there and afraid what might happen to all of them. He escorted Lola and the boy to a small cleaning room where he did not think anyone else would see her or hear them talking. He had to think. They must return to the hacienda. They were still arguing when all the lights went out and they heard explosions and gunfire.

Then there was more gunfire in the tunnel and it was closer.

'Sit in the corner and be very quiet,' said Manuel as he quickly moved mops and supplies to conceal their hiding place. The room was lit softly by a red battery emergency light.

'Bless you, Manuel,' she said as the door flew open. Lola shuddered, clasping Pedro tight. Pedro did not say anything, he just sat staring as a small gecko climbed up the faint red-tinged wall, stopped, and then quickly scurried into a small hole as the door crashed open.

Manuel dropped his gun and raised his hands. Jay Hernandez scanned the small room and saw nothing other than cleaning supplies. He ordered the small man who had surrendered and looked frightened into the hall, closed the door, and prodded Manuel up the tunnel.

'Silencio, niño.' Silence was not hard for Pedro, he hardly ever spoke. He watched in the dim light for the gecko to return but it too was hiding and silent.

Nearly all team members were now inside the hacienda walls and only two remained outside. They methodically moved from building to building covering each other. Mac entered what appeared to be staff quarters and motioned for a woman in there to move out the door when a naked, armed man jumped out of the closet. Mac killed him easily with two short bursts but the angry woman stabbed Mac from behind. She was as furious as she was afraid. The cartel man was her protector and anyone else, especially the army, was her enemy.

Nielly had been talking on his radio and could not react in time to save Mac. He hit the woman in the back of the neck with his rifle and she slumped to the floor.

'Medic, building six,' ordered Nielly. Mac was still standing but getting wobbly.

'Sit, Mac. I don't want you falling over.'

Mac complied and said, 'I told myself I wasn't going to get shot again, I should have said knifed.' The knife was buried deep in the right side of his neck. Nielly didn't like its position. Jeff, their medic, nearly as qualified as any doctor and probably more so in acute care of various wounds, rushed into the room.

Mac smiled as Jeff kneeled and used their newfound llama quip—'Spit happens.' 'Guess you need to practice on someone, Jeff,' added Mac.

'Cut the humor, Mac. I don't want you moving or talking. Understood? And don't answer that.'

Jeff looked at Nielly. 'I don't like the knife's position. Maybe just fractions of an inch from his artery. It's buried deep in the soft tissue but is not yet bleeding much. I'm afraid to take it out and afraid to leave it in.'

'Is that your best needle technique, Jeff?' quipped Mac as Jeff injected morphine while he talked to Nielly.

'You're just full of jokes tonight, aren't you, big guy. And if you talk again it will be the last needle prick you feel for a while. I want you to remain completely still, Mac—it's important, don't screw around. I would rather you stay awake and help keep your neck immobilized, but I'll put you under if you talk again.'

Mac and everyone else had long developed a high pain tolerance both by necessity and because of respect. They didn't complain and they ignored pain. The outward bravado was something they practiced but underneath they were all realists. He knew that the doc wouldn't tell him to do something unless it was necessary.

'I have to remove it. Can't take a chance on it moving and doing more damage,' Jeff decided. Mac didn't say a word as Jeff injected the area with local anesthetic. He then straddled Mac and carefully pulled the deeply buried knife slowly out, applying slight pressure away from Mac's artery.

'Stay with him, Jeff. I'm about to call for the choppers to pick us up. I'll have Marilyn land just outside this door so we can load Mac. ETA should be about forty minutes,' Nielly said. Then he pulled the woman up and passed her to another team member who took her to the courtyard and put her in with two cartel men.


Jim, Tom the tech, and Brush worked their way through a building that looked as plush as any NY office. It was not large but one befitting a billion dollar industry.

Brush shook his head. 'I think you convinced me, pal. It's our war on drugs that makes these people so rich. It might make sense if it wasn't just another war we've already lost.'

They went down some steps leading to a hall.

The walls were made of concrete block and lit with low-light, emergency, battery-operated lights just like the ones illuminating Lola and Pedro's sanctuary. All members of the Special Forces preferred their small lights attached to their headgear and weapons, and to a lesser degree their night vision. They trained extensively in low light and no light and felt a secure advantage in the dark.

Jim looked at his watch; it was 02:33. 'Time to get the hard drives and get out of here,' he said.

Najma, sitting in the back of a cab, was nearing the Cabo San Lucas airport. 'Soon I shall be with my son,' she said to herself. A buzz she had never felt before vibrated her cells and raised her libido. *I will have the pilot fly at maximum speed. I will give my little boy a morning kiss and look into his dark brown eyes as the morning sun turns them to fairy gold.*

Guillermo was entering a suite at the San Sebastian Continental in Cuba. He had a successful discussion with the Cuban finance minister as they laid the plans for transferring money from the London banks. The minister was like Guillermo, educated, sophisticated, and possibly as dangerous, but money was a strong catalyst to friendship. They adjourned shortly after midnight and escorts quickly moved Guillermo to his hotel in a new black limo that contrasted sharply with the vibrant colors on the fifties and sixties vintage American cars that still cruised the streets of Havana. After two more brief meetings—one with Raul Castro, a courtesy that was extended to him and few others—Guillermo would leave for his headquarters in Mexico, the hacienda, his home.

Tom moved down the hall, stopped, and held up a closed fist. Jim and Brush both stopped in midstride and stood motionless. Tom had seen a small light beep near a motion detector and then looked up and saw a similar LED light behind a miniature convex plastic dome on the ceiling. He knew from the diagrams that the halls were monitored but had been assured that with the electricity out and no backup generators, the monitors would be out of action. The diagrams showed no other backup power for their security devices. They must have added it recently and not updated their computer files.

Tom wore a video camera, however, the people watching the monitors, including Heather and Glenda, could not see Jim and Brush. Heather knew that Jim was close behind and sucked in a small breath when Tom held up his hand and stood motionless. Glenda rose slightly in her chair squinting. The hall looked sterile and forbidding. The floors, ceiling, and walls were all the same indistinct gray-tan paint. Captain Fuller unrolled the blueprint of the building that the Wolf Pack had given him. 'The first door is on the left in about seven meters.'

Tom stood motionless wondering. *Where was the backup power? Who was monitoring them?* He had no choice, no time, he had to move. He pointed at Jim and Brush and closed his fist, signaling for them to stay put and walked quickly down the hall, wondering what other changes had not been brought up to date on the computers. *What would I do to protect a sophisticated computer system? What would Brad, the imported hacker, want to protect his computer domain?* The blank hall was a trap, he just didn't know what the trap would be. He turned. His video camera pointed toward Jim and Brush. Heather and Glenda got a quick low-light image of them. He motioned for them to pull back. As soon as they started moving back toward the entrance, he pulled a small package from his side, twisted a knob, stuck it on the door, and sprinted toward the stairs yelling, 'Out. Now.' They watched the image of Jim and Brush running down the corridor trailed by Tom.

They raced up the stairs and Tom slammed the door then motioned them to the side.

'Gas. They re-rigged the corridor and didn't update the diagrams on the computer. I noticed gas valves along the door.' Suddenly there was a large muffled explosion and the door he had just closed blew straight out into the courtyard.

'Gas masks on. Let's get back down there and get to work on their computers.'

'I don't think I can take any more. I need some air, Glenda, but I can't make myself leave,' said Heather. Thoughts of getting Najma completely left her. She didn't care about revenge or justice. She wanted to be home with Jim safe, snuggled up, letting the world take care of itself. She wanted to be with her llamas and plants. She didn't want to be here in Arizona or watching the monitors, yet she had to stay. *But what if Jim is killed right in front of us?* She got angry and told herself not to think such things...*Hang on...Hang on, it will be over soon.* She started to cry. *I can't do this.* She held her head low and put her hands on the sides of her head trying to cover the flow of tears. No one saw. No one looked at her as they were all staring at the computer screen images of a live action mission they had never seen before.

Most never would again; the video and uplinks were unique to Nielly's Special Forces team and usually only watched by their own technician, who often observed things that they missed seeing on the ground. A new tactic was proving to be very useful—placing two to three cameras in strategic locations on the ground. Tom monitored these remote cameras and advised them of opposition movements. Battles were fluid. People moved, Tom observed and reported. The team thought of it as seeing around corners.

Nielly was the first through the door of what they had dubbed building eight. They had expected to take the hacienda easily but it also left them feeling that something would change for the worse. It was ironic that a hard fought battle left them relieved, knowing it was over and an easy one left them uptight.

A young boy stood in the room awkwardly aiming a pistol at

Nielly. They locked eyes for a second and Nielly could see the brave determination in the boy. Nielly had a flash of a recurring daydream where a child shot him in the stomach. He could sense the boy tensing. *He is going to fire. My dreams finally turn to reality.*

There had been continued scattered brief resistance from cartel members but the speed and efficiency of the night attack by Nielly's Special Forces prevented any other serious injuries. The hacienda was almost secured.

No matter how well they planned there would always be something unforeseen. The boy protecting his family, his turf from the invaders, a brave young soldier doing his duty. The young boy held a gun, making him dangerous, but Nielly was too experienced to die like this. He threw his rifle up and to the right, distracting the boy, and simultaneously dived down and to his left. The boy pulled the trigger following Nielly's movement but he had been distracted and was late moving the heavy weapon back to where Nielly landed. The bullets hit the doorframe and the gun jumped in the boy's hand. Nielly pivoted on his hands swinging a leg around toward the boy. His foot connected with the boy's small legs knocking him down and the gun clanged on the stone floor and skidded a few feet away.

'Nice work, boss,' said Nielly's backup at the door as he pulled the flailing boy from the floor. 'This one needs extra guards, a regular little wildcat.'

Fuller watched Nielly amazed and wondered how he would react in the field. He had never seen any action. Nielly probably could have shot the boy. Many would have. Children can kill you just as easily as anyone else can. A lesson learned usually through experience, but Nielly had chosen a different resolution. One he would sleep better with. His nightmare remained a dream and not a reality.

'Pickup ETA, eleven minutes,' he said to his team.

Jim, Brush, and Tom "Teckie" had rushed back into the underground hallway through the detonated door and found three men dead inside the room. Judging from their faces they had died in agony.

'Some sort of bad gas,' said Brush and raised his eyebrows behind his plastic covered mask. 'It would seem advisable not to breathe it.'

'Yep, gas killed them, not the explosion. They thought the gas would only be in the hallway. Slight planning error. Something like Sarin, otherwise we would be dead from skin contact,' responded Jim.

'I guess I can live with the thought that whatever it was it didn't kill by skin contact. Glad you didn't suggest that possibility earlier. I would have let you tiptoe in alone and give me the all clear,' said Brush. 'Sounds right, they probably would not want nerve gas lingering on surfaces in the halls. They might get some on themselves when they left.'

'That was my fervent hope, partner.'

Teckie was inspecting the dead men. 'This one is our big-time US hacker, Brad. They can identify him from our video. Unfortunately, we were hoping to catch him alive. The Wolf Pack wanted to bleed his mind about their computer systems. Must do this...' he said as he removed a long-bladed black knife and quickly cut off Brad's hand. 'I need this for fingerprints and they can identify the type of gas they used from the blood.'

'Oh my god,' said Heather.

'He's dead,' said Glenda. 'Think of it like an autopsy.'

'We need it more than he does,' said Brush. 'You guys seem to like the Busse Boss Jack knife. Prefer something smaller, myself, like the Sog Seal Pup.'

'Better hustle up if we are going to get the hard drives,' said Jim.

'You two start on those computers over there, I'm going to try to boot this one and see what I can see,' said Teckie, then added, 'Look at this,' as he picked up a small rectangular box. 'I was just reading something from the NSA about these. I think it's a hardened browser that you plug into your computer. Bleedin' cool!'

They worked furiously, pulling the computer parts they wanted loose from the stands. They needed them fast and had brought a small kit containing battery-operated tools to quickly unscrew, grind, or sever as needed. Brush placed his and Jim's rucksacks on the floor and tossed several padded canvas bags on a desk near the computers.

'Pickup ETA, ten minutes,' came through their com devices.

Teckie hit the desk in frustration. 'I can't get past their password, not enough time.' He started to look around and grab anything he thought looked interesting, especially any unknown devices. The first item he put in his bag was the device he thought might be a hardened browser. If it was what he suspected, it might take them directly to some interesting information on a remote server somewhere in the world. 'Friggin' righteous,' he whispered to himself as he grinned inside the gas mask.

'Time to pack up and leave,' said Brush.

'Not a good idea yet, Major McGuire,' said Teckie. 'We need all of this we can carry.'

'We get what we can, let's not push our luck,' added Jim supporting Brush's comment.

Glenda blushed back in the control room. She didn't think of Brush as a major, just as the man she was starting to love. Her anxieties were lessening; just a few more minutes and he would be on his way back to her.

'What the…!' said Teckie. 'Timer going with 4:59 showing and counting down. This place must be wired, probably something to destroy the computing system.'

'See if you can find the explosives and figure out if it is just the computers or something larger,' ordered Jim. 'You hear that, "leader"? Anyone else spot anything?'

'Acknowledge; negative, no others observed. Get out here now, choppers in two minutes,' said Nielly. 'I'm bringing the small bird directly into the compound. I want it loaded and gone before that goes off. If this place blows, so much the better.'

'I want all of you on that bird and in the air in max three minutes,' added General Crystal.

'Move everyone out the gate now. Get the injured cartel and the others loaded and into the choppers as soon as they touch down,' ordered Nielly.

'In one minute we leave with whatever we have,' said Jim.

'We're not going to get them all,' said Brush. 'How about I just grab these three computers and hustle them out and you bring our bags of goodies.'

'Sounds like a plan,' said Teckie. 'I can get my bag and grab two more, Brush, if you can hustle them off from the shelves.'

As Brush pulled out one of the computers, a gecko jumped to the wall. 'How'd you get in here, little guy?' Brush asked as he rushed. 'Cute little bugger, aren't you, but this isn't the place for you to be.' He quickly reached out to grab it but it was far too fast. It jumped to a desk, down the side, and into one of their canvas bags. *Smart too, you want to leave with us.*

'This is it. Kind of thinking we best exit this hole fast. I want to

*my miho,* she thought and smiled to herself. The small feeling of pleasure which that thought brought to her surprised her, as did the smaller still but recognizable feeling of arousal titillating her mind and body. How could the little boy, her little boy, do this to her, make her feel these things? Was it normal for mothers to feel attraction to their sons? 'Yes,' she decided aloud, 'why not? He belongs to me.' The pilot didn't look at her as she spoke into her mic, he was too afraid. Najma looked at her watch. It would be after four o'clock in the morning when they flew by the hacienda.

# Chapter 37

Get out, Marilyn,' said Jim. 'RPMs aren't coming up to full speed, something's wrong.'

'Forget it, pull in power now—get over the wall fast.'

Glenda involuntarily raised her hand to her mouth. Heather's face was distorted with anguish. Teckie was looking back toward the building with his video camera when the building erupted in flames. Chunks of concrete flew in the air. Suddenly the camera sent a chaos of blurred images to the operation center's monitors. Then it went blank.

Eyes darted to another monitor. Heather and Glenda both watched on Nielly's camera as he turned toward the explosion. They stared as the image of the Huey with Jim, Brush, and the others shuddered, was knocked sidewise, began to spin six feet off the ground, then hit the ground, rotor blades slashing stone pavement, finally tipped fully on its side, kept sliding and slammed into the hacienda wall next to the gate.

'Nielly, get your people over there,' ordered the general. He didn't need to give that order to Nielly. His team was already racing toward the crumpled remains of the helicopter.

'Status?' said General Crystal.

'Shit,' said Nielly.

Heather couldn't cry or speak, she sat frozen. Jim couldn't be gone, killed right in front of her eyes. Her mind reeled with thoughts of him and their life together, the ranch where they belonged, in each other's arms, delivering llama babies, picking berries, making love on the hillsides, in the wilderness, and under the stars. She couldn't survive without him. *Please let him be alive*, she pleaded to whatever forces were out there.

'Two dead, maybe three,' said Nielly. The door gunner and another of his men were obviously dead. Marilyn looked crushed in the front. He couldn't tell if she was still alive. If there was any good news it was Mac lying on the floor and Jeff still restraining his head. Two men pulled the door gunner out and then carefully removed Mac with Jeff's help. Two others were trying to pry open the cockpit and get to Marilyn.

'Oh my god, where are they?' cried Heather.

Images jumped on the screens as several others made it to the wrecked chopper just as Brush stumbled out onto the hacienda's stone covered ground. Relief swept through Glenda but she immediately looked at Heather hoping that Jim was also alive. Heather's expression was completely blank, lips slightly parted, hope mixed with fear; she stared at the snowy images projected by the jumping videos. Then as Glenda watched, Heather's lips closed and the corners of her mouth turned up slightly.

Glenda looked at the monitor. Brush was back in the chopper and passing Jim out. He was moving, bloody but alive. Brush appeared uninjured as he looked directly at the SF member's headgear and grinned. Glenda shook her head as she looked at this crazy grinning man, her man. They couldn't see each other but they both knew, they could feel each other on the end of the electromagnetic wave carrying their signal. 'You're a lunatic and I love you,' she said none too softly to his face in the monitor.

Their elation immediately changed, watching the two bodies being moved away. They didn't know the dead men but their happiness was tempered seeing the fragility of life. They watched expectantly as Jeff worked on Jim and hoped that Marilyn was not dead.

Sheilla found she had been holding her breath and let out a loud whoop as she pushed back from the monitor and spun around in her chair, auburn hair flying out like a whirling dervish's skirt. Her crew jumped out of her way.

'Oh man, I thought they had bought the farm. Every time I am involved with those two there's a helicopter crash.' She toggled her radio, she couldn't help herself. She had to say something to Heather and Glenda Rose. 'Hey, you two, if you're done holding your breath, I just wanted to say I'm glad they're OK but sorry about the others.'

'Thanks, Sheilla. That makes three of us!' answered Glenda. The TOC team looked at her and Heather. 'Correction, ladies, that makes quite a few of us.' The TOC team now felt like they were almost old friends with Jim since he first glided to the mine, such a short time ago.

A moment's smile had turned to worry as Heather tried to tell how badly Jim was injured. Jeff, the medic, was examining him on the ground. He applied a compress to his side and instructed Brush to hold it and then taped it.

Jim was regaining consciousness and through blurry eyes saw

Brush kneeling over him. Seconds later he gave him a wink. He looked at Jeff and asked, 'What's the damage?'

'Small puncture to your side, maybe a cracked head but nothing that will put you in the nursing home yet, Colonel,' he said as he quickly moved toward the cockpit, where a bloody Marilyn was being pulled onto the cold stones.

Mac was already on a stretcher and being moved to the Chinook as were the two dead men. Marilyn's contorted body was placed on a stretcher as Jeff walked by her side. 'Marilyn's not good and I can't tell the extent of her injuries. Several fractures and a compound fracture of the leg but… we need to get her to the hospital as soon as.' She and Mac were loaded and the bags containing the computer hard drives quickly followed.

'Backup choppers are on the way. Make your personnel switches then we're out of here as soon as you say the word,' said the general.

'Looks like I spoke too soon, Will. Should have known better, just haven't been out in the field for a while. Nothing is ever over until it is,' said Whitcuff.

'You're a go,' said Nielly. The general started to pull in power and hesitated for just a fraction of a second as he saw Brush propping up a bandaged Jim just inside the hacienda. 'He shouldn't have stayed,' said the general. 'But what should I expect, eh,' as he shook his head then gave them a thumbs-up.

Nielly had tried to load Jim and Brush but they refused to go. Nielly left two guardian angels. The Chinook was near capacity and he needed to swap the four men in order to take the wounded. Leaving four of his men would have been his preference but Brush and Jim wouldn't go, so he elected to leave two GAs to watch out for them. The GAs wasted no time moving to defensive positions and were quickly lost from sight, Roberta back to her old position and the other GA on the wall watching over the inside of the hacienda. The big helicopter lifted into the night sky just as a single engine Cessna passed high overhead.

'Drone has a small aircraft above at 7,000 feet, to your south.'

'Roger, keep us informed,' said the general turning the Chinook to the north and toward the two countries' political line in the dirt.

The drone continued to monitor the single engine plane as it lost altitude and turned southeast. After a few minutes, the Chinook and the plane were separated by enough miles and the TOC relaxed. 'Plane is no threat.'

'Roger that, backup ETA?' asked the general.

'Fifty-five minutes. Will keep you informed of location.'

Najma glared at the hacienda below. They had seen the violent explosion when they were over forty miles away: a bright ball of flames erupting from the dark desert. 'We go straight to the airport?' said the pilot hopefully.

'No, get us lower but stay south,' she commanded through clenched teeth. A large helicopter, a Chinook was lifting off in front of the hacienda. It headed north. *The Americans,* she thought. *What had they done to her boy?*


'How you feeling, buddy?'

Jim looked at Brush and shook his head noting not one single visible scratch on the Canadian. 'If we're stuck here for a while, let's take a little look around,' he said. Brush eyed him for a second. 'Where to then? Think our lady might be here after all?'

'Kind of doubt it. Let's take another look at the staff quarters.' He didn't have to tell Brush to be careful. The GA on the wall watched the two agents disappear through a door.

# Chapter 38

I remember using this internet café once, a long time ago when I didn't want to use my personal computer,' said Amir. 'You know the old days when we wanted to hide our identity, not have someone see our IP address.'

Sharon just shook her head and looked at Yousef as they crossed the street from South Kensington tube station and walked along the north side of Marringten Place. The 'out of business' internet café looked dingy and small.

'All the computers used to be in the basement,' said Amir.

'Keep your heads down, look at the pavement,' ordered Felix who walked just behind them.

They crossed the street and approached a dirty glass door. It opened as they neared and they saw the large shape of Ox standing inside, just beyond the outside light.

The shop was old and ugly as Ox closed the door behind them. He pointed toward wooden steps that descended to a basement, the one Amir remembered. A weak light illuminated the way at the bottom. Felix pushed by them and stepped through a thick black curtain into a narrow hallway lit by another low wattage bulb. It felt eerie in the dim light and looked as though no one had thought to clean or paint for dozens of years. It smelled of old dust.

'A witches' den,' whispered Sharon.

'Your new home, señorita, where we shall take up housekeeping together,' sneered Felix the rat.

Sharon bit her tongue and smiled. 'You talk big but I think Ox has more to offer.'

'One day, maybe you will see just what it is that I offer.'

He opened a door and the soft glow of dozens of computer screens illuminated a large decaying room. The computers were on tables just like an internet café and barely visible behind them in the dim light were more chairs and empty tables. Refrigerators and sinks lined the back wall. Much of it was old and dirty, some of it looked new but haphazardly pieced together.

Rameriz stood up from behind one of the computers. 'What do you think of our new facilities?'

Sharon tried to sashay toward him. 'Pretty impressive. An old internet café, lots of bandwidth. A perfect headquarters for our project.'

*She is playing her new role well,* thought Rameriz. He had listened to the tapes and knew what her plan was, but she had good understanding of computers and was not really that bad to look at either. He knew she was role-playing but she had also said that she really was attracted to him.

'Follow me.' He motioned to them. Past the tables and the kitchen area was another door and a hall with doors lining the side. The walls were made of raw plywood and looked new. He opened a door and walked in. There was a small bed, a table with a light, and nothing else other than hooks along the wall. 'Make yourself at home,' he told her with a sardonic look.

She stared at him dumbfounded, trying not to look upset.

'Not as plush as you deserve but better than the men's bunks in the back.'

Amir groaned. He couldn't stand to be close to other men and had hated every moment when he was a young student in a dormitory.

Sharon recovered a little and tried to make light of it in her new role as a happy accomplice. 'Guess you have thought of everything,' she said thinking to herself that it was their new jail. *Why put me in a separate room?* She didn't think it was to protect her modesty and wondered if they would ever leave this place alive.

'We will work from here and perfect our plan and techniques for extracting the money from the bank.' Rameriz smiled.

'It's weeks away, you can't mean we are staying here that long,' said Amir with his eyes wide and mouth hanging open.

'A small inconvenience to pay for all the money you will have by next year,' replied Rameriz.

Yousef's mind was reeling. From the light into the dungeon. Little by little they had been maneuvered and talked into this hole. He could not help but feel he would never see the outside again. Just as Sharon had thought moments ago. 'A life sentence,' he said to Sharon when Rameriz had left.

In the control room, others were also looking at screens. 'How come, Gordon,' asked Glenda, 'everyone is mostly careful with what they say but we are looking at full video that tells anyone monitoring exactly who and what is going on? You know a picture is worth a thousand words.'

Gordon smiled, as this was his favorite topic. 'In audio cryptography we use a completely different method from optical, or rather the video we are watching. We modify the images using the wave interference property of light. The privacy is perfect and the modified images that someone else might see are non-suspicious.'

'So the video transmitted from Mexico looks like something completely different than we see here? But can't some of the agencies like mine figure this out?'

'Yes to the first question but the FBI, if you will forgive me, is way behind the curve. The National Security Agency is closer but it's important to the military to see what's happening real time on the battlefield. NSA, FBI, and others aren't as concerned. It's the drone development driving this too, as we don't want anyone intercepting the live video they feed back to us.'

Glenda was interested but barely took her eyes off the screen hoping to see Brush and Jim come out of the building. She glanced at Heather who sat staring at the images of the hacienda, as the two GAs and the watcher provided the only images now. Heather might normally have been scientifically interested in what Gordon was saying but she allowed none of his words into her brain. She was fixated on getting Jim back.

'There they are,' she whispered to the screen, as Jim and Brush came out one door and headed toward the main house in the hacienda.

'Lieutenant, chopper's back and your computer parts are on the way here,' said Captain Fuller.

Jake reached over and five-knuckled Jason. Fuller shook his head and walked out, seeing his fellow officer acting like a teenager with an enlisted man.

'Cool, man,' said Jason.

'Got that right,' said Jake. 'Ramsey Mann was a cool hacker dude and now he's getting cooler by the minute.' He laughed at his macabre joke.

'You're crude,' said Misa. 'The poor guy is dead, have a little respect.'

Jake looked at the lieutenant, raised a corner of his lip, rolled his eyes, and then said, 'Well what is cool is that we are going to have a Wolf Pack feeding frenzy when we get his hard drives. It might be about the most fun thing that has ever happened to me. Even if he defected to the cartel, Mann was one smart dude and I'm looking forward to this.'


'Alejandro, you take care of the security cameras in this area?'

'I did, boss, pulled up their archives and replaced the data for the last week with video from a month ago. Same weather pattern. Sixteen cameras in just a few blocks. They'll never know.'

'Good. Any sign of anything in the government's computers about us?'

'Nothing here or over the water. Just the same old stuff. DEA on the border chasing people near Douglas and having lots of problems with their equipment over the last few hours. They've been border-blind most of the night near our home turf.'

'Keep on it. I just want to know if there is anything that will affect us here. Don't care about their little drug operations back home. They won't affect us.'

Rameriz started to walk away and then turned back to Alejandro. 'But if you see any big DEA operations planned, let me know.' His job now was the bank break-in but Guillermo would have Felix kill him in an instant if he let anything important slip that would cost the cartel lots of money. Their game was monitoring everything in the US and Mexican governments but not interfering in any of the government operations unless it would cost them too much. That was Guillermo's decision to make, his responsibility was to supply information. Guillermo selectively chose to allow the DEA small successes. It was better to let the DEA succeed occasionally so that they did not become suspicious.

'These bags better be worth something. My team paid a price to get them, so I want to know if you find anything important. It will make me feel a little better knowing it did some good,' said Nielly as he set the canvas bag on a desk next to Jake. 'Where do you want the rest of this stuff?'

'Right here, my man,' said Josh with a gleam in his eye. The two SF men that had followed Nielly into the room carrying the computer chuckled and set them down.

'What's that sign mean, "Wolf Pack"?' asked one of them.

'Man, that's us,' said Josh. 'We're the Wolf Pack, this is our den.'

Just as Nielly closed the door, a loud beat vibrated through it.

The man next to Nielly said, 'Heh, good stuff.'

'Sounds like Dire Straits. Weird bunch in there though.'

'No weirder than us but they have good taste in music.'

The driving beat worked its way into the TOC and then into Heather's consciousness. A little worry left her as she felt the beat. The Stones were her favorite but Dire Straits were a strong second. It was a good omen and she instantly felt somewhat better.

'Turn that noise off, Jake. And give me one of those hard drives,' yelled Misa over the din. 'Don't you have Berlioz or Mozart or something that lets a person work in peace?'

'Jesus, old people,' mumbled Josh as he plugged in his earphones and huddled over his computer, chair-dancing to the silent music as he tapped his fingers in rhythm on his keyboard.

As the Cessna neared the hacienda, a large flash lit up the building in the compound. 'Very bad,' said the pilot.

'Shut up and fly a little closer,' commanded Najma.

She had been looking at the desert east of the hacienda, thinking about holding Pedro, when the explosion erupted. What caught her attention was a tiny spark of light from a ridge just east of the compound. The flash from the explosion had reflected off GA one's scope. She shifted her gaze to the hacienda and anger boiled in her brain. 'Veer south and get me down on the ground now.'

'You mean the airport, señ...señora?'

She grabbed the yoke and banked sharp to the right, heading south, then pushed the yoke in. The plane dove steeply toward the desert then just as abruptly she did a steep bank to the east. She pulled the nose up and the throttle out, slowing to a glide. 'You want me to land this thing or do you want to get me down right there?' she hissed as she pointed.

'Madre Dios, Madre Dios,' he mumbled as he crossed himself and took the yoke.

'As soon as you're near the ground, turn out your wing lights.'

Both the GA and the drone watched the small plane. The TOC lost interest when it headed away from the hacienda and disappeared south over the horizon. They assumed it was heading to an airport south of their location.

The pilot looked terrified as he pulled in full flaps and slowed the plane as much as he dared without stalling it. 'We will die and ruin Guillermo's plane. It is rugged country, señori...señora.' Using Guillermo was the strongest appeal he could think of.

'Land now or I put a bullet in your head.' Najma pushed the

barrel of a small PPK hard against his right ear.

Moments later, at just below forty miles per hour, the Cessna crashed through cacti and brush, bounced violently over a rock, and pitched nose-down into a shallow gully. The propeller, still turning, banged to a sudden stop against a rock. Najma pushed the light-weight door open with her shoulder, jumped out, pulled the seat forward, and grabbed a large duffle bag from the rear, dropping it on the ground.

She unzipped the bag, extracted a Glock pistol and her 22 car-bine along with several clips for each. Then she removed a silenced MP-5, which she slung over her shoulder, and lastly a night vision scope, knife, and a small Maglite. With the low red light in the cockpit, her eyes were already adjusted to the dark desert. The silver light of night softly illuminated the arid landscape; dawn was hours away and the sun still lingered well below the eastern horizon. Najma moved around the plane. *I must hurry,* she thought, *not much time.*

'Alto, señorita, help me, por favor?' Blood was dripping down the pilot's face from a large gash as he opened the door and fell onto the desert pavement. He waved his right hand at the plane. 'Radio for help!' he moaned. Najma raised her small carbine and shot him in the head before hurrying off to the north.

Amir looked sullen lying on a cot in his small cubicle. Losing his home to these yobs and then forced into this dungeon for weeks was more than his mind could bear. He did not know that a small group was busily working in his house, assiduously cleaning and removing all traces of the cartel's existence.

Sharon looked around at the six people working on computers. Lazio, Alejandro, and of course Rameriz were there but she had never seen the other three, one woman and two men, before. Ox was seated near the door with his back to the wall. He grinned at her as she scanned the dingy room.

'Let's have tea,' suggested Yousef. 'I'll start the water and you can come back in a few minutes.'

'Did you see any sweetener?'

'No, but there's sugar on the counter by the microwave.'

Sharon marched over to the huge figure of Ox. 'Get up, you lard ass, and go out and get me some artificial sweetener. I don't like tea without it and no tea means no work.' He just stared at her and didn't move, not even a blink.

'Just put it on that list on the board and someone will get it for you,' said Lazio, who had overheard her. 'There will be two trips a day so put anything down on the list you want.'

'We're in jail here,' grumbled Yousef as Sharon dropped heavily into a chair with a scowl.

She took a deep breath and looked at Yousef and mouthed, 'Bugs.' He nodded his head. She turned hers to the front to see if Ox was still at the door. He was, but Felix had walked in and was coming straight toward them. 'And here comes the cockroach,' said Sharon.

'Go get your buddy and bring him out here,' ordered Felix.

Yousef stood and looked down on the little weasel and wondered if he shouldn't just try to do something. Felix, understanding his thoughts, stared back hoping he would. The thought vanished as Amir walked in while Sharon tried for all she was worth to look longingly at Felix. *I'm no good at this,* she thought. *He knows I am just putting him on.* Felix did know, but then like many men he thought that women sometimes desired him. *Maybe the look was real, maybe she likes being a prisoner,* he persuaded himself.

As Amir and Yousef walked back toward the table, Felix held out a bag and said, 'I need some more cups and saucers. Put one in here, each of you.' They all did, Amir not even caring why he wanted them while Sharon wondered why they would want their fingerprints on cups and saucers.

'Put this hat on. Let's go,' said Felix to Amir as they walked to the door. 'After you, señor.'

They retraced their earlier walk past South Kensington station. 'Keep your head down, look at the pavement,' ordered Felix who also wore a hat and oversized coat.

'Where are we going?'

'Shut up and keep walking.'

Ten minutes later Amir was feeling happier. They were nearing his house.

'Open the door.' They walked in. 'Close it, stupido. Make yourself at home, you're staying here.' A sense of relief flooded through him. Maybe they recognized his importance to them. Guillermo was giving him his true status while his two underlings stayed in the internet café hole.

'Move into the kitchen.' As they entered Felix said, 'Open the dishwasher and don't touch it again or I'll cut off your fine little hands. Comprende? Now put these cups inside and close the door, and don't forget, hands off.' Felix knew he was smart but sometimes his little jokes made him think he really was cleverer than everyone else. *Hands off,* he repeated to himself as he walked away leaving Amir in a state of confusion.

Amir eventually felt brave enough to walk out of the kitchen. Felix was sitting in the living room. The house looked spotless. 'What I am supposed to do?'

'Do whatever you want. You are staying here for now.'

'Find anything interesting?' asked Jake.

'I think it's the jackpot of all time,' answered Josh.

'Out with it then.'

'Just look for yourself. I want to see what's on the other hard drives. Some pretty cool stuff, I'll bet.'

'I've got some seriously interesting things here,' said Vidya. 'Looks like they know everything that is going on in the DEA's computers and they have several people also supplying them with information for other government agencies both, in the US and Mexico. These guys were wired in, no wonder they wanted to incinerate this.'

Jake spent an hour going over the information on the hard drive that Josh had found. Suddenly he burst out. 'Man oh man, these guys are going to take millions from a bank. Josh, get Captain Fuller in here.'

'I told you it was good stuff.'

Captain Fuller came in and Jake summarized. 'I better get General Whitcuff on the horn for this. This is out of our league,' said Fuller, reaching for the phone.

'General Whitcuff, sir, Captain Fuller.'

'What is it, Captain?'

'We have found something that is critical, more than one thing actually, but this one seems big, sir.'

'I'll be there in thirty minutes.'

'He's coming here, so let's talk about what we've found so far, I want to give him a coherent summary,' said Fuller.

'Yousef, I need your help on something,' said Sharon. 'Rameriz has me working on the bank protocols. Come and look at this and tell me what you think.'

Sharon started to type as Yousef watched.

*This is safe. I found a keystroke grabber on the computer but I've disabled it while I'm writing this. Any ideas on how we get out of this mess? And what do you think they are doing with Amir and our finger-prints? Go back and think about it and see if you can...*

'You two have a problem I can help with?' asked Rameriz. 'You have a lot of work to do. What's the problem?'

'I just wanted to ask Yousef about these protocols, he knows more about it than I do. I want to get this right. I'm thinking about all the money I'm seeing here in my bank account.'

Rameriz looked at her for a second. She was lying about what they were doing. But he had been thinking about what El Padrino had in store for him after this and he decided that the cartel leader would not want any loose ends, meaning that he would be eliminat-ed just like Sharon and Yousef. Maybe between the three of them they could find a way out of this. He couldn't trust any of the others in his group. 'OK, go ahead and work on it together.'

As Sharon looked at Rameriz, she felt something in his eyes. Rameriz knew that she knew a lot more than Yousef about the banks' protocols. If so then he knew that her reason for talking to Yousef was bogus. Could he be giving her a message?

Guillermo didn't usually drink much but after the meeting with the Cubans, he felt like celebrating. He had had two mojitos, his favorite drink, along with some fish his chef had prepared that was a gift from the Cubans. *I'm rich,* he thought, *very rich. Mary will marry someone European and I will have a noble legacy with lots of grandchildren. Mexico will be far in the past. I have power but what is there left to do? Soon maybe I will move to Monaco and keep a fine house in Paris and London or maybe in the English country-side.* He had within his reach what he always wanted but he couldn't help feeling listless. He pushed a third mojito aside. He was unhappy and did not understand why.

'Attention,' reverberated through the TOC and the Wolf Pack's den. Seconds later, both generals strode into the room accompanied by Nielly.

'At ease, gentlemen and ladies,' said Whitcuff as he looked at Misa and then at both Heather and Glenda as they walked into the room. 'Captain Fuller has been keeping us up to date. We'll soon get Jim and the others out,' he added as he looked at Heather. 'This is about computers. Maybe you and Glenda could let me know if anything important changes at the hacienda.' They both took the hint and left the room closing the door behind them.

'Let's get to it then. What did you find?'

'There is enough here to keep us busy for weeks. Besides finding some unique approaches to computer security, which may prove invaluable, we've found several informants in US and other governments as well as back doors into DEA and other agencies.'

'What do you mean "back doors"?' asked Whitcuff.

'The cartel had ways of monitoring what was going on in several computers including those of the DEA, NSA, and FBI. They knew what was going to happen before it happened. Interestingly, we have just checked a few but it seems that they knew about operations against them and did nothing about it. If so then that implies that they valued the information so much they were willing to selectively allow operations that cost them. We need to do a lot more checking.'

'You need more help on this?'

'No, sir, it would just slow us down now. The four of us will work around the clock and brief you tomorrow about what we find out. Josh, brief the generals, since you are the one that found out about London.'

'This will knock your socks off, sir!'

'Josh, please just explain,' ordered Fuller.

Sam Whitcuff held up his hand as if to say it was OK and not to interrupt. 'Proceed, Sergeant.'

'They are planning to rip off at least one bank in London for nearly a half a billion pounds, at least as near as I can figure so far. That's approximately eight hundred million dollars. In short they are going to make it look at first like a millennium bug problem. Pass the money to Cuba and then I don't know what else happens after that.'

'Why Cuba?' asked Will Crystal.

'I think that Ramsey Mann, their computer specialist, must have been employing game theory,' said Misa. 'Steal the money and at first it looks like a computer error and later the bank finds out the money has gone to Cuba. It's like that nuclear thing back in the 1960's. Who is going to go to war with Cuba over some money? The British government will be too embarrassed that their systems are so poor and to prevent a run on banks they will probably cover it up. Seems rather brilliant to me. I don't have any idea how the cartel then gets it but I'll bet the information is on the hard drive Josh is looking at.'

'That it?' asked General Whitcuff.

'No,' said Jake. 'Vidya is looking at a device that we have only heard people talk about. It looks like a little box you plug into your computer and it uses a hardened browser to communicate.'

'No idea what that is, son. Explain.'

'It's a sophisticated way of communicating without anyone being able to eavesdrop.'

'Anything else?' No one said anything. The general looked at them all, 'Good work, give this your full attention, everyone. You can have anything or anyone you want.'

'As long as Vidya and Misa stay to help. Anyone else would just get in our way,' replied Jake.

'Captain Fuller, I want your full attention on Mexico until everyone is out. Lieutenant, you let me know directly if you find anything new and don't bother Fuller. We'll be in the conference room. Understood? I am going to need a complete report within the hour.'

The two generals walked immediately down the military-gray painted hall and into a conference room. General Whitcuff's adjutant was waiting. 'Get the chief of staff on the horn. Even the desk jockeys in Washington should be up by now. Then get into the computer room and write a brief. Work with the lieutenant and leave Fuller alone, he has other duties right now. This will likely go to the highest level so get the details included but make it succinct. Don't take the computer team away from the work any longer than necessary.'

'How are you going to play this, Sam?'

'I'll try to keep you out of it for now, if I can, Will.'

'Chief of staff on the line, sir.'

'Good morning, Chief.'

'You still in this army, Sam? Thought you would be transitioning to the golf course by now.'

'Not quite out to pasture yet, Rufus. I got something you are going to want to evaluate with urgency. My computer team here has gotten some information from a drug cartel's computer and it appears to have some important international aspects. In short, this drug cartel has people in London preparing to extract nearly a billion dollars from one of their banks. A brief will be sent within the hour. And it seems that the cartel has access to our most sensitive government computers.'

'Jesus, Sam. You sure about this?'

'I'm no computer expert but I trust the information from my staff.'

'I know you well enough to bump this along on your word, Sam, and for now off the record, but I'll need strong substantiation. The Joint Chief will have our asses if we get the politicians involved and this doesn't play out right.' Will said when Sam put the phone down.

'The intel looks good, Will, I'll leave the politics to you.'

'He's going to want a complete report, sooner rather than later, Sam.'

'No question and I'm going to have to give it to him. If this info is right, I might be able to retire with another medal, regardless of how the information was obtained, but you're not ready to retire yet. The diplomats are going to want someone to hang this on and I suspect that will be you. Invading a sovereign nation without briefing Washington isn't going to sit well with anyone.'

'Actually, Sam, I think we'll both be OK. I'm going to make some calls but I think with the information we've found, we can make this play out right for everyone. Mexican government can take credit for the raid. The Drug Enforcement Agency will be ticked but the State Department will want to claim the operation for themselves and since we will point out that the DEA and other agencies are leaking information to the cartel—I wouldn't want to be in any of their shoes.'

'Hope you're right. OK, I'll give them what we have about the banks and stall other parts about how the information was obtained as best I can until you get something worked out. You're connected to the political types, Will, and it's your backside that needs protecting, not mine. I just want to keep my pension and pride if I can.'

'Lazio, you and Alejandro have three new techs to supervise and I want you to report to me every day at eighteen hundred. Assign one bank each and watch it closely. I want to be in the three banks' systems securely by the end of the week. Remember we are only going to extract money from one of them but we will cause a "millennium bug" problem in all three. We won't choose which bank to take down until just before we are ready to remove money. I'll supervise our two captives.'

Rameriz had figured out that El Padrino would remove all evidence from the bank raid and he was worried that he would be one of the pieces of evidence to disappear. He had been certain that El Padrino would want to keep him as he was a valued member of the cartel and next to Ramsey Mann, their most skilled computer technician. *But compared to the huge amount of money at stake,* he wondered, *am I valuable enough to keep or will it be more important to erase all details of the heist, including me?* In the middle of the night he had an idea for a plan that might protect himself but it would mean turning against the cartel. He needed to think about it more and find a way to test Sharon as she would have to go along with it.

Sharon was starting to warm to Rameriz. At first he seemed hard but she was detecting cracks in his veneer. She wondered if he would turn on the cartel given the chance and if so, how would that help her and Yousef?

Rameriz studied Sharon and then said, 'I am going to give you access to some of our security measures. I want you to monitor all our systems for anyone trying to hack in.'

'So now I am a white hat hacker working for a black hat hacker. Life is confusing sometimes,' she joked.

Rameriz sat next to her and gave her authorization to most but not all of their internal security measures. 'Let me know instantly if there is any intrusion.' He planned to penetrate their own computer system, posing as the UK government and see how Sharon handled the invasion. He would give her a couple of hours to settle in with her new task before testing her.


'I've studied this, Jake. At first I thought we could just install their hard drives and act like we are the cartel at the hacienda but it's far too dangerous,' said Misa. 'But using this new browser that they have, I think I can get into their system in London and monitor it.'

'Neat, I like it. Jas, come here. Show us how this hardened browser works. OK, I like it. Go talk to General Whitcuff and explain what you want to do. I think we had better clear this with him.' The general's adjutant nodded letting him know that was the right course to take. 'And tell him that his adjutant will be back with a report in a few minutes.'

Misa tapped on the partially open door and was motioned in by General Whitcuff. Both generals were talking on the phone. He pointed to a chair and Misa sat down. General Crystal was negotiating politics with the president's chief of staff and Whitcuff was talking to his son who was teaching at West Point. WillHwatched Misa as she sat down, thinking she was a bit of a strange sort of woman but with the thickest blond hair he had ever seen. He was not used to university types and this woman was obviously smart but seemed timid communicating. Maybe that was the norm for these ivory tower types. He was used to someone spitting out what they wanted when in his presence. This woman just looked straight into his eyes but said nothing.

'Do you have something for me, Miss…?'

'Misa is fine, General. Yes. I think I can safely get into the cartel's system in London and see what they are doing.'

'Probability of getting found out?'

'I think nil, General.'

It caught him off guard when she said 'I think,' he wanted certainty. 'Think you can or sure you can?'

Misa stared back and the general was about to tell her to spit it out when she said, 'I'm pretty certain.'

Now the general stared at her for a moment before saying, 'We can't risk alerting anyone without certainty.'

Misa pulled her hand through her hair and then touched her button nose. 'I can do it without getting caught.'

'You talk to the lieutenant?'

'Yes and he agrees but wanted to clear it with you first.'

'Get with it then and tell him to send my adjutant back in here with that report.' And then added, 'If you would, please.'

'Yes, I am supposed to tell you he will be done in a few minutes.'

Misa, who was strong willed and skilled, jumped when the general barked, 'Get with it,' and then couldn't help but like him for softening his tone. She respected the simple, straightforward attitudes she was seeing in the army personnel. She could handle what seemed to some the most complex computer problems but she found it difficult to deal with people and their infinite complexities.

She had never felt as though she belonged with any group of people. Things were different with Vidya. She thought they understood each other.

She smiled a genuine and rare smile. 'I'll do my best, sir.'

The jet's steward handed El Padrino a telephone. Guillermo took the handset wondering what little problem the head of the cartel was having now. The time was right for the cartel leader's departure—it was Guillermo's time to assume leadership in reality not just in principle. All of his listlessness disappeared at the thought of possessing absolute power over the cartel, retirement could wait a little longer. 'Yes,' he answered.

'Sir, this is Berto.'

Guillermo was puzzled. 'What is it, Berto?' he said irritably. He was not his usual suave self after having his pleasant thoughts of the future interrupted and he was not used to having a business manager call him directly.

There was a pause, which irritated Guillermo even more before Berto said, 'I have some disturbing news.'

'Yes, yes, get on with it.'

'Your hacienda has been destroyed.'

Guillermo sat straight in his chair. 'What? How?'

'I don't know, sir. I received a call from Major Guteriz, the police chief at Tubutama.'

'I know who he is; tell me what has happened.'

'I don't know, sir, just that there is no contact with anyone at the hacienda. A police car with four men went to investigate and they were killed. No one will go near now and Guteriz said there are no answers to his calls.'

'Tell Guteriz that I said he better get to the hacienda and give me some answers in one hour and then have him call me directly.' Guillermo threw the phone onto the floor. 'Get the captain back here now,' he commanded the steward.

'Change course to Hermosillo, Captain.'

'Anything new, Sam?' asked the US Army Chief of Staff.

'Nothing new on our end, sir.'

'State Department seems to believe your information. British authorities are fixing to crash the drug cartel's party. I have no idea what they plan. I'm out of the loop now. That is unless this proves to be wrong and then we both are going to be back in the loop in a hurry, as they will need someone to take the blame. Call with anything new then.'

'Roger that, Rufus.'

Sam Whitcuff studied his old friend Will for a moment. 'How'd you get so connected with the politicians? Our chief of staff is out of the loop now but it sounds like they believe the information you passed along. And it seems you are in the loop.'

'Long story, Sam, and sometimes not as good a place to be as it seems.'

After an hour, Guillermo, barely able to control his rage, called Berto. There had been no call from the police chief to either of them. Berto had no further information. Guillermo was used to getting what he wanted. 'I want information and fast, before we land—and get a dozen men to meet me at Hermosillo airport in thirty minutes. Don't alert the police but make sure that everyone is alert at the fort,' he snapped as he called his old Hermosillo headquarters. Guillermo preferred the hacienda but the security of the old fort offered safety. Who was attacking him and why? *I need information now,* he thought, slamming his first on the table, *but my primary people are gone. Dead?*

'Slow, slow,' said Guteriz to his driver. 'I don't like this,' he said as he crossed himself. 'There, the car we sent up earlier. Stop.' He turned to the man in back. 'Careful, go take a look.'

The GA watched calmly from the wall of the hacienda, as did Roberta. One man got out of the car and ran along the side of the road. He could take them out now, just as he had the others—easy shots at 700 meters. He decided to watch and wait. They would approach and they could not escape.

'I'll take them. Better they think any fire comes from the hacienda.'

'OK with me, I don't like shooting cops even if they are cartel cops,' said Roberta.

*Women,* thought the GA. She was every bit as good at her job as he, but their job wasn't to think or worry about details and these weren't really cops, just cartel dressed up as pretend keepers of the peace. They were just as bad as the cartel and, from their briefing, worse to the local population.

The young police officer waved at Guteriz's car to approach.

'Move up then,' ordered Guteriz. He turned to the two remaining men in the back. 'Get out, one of you on each side of the road. Watch the hacienda.'

'All dead,' said the young police officer, who wished he were somewhere else. 'It feels evil here, Captain.'

'They pay our salary and you do what you're told.' Guteriz looked at him. 'Move up the road toward the gate, you two do the same and stay to the side.'

He turned toward the car. The GA fired at the man on the left of the road first and immediately panned his scope to the car driver. Both were dead before Guteriz heard the shots. He turned back to the hacienda just as a bullet tore through his chest.

'Run, little rabbits,' mouthed the GA. He gave them a few seconds and carefully adjusted himself before killing the young policeman and then with lightning speed, moved his scope to the one remaining man and caressed his trigger. Five dead in less than ten seconds. Five less pretend cops to brutalize the community.

Najma heard the shots as she moved closer to the watcher, who remained on the ridge focusing on the hacienda in front of him. Suddenly he felt a small thump in his back, then a creeping pain in his rib cage. He didn't comprehend what was happening as all his senses were now focused on the pain coming from his back. He settled sideways as his grip weakened and his rifle stock pivoted down, suspended between the two tripod feet supporting the barrel. A faint shadow appeared. *Plato's cave.* His thoughts drifted. *Was this reality?* Shadows on his wall couldn't hurt him but the pain was real. Two soft red flashes penetrated his thoughts and ended his life just as he had ended so many before.

Najma studied the man and the gun. It was just luck that she had spotted him. Were there others? She scanned the other ridges and looked at the sniper rifle. If there were, she would die approaching the hacienda. But she had to; no one could keep her from her boy.

'In place at target one.'

'Go,' said the SAS major.

As the door blew into the hall, Ox turned, raised his pistol, and died from a quick burst by a black-clad special services soldier. Men quickly moved past Ox's body into Amir's house. Seconds later

Amir was lying, hands outstretched, on his bedroom floor.

The major motioned and his men rammed the door to the computer center and moved rapidly in and down the stairs. Felix had more warning than Ox. As soon as he heard the crash and footsteps, he jumped to the side and behind a computer desk. The lights went out and the computer screen darkened.

He was the only one to move in the computer room before the SAS rushed through the lower door. Felix the Rat swung his pistol around in the dim light and stared at Sharon not more than a few feet behind him. He grinned, raised his pistol, and shot Rameriz, then Alejandro, as was his duty, and through a hail of bullets, he managed to fire one last shot. A red ooze appeared in the center of Sharon's chest and she looked uncomprehendingly down at it before her arms dropped to her sides, her head lulled down, and she slipped to the floor. Felix should have done his duty and killed the cartel computer staff but when he realized he would soon die he decided to kill the punta that had implied he was not a real man.

'Medic.'

A two man team descended into the room and checked Sharon. 'Get her into the ambulance but I doubt they can sort her out.'

The Special Services quickly bundled the bodies into an unmarked truck and then drove off and disappeared. The streets at both the house and the internet café had been cordoned off. Plainclothes Special Service soldiers secured the buildings with uniformed officers at the ends of the blocked streets. Forensics teams were the first to enter the buildings after the Special Services.

The major in charge of the combined task force lit a cigarette and leaned against the internet café building, relaxed. He called his second in command at Amir's house. 'Send in the computer specialists when forensics is finished.'

A dazed Yousef along with the remaining cartel computer team were hustled into a black truck, which quickly disappeared, sirens wailing, past South Kensington in a convoy to an undisclosed location.

The Mexican president in his proclamation stated that his government had caused a serious blow to one of the most powerful cartels in Mexico. Their leader, Guillermo Vasquez, would soon be found and likewise punished for his crimes against Mexico. A bold statement that would never come to pass.

Will Crystal hung up the phone and looked at Sam. 'Looks like your retirement is secure and you'll go out with a medal.'

'Never doubted you for a minute.'

'The Brits captured the cartel's computer center and the house with little resistance. We already know what they will find. I doubt you will get much shut-eye as you'll be in front of a committee in Washington before the day is out.'

'And I was just starting to enjoy this,' lamented Sam. 'What'll happen to the cartel members?'

The Mexicans would be interrogated over several days. They would then be returned to Mexico by special extradition request of the president of Mexico. Their fate was to be publicly hanged as an example of what happened to transgressors in the Mexican government's war on drugs. Amir and Yousef became familiar faces on the newspaper covers as information leaked to Britain's tabloid press before their trial and finally imprisonment.

# Chapter 39

A ttention,' commanded Gordon as General Crystal walked into the control room.

'At ease. I'm going to be in and out so let's stay that way for the rest of the day. What's the situation at the hacienda?'

'Chinook's estimated time of arrival is three minutes,' said Captain Fuller.

The general looked at Heather and then Glenda Rose. 'They're both fine,' said Heather. 'They have been moving in and out of the buildings.'

'Two vehicles have approached and both have been neutralized,' added Captain Fuller. 'The big bird is landing now. It is going to take some work to get the Huey in a sling.'

'Why bother doing that?' asked Heather and then, 'What are they going to do with all the people from the hacienda?'

'Answer to your first question, we can't very well leave a US military helicopter there; and to your second, it will be up to the politicians to decide their fate. They are being separated and questioned. Part of Nielly's group is working with our Criminal Investigation Division, CID, to make certain that no cartel members slip through into the civilian group. I expect that the cartel members will be secretly returned to the Mexican military. As soon as we leave the hacienda, the president's special military units will arrive and no doubt send images of the dead cartel members to the press.'

'Your rules are a bit different from what I am used to, General,' said Glenda.

'Happens that way sometimes,' replied the general. 'The Mexican president will send an investigative group to the hacienda tomorrow after the military secures it. They will collect everything belonging to the cartel. They will be told it was a Mexican special military operation. Their presence should help deflect any thoughts of US involvement.'

The backup Huey arrived at the hacienda first and did a brief flight around the hacienda. 'No activity sighted.'

'We see no activity with the drone.'

'Big Bird Two, you are cleared to land inside the hacienda.'

The big Chinook landed next to the hacienda's gate. The men quickly set about preparing the Huey. It would take a while to load the pieces and secure it well enough for extraction by the Chinook. The mood was somber. The broken Huey was a symbol of death. Just metal, plastic, grease, and oil but in a sense it was a living thing a short time ago and now lifeless as were two of its inhabitants.

'How long will it take, Captain Fuller?' asked Glenda.

'Unknown with certainty but I was told less than an hour. After the Chinook starts back, the Huey picks up the two GAs and then the watcher on the ridge.'

'Captain Fuller, what happens to the people brought in from the hacienda? How do you really tell which ones are bad guys and which are just people caught there, needing work or maybe even enslaved?' asked Heather.

'I don't think any of us can answer that for sure,' said Nielly as he walked in the door. 'General, I have put together a list of everyone we brought back, with recommendations.'

'Let's talk in the conference room,' boomed the general as he walked off rapidly followed by Nielly.

'Well, he certainly got his voice back,' said Heather. *Soon, soon,* she thought, *he should be on his way back in one more hour.*

'Before we discuss the captives, Nielly, I want to congratulate you on a good mission. Things always go wrong, as you well know, but as far as I am concerned, your team's performance was outstanding.'

'Thanks, General, I appreciate that. I'm not so sure myself. We will have to do substantial review to see where things went wrong and what we could have or should have done differently. I hate losing anyone even though we all know it can happen every time we go out. Marilyn sends her regards as one chopper pilot to another. She said you were a damn good pilot.'

The general smiled. 'I'm glad she's survived.'

'She'll be out of action for some time; she may not even be able to return to our unit. I think that would hurt her more than anything.'

'First of all, we are missing all three of the people that were our primary mission targets. No one knows what happened to the DEA informant, Lola. It is hard to get much from anyone since they have no idea where they are or who we are. Two of the staff, though, said that Lola was taking care of a small child for Najma, if that makes any sense to you. Najma was apparently away as was the cartel lieutenant, Guillermo, who is actually running the cartel for the old leader. I am surmising that the old leader is the one in the safe room. He was confirmed at the hacienda but is unaccounted for. No one has any idea where Lola or Najma are now.'

'Strange turn of events. We set out to catch a terrorist and instead save the Brits from a financial disaster.'

'We did some real damage to the largest cartel in Mexico.'

The general didn't want to tell Nielly after his losses that yes, they had hurt the cartel but it would just be one unremembered battle in a larger fight. 'Give me your recommendations.'

'I've put everyone into groups. The larger group, A, are either cartel or supporters. None of them have any idea where they are or who took them. Here are two names of cartel members I think we should interrogate further as they look likely to cooperate and maybe provide us with some information. The rest I would give to the Mexican government straightaway and get them out of our hair, as we discussed before the mission.

'Group B are the civilians I am reasonably certain are just locals employed by the cartel. They don't know they are on US soil. I suggest you pull a ruse by offering to bring them to the US; drive them or fly them around, and then give them asylum.

'The last group of six women and two men are a tougher choice. We put a lot of questions to them and all eight, I believe, would want to stay in the US but all have some allegiance to the cartel. If they go home, the cartel will find them and not ask questions as nicely as we did. The missing boy I mentioned may be the sole survivor of the family massacre in Tubutama. Sheilla and her analysts have been helping with this and helping to profile them. Sheilla is convinced that the boy survived and watched his family be killed by our nasty lady.

'Well done, Nielly.'

'I wish I could agree it was well done, General.'

'It's never easy but pushing won't bring your men back. Your people have been non-stop since I brought you out here. Might as well get them some stand-down time. I want status reports on your injured. You tell Marilyn to get well and that's an order. I'd like nothing better than to go flying with her again.'

'We are going to start loading up. It looks like the rest of my group will be here in about an hour. They report no problems. We'll get some sleep after our gear is taken care of, stay here for the night, and head back to our home base tomorrow for some rest and relaxation.'

'I'll be staying here,' said Will Crystal, 'until this thing winds down and that might be a while as we fill Washington in. Lots of paperwork and if there is anything good about being a general it is that I don't have to write it, just approve it. Dinner later with you, Jim, Brush, Glenda, Heather, and Whitcuff, what do you say?'

'If I can keep my eyes open, it's a date.'

'Attention.'

'At ease. I thought I told you to knock it off for the rest of the day, Specialist Gordon.'

'Sorry, sir.'

The general turned to the Wolf Pack. 'Your work proved to be of high value. Well done. Your base commander and some of the higher-ups have learned just how valuable technology will be to the army. The cartel bank heist is history, thanks to you.'

'What happened with it?' asked Jake.

'The Brits have several special operations groups and they apparently have all members of the cartel and some others in custody. They are quite happy and that means that our higher-ups are happy, so all is well. It's their problem now and the last we and probably anyone else will hear about it. The Brits may want to discuss the computer issues with you. They were especially interested in talking to Misa, as they know something about her history at Oxford. Misa, you'll need approval about what you can discuss and the State Department will want someone present. How long do you need to finish up finding out all you can from this?'

'Could be a while, General,' answered Jake.

'Define "a while" for me, Lieutenant.'

Jake looked around and offered, 'A week maybe.'

'It's impossible to say accurately,' said Misa.

'I'll talk to General Whitcuff, but I am sure he will want you working on this for as long as it is productive.' He looked at Misa and then the Malaysian, Vidya. 'I'm pleased you two volunteered to stay and work on this. Will you stay until it is finished?'

They both spoke at the same time. 'Yes, we will, glad we could help. It's been a blast.' And Misa winked at Vidya.

'Get a report to Captain Fuller every six hours,' said Will Crystal. 'This turned out very well.' And he walked to the ops room wondering how old Misa was. She wasn't that much younger, maybe late thirties to his fifty-four years. To his eye, very intelligent and attractive. It was not something that he gave much thought to. He had always thought his job and a relationship were incompatible. He dismissed it from his mind. When was the last time he had even had time to think about a woman? *Well not that long ago, Shiella too. Starting to think about women, maybe I am ready to retire*, he thought.

Just as he was about to enter the operations room, the door burst open and Captain Fuller almost knocked him over. 'What's the big rush, Captain?' he boomed.

'We got a situation, I was just coming to advise you, sir.'

# Chapter 40

This will be my headquarters now. They attacked my hacienda, it may happen here. Be ready,' said Guillermo.

'Sí, señor.'

'I want the office staff here in thirty minutes.'

'They are arriving now.'

'I want you back here in twenty minutes.'

'Sí, Sí.' His second in command, *Temporary second*, he thought, ran off.

Was this what he was left with, second line leaders? Raul would have been useful. But the devil-woman might still be alive and in many ways she was better than Raul, at least smarter but she did not understand Mexicans. The men feared her, he was certain, but that in itself did not make her an effective lieutenant for him. He had plenty of men to draw on. He would quickly start to assemble them and begin building what he had so painstakingly built before. *I will get what I want and I will make those people who have harmed me pay*, he thought.

Four people sat in Guillermo's office. 'Get my daughter on the phone first, and then Guteriz in Tubutama. Mercedes, stay here with me. Manuel, I repeat, make sure that this place is protected. Start bringing in as many people as needed and get Cortez here by tonight. Report back to me in one hour.'

'*Hijo de la chingada. Guillermo is going to replace me. I could be his lieutenant here. Why replace me? Worse,* Manuel thought. *Cortez does not like me and I don't like him, a real asshole.*

'Now, Mercedes. You will work here with me and act as my personal assistant. Speak only English.'

'Yes, Mr. Vasquez.'

'We are going to be using the telephone a lot and I want you to answer all calls using our company name.' Just as he said it, one of the three phones started to ring. Mercedes immediately picked it up.

'Euro Americana,' she said pleasantly.

Next, Mercedes placed a call to Guillermo's daughter, Mary. Her eyes widened for a second and she pushed the hold button. 'A man is answering for your daughter,' she told Guillermo. He grabbed the phone from her.

'Who is this? Where is my daughter? And what is your business answering?'

'My business, Mr. Vasquez, is making sure people like you do not get to enjoy the benefits of British hospitality,' said a smooth English voice.

'I wish to speak to my daughter.'

Mary came to the phone, sounding confused and upset but not frightened. 'Papa, what is going on? They expelled me from school and said you were a criminal and I was a bad influence and could not stay here. Can't you fix it so I can stay with my friends?'

The man's voice replaced hers. 'Now that you have talked to her, I will answer for her. She will be placed on a plane to Mexico tomorrow after she answers some questions. She has indeed been expelled from the ladies' college and neither of you will be allowed to enter the United Kingdom again unless, that is, we are successful in extraditing you, which I assure you, we will be.'

'Who is this?'

'It is not important who I am, just provide me with your contact details so we can advise you of when she will arrive. Your other employees here will be subject to further questions and will not be leaving this country for some time.'

Guillermo was stunned. He put down the phone and turned to Mercedes. 'Get me these people on the line in this order. First, Sir Peter Brandt,' and he proceeded to give her a number of English government contacts and others in and out of Mexico.

Guillermo realized that he was probably the cartel's official leader now. His old boss was probably dead. But what was he the leader of? If the hacienda was gone along with his some of his strongest people, and his computer groups in both Mexico and London were gone too, he would be very much poorer than he was just hours ago. Would the Cubans abandon him?

'Get someone to get Ortega in Cuba on the line in one hour. I will have to inform him of the change but I need information first.' *I need it now,* he said hissing in his mind. *My power is diminished and I can't get it back without knowledge.*

'Sir Peter Brandt is not available,' said Mercedes after a few minutes. 'I have not been able to get the others you gave me either. They are all out.'

Guillermo realized that his contacts would not talk to him. Astonishment was changing to anger with each passing minute. His world had changed. At first he thought he could resolve the issue with Mary's school. If his life had changed then so would that of those who caused him this humiliation. He had fought many battles and his old determination took hold. He would regroup; consolidate his power so that no one would deny him or his daughter their rightful places in society.

He must switch priorities and accept his new circumstances. His hacienda and London group had vanished. 'Mercedes, I want you to stop everything to do with England and start to contact all of our people in and out of the Mexican government. I want information about the hacienda. Get me Floriano first.'

Differing from the United Kingdom, everyone was available to him or his staff in Mexico. But not one person had any idea concerning the attack. General Floriana was at the top and it was impossible to think that he would not know of a military action. Guillermo decided his immediate priority was defensive. *I must first consolidate my organization, protect it, and then make money to regain power,* he said to himself.

# Chapter 41

The big Chinook raised the damaged Huey into the air and lumbered north toward the border. The backup Huey loaded the GA at the hacienda and the two that had remained on the ground to secure the cables to the Chinook. It made a swooping turn back to its right toward the small rise down the road where the penultimate GA, Roberta, guarded their exit, and then headed for the watcher who had been on the ridge for over two days now.

'We've lost contact with him, so stay on the alert as we near his position,' radioed Nielly from base. The chopper stayed low and south of the ridge and then circled behind it and climbed. There was no movement, no signal, no communication.

'Doesn't feel right. We lose radio frequently but he knows he is the last out and would have signaled another way if his com failed,' said Roberta.

'Put us down behind that rise to the east,' said the other GA. 'Roberta, you're out there and then take me over to the higher point north and east. We'll set up again with two of us to cover you two while you check this out.'

The chopper settled just out of sight of the ridge. Roberta moved quickly to the top of the rise and surveyed the area. The two Special Forces men jumped out and split up toward opposite sides of the ridge but stopped just short of exposing themselves. The chopper moved off north and dropped the second GA.

'Go.'

The two men moved rapidly toward the ridge using ground cover. 'No movement,' reported both GAs. The two men closed to within thirty meters. One took a covering position and the other, a corporal, the newest and lowest ranking man in the unit, moved to within ten meters and stopped. They continued until both converged on the position.

'Shit,' said the corporal.

'What?' said Nielly.

'He's dead, no one in sight.'

Nielly was taken aback. *Who could have gotten to his GA and who in the hell could penetrate his defenses?* 'Tell me what you see. Anything that might tell us who got to him. And for Christ's sake be careful. Make sure someone didn't booby-trap him or his position.

The GA in charge, George, said to the pilot, 'Evac them when they're ready and then extract us, starting with me first and Roberta last.' There was no need to tell anyone to be watchful. They had lost one of the founding members of their team.

The chopper hovered low at the top of the ridge and the two SF men slung their team member in and then his equipment. The chopper banked left and picked up the GA in charge and then Roberta. It had been six years since they had lost a guardian angel.

The corporal said in a subdued voice, 'Watcher was shot with small-gauge weapon. No evidence other than small footprints.'

The men in the Chinook were clearly upset. No one had heard anything. 'Could only mean one thing,' said Brush just as the general called saying, 'We have to get both choppers over the line in twenty minutes max.'

'We'll advise,' said Jim.

'What d'ya think, partner? Our lady is still there it seems,' asked Brush.

'The SF can't stay on this side of the border. Guess that leaves us. Let's go flying.'

It took Brush a second to understand what Jim had in mind. 'Interesting idea. It's never dull for us, is it?'

'Turn the Chinook back to just north of the border and take us to twenty-six thousand,' ordered Jim. The SF all looked at him wondering what would come next.

'Think that will get us there? Our paragliders have a better range.'

'Glide ratio is over seven to one. Close at least,' said Jim with a small grin.

'Just great,' mumbled Heather back in the control room.

'Move to these coordinates,' said Brad, who was not only the drone controller but also quick at math. He rapidly calculated the distance and glide angle. 'That will give you the exit coordinates with the shortest distance.'

'Let's get to work,' said Brush as he moved to the containers holding the new super-gliders that Nielly had shown them.

'Which do you want, Brush?'

'I said I wanted to be Batman, remember? You get the super-glider. Have to find a parachute for you though. They're bound to have some on board.'

'Sorry, sir, not a one on board; makes me feel sorta helpless up here, too.'

'Well, I want to get down fast anyway so I think I'll just have to see how it lands,' said Jim as he opened the crate that housed the bobsled-like glider. 'I have to admit it is a pretty looking piece of engineering.'

Brush wasn't about to remind Jim that a gliding landing was still in trial.

As if reading his mind, Jim said, 'Gliding is one thing, Brush, but flying the Batman outfit could get a guy in a lot of trouble.'

'Nielly said he flew it. If he did, I can.'

'I think Nielly meant he flew it after reading the manual.'

'There's probably some instruction in the box, I'll read it on the way.'

'You idiot, you know we can still hear you,' said Glenda. 'What are you doing?'

'Hey, sweetie, I thought you were supposed to listen and not talk to us.'

Brush was getting all kinds of looks from the men in the Chinook. He ignored them and, secretly pleased, continued to talk to Glenda.

'Not doing much now but I was thinking about a nice quiet dinner later—you up for that?'

'OK, I see what you are up to. How are you planning to get to that dinner?' asked General Crystal.

'Think we're going to need a ride, maybe you can arrange for one where those ironwood collectors started from?' said Jim. 'We still have eyes up?'

'Yes,' blurted out Brad. He was feeling left out as his drone so far had spotted nothing useful. Maybe that would change.

'We need to get a good look at our destination. Can you do that?'

Brad looked at General Crystal. 'It means going over the border again, sir.'

'Get a move on it. They need info,' said General Crystal.

Brad looked pleased. Glenda and Heather, however, looked anything but pleased. 'You get back here, mister, or we're kaput,' said Glenda.

'Guess we've got a date later, then,' Brush said as he smiled at the men around him.

'Brush, I can see you grinning. I'm not kidding.'

'We'll both be there,' added Jim.

'I know you will,' was all Heather could say, but she felt anything but certain that he would be. She felt sick and all her fears and experiences of the last few days knotted her stomach so tight she started to feel nauseous and light-headed.

# Chapter 42

Y ou've got a lot of balls, Major, jumping out in that thing.'

'I seem to recall Nielly saying it was a piece of cake.'

The three Special Forces men helping him into the black-winged apparatus just looked at each other.

'This is how you ignite the mini turbo jets. And try not to run into anything hard on the way down. The carbon fiber is light but a little brittle.'

'How come no parachutes on board?' asked Brush.

'They're on the other Chinook. Let's send an image of "Batman Resurrected," ' said the sergeant. 'Give us a grin.' Brush did and the operation center broke out into a yelling frenzy, which caused the four computer compatriots to leave their den and rush in. All that is, except Glenda Rose who understood now that she loved this guy, respected him, but was going to make sure that his 'Batman Days' ended today. Dangerous activities were one thing but stunts were another. This was crazy. They could have flown back in the Chinook and within an hour been up in the air with Ram parachutes. 'Damn him anyway,' she mused when she realized there was no way she wanted to change this man, her man.

'Only slightly nose up and wings absolutely level if you're going to try to land that thing,' said Nielly over the com. 'Sticking a wing in or hitting the tail first will send it tumbling.'

'He's right, Major. That's what happened to our last one. This one hasn't been flown yet and has a few engineering modifications from the last one, which means it might be better than before—or maybe not. Good luck.'

Four men picked up Brush, ensconced in his rigid black outfit, and held him near the edge of the ramp. Two others moved the bobsled-glider onto a specially made launch cradle.

'Give us the word when you want to go. You will both be about the same speed and that's fast, not like freefall, less resistance to slow you down.'

'Ready when you are, buddy.'

'No better time,' said Jim. 'Let's do it, Go.' Brush was moved to the very edge then gently tossed out facedown. Just after, Jim's glider was nudged off its cradle into the clear, high-pressure haze of the November predawn morning.

'Does Batman yell anything like Hi Ho Away?' asked Brush as though he was sitting at a Starbucks chatting instead of racing across the sky toward the hacienda.

'Sounds more like the Lone Ranger,' replied Jim.

'What's their plan, Will?' asked General Whitcuff as he walked in and, for the first time, no one even noticed him. Everyone was still mesmerized by the tiny disappearing specks as they crossed back into Mexico for the third time in as many days and disappeared south.

'No plan, just get Najma,' replied Will. 'Specialist, you see anything with the drone?'

'Nothing yet, sir. Its ETA at the hacienda is five minutes.'

General Whitcuff arched an eyebrow at Will Crystal. 'DEA is back on the border and in the sky, so they might detect the drone.'

'It will be the way of the future, Sam. No personnel means we haven't technically violated their airspace.'

'Unless it crashes. In that case it will have US Army written all over it.'

'I'll get it back in one piece, sir,' said Brad.

'Hacienda is in sight.'

'Keep it high and wide at first,' said Captain Fuller, who was standing over Brad, watching the video images sent by the drone.

Brad toggled his joysticks and climbed his drone to three thousand feet above the hacienda and three-quarters of a mile away. 'It should be impossible to spot at that distance. When you say the word, I'll bring it in closer from the east side where the watcher was.'

Everyone became silent. Sadness for the watcher they had grown accustomed to talking to on the ridge and a state of anxiety replaced their earlier exuberance following Jim and Brush's departure.


Najma had looked for a radio on the dead man but found nothing except lots of electronic devices she had not seen before. A well-worn but spotless sniper rifle that had been fired recently lay by the dead man. There was no indication of his nationality but his equipment was sophisticated. *Must be American. Associates of the agent? Yes*, she thought. *There will be others.* She scanned in all directions. *If there are more, I will be an easy target.* After several minutes she decided that she had no other choice and with the field of view that this sniper had had, there was no need for others on this side of the hacienda. *Yes, others will be in front but not here.*

She worked her way closer to the hacienda and saw no one else and then she was at the southeast tunnel entrance. Still there was no one in sight as she started to work her way through the long hall. Suddenly, she stopped as she heard the thudding of helicopter blades. She quickly turned back to the entrance and peered out. The helicopter was in the hacienda but she couldn't see it. She needed to be somewhere higher and inside.

'You're just a tiny speck,' said Brush.

'Best to keep it that way. You were zigging back and forth and my little sleigh doesn't have a seat belt if you bump into me.'

'Well, I was just testing it out,' said Brush a little defensively. 'It's kinda sensitive. Will be interesting to see how it slows down to land when we get there.'

'I thought I better watch this,' said Nielly as he walked in.

Heather looked at him with a questioning face.

'They're both good pilots and survivors. They'll be fine.' He sounded more confident than he was. The Batman and the super-gliders had only been test-landed on big grassy fields with medical help standing by. The glider that Jim was flying was very stable in the air but had broken apart on its first landing. This would be the first field test of the newest model.

'Objective in sight,' said Jim. 'Anything from the flyover?'

'Completely still and quiet. We are going to fly over one more time and head west to take a look at the road and then we have to bring it back as it is getting low on fuel,' said Brad, a little disappointed that the drone had seen nothing useful.

'Catch up with you later, buddy,' said Brush veering to the southeast. Jim had to have the smoothest place to land and the only option was the long drive at the front of the hacienda. Brush would try to slow himself down with the mini thrusters and land as close to the tunnels as he could.

Lola listened at the door to their small room. It seemed as though time was moving so slowly. She heard no noises from the hall. She peeked out the door and still could not hear anything and there was no one in sight. 'Pedro, be very, very quiet and follow me. Can you do that?'

'Sí, señora.' He looked one last time at the spot where the gecko had disappeared. It must be safe in its home.

Lola peeked out the door again, ready to leave, when she thought she heard a noise like a shoe scuffing the concrete floor. *My imagination? We must get to the outside.* And then a wave of fear took hold of her and she felt as though her breath was being squeezed from her body. She was trembling so much she had to use two hands to steady herself so she could close the door soundlessly, but still it made a small clink as she pulled it.

In the faint emergency lighting she had seen the she-devil; Najma was slowly moving toward them.

Najma stopped, listened, motionless and then moved on down the hall.

'Madre Dios, Silencio, miho,' Lola whispered as she trembled uncontrollably. Pedro looked at her, reached up, and took hold of her hand. There was no other sound; she waited, feeling exhausted but there was nothing. The evil woman had passed. *What should we do?* As she tried hopelessly to control her fear, the small room suddenly felt like a prison. They must go. They couldn't stay. Here they would die. The hacienda was death. The desert, as harsh as it could be, was life.

Jim slowly raised a lever that controlled the flaps on the glider. It started to jump around and he pushed them in slightly. The ground started to rush by as he got closer. He was lined up on the road and, unlike a plane, he had to point the nose down at the dirt road. He couldn't slow it down and lose altitude by pulling back the power like he was used to with planes. Just above the gravel drive, he leveled out and tried the flap lever again. The glider hit the air cushion between it and the ground and floated up. He was nearing the hacienda and he still felt like he was in a rocket.

He skimmed over the two vehicles and the bodies of Guteriz and the other policemen. He tried raising the nose and adding more flaps. It swerved and jumped but was slowing a little. He had to get it down on the drive before he ran out of space.

Brush stood looking at the broken remains of what had been his carbon fiber winged glider. 'Maybe better luck next time,' he mused out loud. 'Maybe I should have flattened myself out more to my direction of flight before igniting the thrusters.'

It was one of Heather's and the sergeants' ironwood trees that eventually stopped him. He had come in far too fast. Clichés popped into his thoughts. *Live and learn. All's well that ends well.*

'Brush, Brush,' said Glenda shaking her head from side to side as they heard him speak at the operations center. Nielly made a fist to the ceiling and said, 'Yes.' Brad and Captain Fuller did a knuckle touch. A whoop could be heard from Sheilla's group at Fort Lewis.

The glider touched the ground, bounced, started sliding sideways on the road, caught one of the razor wings, and began spinning as it slid off the road and into a small ditch coming to an abrupt stop.

'You ready, partner?' said Jim.

'As ever, ready when you are, pal.' The operations center staff erupted yet again, all yelled and jumped up from their chairs slapping shoulders and Heather gave Nielly a kiss on the cheek and then looked at Sam Whitcuff and did the same. Misa gave General Crystal a short peck on the cheek and then gave Vidya a long, tight hug. They looked at each other and he lightly kissed her on the lips.

'I'm starting to feel sorry about retiring from this new army,' said Sam.

Lola held her breath and cracked the door ever so slightly. She neither heard nor saw anything. She opened it a little farther and peered back down to where Najma had been. She was gone, but there was a slight bulge near the left side wall. She stared at it. It was stationary. 'Nos vamanos, Pedro,' and she held her finger to her lips and slowly opened the door.

'Want to change the plan, partner?'

'Nope. I'll check out the courtyard and the gate wall while you work your way through the tunnel,' said Jim.

Neither had to tell the other to be careful. But in the TOC Heather softly whispered for them to be.

'Sounds like we have a plan after all, eh.'

# Chapter 43

Najma stopped behind a support post along the left tunnel wall. She waited patiently, listening. She was a stalker and could sit waiting for hours if need be. However, she neither sensed nor heard anything. She silently moved into the tunnel and ghost-like moved toward the hacienda. As she passed a door on her right, her sensitive nostrils smelled something. She couldn't place it and stopped; a cleaning agent. She moved on and stopped again, listening. Nothing.

The hacienda seemed completely deserted but she continued to move cautiously. She emerged into an empty room. There was an electronic card swipe alongside a lone door but fortunately, the door stood open. The next room looked like a room used by cartel guards. The furniture was tipped and broken, and the damp bloodstains on the floor and chunks of adobe missing told her there had been a recent battle. She sniffed and the smell of death filled the air. Still no sign of anyone but she knew that there were bodies close.

Pedro was gone, she was certain but she still had a need to get to her rooms and that of the Mexican woman watching him and see for herself. She emerged into the courtyard and saw further evidence of the recent battle. Bodies were scattered and slumped. At the entrance to her room, the emptiness angered her. She slammed the door and walked out toward El Padrino's house. Pedro should be here. They should be together. She should be holding him and wanted him in her arms right now. 'Fucking people, no one has the right to take my son,' she cursed and stormed toward Guillermo's house.

Nothing seemed disturbed. She wandered around for a few seconds and then she saw a cell phone lying on the floor next to a wall. It was not a booby trap, the location was too obscure. Nevertheless, she slid a book across the floor. It moved and nothing happened. She stooped and picked it up looking at it from all sides and then tossed it onto a sofa. Still nothing. She retrieved it and opened the lid, pushed a key, and it came on. She quickly looked in the contact list and saw a G—must be Guillermo, and she pushed call.

'Euro Americana,' answered Mercedes pleasantly.

'I want to speak to Guillermo.'

'Whom shall I say is calling?'

'Just get him on the phone, now—tell him I am at the hacienda.'

'Sirs,' said Marcus Gordon as he pulled a headset off and turned toward the generals. 'I just intercepted a cell phone conversation with a woman saying she is at the hacienda.'

General Crystal immediately walked to a computer station and flicked the mic on. 'Female at your location using a cell phone.'

'Roger that. If I ever tell you I want to go bobsledding again, I hope you will teach me some wisdom,' said Jim as he stood up shaking off dust before extracting several cactus thorns from his calf and attempting to push his throbbing side to the back of his mind.

'Glad you're alive, try to stay that way,' said Will Crystal as he smiled at Heather.

'I thought you had the easy one, partner,' said Brush. He approached the tunnel and then crouched down behind a small mound of sandy gravel.

Jim was already running toward the hacienda gate. He stopped at one hundred meters, surveyed it carefully, and saw no sign of anyone. But then he wouldn't see her, would he? She was a huntress; she would lay in wait for her prey, then carefully stalk it.

'What has happened?' commanded Guillermo.

'I've seen no one alive. There's been a fight—several bodies.'

'I sent men. Any sign of cars or anyone out on the entry road?'

'I have seen no one. I will look and call back.'

'Where are you now?'

'I am in your house; that is where I found the cell phone.'

'Go to the large bedroom. There is a catch on the side of the left nightstand. Release it.'

She walked into the bedroom. 'No need, it is open.'

'Go down the steps and see if the safe room is closed.'

'It is and looks as though it has been fused.'

Guillermo reasoned that the old man had sealed himself in. 'Go back up and close the latch of the nightstand. I'm going to send more men. Watch for them and do not mention the nightstand,' said Guillermo.

*A panic room with someone inside he does not want to let out,* reasoned Najma, filing the information away for future use.

'I will go outside and call you back.' Najma walked outside and looked down the drive. She saw a man running toward the hacienda and jumped out of sight, running immediately up the steps to the wall next to the gate. When she peered out of the guardhouse, the man had disappeared. She stayed still and watched. He was there and would move soon enough. Minutes later the man ran to his left and toward the side of the gate that would put him below where she was. He was cautious but not timid, she thought. *The agent? But if he were responsible for what happened at the hacienda why would he approach from the road? He would know it was deserted.* She could think of no explanation. *Probably not him; one of Guillermo's men. The man was cautious. Too cautious.* She watched and waited. Time had no meaning for her as she waited. A huntress remains still, waiting to ambush.

Brush carefully approached the tunnel and peered around the corner. He moved his foot, heard a crunch, and looked down to see a beetle. He had inadvertently stepped on it. Just a few feet ahead was another crushed beetle, still wet from where someone had recently stepped on it. She had come this way after she killed the watcher. Najma.

'At the tunnel entrance and she has been this way,' said Brush quietly to Jim.

'Outside the entrance, will sit tight until you get aboveground.'

Heather whispered, 'Careful.' *Careful, Jim, careful, please be careful, she's a killer,* she kept saying to herself as if willing Jim to hear. Sheilla gripped the arms of her chair at the BWL as she listened, straining as if she could hear better leaning forward and still. The Fort Huachuca operations center all sat motionless watching empty screens and listening to the silence that followed Jim's last words. With only audio, their sense of reality changed. *Blind but not deaf,* thought Sheilla.

# Chapter 44

What's that?' Nielly pointed at the drone video he was watching. 'It looks like a plane.' Brad flew the drone south. 'Take it in a little lower,' ordered Nielly. 'I don't want to risk someone hearing or seeing us on the ground.'

'Not a problem,' said Brad as he zoomed in on the plane.

'That's good,' said Nielly. 'This is useful. You know your stuff.'

Brad tried to keep from smiling. His first real mission. At that exact moment, he fell in love with his drones.

'There's a body lying outside,' said Nielly.

'On the pilot side with the door open,' added General Crystal, as General Whitcuff, Fuller, and Nielly hovered over Brad.

'A Cessna 206,' noted Will Crystal. 'Probably how our lady ended up in the area. Leaves bodies wherever she goes. Send the tail number up to Sheilla and see if we can find out who owns it. Even though it probably won't help us much.'

'General, what if they need help?' asked Nielly. 'What do you want me to do?' he added softly, watching Heather and Glenda to make sure they did not hear him.

'As usual, just like other wars, we do it and face up to it after. Stand by at the airport. If you're needed, I'll let you know and you can get airborne, but stay on this side of the border until I tell you to cross. Who's meeting them at the rendezvous in Mexico?'

'The two sergeants are on their way back now. They took Sergeant Hernandez's personal 4x4. Left about an hour ago,' said Nielly as he turned toward the door.

'There's a small plane wreck and body about seven klicks southwest,' said Will into the mic. 'Makes sense. Our friend came up behind the ridge and is probably somewhere near you now.' He wanted to add 'Be careful' but he didn't want to insult them by saying the obvious.

'Entering the tunnel,' whispered Brush. 'Keep your...' He went silent and listened. 'Someone approaching.'

Lola and Pedro were walking toward freedom. The bulge on the wall that had scared her proved to be nothing. Her heart was still beating fast. She didn't know what had happened to Manuel. He had really been her friend after all. He had hidden them and not said anything. Had the cartel taken him? *I hope he wasn't hurt for helping us,* she said to herself. They could see a faint glow ahead. The first glimmers of dawn were lighting the eastern horizon. Why were there no guards? The stillness made her afraid. Pedro said nothing and walked holding her hand tightly.

They stopped and looked out the open door. Were there men outside? 'Stay still, little one. Do not move.' She walked slowly toward the tunnel entrance and looked outside at the dim warm glow illuminating the red desert soil. She saw no one and timidly started to walk out and then changed her mind and moved back to Pedro. There was a door next him. It was a guard station that Manuel had told her about. She peeked inside. No one. 'You stay here, little one, and be very quiet while I look outside.'

Brush waited. Najma moved like a cat but this was not her. The feet shuffled so he could not tell for sure, but it might even be two people. It must be someone who had eluded them earlier. He lowered himself to the ground and looked around the corner; a short woman in a skirt disappeared through a door. He could see no one else. He moved to the door. He listened and thought he heard a woman speaking in Spanish. He opened the door. The woman turned fearfully toward him. She was unarmed.

'Commo se llama, señora?'

'Mona, señor,' she said her voice barely audible. She did not know why she gave a false name. It had just come out that way.

The DEA contact—but the name was not right. 'Do not be afraid. Where did you come from?' Then Brush saw a small shoe just behind her long dress. He motioned for her to move.

She reached around behind her and half tugged and half coaxed a small boy into view. 'Tell him your name, niño.'

'Pedro, señor.'

She used 'niño,' suggesting he was her son but the DEA informer did not have a son except for the one killed by the cartel, according to what General Crystal had been able to learn from his DEA contact. It didn't make any real difference. 'Your name is Mona or is it something else?'

She looked at the floor and whispered, 'Lola, Señor. Lo Siento. I am sorry. I was afraid.'

'You're safe now. I will call and let the others know we have found you.

'Jim, looks like our DEA insider and she has a small boy with her,' said Brush.

'Good, you found her. Hum, the safest place for her and the boy would be in the desert, hidden, or in a room in the tunnel but I think you have to keep her with you. Bring them through the tunnel and find a place where they can hide until we locate our lady. I have a feeling she is close and it's hard for me to get inside until you get here to cover my approach,' said Jim.

'Or she finds us,' added Brush. 'Lola, Pedro, will you please come with me.' Brush squeezed his shoulder and gently scooped up Pedro. They walked back through the tunnel with Brush trying not to show that he was on alert, looking for Najma. As they neared its end, Brush found a room just before the stairs. The farther he took them the more dangerous it would be and above the stairs there would be bodies. Here was as good a place as any. 'I'm leaving them in a room at the end of the tunnel. I don't know enough Spanish to tell them to stay.'

'Give her your earpiece,' said Jim. He told her they would take good care of her and the boy and for them to do as Brush said. Lola nodded several times, passed back his earpiece, and smiled.

'I'm out and looking over the courtyard,' said Brush. 'Our lady is here somewhere. I think I should sit tight. I've got good position and about the only way she could be watching is from the wall.'

'Moving toward the gate,' responded Jim.

Najma, the huntress, was pleased. The American didn't know she was there watching him. *The advantage is mine.* She watched her prey or at least the position where he last was. *He is smart.*

*He is watching and will move in slowly*. She would wait until he passed through the gate and kill him at close range. *There is no cover inside the gate and he will be exposed to me. He will know it is me that has beaten him.*

Jim moved forward to a new position and scanned the hacienda, especially the wall. He was most vulnerable to anyone above him. He moved to his left and decided to keep moving sideways and north, and then move in tight against the wall and back toward the gate. Najma watched him move.

'No sign of her yet, buddy,' said Brush.

'I'm alongside the wall and moving toward the gate.' Then he stopped, ducked, and turned back to the west. He heard a distant noise and saw a dust plume far down the entry road. 'Company on the way, driving up the road. I'll have to move inside.'

Najma couldn't see Jim but she could see approaching vehicles. She adjusted her position slightly so she could see the inside of the gate.

Brush caught the motion. She had barely moved and he would not have seen her except that he happened to be watching the exact spot where she was hiding. 'I got her. She's above the entry gate on your side next to the watch bunker. I don't have a good shot.'

'I can't stay out. I'll have to move in.' Jim left his cover and sprinted to the wall next to the gate. 'Distract her and I'll move in and below her...now.'

Brush immediately fired one carefully aimed shot. He saw her turn and then fired a short burst at her position, waited a second and fired another. Jim appeared inside and below her. As bullets and adobe erupted around him, he caught a slight movement down the wall to his right. Najma had managed to shift her position using a short inside wall for cover. Brush returned fire and then said, 'You can move to the other side of the gate but you will be exposed in the courtyard if you try to come in. Move as soon as I fire.'

'Company is three trucks approaching fast, thirty seconds at most,' said Jim as he bolted straight in. He would be exposed to Najma but did not want the approaching vehicles to see him. 'Coming straight at you.'

More flying adobe erupted around Brush and this time from thirty feet farther down the wall.

Najma wanted to make it look like her direction was north along the wall and then she would double back. It worked— Brush was watching for her to reappear in the direction she had been heading. Now she was back near her original position. The man from outside, the American agent, was running directly below her, exposed in the courtyard. She caressed the trigger and held him in the sight for a fraction of second before lightly squeezing her killing round.

As Jim ran, he remembered his last encounter with Najma, and how she had doubled back and taken up the attack. He could feel her eyes on him now. It wasn't second sight but cold reason. He knew he had run straight as far as he could. An instinct, a guess—he abruptly dodged to his right, faked switching back, and went farther to his right as her bullets tracked his every move.

He moved back toward an open door. As if an illusion, Pedro appeared framed by the doorway. How did the child get there? He had to distract Najma from the boy. She would kill him. He saw Pedro's face and instantly two young girls' faces replaced the boy's. His mind reeled back to Vietnam. The girls died for the thousandth time with their mother as he relived the decision that had plagued him since. The flashback seemed to last an eternity but in reality only an instant. He had to save the boy.

In amazement, he heard a long eerie wail from the wall and then, 'Run to me. I am your mother now. Run, I will protect you.' *Could she be saying that to the boy?* But the boy didn't move.

He was several feet away from the door when Brush fired again at Najma. Jim lunged toward the side of the building. Then the red dust on the paving stones rose to meet his face and his world turned to blackness.

A small gecko scurried down the wall next to Najma. She saw red blood mixed with red soil. She moved her eyes from her kill to the movement of the green gecko and back again to the American. For a second she admired the color red—Jim's blood and the iron rich soil on the paving stones as they mixed, then she watched the same red fluid draining from her onto the stone wall at her feet, as her world too, turned to blackness.

Brush saw blood spray into the lightening sky and splatter onto the wall behind Najma. 'About time for her. Let's get a move on, company just drove in,' said Brush as three trucks filled with Guillermo's men skidded into the compound.

There was no answer. Brush looked to his left and saw only a trickle of blood running across the red soil from Jim's head. 'Shit,' he muttered, as he ran the few feet along the front of the building.

In the operations room, everyone shared a moment of accomplishment as they assumed that Brush had killed Najma. Then there was complete silence after Jim failed to respond and

Brush's exclamation.

'Oh, no.' Heather covered her mouth with her hand and gaped at the blank screen.

At Fort Lewis, Sheilla slammed her fist on her desk and stared at the wall behind her desk, waiting for what Brush would say next.

Brush looked first at Jim and then at the trucks' doors as they opened. He had no choice. *I hope I don't kill you, old friend,* he mumbled as he picked Jim up off the ground and swiftly carried him through the door of the building. He laid him gently on the floor just as the sound of automatic weapons exploded in the courtyard and pieces of the door and the building flew in all directions.

Brush ignored the bullets and flying debris. 'I don't like what I see, General. It's a large crease on his head. It's deep but he's alive. I can't look closer until my guests outside give me some time. Not much I can do, let's get him out of here fast.'

'Nielly, you're a go. Get down there stat. You have a medic?'

'Never leave home without one and, General, I took a chance and left as soon as we heard, ETA twenty minutes.'

Nielly should have waited for the general's authorization but he was damn glad he hadn't. Seconds would make the difference to Jim and an outnumbered Brush. Even so, twenty minutes was a long time in a firefight and the odds were not good.

'Good choice!'

'Sooner the better, Nielly,' added Brush.


Glenda, who rarely showed emotion, let out a gasp. Heather ran from the room as tears streamed down her face. She needed to be any place away from people. Glenda stared straight ahead listening, hoping, urging Nielly to get there.

'Señor.' Lola appeared holding Pedro. Brush waved them away. He didn't know Spanish. As if waking from a dream, Jim opened his eyes. A mother and her child were there. *But who were they? Where were they?* The sounds of shooting entered his consciousness. He struggled to his knees and crawled toward them. Disparate thoughts formed. *Mexico, hacienda, Najma.* Lola pulled Pedro to her and the man dripping with blood slowly moved over the floor in their direction. 'Vamanos, señora,' he uttered in a raspy voice.

She moved back through the door and for a second was more frightened of the bleeding man than the shooting.

Bullets and adobe chunks sounded like steel raindrops on a metal roof. *At least a dozen,* Brush thought as he quickly and effectively shot one, then another and another. The cartel men had brazenly started to move in the open toward Brush. Five of the cartel's men died before the others scattered for cover. Brush changed his clip.

They now fired more carefully aimed shots. Splinters wedged in his cheek and chunks of adobe hit his hand. They were moving cautiously to his sides. They would soon flank him and there were windows to his right. He jumped back and turned a table over in a crazy attempt to protect Jim. But Jim wasn't there. He moved back a few feet from the door and focused on the window to his right. A head appeared, glass shattered, and blood erupted from the man's head as Brush shot him. Brush immediately moved back to the door but on the opposite side as he tried to watch both the window and the door. A man jumped in clear view and fired on full automatic through the door. The man's clip empty, Brush shot him and in the ensuing silence, heard the faint thump of a Huey approaching. The sound immediately made him feel secure and safe. It was a sound that never left those that had depended on the choppers for their rescue. *The finest music in the world,* he thought, as the thump grew louder.

The firing stopped outside. Brush moved to the door. If his count was right, there were six cartel soldiers remaining. 'Make it six left,' he said to Nielly. Brush spun around as a shot was fired behind him. His eyes trailed the smeared blood on the floor to the inner door. Jim was propped up just inside the door and had his rifle pointed at the window behind Brush. A man was slumped over the windowsill.

Brush beamed. 'Nice to see you up and about, partner!' And then added, 'You don't look your usual debonair self. You probably scared Lola and the boy right back out the tunnel.'

Jim gave him his lopsided grin while blood dripped from his chin and nose onto the floor. Brush dropped his jaw as the small boy peeked around the corner and put his head on Jim's shoulder. Pedro seemed unafraid of the wounded man and so Lola overcame her own fear. She would trust the boy's instincts and these men seemed different from most she had met. Lola tried to put a cloth on Jim's blood soaked head.

Brush moved toward them keeping an eye on the door and quickly had her press to stop the bleeding. 'That is a sight,' said Brush, 'I never...we are all one big happy family here. General, I can't say I am displeased to hear a Huey but it won't be exactly like the old days if you aren't flying it.'

'Five at five,' ordered Nielly. The Huey moved in slow motion approximately five feet above the ground and five of his men exited. It then swooped toward the hacienda wall and floated up over it. The door gunner fired on the trucks killing three while the GA jumped onto the wall and took up a protective position. Two of the cartel climbed in a truck and raced through the gate only to be met with a barrage from the five men outside. The remaining man threw his gun down and lay spread-eagled on the ground without anyone telling him to do so.

The chopper hovered over the entry road, waiting for the five men on the ground to enter the gate. 'Coming out of the building across from the gate,' said Brush.

Glenda shuddered in relief and tearful happiness. Then she rubbed her forehead and tilted her head back. He would be coming back to her. She jumped from her chair and moved out of the room.

'Where'd the woman go that came out a few minutes ago?' she asked the sergeant outside. He pointed at a door. Glenda walked in and took hold of Heather. Heather's first instinct was to push her away but then she collapsed sobbing as she wrapped her arms around Glenda.

'He is OK, Heather. He'll be coming back to you, both of them will.'

General Crystal was the first to break the silence. 'Call off the rendezvous, bring the sergeants back.' The room remained silent, waiting.

'Land as close as you can,' ordered Nielly.

Before the helicopter touched down, Nielly and the medic jumped out with a stretcher and ran inside following Brush.

'Clear,' came over the radio as the men outside secured the

prisoner and checked the bodies.

'Help him onto the stretcher.' Brush gently held an arm while Nielly held the other and Jeff took his feet, together they carefully laid Jim on the stretcher. Jeff undid Lola's makeshift bandage and inspected the wound. 'It's deep but not through the skull, however the impact may have caused some internal damage.' He sprayed the wound with antiseptic and wrapped white gauze around Jim's head. The white quickly changed to pink and then to red. 'He's lost a lot of blood. Let's get him loaded and I'll get a transfusion started.'

The boy stood by him as Jim was lifted, looked at his unfocused eyes, and said, 'Pedro.'

'It seems you have made a friend, eh. But I'm not at all sure why, looking like you do,' Brush joked.

Jim tried to focus on the boy and, despite his condition, he felt contented. He had saved him. Then the world once again turned to darkness but this time no one came to torment him with his failures.

'I wish we could keep him awake as he will have a serious concussion at a minimum. But then I don't know why he was awake at all after getting slammed in the head like that,' said Jeff.

The team bound and blindfolded the cartel soldier. The others were dead. Brush ran across the courtyard and up the steps to where Najma lay with flies already buzzing around her. *The woman was a devil,* he thought, *but a beautiful one even in death.* He bent over her and caught a slight movement. She wasn't dead. He felt for her pulse and at first could not find one. None too gently he pulled her up and onto his shoulder and moved back down the steps and into the chopper. Jeff looked at her and gave her a shot of morphine. 'That will keep her happy in case she wakes up, but my guess is she won't survive the trip back,' he said.

'Get a blindfold for the woman and the boy,' said one of the men.

'No, they've been through enough,' said Nielly.

Lola tried to take Pedro away from the stretchers but Pedro pulled toward Najma. Her hair was pulled back on one side exposing the birthmark behind her ear. Its redness was diminished by her blood soaked clothes.

'She has been touched by the gecko,' he said. Brush looked at the birthmark. It contrasted with the beauty of her tawny colored face and black hair. A spot of ugliness that matched her mind but not her face.

'It looks like a starfish to me,' said Brush.

Pedro turned to Lola and said a few words which she explained to the others. 'I see starfish in book before. I try to explain but he does not know what starfish is. He says it is hand of gecko,' she told Brush.

The GA was the last on board as the Huey lumbered up with a full load, moved above the wall, dipped its nose, and headed back over the line for the last time.

# Chapter 45

Heather heard the Huey as it approached. An ambulance was standing by. The chopper swooped in and landed quickly next to it. Heather rushed into the helicopter. Jim was unconscious.

Holding him with tears streaming, dripping from one cheek and soaking gauze on the other side, she whispered to him, 'I love you. I'm here. I know you can't hear me but soon you will be able to.'

They rushed him into the ambulance and, sirens blaring, it sped the short distance to the base hospital. *Déjà vu,* she thought as the same emergency team that not so many days ago received her at the hospital now attended to Jim.

They pushed him into a cubicle, quickly examined his wound, checked his vital signs, and moved him into the X-ray room. The hospital staff seemed to be completely dedicated to Jim.

The emergency room doctor walked up. 'Wish I could say it was nice to see you again and it would be but not under these circumstances. I can't say much until I have the X-rays.'

'Please tell me what you think.'

He hesitated for a second as he could only guess. 'The outward damage is not critical. Until the X-ray I won't know for sure if his skull is fractured.' She looked at him. Reluctantly, he said, 'I don't think it is. If there's no fracture then we'll do several tests to see if there is any brain trauma.' Again he hesitated. 'My hope is no, but there is no way I can say anything about that for sure.'

'Thank you, Doctor. I appreciate you telling me what you think.'

'How is your cheek?'

'I really don't know, I haven't had time to even give it a thought.'

'Dr. Morrel is on his way down and he can look at it again. General Whitcuff called but he didn't need to. I called Dr. Morrel as soon as the helicopter radioed me. Said he had never worked on a couple before, something about a matched set. He wants to see your cheek, so he was happy to come down.'

The radiologist rushed in. 'No fractures. There is a shallow furrow in the bone. I would call it a very close call.'

'Good news, Heather. We'll do several tests now. I'll let you know as soon as I can if there is anything else. I have an emergency to attend to. See you later.'

*Najma*, thought Heather. *Here in the same hospital.* A gurney followed by two military policemen was moved past her into a cubicle. The emergency doctor followed them into the room. From the other direction a gurney with Jim on it was pushed back into his cubicle. She rushed in. No one told her to leave as she watched them work methodically, hooking him up to a heart monitor, rearranging his IV, and examining his eyes in a nonstop flurry of activity.

'Heather, my dear. How are you?' said Dr. Morrel as he entered and looked at Jim's chart, then checked his vital signs. He left the room and reappeared a few minutes later in a green gown, cap, and gloves. Another man wearing a similar gown and pushing a cart followed him in. He removed the head bandages and examined the wound. The other man supplied him with the tools he needed in quick succession.

Nearly an hour later, he stopped and patted the still unconscious Jim on the shoulder. 'Now, Heather, let's move to another room and take a look at you while I tell you how wonderful your partner will look in no time.'

'Can't you look here? Please. I don't want to leave him.'

Not used to being countermanded, the doctor had to stop himself from saying no and instead said, 'Yes, let's take a look here then. Please sit in that chair.' He snapped new latex gloves on. 'Let's see. Looks marvelous. Must have been an excellent surgeon.' He smiled at her.

'I think I had the best.' She smiled back.

'You will have minimal scarring.' He hurried into the next sentence as if knowing that she wasn't concerned about herself. 'Jim, however, will have quite a large scar but it won't show at all beneath his hair. I would like to examine you one last time, maybe in a week,' he added as he applied a new and much smaller dressing to her cheek.

'Thank you, Doctor. You've been very kind.'


Jim was moved to a room with a glass window where a nurse sat monitoring him. Heather sat in a chair next to the bed, also watching him. They had both been lucky. Ralphy had moved so far from her thoughts that it was as if an old friend had entered again when she thought that he, too, had been lucky. Then there was Marilyn, she would visit her soon. But others had not been so lucky. Nicola and Kristina caused her the most grief, but Nielly had lost three members of his special unit and two others were injured. She didn't really know Mac but she did feel, in a strange way, that she had gotten to know the dead watcher. She didn't even know his name.

The nurse rapped on the window and pointed at Jim. His eyes were open and looking at her. Two nurses and another doctor rushed into the room. They did some quick checks, asked Jim if he could see them. He nodded but didn't say anything. 'We'll be close by if you need anything,' they told him and then they left the room.

'Hi, beautiful.' His smile tilted to the same side as a bulge on his massive head bandage.

'Hi, lover.' Tears she didn't know that she had streamed once again down her face as she lightly kissed him on the lips and squeezed him for all she was worth.

Another hour passed and there was a tap on the door as Glenda, Brush, and the general walked in. Glenda looked at Jim and gave Heather a hug and big smile.

'Not sure if I find you that appealing in your new headgear. Never really liked turbans,' said Brush.

Will Crystal moved over to the bed. 'We've talked to the doctor and all the tests coming back indicate you will be fine. But you are going to need some recovery time and this isn't one to shortcut.' He looked sternly at Jim. 'You stay here and rest; your part in this is over. That's an order!'

'Thank you, General,' said Heather, 'maybe he will listen to both of us.'

'I'm going to leave you for a while as you need to rest here and I am being inundated with paperwork requests from Washington.' He paused. 'Good work, Jim, and you too, Batman. We accomplished our mission. Najma won't be terrorizing anyone again.'

'Is she dead, General?' asked Jim.

'She is right down the hall in critical condition. Docs don't give her much of a chance. See you later, Jim. Heather, could I have a word with you?'

They moved out into the corridor.

'I know you have your hands full with Jim but I would like to ask you a favor. The woman, the DEA informant, Lola, has a small boy with her. It was his family that was murdered by Najma.'

'That's awful. Is he OK? How old is he?'

The general couldn't help but smile. Heather's questions.

'He seems to be OK but he is very quiet and it's hard to say how he will be. I am not sure what his age is, close to six years old maybe. If you can find a moment when Jim is resting, would you be willing to go talk to them? They're being held at the airport. They are being treated well but are still pretty scared. You speak Spanish and they need a non-military friendly face. I'll leave Sergeant Murphy outside. Just have him get anything you need here or if you are comfortable breaking away to talk to them, Murphy can call Nielly and let him know you are coming.'

'I can't leave Jim,' she said immediately. But then she remembered the little boy and said, 'I'll go as soon as I can.'

Several hours passed. Jim went in and out of sleep but they were able to talk. Several people came by to see how Jim was doing but General Whitcuff was the only other one admitted. 'I haven't had this much excitement for years and truthfully maybe never before. You two are something else, Ram chutes, Batman outfits. Glad you are doing fine. Good…very good job, Colonel. I'm proud to have served with you.'

Heather and Jim talked about all the things that were important to them, their home and friends. They didn't talk about Mexico. They had lived and breathed it for so many days, there was nothing else they wanted to say now.

'Will asked me to go to the airport to talk to the woman and the little boy. He says they are frightened and a friendly face might make them feel better.'

'I want you to go now. I'm fine. The boy is special. I don't know why he is, he just is. I'm not sure if he saved me or if I have this scrape because of him or if it touches something in me that goes back a long way.'

'The girls in Vietnam and their mother?'

'Yes.'

'I'll go now then.'

'Thanks, sweetie. I'll be fine and try to sleep.'

'I'll stop by Marilyn's room on the way out and see how she is doing. I hardly know her or any of them other than Nielly, but they all almost seem like family now.'

'It works that way. Give Marilyn my regards.'

Heather walked out of the room for only the second time since they had entered the hospital.

'There is a woman, Marilyn. Where is her room?' she asked an orderly.

'Just two doors down the hall, ma'am.'

Heather looked down the hall. Just beyond where the orderly had said Marilyn's room was, she saw an MP stationed at the door. They were all here together. Enemies and friends. *A strange world,* she thought. Najma didn't represent the same thing to her anymore. Too much had transpired. She had seen and learned too much about another world in Mexico and through the video cameras. She thought about the parallel universe hypothesis. Maybe the other worlds were here all together operating simultaneously. Each person living in their own world.

Marilyn was awake but was hardly recognizable. Where her

face wasn't covered with bandages, it was hideously bruised in dark, angry colors. Her leg was in traction, both arms in casts. One hand looked undamaged protruding from a cast that ran to her shoulder.

Heather smiled. 'Can you talk, Marilyn?'

Marilyn nodded her head slightly and managed to get out, 'Better than I can walk.'

'You guys are all the same. I just wanted to tell you how much I admire you. You are braver than any woman I have ever met and more skilled than most men. Jim sends his regards and I really hope that when you are better we can get together sometime.'

Marilyn tried to smile but for the first time since entering the army she felt vulnerable and a tear trickled slowly down her cheek. *Heather understands. But I can't share this with the men,* she thought allowing herself the moment of weakness.

'I'll stop by again soon.'

*What a woman. My little scar is nothing compared to her damage,* Heather thought as she went out of the hospital.

'Murphy, the general said you could call Nielly on the way to the airport.'

'Sure thing, ma'am.'

The guard motioned toward the big hangar and Heather was shocked to see the two old sergeants standing out in front.

'You two are completely crazy but I love you. I'm so glad you are alive and back,' she told them happily. The two sergeants almost blushed. They had survived before and they had survived this time and they felt on top of the world. It was what they lived for. Nielly walked over and Master Sergeant Smith and Sergeant Jay Hernandez saluted smartly.

Nielly saluted back and then shook both their hands. 'Good job, you two.' After a pause he turned to Heather and said, 'Let's go meet the boy and the woman.'

He walked her into the large hangar past two white-hatted military police and then to a large storage container standing alongside several others in a neat row. Guards saluted as they walked by until Nielly stopped at one labeled with a large white number three. The guard opened the door and inside was a female doctor and two more guards. The three dwarfed a petite Mexican woman sitting on a chair with a small boy clinging to her.

Heather walked to the woman who looked nervous; the boy clung tighter as she approached. Heather turned to Nielly. 'Do you think we could be alone?'

'You three, wait outside but I'll stay for the time being.'

'Thank you,' said Heather as she turned back to the woman. 'Como se llama, señora?' she asked and smiled at both of them.

'I am Lola and this is Pedro.' The boy released his hold on Lola a little and stared at Heather.

'Are you both OK?'

'Esta bien.'

The boy who had not released his grip on Lola since they left the hacienda looked at the floor and moved toward Heather. He shyly looked up at her and as she bent down to him, he touched the bandage on her cheek. 'Esta bien,' she said. She reached out to little Pedro and took his hand as her eyes filled with tears.

'Let's get them out of here, Nielly. Take them to our house. Glenda could watch them and you could leave a guard at the doors if you need to.'

'I'll talk to the general and see what he says.'

Heather sat and talked with them for several minutes. As each minute passed, Lola and Pedro looked less frightened and Heather was more and more taken with Pedro.

'I talked to General Crystal and he gives it his OK. I'll get them settled in.'

'And post the guards?'

'Yes, that, too.'

Heather turned to Lola. 'Everything will be fine, Lola. You will be taken to my house where you will be safe.' She looked at Pedro, smiled, and walked him to Lola. Pedro took her hand and walked with his head down. 'The major will take you,' she told them.

She hadn't mentioned Jim to them and thought she would. 'I have to get back to the hospital. The man that was injured and brought back with you is my friend.'

'He is a brave man, señorita. He and other man saved Pedro.' Then Lola started to cry as she realized for the first time that they were safe and away from the cartel and their devils.

Heather bent over and gave Lola a hug, then kissed Pedro on top of his head, smiled, and left with Nielly.

'I will be at the hospital but will come home as soon as I can and see how they are doing.'

'Don't worry, we'll take good care of them.'


'What are you going to do with them, General? I think you should send them to the BWL,' said Nielly. 'Let Sheilla's analyst, the profiler that has psychological training, talk to them along with a counselor from the VA. You could keep them on base there for a while. I've been talking to Sheilla and she is agreeable. The boy probably needs some evaluation and the woman is going to need a new identity. There is a large Mexican community in eastern Washington. Perhaps you could place them up there. None of my business, but the woman deserves our help after spying for the DEA and we both know they won't do anything except just kick her loose. The boy seems a good kid. My guys have been giving him Cokes and candy and they all want to adopt him.'

'Appreciate your opinion, Nielly. I'll give it all some thought.'

'Let me know what you decide and I'd like to know what happens to our psycho-lady as well. We're off first thing in the morning, General. As usual it's been interesting. Mac is going back with us but Marilyn will stay here until she can be transported.'

Hours went by as Jim drifted in and out of sleep. He and Heather talked about the woman and the boy and the minor things that make up everyday life and seem to become a privilege after traumatic events. Evening neared.

'I want to sleep some, special one. Why don't you check on the woman and the boy?'

'You sure?'

But Heather wanted to go see the little shy brown boy again. He was so fragile, soft, and sensitive. The look in his eyes as he walked over to her in the shipping container stirred something inside her.

She bent over and softly touched Jim's forehead with hers, looked into his eyes, the same eyes that had always been there.

# Epilogue

Y ou's two is always bringing animals back but not this kind—what's this little fella's name?' asked Duane.

'Say hello, Pedro,' said Heather. 'This man will show you how to be a real cowboy.'

Pedro reluctantly let go of the giant tan wolfhound and timidly raised his hand toward Duane.

'Never thought you two would get around to having a family,' said Duane, 'and now there's a whole house full.'

Jim laughed.

'You're the best family there is, Duane,' said Heather. Lola, looking pleased with herself, brought in a cup of chamomile tea and set it next to Jim. 'She's taken over the role as his private nurse for the last week at Fort Huachuca and now she knows everything he likes,' she told Duane.

Heather had talked to Duane on the phone and explained that they were OK but would be delayed getting back to the ranch. Jim's doctor wanted to make sure that Jim's wound was healing properly. They told Duane there was lots of paperwork and there was another problem they needed to deal with but didn't tell him what it was—they had wanted to surprise him with Pedro.

The State Department, with some prodding from the general, had arranged to have Lola and Pedro transferred to Wolf Canyon Ranch. Lola was given asylum and was being fast-tracked for citizenship. Heather and Jim were officially given custody of Pedro.

They had arrived two days ago, chauffeured in General Crystal's Huey. Rosie immediately greeted Pedro with a big lick and the two had become inseparable. Rosie had been allowed to lie next to Jim's bed, a rarity on the ranch to let any of the animals into the house. It wasn't lack of love for them but just a practicality. The house was an island in the middle of a sea of beauty but also dust, dirt, and manure.

Pedro had wanted to sleep there too, but he had a room of his own. Still Jim would often wake up in the morning to find Pedro lying on the floor with his arm around Rosie.

'Guess it's time to tell me what you two have been up to,' grinned Duane. 'You's all been keeping me in the dark for the last few days and it's time now. I want to hear the story.'

Jim looked at Heather knowing she didn't want to relive her role in Mexico. 'We'll tell you another time, Duane, if that's OK.' It wasn't a question and Duane understood that there was a reason and he would have to wait.

'Duane, you get on home and collect Betty Lou, Ben, Loretta, and anyone else you want to bring back tonight. We're going to have a small party for Jim's birthday,' a happy Heather told him.

'What party? Not sure I want to have a party,' said Jim.

'Guess you don't have any choice, my sweet. It was going to be a surprise but I know you don't like them.'

The telephone rang and Heather answered.

'Brush and Glenda are back from Alaska,' she said.

*Wonder if it's significant that he finally made it to Alaska and with Glenda,* Heather mused.

'Hope you two enjoyed yourselves... Yep, I know you're coming over with the general.' She was repeating some of the conversation for Jim. 'And the general is going to be the taxi service, bringing both of you and Sheilla, and then picking up JT and Ralphy in Seattle. I think they get on really well together,' continued Heather.

'The general said he offered to provide transport for Misa and Vidya but they are still embroiled in their computer stuff at Fort Huachuca. The army has hired them as consultants and they are all now in a special unit with Josh and Jake, still calling themselves the Wolf Pack. We'll tell you more when you get here,' said Heather.

Jim listened and watched her as she talked. She seemed fine but he knew that scars could run deep. Her external scar was healing fast, he could only hope that the internal ones would, too. The woman that had loved solitude had metamorphosed into a different person. Her extended family, born in adversity, now seemed to be her life. Jim looked at Pedro and Rosie. A hazy image of Vietnam and the village drifted through his mind and then disappeared.

Heather passed the phone to Jim. 'Hey, Brush, you finally made it to Alaska...Tell Glenda hi and see you both soon... The two sergeants? Both got medals and retired to Mexico. I wished they liked colder climates, they could work here. Heather has good judgment, they are fine men.'

Jim looked at Pedro. He was an exceptionally nice boy. He seemed happy that Lola was here but had formed an attachment to Jim and Heather that he couldn't explain. *Some things are not explainable with logic,* Jim thought. Why had the boy touched him at the hacienda and why had he walked to Heather inside the container and touched her face? He set it aside; sometimes there was no reason for the way things happened.

As he continued to watch Rosie bask in the affection from the boy, a feeling of happiness came over him. He had never been sure if he wanted a child but had always thought that out there somewhere, a child would be thrust into his existence. Fate.

Duane went home to get Betty Lou, Loretta, and Ben. The hours passed as Heather, Rosie, Jim, Lola, and Pedro watched the blue sky turn to gray and then it snowed. Huge flakes floating and shifting from side to side. Pedro stood with his mouth open as the outside world turned to a glistening white.

Then they heard the familiar thump as a Huey entered their canyon and landed in a maelstrom of blowing snow just below the house. Soon the house filled with the sounds of people and the general walked up the stairs.

'Wanted a minute with you before the others get all your attention. How you feeling?' boomed Will Crystal.

'Really good,' answered Jim. 'Quite a change from a few weeks ago, now I'm a family man! How have you been enjoying Washington?'

'Our little adventure crossed over a lot of agency lines. Lots of small fires to put out and egos to assuage. Not sure if that is going to be the job for you, Jim, when you take over.'

'Lots of time for that. You're not leaving for a while. Talked to Nielly lately? Anything new with Najma? I heard about the bank thing and the British.'

The general laughed. 'You're sounding just like Heather with the back-to-back questions. No idea what Nielly is doing. Off somewhere or other. But he apparently welded the door to a safe room at the hacienda. We surreptitiously advised the local authorities to let them know but the word is the cartel and police apparently won't let anyone near the place. That is if anyone wanted to go near it. The locals say it's haunted by the devil-lady and won't go close to it, cartel or no cartel. But then the Mexican authorities got their special anti-drug unit to remove the cartel's leader from the safe room. State Department just heard that the Mexican president has announced he is going to execute him, claiming he was captured after the successful raid on the cartel's headquarters by his special anti-drug unit.'

'There's no death penalty in Mexico.'

'Guess he's making a rule change,' responded the general.

'Najma?' asked Jim.

'Our woman is a conundrum. Can't prosecute her as we grabbed her "illegally" from Mexico. Probably would prove to be a psycho if evaluated and we wouldn't be able to prosecute her because of that. She now has a fifty-fifty chance of surviving and if she does she will most likely get sent to a secret detention center the state department is just beginning to operate at Guantanamo Bay and be held there indefinitely. My guess is she will never leave. Probably best all around, though, if she doesn't make it.'

Brush walked up the stairs grinning. 'See you tamed down your turban a little, eh. Down to a normal size bandage now. Hello, Pedro. Looks like you have made a friend.'

'Yes.' He looked down and rubbed the Irish wolfhound's stomach with his tiny hands.

'How was Alaska?' Jim asked.

'Everything I ever thought it would be, partner.'

Both Will and Jim looked at Brush, waiting. They knew Alaska was a childhood dream fulfilled for Brush but what they really wanted to know was how he and Glenda were getting on.

Brush understood what they wanted and just stood smiling back.

'Guess we got our answer in as few words as possible—no words,' said Will.

To anyone that did not know Brush as well as they did, it wouldn't be an answer at all but his look and lack of a smart answer told them everything they needed to know. Brush was finally serious about someone.

The general couldn't help but smile thinking his playboy agent was going to finally settle down. 'What the devil is that music?'

'The Stones,' said Brush. 'Her favorite.'

'One of mine, too,' said Jim. 'Especially this album, "Bridges of Babylon."'

'This is like your coming-out party, Jim. Time to stop being an invalid. Let's get downstairs,' said Brush.

Jim swung his feet over the bed and leaned toward Pedro. 'Come on, son, and bring Rosie with you. Looks like she's your dog now.'

Lightning Source UK Ltd.
Milton Keynes UK
UKOW04f1825020714

234462UK00001B/16/P

Title: A Far Country, Book 1
Author: Winston Churchill
Language: English

# A FAR COUNTRY

By Winston Churchill

## BOOK 1.

## I.

My name is Hugh Paret. I was a corporation lawyer, but by no means a typical one, the choice of my profession being merely incidental, and due, as will be seen, to the accident of environment. The book I am about to write might aptly be called The Autobiography of a Romanticist. In that sense, if in no other, I have been a typical American, regarding my country as the happy hunting-ground of enlightened self-interest, as a function of my desires. Whether or not I have completely got rid of this romantic virus I must leave to those the aim of whose existence is to eradicate it from our literature and our life. A somewhat Augean task!

I have been impelled therefore to make an attempt at setting forth, with what frankness and sincerity I may, with those powers of selection of which I am capable, the life I have lived in this modern America; the passions I have known, the evils I have done. I endeavour to write a biography of the inner life; but in order to do this I shall have to relate those causal experiences of the outer existence that take place in the world of space and time, in the four walls of the home, in the school and university, in the noisy streets, in the realm of business and politics. I shall try to set down, impartially, the motives that have impelled my actions, to reveal in some degree the amazing mixture of good and evil which has made me what I am to-day: to avoid the tricks of memory and resist the inherent desire to present myself other and better than I am. Your American romanticist is a sentimental spoiled child who believes in miracles, whose needs are mostly baubles, whose desires are dreams. Expediency is his motto. Innocent of a knowledge of the principles of the universe, he lives in a state of ceaseless activity, admitting no limitations, impatient of all restrictions. What he wants, he wants very badly indeed. This wanting things was the corner-stone of my character, and I believe that the science of the future will bear me out when I say that it might have been differently built upon. Certain it is that the system of education in vogue in the 70's and 80's never contemplated the search for natural corner-stones.

At all events, when I look back upon the boy I was, I see the beginnings of a real person who fades little by little as manhood arrives and advances, until suddenly I am aware that a stranger has taken his place....

I lived in a city which is now some twelve hours distant from the Atlantic seaboard. A very different city, too, it was in youth, in my grandfather's day and my father's, even in my own boyhood, from what it has since become in this most material of ages.

There is a book of my photographs, preserved by my mother, which I have been looking over lately. First is presented a plump child of two, gazing in smiling trustfulness upon a world of sunshine; later on a lean boy in plaided kilts, whose wavy, chestnut-brown hair has been most carefully parted on the side by Norah, his nurse. The face is still childish. Then appears a youth of fourteen or thereabout in long trousers and the queerest of short jackets, standing beside a marble table against a classic background; he is smiling still in undiminished hope and trust, despite increasing vexations and crossings, meaningless lessons which had to be learned, disciplines to rack an aspiring soul, and long, uncomfortable hours in the stiff pew of the First Presbyterian Church. Associated with this torture is a peculiar Sunday smell and the faint rustling of silk dresses. I can see the stern black figure of Dr. Pound, who made interminable statements to the Lord.

"Oh, Lord," I can hear him say, "thou knowest..."

These pictures, though yellowed and faded, suggest vividly the being I once was, the feelings that possessed and animated me, love for my playmates, vague impulses struggling for expression in a world forever thwarting them. I recall, too, innocent dreams of a future unidentified, dreams from which I emerged vibrating with an energy that was lost for lack of a definite objective: yet it was constantly being renewed. I often wonder what I might have become if it could have been harnessed, directed! Speculations are vain. Calvinism, though it had begun to make compromises, was still a force in those days, inimical to spontaneity and human instincts. And when I think of Calvinism I see, not Dr. Pound, who preached it, but my father, who practised and embodied it. I loved him, but he made of righteousness a stern and terrible thing implying not joy, but punishment, the, suppression rather than the expansion of aspirations. His religion seemed woven all of austerity, contained no shining threads to catch my eye. Dreams, to him, were matters for suspicion and distrust.

I sometimes ask myself, as I gaze upon his portrait now, the duplicate of the one painted for the Bar Association, whether he ever could have felt the secret, hot thrills I knew and did not identify with religion. His religion was real to him, though he failed utterly to make it comprehensible to me. The apparent calmness, evenness of his life awed me. A successful lawyer, a respected and trusted citizen, was he lacking somewhat in virility, vitality? I cannot judge him, even to-day. I never knew him. There were times in my youth when the curtain of his unfamiliar spirit was withdrawn a little: and once, after I had passed the crisis of some childhood disease, I awoke to find him bending over my bed with a tender expression that surprised and puzzled me.

He was well educated, and from his portrait a shrewd observer might divine in him a genteel taste for literature. The fine features bear witness to the influence of an American environment, yet suggest the intellectual Englishman of Matthew Arnold's time. The face is distinguished, ascetic, the chestnut hair lighter and thinner than my own; the side whiskers are not too obtrusive, the eyes blue-grey. There is a large black cravat crossed and held by a cameo pin, and the coat has odd, narrow lapels. His habits of mind were English, although he harmonized well enough with the manners and traditions of a city whose inheritance was Scotch-Irish; and he invariably drank tea for breakfast. One of my earliest recollections is of the silver breakfast service and egg-cups which my great-grandfather brought with him from Sheffield to Philadelphia shortly after the Revolution. His son, Dr. Hugh Moreton Paret, after whom I was named, was the best known physician of the city in the decorous, Second Bank days.

My mother was Sarah Breck. Hers was my Scotch-Irish side. Old Benjamin Breck, her grandfather, undaunted by sea or wilderness, had come straight from Belfast to the little log settlement by the great river that mirrored then the mantle of primeval forest on the hills. So much for chance. He kept a store with a side porch and square-paned windows, where hams and sides of bacon and sugar loaves in blue glazed paper hung beside ploughs and calico prints, barrels of flour, of molasses and rum, all of which had been somehow marvellously transported over the passes of those forbidding mountains,—passes we blithely thread to-day in dining cars and compartment sleepers. Behind the store were moored the barges that floated down on the swift current to the Ohio, carrying goods to even remoter settlements in the western wilderness.

Benjamin, in addition to his emigrant's leather box, brought with him some of that pigment that was to dye the locality for generations a deep blue. I refer, of course, to his Presbyterianism. And in order the better to ensure to his progeny the fastness of this dye, he married the granddaughter of a famous divine, celebrated in the annals of New England,—no doubt with some injustice,—as a staunch advocate on the doctrine of infant damnation. My cousin Robert Breck had old Benjamin's portrait, which has since gone to the Kinley's. Heaven knows who painted it, though no great art were needed to suggest on canvas the tough fabric of that sitter, who was more Irish than Scotch. The heavy stick he holds might, with a slight stretch of the imagination, be a blackthorn; his head looks capable of withstanding many blows; his hand of giving many. And, as I gazed the other day at this picture hanging in the shabby suburban parlour, I could only contrast him with his anaemic descendants who possessed the likeness. Between the children of poor Mary Kinley,—Cousin Robert's daughter, and the hardy stock of the old country there is a gap indeed!

Benjamin Breck made the foundation of a fortune. It was his son who built on the Second Bank the wide, corniced mansion in which to house comfortably his eight children. There, two tiers above the river, lived my paternal grandfather, Dr. Paret, the Breck's physician and friend; the Durrets and the Hambletons, iron-masters; the Hollisters, Sherwins, the McAlerys and Ewanses,—Breck connections,—the Willetts and Ogilvys; in short, everyone of importance in the days between the 'thirties and the Civil War. Theirs were generous houses surrounded by shade trees, with glorious back yards—I have been told—where apricots and pears and peaches and even nectarines grew.

The business of Breck and Company, wholesale grocers, descended to my mother's first cousin, Robert Breck, who lived at Claremore. The very sound of that word once sufficed to give me a shiver of delight; but the Claremore I knew has disappeared as completely as Atlantis, and the place is now a suburb (hateful word!) cut up into building lots and connected with Boyne Street and the business section of the city by trolley lines. Then it was "the country," and fairly saturated with romance. Cousin Robert, when he came into town to spend his days at the store, brought with him some of this romance, I had almost said of this aroma. He was no suburbanite, but rural to the backbone, professing a most proper contempt for dwellers in towns.

Every summer day that dawned held Claremore as a possibility. And such was my capacity for joy that my appetite would depart completely when I heard my mother say, questioningly and with proper wifely respect —

"If you're really going off on a business trip for a day or two, Mr. Paret" (she generally addressed my father thus formally), "I think I'll go to Robert's and take Hugh."

"Shall I tell Norah to pack, mother," I would exclaim, starting up.

"We'll see what your father thinks, my dear."

"Remain at the table until you are excused, Hugh," he would say.

Released at length, I would rush to Norah, who always rejoiced with me, and then to the wire fence which marked the boundary of the Peters domain next door, eager, with the refreshing lack of consideration characteristic of youth, to announce to the Peterses—who were to remain at home the news of my good fortune. There would be Tom and Alfred and Russell and Julia and little Myra with her grass-stained knees, faring forth to seek the adventures of a new day in the shady western yard. Myra was too young not to look wistful at my news, but the others pretended indifference, seeking to lessen my triumph. And it was Julia who invariably retorted "We can go out to Uncle Jake's farm whenever we want to. Can't we, Tom?"...

No journey ever taken since has equalled in ecstasy that leisurely trip of thirteen miles in the narrow-gauge railroad that wound through hot fields of nodding corn tassels and between delicious, acrid-smelling woods to Claremore. No silent palace "sleeping in the sun," no edifice decreed by Kubla Khan could have worn more glamour than the house of Cousin Robert Breck.

It stood half a mile from the drowsy village, deep in its own grounds amidst lawns splashed with shadows, with gravel paths edged—in barbarous fashion, if you please with shells. There were flower beds of equally barbarous design; and two iron deer, which, like the figures on Keats's Grecian urn, were ever ready poised to flee,—and yet never fled. For Cousin Robert was rich, as riches went in those days: not only rich, but comfortable. Stretching behind the house were sweet meadows of hay and red clover basking in the heat, orchards where the cows cropped beneath the trees, arbours where purple clusters of Concords hung beneath warm leaves: there were woods beyond, into which, under the guidance of Willie Breck, I made adventurous excursions, and in the autumn gathered hickories and walnuts. The house was a rambling, wooden mansion painted grey, with red scroll-work on its porches and horsehair furniture inside. Oh, the smell of its darkened interior on a midsummer day! Like the flavour of that choicest of tropical fruits, the mangosteen, it baffles analysis, and the nearest I can come to it is a mixture of matting and corn-bread, with another element too subtle to define.

The hospitality of that house! One would have thought we had arrived, my mother and I, from the ends of the earth, such was the welcome we got from Cousin Jenny, Cousin Robert's wife, from Mary and Helen with the flaxen pig-tails, from Willie, whom I recall as permanently without shoes or stockings. Met and embraced by Cousin Jenny at the station and driven to the house in the squeaky surrey, the moment we arrived she and my mother would put on the dressing-sacks I associated with hot weather, and sit sewing all day long in rocking-chairs at the coolest end of the piazza. The women of that day scorned lying down, except at night, and as evening came on they donned starched dresses; I recall in particular one my mother wore, with little vertical stripes of black and white, and a full skirt. And how they talked, from the beginning of the visit until the end! I have often since wondered where the topics came from.

It was not until nearly seven o'clock that the train arrived which brought home my Cousin Robert. He was a big man; his features and even his ample moustache gave a disconcerting impression of rugged integrity, and I remember him chiefly in an alpaca or seersucker coat. Though much less formal, more democratic—in a word—than my father, I stood in awe of him for a different reason, and this I know now was because he possessed the penetration to discern the flaws in my youthful character,—flaws that persisted in manhood. None so quick as Cousin Robert to detect deceptions which were hidden from my mother.

His hobby was carpentering, and he had a little shop beside the stable filled with shining tools which Willie and I, in spite of their attractions, were forbidden to touch. Willie, by dire experience, had learned to keep the law; but on one occasion I stole in alone, and promptly cut my finger with a chisel. My mother and Cousin Jenny accepted the fiction that the injury had been done with a flint arrowhead that Willie had given me, but when Cousin Robert came home and saw my bound hand and heard the story, he gave me a certain look which sticks in my mind.

"Wonderful people, those Indians were!" he observed. "They could make arrowheads as sharp as chisels."

I was most uncomfortable....

He had a strong voice, and spoke with a rising inflection and a marked accent that still remains peculiar to our locality, although it was much modified in my mother and not at all noticeable in my father; with an odd nasal alteration of the burr our Scotch-Irish ancestors had brought with them across the seas. For instance, he always called my father Mr. Par-r-ret. He had an admiration and respect for him that seemed to forbid the informality of "Matthew." It was shared by others of my father's friends and relations.

"Sarah," Cousin Robert would say to my mother, "you're coddling that boy, you ought to lam him oftener. Hand him over to me for a couple of months—I'll put him through his paces.... So you're going to send him to college, are you? He's too good for old Benjamin's grocery business."

He was very fond of my mother, though he lectured her soundly for her weakness in indulging me. I can see him as he sat at the head of the supper table, carving liberal helpings which Mary and Helen and Willie devoured with country appetites, watching our plates.

"What's the matter, Hugh? You haven't eaten all your lamb."

"He doesn't like fat, Robert," my mother explained.

"I'd teach him to like it if he were my boy."

"Well, Robert, he isn't your boy," Cousin Jenny would remind him.... His bark was worse than his bite. Like many kind people he made use of brusqueness to hide an inner tenderness, and on the train he was hail fellow well met with every Tom, Dick and Harry that commuted,—although the word was not invented in those days,—and the conductor and brakeman too. But he had his standards, and held to them....

Mine was not a questioning childhood, and I was willing to accept the scheme of things as presented to me entire. In my tenderer years, when I had broken one of the commandments on my father's tablet (there were more than ten), and had, on his home-coming, been sent to bed, my mother would come softly upstairs after supper with a book in her hand; a book of selected Bible stories on which Dr. Pound had set the seal of his approval, with a glazed picture cover, representing Daniel in the lions' den and an angel standing beside him. On the somewhat specious plea that Holy Writ might have a chastening effect, she was permitted to minister to me in my shame. The amazing adventure of Shadrach, Meshach and Abednego particularly appealed to an imagination needing little stimulation. It never occurred to me to doubt that these gentlemen had triumphed over caloric laws. But out of my window, at the back of the second storey, I often saw a sudden, crimson glow in the sky to the southward, as though that part of the city had caught fire. There were the big steel-works, my mother told me, belonging to Mr. Durrett and Mr. Hambleton, the father of Ralph Hambleton and the grandfather of Hambleton Durrett, my schoolmates at Miss Caroline's. I invariably connected the glow, not with Hambleton and Ralph, but with Shadrach, Meshach and Abednego! Later on, when my father took me to the steel-works, and I beheld with awe a huge pot filled with molten metal that ran out of it like water, I asked him—if I leaped into that stream, could God save me? He was shocked. Miracles, he told me, didn't happen any more.

"When did they stop?" I demanded.

"About two thousand years ago, my son," he replied gravely.

"Then," said I, "no matter how much I believed in God, he wouldn't save me if I jumped into the big kettle for his sake?"

For this I was properly rebuked and silenced.

My boyhood was filled with obsessing desires. If God, for example, had cast down, out of his abundant store, manna and quail in the desert, why couldn't he fling me a little pocket money? A paltry quarter of a dollar, let us say, which to me represented wealth. To avoid the reproach of the Pharisees, I went into the closet of my bed-chamber to pray, requesting that the quarter should be dropped on the north side of Lyme Street, between Stamford and Tryon; in short, as conveniently near home as possible. Then I issued forth, not feeling overconfident, but hoping. Tom Peters, leaning over the ornamental cast-iron fence which separated his front yard from the street, presently spied me scanning the sidewalk.

"What are you looking for, Hugh?" he demanded with interest.

"Oh, something I dropped," I answered uneasily.

"What?"

Naturally, I refused to tell. It was a broiling, midsummer day; Julia and Russell, who had been warned to stay in the shade, but who were engaged in the experiment of throwing the yellow cat from the top of the lattice fence to see if she would alight on her feet, were presently attracted, and joined in the search. The mystery which I threw around it added to its interest, and I was not inconsiderably annoyed. Suppose one of them were to find the quarter which God had intended for me? Would that be justice?

"It's nothing," I said, and pretended to abandon the quest—to be renewed later. But this ruse failed; they continued obstinately to search; and after a few minutes Tom, with a shout, picked out of a hot crevice between the bricks—a nickel!

"It's mine!" I cried fiercely.

"Did you lose it?" demanded Julia, the canny one, as Tom was about to give it up.

My lying was generally reserved for my elders.

"N-no," I said hesitatingly, "but it's mine all the same. It was—sent to me."

"Sent to you!" they exclaimed, in a chorus of protest and derision. And how, indeed, was I to make good my claim? The Peterses, when assembled, were a clan, led by Julia and in matters of controversy, moved as one. How was I to tell them that in answer to my prayers for twenty-five cents, God had deemed five all that was good for me?

"Some—somebody dropped it there for me."

"Who?" demanded the chorus. "Say, that's a good one!"

Tears suddenly blinded me. Overcome by chagrin, I turned and flew into the house and upstairs into my room, locking the door behind me. An interval ensued, during which I nursed my sense of wrong, and it pleased me to think that the money would bring a curse on the Peters family. At length there came a knock on the door, and a voice calling my name.

"Hugh! Hugh!"

It was Tom.

"Hughie, won't you let me in? I want to give you the nickel."

"Keep it!" I shouted back. "You found it."

Another interval, and then more knocking.

"Open up," he said coaxingly. "I—I want to talk to you."

I relented, and let him in. He pressed the coin into my hand. I refused; he pleaded.

"You found it," I said, "it's yours."

"But—but you were looking for it."

"That makes no difference," I declared magnanimously.

Curiosity overcame him.

"Say, Hughie, if you didn't drop it, who on earth did?"

"Nobody on earth," I replied cryptically....

Naturally, I declined to reveal the secret. Nor was this by any means the only secret I held over the Peters family, who never quite knew what to make of me. They were not troubled with imaginations. Julia was a little older than Tom and had a sharp tongue, but over him I exercised a distinct fascination, and I knew it. Literal himself, good-natured and warm-hearted, the gift I had of tingeing life with romance (to put the thing optimistically), of creating kingdoms out of back yards—at which Julia and Russell sniffed —held his allegiance firm.

## II.

I must have been about twelve years of age when I realized that I was possessed of the bard's inheritance. A momentous journey I made with my parents to Boston about this time not only stimulated this gift, but gave me the advantage of which other travellers before me have likewise availed themselves—of being able to take certain poetic liberties with a distant land that my friends at home had never seen. Often during the heat of summer noons when we were assembled under the big maple beside the lattice fence in the Peters' yard, the spirit would move me to relate the most amazing of adventures. Our train, for instance, had been held up in the night by a band of robbers in black masks, and rescued by a traveller who bore a striking resemblance to my Cousin Robert Breck. He had shot two of the robbers. These fabrications, once started, flowed from me with ridiculous ease. I experienced an unwonted exhilaration, exaltation; I began to believe that they had actually occurred. In vain the astute Julia asserted that there were no train robbers in the east. What had my father done? Well, he had been very brave, but he had had no pistol. Had I been frightened? No, not at all;

I, too, had wished for a pistol. Why hadn't I spoken of this before? Well, so many things had happened to me I couldn't tell them all at once. It was plain that Julia, though often fascinated against her will, deemed this sort of thing distinctly immoral.

I was a boy divided in two. One part of me dwelt in a fanciful realm of his own weaving, and the other part was a commonplace and protesting inhabitant of a world of lessons, disappointments and discipline. My instincts were not vicious. Ideas bubbled up within me continually from an apparently inexhaustible spring, and the very strength of the longings they set in motion puzzled and troubled my parents: what I seem to see most distinctly now is a young mind engaged in a ceaseless struggle for self-expression, for self-development, against the inertia of a tradition of which my father was the embodiment. He was an enigma to me then. He sincerely loved me, he cherished ambitions concerning me, yet thwarted every natural, budding growth, until I grew unconsciously to regard him as my enemy, although I had an affection for him and a pride in him that flared up at times. Instead of confiding to him my aspirations, vague though they were, I became more and more secretive as I grew older. I knew instinctively that he regarded these aspirations as evidences in my character of serious moral flaws. And I would sooner have suffered many afternoons of his favourite punishment—solitary confinement in my room—than reveal to him those occasional fits of creative fancy which caused me to neglect my lessons in order to put them on paper. Loving literature, in his way, he was characteristically incapable of recognizing the literary instinct, and the symptoms of its early stages he mistook for inherent frivolity, for lack of respect for the truth; in brief, for original sin. At the age of fourteen I had begun secretly (alas, how many things I did secretly!) to write stories of a sort, stories that never were finished.

He regarded reading as duty, not pleasure. He laid out books for me, which I neglected. He was part and parcel of that American environment in which literary ambition was regarded as sheer madness. And no one who has not experienced that environment can have any conception of the pressure it exerted to stifle originality, to thrust the new generation into its religious and commercial moulds. Shall we ever, I wonder, develop the enlightened education that will know how to take advantage of such initiative as was mine? that will be on the watch for it, sympathize with it and guide it to fruition?

I was conscious of still another creative need, that of dramatizing my ideas, of converting them into action. And this need was to lead me farther than ever afield from the path of righteousness. The concrete realization of ideas, as many geniuses will testify, is an expensive undertaking, requiring a little pocket money; and I have already touched upon that subject. My father did not believe in pocket money. A sea story that my Cousin Donald Ewan gave me at Christmas inspired me to compose one of a somewhat different nature; incidentally, I deemed it a vast improvement on Cousin Donald's book. Now, if I only had a boat, with the assistance of Ham Durrett and Tom Peters, Gene Hollister and Perry Blackwood and other friends, this story of mine might be staged. There were, however, as usual, certain seemingly insuperable difficulties: in the first place, it was winter time; in the second, no facilities existed in the city for operations of a nautical character; and, lastly, my Christmas money amounted only to five dollars. It was my father who pointed out these and other objections. For, after a careful perusal of the price lists I had sent for, I had been forced to appeal to him to supply additional funds with which to purchase a row-boat. Incidentally, he read me a lecture on extravagance, referred to my last month's report at the Academy, and finished by declaring that he would not permit me to have a boat even in the highly improbable case of somebody's presenting me with one. Let it not be imagined that my ardour or my determination were extinguished. Shortly after I had retired from his presence it occurred to me that he had said nothing to forbid my making a boat, and the first thing I did after school that day was to procure, for twenty-five cents, a second-hand book on boat construction. The woodshed was chosen as a shipbuilding establishment. It was convenient—and my father never went into the back yard in cold weather. Inquiries of lumber-yards developing the disconcerting fact that four dollars and seventy-five cents was inadequate to buy the material itself, to say nothing of the cost of steaming and bending the ribs, I reluctantly abandoned the ideal of the graceful craft I had sketched, and compromised on a flat bottom. Observe how the ways of deception lead to transgression: I recalled the cast-off lumber pile of Jarvis, the carpenter, a good-natured Englishman, coarse and fat: in our neighbourhood his reputation for obscenity was so well known to mothers that I had been forbidden to go near him or his shop. Grits Jarvis, his son, who had inherited the talent, was also contraband. I can see now the huge bulk of the elder Jarvis as he stood in the melting, soot-powdered snow in front of his shop, and hear his comments on my pertinacity.

"If you ever wants another man's missus when you grows up, my lad, Gawd 'elp 'im!"

"Why should I want another man's wife when I don't want one of my own?" I demanded, indignant.

He laughed with his customary lack of moderation.

"You mind what old Jarvis says," he cried. "What you wants, you gets."

I did get his boards, by sheer insistence. No doubt they were not very valuable, and without question he more than made up for them in my mother's bill. I also got something else of equal value to me at the moment, —the assistance of Grits, the contraband; daily, after school, I smuggled him into the shed through the alley, acquiring likewise the services of Tom Peters, which was more of a triumph than it would seem. Tom always had to be "worked up" to participation in my ideas, but in the end he almost invariably succumbed. The notion of building a boat in the dead of winter, and so far from her native element, naturally struck him at first as ridiculous. Where in Jehoshaphat was I going to sail it if I ever got it made? He much preferred to throw snowballs at innocent wagon drivers.

All that Tom saw, at first, was a dirty, coal-spattered shed with dim recesses, for it was lighted on one side only, and its temperature was somewhere below freezing. Surely he could not be blamed for a tempered enthusiasm! But for me, all the dirt and cold and discomfort were blotted out, and I beheld a gallant craft manned by sturdy seamen forging her way

across blue water in the South Seas. Treasure Island, alas, was as yet
unwritten; but among my father's books were two old volumes in which I
had hitherto taken no interest, with crude engravings of palms and coral
reefs, of naked savages and tropical mountains covered with jungle, the
adventures, in brief, of one Captain Cook. I also discovered a book by a
later traveller. Spurred on by a mysterious motive power, and to the great
neglect of the pons asinorum and the staple products of the Southern States,
I gathered an amazing amount of information concerning a remote portion
of the globe, of head-hunters and poisoned stakes, of typhoons, of quee
war-craft that crept up on you while you were dismantling galleons, when
desperate hand-to-hand encounters ensued. Little by little as I wove all this
into personal adventures soon to be realized, Tom forgot the snowballs and
the maddened grocery-men who chased him around the block; while Grits
would occasionally stop sawing and cry out:—"Ah, s'y!" frequently adding
that he would be G—d—d.

The cold woodshed became a chantry on the New England coast, the
alley the wintry sea soon to embrace our ship, the saw-horses—which stood
between a coal-bin on one side and unused stalls filled with rubbish and
kindling on the other—the ways; the yard behind the lattice fence became a
backwater, the flapping clothes the sails of ships that took refuge there—on
Mondays and Tuesdays. Even my father was symbolized with unparalleled
audacity as a watchful government which had, up to the present, no inkling
of our semi-piratical intentions! The cook and the housemaid, though
remonstrating against the presence of Grits, were friendly confederates;
likewise old Cephas, the darkey who, from my earliest memory, carried coal
and wood and blacked the shoes, washed the windows and scrubbed the
steps.

One afternoon Tom went to work....

The history of the building of the good ship Petrel is similar to that of
all created things, a story of trial and error and waste. At last, one March day
she stood ready for launching. She had even been caulked; for Grits, from
an unknown and unquestionably dubious source, had procured a bucket of
tar, which we heated over afire in the alley and smeared into every crack. It
was natural that the news of such a feat as we were accomplishing should
have leaked out, that the "yard" should have been visited from time to time
by interested friends, some of whom came to admire, some to scoff, and all
to speculate. Among the scoffers, of course, was Ralph Hambleton, who
stood with his hands in his pockets and cheerfully predicted all sorts of dire
calamities. Ralph was always a superior boy, tall and a trifle saturnine and
cynical, with an amazing self-confidence not wholly due to the wealth of his
father, the iron-master. He was older than I.

"She won't float five minutes, if you ever get her to the water," was his
comment, and in this he was supported on general principles by Julia and
Russell Peters. Ralph would have none of the Petrel, or of the South Seas
either; but he wanted,—so he said,—"to be in at the death." The
Hambletons were one of the few families who at that time went to the sea
for the summer, and from a practical knowledge of craft in general Ralph
was not slow to point out the defects of ours. Tom and I defended her

passionately.

Ralph was not a romanticist. He was a born leader, excelling at organized games, exercising over boys the sort of fascination that comes from doing everything better and more easily than others. It was only during the progress of such enterprises as this affair of the Petrel that I succeeded in winning their allegiance; bit by bit, as Tom's had been won, fanning their enthusiasm by impersonating at once Achilles and Homer, recruiting while relating the Odyssey of the expedition in glowing colours. Ralph always scoffed, and when I had no scheme on foot they went back to him. Having surveyed the boat and predicted calamity, he departed, leaving a circle of quaint and youthful figures around the Petrel in the shed: Gene Hollister, romantically inclined, yet somewhat hampered by a strict parental supervision; Ralph's cousin Ham Durrett, who was even then a rather fat boy, good-natured but selfish; Don and Harry Ewan, my second cousins; Mac and Nancy Willett and Sam and Sophy McAlery. Nancy was a tomboy, not to be denied, and Sophy her shadow. We held a council, the all-important question of which was how to get the Petrel to the water, and what water to get her to. The river was not to be thought of, and Blackstone Lake some six miles from town. Finally, Logan's mill-pond was decided on, —a muddy sheet on the outskirts of the city. But how to get her to Logan's mill-pond? Cephas was at length consulted. It turned out that he had a coloured friend who went by the impressive name of Thomas Jefferson Taliaferro (pronounced Tolliver), who was in the express business; and who, after surveying the boat with some misgivings,—for she was ten feet long,—finally consented to transport her to "tide-water" for the sum of two dollars. But it proved that our combined resources only amounted to a dollar and seventy-five cents. Ham Durrett never contributed to anything. On this sum Thomas Jefferson compromised.

Saturday dawned clear, with a stiff March wind catching up the dust into eddies and whirling it down the street. No sooner was my father safely on his way to his office than Thomas Jefferson was reported to be in the alley, where we assembled, surveying with some misgivings Thomas Jefferson's steed, whose ability to haul the Petrel two miles seemed somewhat doubtful. Other difficulties developed; the door in the back of the shed proved to be too narrow for our ship's beam. But men embarked on a desperate enterprise are not to be stopped by such trifles, and the problem was solved by sawing out two adjoining boards. These were afterwards replaced with skill by the ship's carpenter, Able Seaman Grits Jarvis. Then the Petrel by heroic efforts was got into the wagon, the seat of which had been removed, old Thomas Jefferson perched himself precariously in the bow and protestingly gathered up his rope-patched reins.

"Folks'll 'low I'se plum crazy, drivin' dis yere boat," he declared, observing with concern that some four feet of the stern projected over the tail-board. "Ef she topples, I'll git to heaven quicker'n a bullet."

When one is shanghaied, however,—in the hands of buccaneers,—it is too late to withdraw. Six shoulders upheld the rear end of the Petrel, others shoved, and Thomas Jefferson's rickety horse began to move forward in spite of himself. An expression of sheer terror might have been observed or the old negro's crinkled face, but his voice was drowned, and we swept out of the alley. Scarcely had we travelled a block before we began to be joined by all the boys along the line of march; marbles, tops, and even incipient baseball games were abandoned that Saturday morning; people ran out of their houses, teamsters halted their carts. The breathless excitement, the exaltation I had felt on leaving the alley were now tinged with other feelings, unanticipated, but not wholly lacking in delectable quality,—concern and awe at these unforeseen forces I had raised, at this ever growing and enthusiastic body of volunteers springing up like dragon's teeth in our path. After all, was not I the hero of this triumphal procession? The thought was consoling, exhilarating. And here was Nancy marching at my side, a little subdued, perhaps, but unquestionably admiring and realizing that it was I who had created all this. Nancy, who was the aptest of pupils, the most loyal of followers, though I did not yet value her devotion at its real worth, because she was a girl. Her imagination kindled at my touch. And on this eventful occasion she carried in her arms a parcel, the contents of which were unknown to all but ourselves. At length we reached the muddy shores of Logan's pond, where two score eager hands volunteered to assist the Petrel into her native element.

Alas! that the reality never attains to the vision. I had beheld, in my dreams, the Petrel about to take the water, and Nancy Willett standing very straight making a little speech and crashing a bottle of wine across the bows. This was the content of the mysterious parcel; she had stolen it from her father's cellar. But the number of uninvited spectators, which had not been foreseen, considerably modified the programme,—as the newspapers would have said. They pushed and crowded around the ship, and made frank and even brutal remarks as to her seaworthiness; even Nancy, inured though she was to the masculine sex, had fled to the heights, and it looked at this supreme moment as though we should have to fight for the Petrel. An attempt to muster her doughty buccaneers failed; the gunner too had fled,— Gene Hollister; Ham Durrett and the Ewanses were nowhere to be seen, and a muster revealed only Tom, the fidus Achates, and Grits Jarvis.

"Ah, s'y!" he exclaimed in the teeth of the menacing hordes. "Stand back, carn't yer? I'll bash yer face in, Johnny. Whose boat is this?"

Shall it be whispered that I regretted his belligerency? Here, in truth, was the drama staged,—my drama, had I only been able to realize it. The good ship beached, the headhunters hemming us in on all sides, the scene prepared for one of those struggles against frightful odds which I had so graphically related as an essential part of our adventures.

"Let's roll the cuss in the fancy collar," proposed one of the head-hunters,—meaning me.

"I'll stove yer slats if yer touch him," said Grits, and then resorted to appeal. "I s'y, carn't yer stand back and let a chap 'ave a charnst?"

The head-hunters only jeered. And what shall be said of the Captain in this moment of peril? Shall it be told that his heart was beating wildly?— bumping were a better word. He was trying to remember that he was the Captain. Otherwise, he must admit with shame that he, too, should have fled. So much for romance when the test comes. Will he remain to fall fighting for his ship? Like Horatius, he glanced up at the hill, where, instead of the porch of the home where he would fain have been, he beheld a wisp of a girl standing alone, her hat on the back of her head, her hair flying in the wind, gazing intently down at him in his danger. The renegade crew was nowhere to be seen. There are those who demand the presence of a woman in order to be heroes....

"Give us a chance, can't you?" he cried, repeating Grits's appeal in not quite such a stentorian tone as he would have liked, while his hand trembled on the gunwale. Tom Peters, it must be acknowledged, was much more of a buccaneer when it was a question of deeds, for he planted himself in the way of the belligerent chief of the head-hunters (who spoke with a decided brogue).

"Get out of the way!" said Tom, with a little squeak in his voice. Yet there he was, and he deserves a tribute.

An unlooked-for diversion saved us from annihilation, in the shape of one who had a talent for creating them. We were bewilderingly aware of a girlish figure amongst us.

"You cowards!" she cried. "You cowards!"

Lithe, and fairly quivering with passion, it was Nancy who showed us how to face the head-hunters. They gave back. They would have been brave indeed if they had not retreated before such an intense little nucleus of energy and indignation!...

"Ah, give 'em a chanst," said their chief, after a moment.... He even helped to push the boat towards the water. But he did not volunteer to be one of those to man the Petrel on her maiden voyage. Nor did Logan's pond, that wild March day, greatly resemble the South Seas. Nevertheless, my eye on Nancy, I stepped proudly aboard and seized an "oar." Grits and Tom followed,—when suddenly the Petrel sank considerably below the water-line as her builders had estimated it. Ere we fully realized this, the now friendly head-hunters had given us a shove, and we were off! The Captain, who should have been waving good-bye to his lady love from the poop, sat down abruptly,—the crew likewise; not, however, before she had heeled to the scuppers, and a half-bucket of iced water had run it. Head-hunters were mere daily episodes in Grits's existence, but water... He muttered something in cockney that sounded like a prayer.... The wind was rapidly driving us toward the middle of the pond, and something cold and ticklish was seeping through the seats of our trousers. We sat like statues....

The bright scene etched itself in my memory—the bare brown slopes with which the pond was bordered, the Irish shanties, the clothes-lines with red flannel shirts snapping in the biting wind; Nancy motionless on the bank; the group behind her, silent now, impressed in spite of itself at the sight of our intrepidity.

The Petrel was sailing stern first.... Would any of us, indeed, ever see home again? I thought of my father's wrath turned to sorrow because he had refused to gratify a son's natural wish and present him with a real rowboat.... Out of the corners of our eyes we watched the water creeping around the gunwale, and the very muddiness of it seemed to enhance its coldness, to make the horrors of its depths more mysterious and hideous.

The voice of Grits startled us.

"O Gawd," he was saying, "we're a-going to sink, and I carn't swim! The blarsted tar's give way back here."

"Is she leaking?" I cried.

"She's a-filling up like a bath tub," he lamented.

Slowly but perceptibly, in truth, the bow was rising, and above the whistling of the wind I could hear his chattering as she settled.... Then several things happened simultaneously: an agonized cry behind me, distant shouts from the shore, a sudden upward lunge of the bow, and the torture of being submerged, inch by inch, in the icy, yellow water. Despite the splashing behind me, I sat as though paralyzed until I was waist deep and the boards turned under me, and then, with a spasmodic contraction of my whole being I struck out—only to find my feet on the muddy bottom. Such was the inglorious end of the good ship Petrel! For she went down, with all hands, in little more than half a fathom of water.... It was not until then I realized that we had been blown clear across the pond!

Figures were running along the shore. And as Tom and I emerged dragging Grits between us,—for he might have been drowned there abjectly in the shallows,—we were met by a stout and bare-armed Irishwoman whose scanty hair, I remember, was drawn into a tight knot behind her head; and who seized us, all three, as though we were a bunch of carrots.

"Come along wid ye!" she cried.

Shivering, we followed her up the hill, the spectators of the tragedy, who by this time had come around the pond, trailing after. Nancy was not among them. Inside the shanty into which we were thrust were two small children crawling about the floor, and the place was filled with steam from a wash-tub against the wall and a boiler on the stove. With a vigorous injunction to make themselves scarce, the Irishwoman slammed the door in the faces of the curious and ordered us to remove our clothes. Grits was put to bed in a corner, while Tom and I, provided with various garments, huddled over the stove. There fell to my lot the red flannel shirt which I had seen on the clothes-line. She gave us hot coffee, and was back at her wash-tub in no time at all, her entire comment on a proceeding that seemed to Tom and me to have certain elements of gravity being, "By's will be by's!" The final ironical touch was given the anti-climax when our rescuer turned out to be the mother of the chief of the head-hunters himself! He had lingered perforce with his brothers and sister outside the cabin until dinner time, and when he came in he was meek as Moses.

Thus the ready hospitality of the poor, which passed over the heads of Tom and me as we ate bread and onions and potatoes with a ravenous hunger. It must have been about two o'clock in the afternoon when we bade good-bye to our preserver and departed for home....

At first we went at a dog-trot, but presently slowed down to discuss the future looming portentously ahead of us. Since entire concealment was now impossible, the question was,—how complete a confession would be necessary? Our cases, indeed, were dissimilar, and Tom's incentive to hold back the facts was not nearly so great as mine. It sometimes seemed to me in those days unjust that the Peterses were able on the whole to keep out of criminal difficulties, in which I was more or less continuously involved: for it did not strike me that their sins were not those of the imagination. The method of Tom's father was the slipper. He and Tom understood each other, while between my father and myself was a great gulf fixed. Not that Tom yearned for the slipper; but he regarded its occasional applications as being as inevitable as changes in the weather; lying did not come easily to him, and left to himself he much preferred to confess and have the matter over with. I have already suggested that I had cultivated lying, that weapon of the weaker party, in some degree, at least, in self-defence.

Tom was loyal. Moreover, my conviction would probably deprive him for six whole afternoons of my company, on which he was more or less dependent. But the defence of this case presented unusual difficulties, and we stopped several times to thrash them out. We had been absent from dinner, and doubtless by this time Julia had informed Tom's mother of the expedition, and anyone could see that our clothing had been wet. So I lingered in no little anxiety behind the Peters stable while he made the investigation. Our spirits rose considerably when he returned to report that Julia had unexpectedly been a trump, having quieted his mother by the surmise that he was spending the day with his Aunt Fanny. So far, so good. The problem now was to decide upon what to admit. For we must both tell the same story.

It was agreed that we had fallen into Logan's Pond from a raft: my suggestion. Well, said Tom, the Petrel hadn't proved much better than a raft, after all. I was in no mood to defend her.

This designation of the Petrel as a "raft" was my first legal quibble. The question to be decided by the court was, What is a raft? just as the supreme tribunal of the land has been required, in later years, to decide, What is whiskey? The thing to be concealed if possible was the building of the "raft," although this information was already in the possession of a number of persons, whose fathers might at any moment see fit to congratulate my own on being the parent of a genius. It was a risk, however, that had to be run. And, secondly, since Grits Jarvis was contraband, nothing was to be said about him.

I have not said much about my mother, who might have been likened on such occasions to a grand jury compelled to indict, yet torn between loyalty to an oath and sympathy with the defendant. I went through the Peters yard, climbed the wire fence, my object being to discover first from Ella, the housemaid, or Hannah, the cook, how much was known in high quarters. It was Hannah who, as I opened the kitchen door, turned at the sound, and set down the saucepan she was scouring.

"Is it home ye are? Mercy to goodness!" (this on beholding my shrunken costume) "Glory be to God you're not drownded! and your mother worritin' her heart out! So it's into the wather ye were?"

I admitted it.

"Hannah?" I said softly.

"What then?"

"Does mother know—about the boat?"

"Now don't ye be wheedlin'."

I managed to discover, however, that my mother did not know, and surmised that the best reason why she had not been told had to do with Hannah's criminal acquiescence concerning the operations in the shed. I ran into the front hall and up the stairs, and my mother heard me coming and met me on the landing.

"Hugh, where have you been?"

As I emerged from the semi-darkness of the stairway she caught sight of my dwindled garments, of the trousers well above my ankles. Suddenly she had me in her arms and was kissing me passionately. As she stood before me in her grey, belted skirt, the familiar red-and-white cameo at her throat, her heavy hair parted in the middle, in her eyes was an odd, appealing look which I know now was a sign of mother love struggling with a Presbyterian conscience. Though she inherited that conscience, I have often thought she might have succeeded in casting it off—or at least some of it—had it not been for the fact that in spite of herself she worshipped its incarnation in the shape of my father. Her voice trembled a little as she drew me to the sofa beside the window.

"Tell me about what happened, my son," she said.

It was a terrible moment for me. For my affections were still quiveringly alive in those days, and I loved her. I had for an instant an instinctive impulse to tell her the whole story,—South Sea Islands and all! And I could have done it had I not beheld looming behind her another figure which represented a stern and unsympathetic Authority, and somehow made her, suddenly, of small account. Not that she would have understood the romance, but she would have comprehended me. I knew that she was powerless to save me from the wrath to come. I wept. It was because I hated to lie to her,—yet I did so. Fear gripped me, and—like some respectable criminals I have since known—I understood that any confession I made would inexorably be used against me.... I wonder whether she knew I was lying? At any rate, the case appeared to be a grave one, and I was presently remanded to my room to be held over for trial....

Vividly, as I write, I recall the misery of the hours I have spent, while awaiting sentence, in the little chamber with the honeysuckle wall-paper and steel engravings of happy but dumpy children romping in the fields and groves. On this particular March afternoon the weather had become morne, as the French say; and I looked down sadly into the grey back yard which the wind of the morning had strewn with chips from the Petrel. At last, when shadows were gathering in the corners of the room, I heard footsteps. Ella appeared, prim and virtuous, yet a little commiserating. My father wished to see me, downstairs. It was not the first time she had brought that summons, and always her manner was the same!

The scene of my trials was always the sitting room, lined with grim books in their walnut cases. And my father sat, like a judge, behind the big desk where he did his work when at home. Oh, the distance between us at such an hour! I entered as delicately as Agag, and the expression in his eye seemed to convict me before I could open my mouth.

"Hugh," he said, "your mother tells me that you have confessed to going, without permission, to Logan's Pond, where you embarked on a raft and fell into the water."

The slight emphasis he contrived to put on the word raft sent a colder shiver down my spine than the iced water had done. What did he know? or was this mere suspicion? Too late, now, at any rate, to plead guilty.

"It was a sort of a raft, sir," I stammered.

"A sort of a raft," repeated my father. "Where, may I ask, did you find it?"

"I—I didn't exactly find it, sir."

"Ah!" said my father. (It was the moment to glance meaningly at the jury.) The prisoner gulped. "You didn't exactly find it, then. Will you kindly explain how you came by it?"

"Well, sir, we—I—put it together."

"Have you any objection to stating, Hugh, in plain English, that you made it?"

"No, sir, I suppose you might say that I made it."

"Or that it was intended for a row-boat?"

Here was the time to appeal, to force a decision as to what constituted a row-boat.

"Perhaps it might be called a row-boat, sir," I said abjectly.

"Or that, in direct opposition to my wishes and commands in forbidding you to have a boat, to spend your money foolishly and wickedly on a whim, you constructed one secretly in the woodshed, took out a part of the back partition, thus destroying property that did, not belong to you, and had the boat carted this morning to Logan's Pond?" I was silent, utterly undone. Evidently he had specific information.... There are certain expressions that are, at times, more than mere figures of speech, and now my father's wrath seemed literally towering. It added visibly to his stature.

"Hugh," he said, in a voice that penetrated to the very corners of my soul, "I utterly fail to understand you. I cannot imagine how a son of mine, a son of your mother who is the very soul of truthfulness and honour—can be a liar." (Oh, the terrible emphasis he put on that word!) "Nor is it as if this were a new tendency—I have punished you for it before. Your mother and I have tried to do our duty by you, to instil into you Christian teaching. But it seems wholly useless. I confess that I am at a less how to proceed. You seem to have no conscience whatever, no conception of what you owe to your parents and your God. You not only persistently disregard my wishes and commands, but you have, for many months, been leading a double life, facing me every day, while you were secretly and continually disobeying me. I shudder to think where this determination of yours to have what you desire at any price will lead you in the future. It is just such a desire that distinguishes wicked men from good."

I will not linger upon a scene the very remembrance of which is painful to this day.... I went from my father's presence in disgrace, in an agony of spirit that was overwhelming, to lock the door of my room and drop face downward on the bed, to sob until my muscles twitched. For he had, indeed, put into me an awful fear. The greatest horror of my boyish imagination was a wicked man. Was I, as he had declared, utterly depraved and doomed in spite of myself to be one?

There came a knock at my door—Ella with my supper. I refused to open, and sent her away, to fall on my knees in the darkness and pray wildly to a God whose attributes and character were sufficiently confused in my mind. On the one hand was the stern, despotic Monarch of the Westminster Catechism, whom I addressed out of habit, the Father who condemned a portion of his children from the cradle. Was I one of those who he had decreed before I was born must suffer the tortures of the flames of hell? Putting two and two together, what I had learned in Sunday school and gathered from parts of Dr. Pound's sermons, and the intimation of my father that wickedness was within me, like an incurable disease,—was not mine the logical conclusion? What, then, was the use of praying?... My supplications ceased abruptly. And my ever ready imagination, stirred to its depths, beheld that awful scene of the last day: the darkness, such as sometimes creeps over the city in winter, when the jaundiced smoke falls down and we read at noonday by gas-light. I beheld the tortured faces of the wicked gathered on the one side, and my mother on the other amongst the blessed, gazing across the gulf at me with yearning and compassion. Strange that it did not strike me that the sight of the condemned whom they had loved in life would have marred if not destroyed the happiness of the chosen, about to receive their crowns and harps! What a theology—that made the Creator and Preserver of all mankind thus illogical!

# III.

Although I was imaginative, I was not morbidly introspective, and by the end of the first day of my incarceration my interest in that solution had waned. At times, however, I actually yearned for someone in whom I could confide, who could suggest a solution. I repeat, I would not for worlds have asked my father or my mother or Dr. Pound, of whom I had a wholesome fear, or perhaps an unwholesome one. Except at morning Bible reading and at church my parents never mentioned the name of the Deity, save to instruct me formally. Intended or no, the effect of my religious training was to make me ashamed of discussing spiritual matters, and naturally I failed to perceive that this was because it laid its emphasis on personal salvation.... I did not, however, become an unbeliever, for I was not of a nature to contemplate with equanimity a godless universe....

My sufferings during these series of afternoon confinements did not come from remorse, but were the result of a vague sense of injury; and their effect was to generate within me a strange motive power, a desire to do something that would astound my father and eventually wring from him the confession that he had misjudged me. To be sure, I should have to wait until early manhood, at least, for the accomplishment of such a coup. Might it not be that I was an embryonic literary genius? Many were the books I began in this ecstasy of self-vindication, only to abandon them when my confinement came to an end.

It was about this time, I think, that I experienced one of those shocks which have a permanent effect upon character. It was then the custom for ladies to spend the day with one another, bringing their sewing; and sometimes, when I unexpectedly entered the sitting-room, the voices of my mother's visitors would drop to a whisper. One afternoon I returned from school to pause at the head of the stairs. Cousin Bertha Ewan and Mrs. McAlery were discussing with my mother an affair that I judged from the awed tone in which they spoke might prove interesting.

"Poor Grace," Mrs. McAlery was saying, "I imagine she's paid a heavy penalty. No man alive will be faithful under those circumstances."

I stopped at the head of the stairs, with a delicious, guilty feeling.

"Have they ever heard of her?" Cousin Bertha asked.

"It is thought they went to Spain," replied Mrs. McAlery, solemnly, yet not without a certain zest. "Mr. Jules Hollister will not have her name mentioned in his presence, you know. And Whitcomb chased them as far as New York with a horse-pistol in his pocket. The report is that he got to the dock just as the ship sailed. And then, you know, he went to live somewhere out West,—in Iowa, I believe."

"Did he ever get a divorce?" Cousin Bertha inquired.

"He was too good a church member, my dear," my mother reminded her.

"Well, I'd have got one quick enough, church member or no church member," declared Cousin Bertha, who had in her elements of daring.

"Not that I mean for a moment to excuse her," Mrs. McAlery put in, "but Edward Whitcomb did have a frightful temper, and he was awfully strict with her, and he was old enough, anyhow, to be her father. Grace Hollister was the last woman in the world I should have suspected of doing so hideous a thing. She was so sweet and simple."

"Jennings was very attractive," said my Cousin Bertha. "I don't think I ever saw a handsomer man. Now, if he had looked at me—"

The sentence was never finished, for at this crucial moment I dropped a grammar....

I had heard enough, however, to excite my curiosity to the highest pitch. And that evening, when I came in at five o'clock to study, I asked my mother what had become of Gene Hollister's aunt.

"She went away, Hugh," replied my mother, looking greatly troubled.

"Why?" I persisted.

"It is something you are too young to understand."

Of course I started an investigation, and the next day at school I asked the question of Gene Hollister himself, only to discover that he believed his aunt to be dead! And that night he asked his mother if his Aunt Grace were really alive, after all? Whereupon complications and explanations ensued between our parents, of which we saw only the surface signs.... My father accused me of eavesdropping (which I denied), and sentenced me to an afternoon of solitary confinement for repeating something which I had heard in private. I have reason to believe that my mother was also reprimanded.

It must not be supposed that I permitted the matter to rest. In addition to Grits Jarvis, there was another contraband among my acquaintances, namely, Alec Pound, the scrape-grace son of the Reverend Doctor Pound. Alec had an encyclopaedic mind, especially well stocked with the kind of knowledge I now desired; first and last he taught me much, which I would better have got in another way. To him I appealed and got the story, my worst suspicions being confirmed. Mrs. Whitcomb's house had been across the alley from that of Mr. Jennings, but no one knew that anything was "going on," though there had been signals from the windows—the neighbours afterwards remembered....

I listened shudderingly.

"But," I cried, "they were both married!"

"What difference does that make when you love a woman?" Alec replied grandly. "I could tell you much worse things than that."

This he proceeded to do. Fascinated, I listened with a sickening sensation. It was a mild afternoon in spring, and we stood in the deep limestone gutter in front of the parsonage, a little Gothic wooden house set in a gloomy yard.

"I thought," said I, "that people couldn't love any more after they were married, except each other."

Alec looked at me pityingly.

"You'll get over that notion," he assured me.

Thus another ingredient entered my character. Denied its food at home, good food, my soul eagerly consumed and made part of itself the fermenting stuff that Alec Pound so willing distributed. And it was fermenting stuff. Let us see what it did to me. Working slowly but surely, it changed for me the dawning mystery of sex into an evil instead of a holy one. The knowledge of the tragedy of Grace Hollister started me to seeking restlessly, on bookshelves and elsewhere, for a secret that forever eluded me, and forever led me on. The word fermenting aptly describes the process begun, suggesting as it does something closed up, away from air and sunlight, continually working in secret, engendering forces that fascinated, yet inspired me with fear. Undoubtedly this secretiveness of our elders was due to the pernicious dualism of their orthodox Christianity, in which love was carnal and therefore evil, and the flesh not the gracious soil of the spirit, but something to be deplored and condemned, exorcised and transformed by the miracle of grace. Now love had become a terrible power (gripping me) whose enchantment drove men and women from home and friends and kindred to the uttermost parts of the earth....

It was long before I got to sleep that night after my talk with Alec Pound. I alternated between the horror and the romance of the story I had heard, supplying for myself the details he had omitted: I beheld the signals from the windows, the clandestine meetings, the sudden and desperate flight. And to think that all this could have happened in our city not five blocks from where I lay!

My consternation and horror were concentrated on the man,—and yet I recall a curious bifurcation. Instead of experiencing that automatic righteous indignation which my father and mother had felt, which had animated old Mr. Jules Hollister when he had sternly forbidden his daughter's name to be mentioned in his presence, which had made these people outcasts, there welled up within me an intense sympathy and pity. By an instinctive process somehow linked with other experiences, I seemed to be able to enter into the feelings of these two outcasts, to understand the fearful yet fascinating nature of the impulse that had led them to elude the vigilance and probity of a world with which I myself was at odds. I pictured them in a remote land, shunned by mankind. Was there something within me that might eventually draw me to do likewise? The desire in me to which my father had referred, which would brook no opposition, which twisted and squirmed until it found its way to its object? I recalled the words of Jarvis, the carpenter, that if I ever set my heart on another man's wife, God help him. God help me!

A wicked man! I had never beheld the handsome and fascinating Mr. Jennings, but I visualised him now; dark, like all villains, with a black moustache and snapping black eyes. He carried a cane. I always associated canes with villains. Whereupon I arose, groped for the matches, lighted the gas, and gazing at myself in the mirror was a little reassured to find nothing sinister in my countenance....

Next to my father's faith in a Moral Governor of the Universe was his belief in the Tariff and the Republican Party. And this belief, among others, he handed on to me. On the cinder playground of the Academy we Republicans used to wage, during campaigns, pitched battles for the Tariff. It did not take a great deal of courage to be a Republican in our city, and I was brought up to believe that Democrats were irrational, inferior, and—with certain exceptions like the Hollisters—dirty beings. There was only one degree lower, and that was to be a mugwump. It was no wonder that the Hollisters were Democrats, for they had a queer streak in them; owing, no doubt, to the fact that old Mr. Jules Hollister's mother had been a Frenchwoman. He looked like a Frenchman, by the way, and always wore a skullcap.

I remember one autumn afternoon having a violent quarrel with Gene Hollister that bade fair to end in blows, when he suddenly demanded:—"I'll bet you anything you don't know why you're a Republican."

"It's because I'm for the Tariff," I replied triumphantly.

But his next question floored me. What, for example, was the Tariff? I tried to bluster it out, but with no success.

"Do you know?" I cried finally, with sudden inspiration.

It turned out that he did not.

"Aren't we darned idiots," he asked, "to get fighting over something we don't know anything about?"

That was Gene's French blood, of course. But his question rankled. And how was I to know that he would have got as little satisfaction if he had hurled it into the marching ranks of those imposing torch-light processions which sometimes passed our house at night, with drums beating and fifes screaming and torches waving,—thousands of citizens who were for the Tariff for the same reason as I: to wit, because they were Republicans.

Yet my father lived and died in the firm belief that the United States of America was a democracy!

Resolved not to be caught a second time in such a humiliating position by a Democrat, I asked my father that night what the Tariff was. But I was too young to understand it, he said. I was to take his word for it that the country would go to the dogs if the Democrats got in and the Tariff were taken away. Here, in a nutshell, though neither he nor I realized it, was the political instruction of the marching hordes. Theirs not to reason why. I was too young, they too ignorant. Such is the method of Authority!

The steel-mills of Mr. Durrett and Mr. Hambleton, he continued, would be forced to shut down, and thousands of workmen would starve. This was just a sample of what would happen. Prosperity would cease, he declared. That word, Prosperity, made a deep impression on me, and I recall the certain reverential emphasis he laid on it. And while my solicitude for the workmen was not so great as his and Mr. Durrett's, I was concerned as to what would happen to us if those twin gods, the Tariff and Prosperity, should take their departure from the land. Knowing my love for the good things of the table, my father intimated, with a rare humour I failed to appreciate, that we should have to live henceforth in spartan simplicity. After that, like the intelligent workman, I was firmer than ever for the Tariff.

Such was the idealistic plane on which—and from a good man—I received my first political instruction! And for a long time I connected the dominance of the Republican Party with the continuation of manna and quails, in other words, with nothing that had to do with the spiritual welfare of any citizen, but with clothing and food and material comforts. My education was progressing....

Though my father revered Plato and Aristotle, he did not, apparently, take very seriously the contention that that government alone is good "which seeks to attain the permanent interests of the governed by evolving the character of its citizens." To put the matter brutally, politics, despite the lofty sentiments on the transparencies in torchlight processions, had only to do with the belly, not the soul.

Politics and government, one perceives, had nothing to do with religion, nor education with any of these. A secularized and disjointed world! Our leading citizens, learned in the classics though some of them might be, paid no heed to the dictum of the Greek idealist, who was more practical than they would have supposed. "The man who does not carry his city within his heart is a spiritual starveling."

One evening, a year or two after that tariff campaign, I was pretending to study my lessons under the student lamp in the sitting-room while my mother sewed and my father wrote at his desk, when there was a ring at the door-bell. I welcomed any interruption, even though the visitor proved to be only the druggist's boy; and there was always the possibility of a telegram announcing, for instance, the death of a relative. Such had once been the case when my Uncle Avery Paret had died in New York, and I was taken out of school for a blissful four days for the funeral.

I went tiptoeing into the hall and peeped over the banisters while Ella opened the door. I heard a voice which I recognized as that of Perry Blackwood's father asking for Mr. Paret; and then to my astonishment, I saw filing after him into the parlour some ten or twelve persons. With the exception of Mr. Ogilvy, who belonged to one of our old families, and Mr. Watling, a lawyer who had married the youngest of Gene Hollister's aunts, the visitors entered stealthily, after the manner of burglars; some of these were heavy-jowled, and all had an air of mystery that raised my curiosity and excitement to the highest pitch. I caught hold of Ella as she came up the stairs, but she tore herself free, and announced to my father that Mr. Josiah Blackwood and other gentlemen had asked to see him. My father seemed puzzled as he went downstairs.... A long interval elapsed, during which I did not make even a pretence of looking at my arithmetic. At times the low hum of voices rose to what was almost an uproar, and on occasions I distinguished a marked Irish brogue.

"I wonder what they want?" said my mother, nervously.

At last we heard the front door shut behind them, and my father came upstairs, his usually serene face wearing a disturbed expression.

"Who in the world was it, Mr. Paret?" asked my mother.

My father sat down in the arm-chair. He was clearly making an effort for self-control.

"Blackwood and Ogilvy and Watling and some city politicians," he exclaimed.

"Politicians!" she repeated. "What did they want? That is, if it's anything you can tell me," she added apologetically.

"They wished me to be the Republican candidate for the mayor of this city."

This tremendous news took me off my feet. My father mayor!

"Of course you didn't consider it, Mr. Paret," my mother was saying.

"Consider it!" he echoed reprovingly. "I can't imagine what Ogilvy and Watling and Josiah Blackwood were thinking of! They are out of their heads. I as much as told them so."

This was more than I could bear, for I had already pictured myself telling the news to envious schoolmates.

"Oh, father, why didn't you take it?" I cried.

By this time, when he turned to me, he had regained his usual expression.

"You don't know what you're talking about, Hugh," he said. "Accept a political office! That sort of thing is left to politicians."

The tone in which he spoke warned me that a continuation of the conversation would be unwise, and my mother also understood that the discussion was closed. He went back to his desk, and began writing again as though nothing had happened.

As for me, I was left in a palpitating state of excitement which my father's self-control or sang-froid only served to irritate and enhance, and my head was fairly spinning as, covertly, I watched his pen steadily covering the paper.

How could he—how could any man of flesh and blood sit down calmly after having been offered the highest honour in the gift of his community! And he had spurned it as if Mr. Blackwood and the others had gratuitously insulted him! And how was it, if my father so revered the Republican Party that he would not suffer it to be mentioned slightingly in his presence, that he had refused contemptuously to be its mayor?...

The next day at school, however, I managed to let it be known that the offer had been made and declined. After all, this seemed to make my father a bigger man than if he had accepted it. Naturally I was asked why he had declined it.

"He wouldn't take it," I replied scornfully. "Office-holding should be left to politicians."

Ralph Hambleton, with his precocious and cynical knowledge of the world, minimized my triumph by declaring that he would rather be his grandfather, Nathaniel Durrett, than the mayor of the biggest city in the country. Politicians, he said, were bloodsuckers and thieves, and the only reason for holding office was that it enabled one to steal the taxpayers' money....

As I have intimated, my vision of a future literary career waxed and waned, but a belief that I was going to be Somebody rarely deserted me. If not a literary lion, what was that Somebody to be? Such an environment as mine was woefully lacking in heroic figures to satisfy the romantic soul. In view of the experience I have just related, it is not surprising that the notion of becoming a statesman did not appeal to me; nor is it to be wondered at, despite the somewhat exaggerated respect and awe in which Ralph's grandfather was held by my father and other influential persons, that I failed to be stirred by the elements of greatness in the grim personality of our first citizen, the iron-master. For he possessed such elements. He lived alone in Ingrain Street in an uncompromising mansion I always associated with the Sabbath, not only because I used to be taken there on decorous Sunday visits by my father, but because it was the very quintessence of Presbyterianism. The moment I entered its "portals"—as Mr. Hawthorne appropriately would have called them—my spirit was overwhelmed and suffocated by its formality and orderliness. Within its stern walls Nathaniel Durrett had made a model universe of his own, such as the Deity of the Westminster Confession had no doubt meant his greater one to be if man had not rebelled and foiled him.... It was a world from which I was determined to escape at any cost.

My father and I were always ushered into the gloomy library, with its high ceiling, with its long windows that reached almost to the rococo cornice, with its cold marble mantelpiece that reminded me of a tombstone, with its interminable book shelves filled with yellow bindings. On the centre table, in addition to a ponderous Bible, was one of those old-fashioned carafes of red glass tipped with blue surmounted by a tumbler of blue tipped with red. Behind this table Mr. Durrett sat reading a volume of sermons, a really handsome old man in his black tie and pleated shirt; tall and spare, straight as a ramrod, with a finely moulded head and straight nose and sinewy hands the colour of mulberry stain. He called my father by his first name, an immense compliment, considering how few dared to do so.

"Well, Matthew," the old man would remark, after they had discussed Dr. Pound's latest flight on the nature of the Trinity or the depravity of man, or horticulture, or the Republican Party, "do you have any better news of Hugh at school?"

"I regret to say, Mr. Durrett," my father would reply, "that he does not yet seem to be aroused to a sense of his opportunities."

Whereupon Mr. Durrett would gimble me with a blue eye that lurked beneath grizzled brows, quite as painful a proceeding as if he used an iron tool. I almost pity myself when I think of what a forlorn stranger I was in their company. They two, indeed, were of one kind, and I of another sort who could never understand them,—nor they me. To what depths of despair they reduced me they never knew, and yet they were doing it all for my good! They only managed to convince me that my love of folly was ineradicable, and that I was on my way head first for perdition. I always looked, during these excruciating and personal moments, at the coloured glass bottle.

"It grieves me to hear it, Hugh," Mr. Durrett invariably declared. "You'll never come to any good without study. Now when I was your age…"

I knew his history by heart, a common one in this country, although he made an honourable name instead of a dishonourable one. And when I contrast him with those of his successors whom I was to know later…! But I shall not anticipate. American genius had not then evolved the false entry method of overcapitalization. A thrilling history, Mr. Durrett's, could I but have entered into it. I did not reflect then that this stern old man must have throbbed once; nay, fire and energy still remained in his bowels, else he could not have continued to dominate a city. Nor did it occur to me that the great steel-works that lighted the southern sky were the result of a passion, of dreams similar to those possessing me, but which I could not express. He had founded a family whose position was virtually hereditary, gained riches which for those days were great, compelled men to speak his name with a certain awe. But of what use were such riches as his when his religion and morality compelled him to banish from him all the joys in the power of riches to bring?

No, I didn't want to be an iron-master. But it may have been about this time that I began to be impressed with the power of wealth, the adulation and reverence it commanded, the importance in which it clothed all who shared in it.…

The private school I attended in the company of other boys with whom I was brought up was called Densmore Academy, a large, square building of a then hideous modernity, built of smooth, orange-red bricks with threads of black mortar between them. One reads of happy school days, yet I fail to recall any really happy hours spent there, even in the yard, which was covered with black cinders that cut you when you fell. I think of it as a penitentiary, and the memory of the barred lower windows gives substance to this impression.

I suppose I learned something during the seven years of my incarceration. All of value, had its teachers known anything of youthful psychology, of natural bent, could have been put into me in three. At least four criminally wasted years, to say nothing of the benumbing and desiccating effect of that old system of education! Chalk and chalk-dust! The Mediterranean a tinted portion of the map, Italy a man's boot which I drew painfully, with many yawns; history no glorious epic revealing as it unrolls the Meaning of Things, no revelation of that wondrous distillation of the Spirit of man, but an endless marching and counter-marching up and down the map, weary columns of figures to be learned by rote instantly to be forgotten again. "On June the 7th General So-and-so proceeded with his whole army—" where? What does it matter? One little chapter of Carlyle, illuminated by a teacher of understanding, were worth a million such text-books. Alas, for the hatred of Virgil! "Paret" (a shiver), "begin at the one hundred and thirtieth line and translate!" I can hear myself droning out in detestable English a meaningless portion of that endless journey of the pious AEneas; can see Gene Hollister, with heart-rending glances of despair, stumbling through Cornelius Nepos in an unventilated room with chalk-rubbed blackboards and heavy odours of ink and stale lunch. And I graduated from Densmore Academy, the best school in our city, in the 80's, without having been taught even the rudiments of citizenship.

Knowledge was presented to us as a corpse, which bit by bit we painfully dissected. We never glimpsed the living, growing thing, never experienced the Spirit, the same spirit that was able magically to waft me from a wintry Lyme Street to the South Seas, the energizing, electrifying Spirit of true achievement, of life, of God himself. Little by little its flames were smothered until in manhood there seemed no spark of it left alive. Many years were to pass ere it was to revive again, as by a miracle. I travelled. Awakening at dawn, I saw, framed in a port-hole, rose-red Seriphos set in a living blue that paled the sapphire; the seas Ulysses had sailed, and the company of the Argonauts. My soul was steeped in unimagined colour, and in the memory of one rapturous instant is gathered what I was soon to see of Greece, is focussed the meaning of history, poetry and art. I was to stand one evening in spring on the mound where heroes sleep and gaze upon the plain of Marathon between darkening mountains and the blue thread of the strait peaceful now, flushed with pink and white blossoms of fruit and almond trees; to sit on the cliff-throne whence a Persian King had looked down upon a Salamis fought and lost.... In that port-hole glimpse a Themistocles was revealed, a Socrates, a Homer and a Phidias, an AEschylus, and a Pericles; yes, and a John brooding Revelations on his sea-girt rock as twilight falls over the waters....

I saw the Roman Empire, that Scarlet Woman whose sands were dyed crimson with blood to appease her harlotry, whose ships were laden with treasures from the immutable East, grain from the valley of the Nile, spices from Arabia, precious purple stuffs from Tyre, tribute and spoil, slaves and jewels from conquered nations she absorbed; and yet whose very emperors were the unconscious instruments of a Progress they wot not of, preserved to the West by Marathon and Salamis. With Caesar's legions its message went forth across Hispania to the cliffs of the wild western ocean, through

Hercynian forests to tribes that dwelt where great rivers roll up their bars by misty, northern seas, and even to Celtic fastnesses beyond the Wall....

# IV.

In and out of my early memories like a dancing ray of sunlight flits the spirit of Nancy. I was always fond of her, but in extreme youth I accepted her incense with masculine complacency and took her allegiance for granted, never seeking to fathom the nature of the spell I exercised over her. Naturally other children teased me about her; but what was worse, with that charming lack of self-consciousness and consideration for what in after life are called the finer feelings, they teased her about me before me, my presence deterring them not at all. I can see them hopping around her in the Peters yard crying out:—"Nancy's in love with Hugh! Nancy's in love with Hugh!"

A sufficiently thrilling pastime, this, for Nancy could take care of herself. I was a bungler beside her when it came to retaliation, and not the least of her attractions for me was her capacity for anger: fury would be a better term. She would fly at them—even as she flew at the head-hunters when the Petrel was menaced; and she could run like a deer. Woe to the unfortunate victim she overtook! Masculine strength, exercised apologetically, availed but little, and I have seen Russell Peters and Gene Hollister retire from such encounters humiliated and weeping. She never caught Ralph; his methods of torture were more intelligent and subtle than Gene's and Russell's, but she was his equal when it came to a question of tongues.

"I know what's the matter with you, Ralph Hambleton," she would say. "You're jealous." An accusation that invariably put him on the defensive. "You think all the girls are in love with you, don't you?"

These scenes I found somewhat embarrassing. Not so Nancy. After discomfiting her tormenters, or wounding and scattering them, she would return to my side.... In spite of her frankly expressed preference for me she had an elusiveness that made a continual appeal to my imagination. She was never obvious or commonplace, and long before I began to experience the discomforts and sufferings of youthful love I was fascinated by a nature eloquent with contradictions and inconsistencies. She was a tomboy, yet her own sex was enhanced rather than overwhelmed by contact with the other: and no matter how many trees she climbed she never seemed to lose her daintiness. It was innate.

She could, at times, be surprisingly demure. These impressions of her daintiness and demureness are particularly vivid in a picture my memory has retained of our walking together, unattended, to Susan Blackwood's birthday party. She must have been about twelve years old. It was the first time I had escorted her or any other girl to a party; Mrs. Willett had smiled over the proceeding, but Nancy and I took it most seriously, as symbolic of things to come. I can see Powell Street, where Nancy lived, at four o'clock on a mild and cloudy December afternoon, the decorous, retiring houses, Nancy on one side of the pavement by the iron fences and I on the other by the tree boxes. I can't remember her dress, only the exquisite sense of her slimness and daintiness comes back to me, of her dark hair in a long braid tied with a red ribbon, of her slender legs clad in black stockings of shining silk. We felt the occasion to be somehow too significant, too eloquent for words....

In silence we climbed the flight of stone steps that led up to the Blackwood mansion, when suddenly the door was opened, letting out sounds of music and revelry. Mr. Blackwood's coloured butler, Ned, beamed at us hospitably, inviting us to enter the brightness within. The shades were drawn, the carpets were covered with festal canvas, the folding doors between the square rooms were flung back, the prisms of the big chandeliers flung their light over animated groups of matrons and children. Mrs. Watling, the mother of the Watling twins—too young to be present was directing with vivacity the game of "King William was King James's son," and Mrs. McAlery was playing the piano.

"Now choose you East, now choose you West,
Now choose the one you love the best!"

Tom Peters, in a velvet suit and consequently very miserable, refused to embrace Ethel Hollister; while the scornful Julia lurked in a corner: nothing would induce her to enter such a foolish game. I experienced a novel discomfiture when Ralph kissed Nancy.... Afterwards came the feast, from which Ham Durrett, in a pink paper cap with streamers, was at length forcibly removed by his mother. Thus early did he betray his love for the flesh pots....

It was not until I was sixteen that a player came and touched the keys of my soul, and it awoke, bewildered, at these first tender notes. The music quickened, tripping in ecstasy, to change by subtle phrases into themes of exquisite suffering hitherto unexperienced. I knew that I loved Nancy.

With the advent of longer dresses that reached to her shoe tops a change had come over her. The tomboy, the willing camp-follower who loved me and was unashamed, were gone forever, and a mysterious, transfigured being, neither girl nor woman, had magically evolved. Could it be possible that she loved me still? My complacency had vanished; suddenly I had become the aggressor, if only I had known how to "aggress"; but in her presence I was seized by an accursed shyness that paralyzed my tongue, and the things I had planned to say were left unuttered. It was something—though I did not realize it—to be able to feel like that.

The time came when I could no longer keep this thing to myself. The need of an outlet, of a confidant, became imperative, and I sought out Tom Peters. It was in February; I remember because I had ventured—with incredible daring—to send Nancy an elaborate, rosy Valentine; written on the back of it in a handwriting all too thinly disguised was the following verse, the triumphant result of much hard thinking in school hours:—

> Should you of this the sender guess
> Without another sign,
> Would you repent, and rest content
> To be his Valentine

I grew hot and cold by turns when I thought of its possible effects on my chances.

One of those useless, slushy afternoons, I took Tom for a walk that led us, as dusk came on, past Nancy's house. Only by painful degrees did I succeed in overcoming my bashfulness; but Tom, when at last I had blurted out the secret, was most sympathetic, although the ailment from which I suffered was as yet outside of the realm of his experience. I have used the word "ailment" advisedly, since he evidently put my trouble in the same category with diphtheria or scarlet fever, remarking that it was "darned hard luck." In vain I sought to explain that I did not regard it as such in the least; there was suffering, I admitted, but a degree of bliss none could comprehend who had not felt it. He refused to be envious, or at least to betray envy; yet he was curious, asking many questions, and I had reason to think before we parted that his admiration for me was increased. Was it possible that he, too, didn't love Nancy? No, it was funny, but he didn't. He failed to see much in girls: his tone remained commiserating, yet he began to take an interest in the progress of my suit.

For a time I had no progress to report. Out of consideration for those members of our weekly dancing class whose parents were Episcopalians the meetings were discontinued during Lent, and to call would have demanded a courage not in me; I should have become an object of ridicule among my friends and I would have died rather than face Nancy's mother and the members of her household. I set about making ingenious plans with a view to encounters that might appear casual. Nancy's school was dismissed at two, so was mine. By walking fast I could reach Salisbury Street, near St. Mary's Seminary for Young Ladies, in time to catch her, but even then for many days I was doomed to disappointment. She was either in company with other girls, or else she had taken another route; this I surmised led past Sophy McAlery's house, and I enlisted Tom as a confederate. He was to make straight for the McAlery's on Elm while I followed Powell, two short blocks away, and if Nancy went to Sophy's and left there alone he was to announce the fact by a preconcerted signal. Through long and persistent practice he had acquired a whistle shrill enough to wake the dead, accomplished by placing a finger of each hand between his teeth;—a gift that was the envy of his acquaintances, and the subject of much discussion as to whether his teeth were peculiar. Tom insisted that they were; it was an added distinction.

On this occasion he came up behind Nancy as she was leaving Sophy's gate and immediately sounded the alarm. She leaped in the air, dropped her school-books and whirled on him.

"Tom Peters! How dare you frighten me so!" she cried.

Tom regarded her in sudden dismay.

"I—I didn't mean to," he said. "I didn't think you were so near."

"But you must have seen me."

"I wasn't paying much attention," he equivocated,—a remark not calculated to appease her anger.

"Why were you doing it?"

"I was just practising," said Tom.

"Practising!" exclaimed Nancy, scornfully. "I shouldn't think you needed to practise that any more."

"Oh, I've done it louder," he declared, "Listen!"

She seized his hands, snatching them away from his lips. At this critical moment I appeared around the corner considerably out of breath, my heart beating like a watchman's rattle. I tried to feign nonchalance.

"Hello, Tom," I said. "Hello, Nancy. What's the matter?"

"It's Tom—he frightened me out of my senses." Dropping his wrists, she gave me a most disconcerting look; there was in it the suspicion of a smile. "What are you doing here, Hugh?"

"I heard Tom," I explained.

"I should think you might have. Where were you?"

"Over in another street," I answered, with deliberate vagueness. Nancy had suddenly become demure. I did not dare look at her, but I had a most uncomfortable notion that she suspected the plot. Meanwhile we had begun to walk along, all three of us, Tom, obviously ill at ease and discomfited, lagging a little behind. Just before we reached the corner I managed to kick him. His departure was by no means graceful.

"I've got to go;" he announced abruptly, and turned down the side street.

We watched his sturdy figure as it receded.

"Well, of all queer boys!" said Nancy, and we walked on again.

"He's my best friend," I replied warmly.

"He doesn't seem to care much for your company," said Nancy.

"Oh, they have dinner at half past two," I explained.

"Aren't you afraid of missing yours, Hugh?" she asked wickedly.

"I've got time. I'd—I'd rather be with you." After making which audacious remark I was seized by a spasm of apprehension. But nothing happened. Nancy remained demure. She didn't remind me that I had reflected upon Tom.

"That's nice of you, Hugh."

"Oh, I'm not saying it because it's nice," I faltered. "I'd rather be with you than—with anybody."

This was indeed the acme of daring. I couldn't believe I had actually said it. But again I received no rebuke; instead came a remark that set me palpitating, that I treasured for many weeks to come.

"I got a very nice valentine," she informed me.

"What was it like?" I asked thickly.

"Oh, beautiful! All pink lace and—and Cupids, and the picture of a young man and a young woman in a garden."

"Was that all?"

"Oh, no, there was a verse, in the oddest handwriting. I wonder who sent it?"

"Perhaps Ralph," I hazarded ecstatically.

"Ralph couldn't write poetry," she replied disdainfully. "Besides, it was very good poetry."

I suggested other possible authors and admirers. She rejected them all. We reached her gate, and I lingered. As she looked down at me from the stone steps her eyes shone with a soft light that filled me with radiance, and into her voice had come a questioning, shy note that thrilled the more because it revealed a new Nancy of whom I had not dreamed.

"Perhaps I'll meet you again—coming from school," I said.

"Perhaps," she answered. "You'll be late to dinner, Hugh, if you don't go...."

I was late, and unable to eat much dinner, somewhat to my mother's alarm. Love had taken away my appetite.... After dinner, when I was wandering aimlessly about the yard, Tom appeared on the other side of the fence.

"Don't ever ask me to do that again," he said gloomily.

I did meet Nancy again coming from school, not every day, but nearly every day. At first we pretended that there was no arrangement in this, and we both feigned surprise when we encountered one another. It was Nancy who possessed the courage that I lacked. One afternoon she said:—"I think I'd better walk with the girls to-morrow, Hugh."

I protested, but she was firm. And after that it was an understood thing that on certain days I should go directly home, feeling like an exile. Sophy McAlery had begun to complain: and I gathered that Sophy was Nancy's confidante. The other girls had begun to gossip. It was Nancy who conceived the brilliant idea—the more delightful because she said nothing about it to me—of making use of Sophy. She would leave school with Sophy, and I waited on the corner near the McAlery house. Poor Sophy! She was always of those who piped while others danced. In those days she had two straw-coloured pigtails, and her plain, faithful face is before me as I write. She never betrayed to me the excitement that filled her at being the accomplice of our romance.

Gossip raged, of course. Far from being disturbed, we used it, so to speak, as a handle for our love-making, which was carried on in an inferential rather than a direct fashion. Were they saying that we were lovers? Delightful! We laughed at one another in the sunshine.... At last we achieved the great adventure of a clandestine meeting and went for a walk in the afternoon, avoiding the houses of our friends. I've forgotten which of us had the boldness to propose it. The crocuses and tulips had broken the black mould, the flower beds in the front yards were beginning to blaze with scarlet and yellow, the lawns had turned a living green. What did we talk about? The substance has vanished, only the flavour remains.

One awoke of a morning to the twittering of birds, to walk to school amidst delicate, lace-like shadows of great trees acloud with old gold: the buds lay curled like tiny feathers on the pavements. Suddenly the shade was dense, the sunlight white and glaring, the odour of lilacs heavy in the air, spring in all its fulness had come,—spring and Nancy. Just so subtly, yet with the same seeming suddenness had budded and come to leaf and flower a perfect understanding, which nevertheless remained undefined. This, I had no doubt, was my fault, and due to the incomprehensible shyness her presence continued to inspire. Although we did not altogether abandon our secret trysts, we began to meet in more natural ways; there were garden parties and picnics where we strayed together through the woods and fields, pausing to tear off, one by one, the petals of a daisy, "She loves me, she loves me not." I never ventured to kiss her; I always thought afterwards I might have done so, she had seemed so willing, her eyes had shone so expectantly as I sat beside her on the grass; nor can I tell why I desired to kiss her save that this was the traditional thing to do to the lady one loved. To be sure, the very touch of her hand was galvanic. Paradoxically, I saw the human side of her, the yielding gentleness that always amazed me, yet I never overcame my awe of the divine; she was a being sacrosanct. Whether this idealism were innate or the result of such romances as I had read I cannot say.... I got, indeed, an avowal of a sort. The weekly dancing classes having begun again, on one occasion when she had waltzed twice with Gene Hollister I protested.

"Don't be silly, Hugh," she whispered. "Of course I like you better than anyone else—you ought to know that."

We never got to the word "love," but we knew the feeling.

One cloud alone flung its shadow across these idyllic days. Before I was fully aware of it I had drawn very near to the first great junction-point of my life, my graduation from Densmore Academy. We were to "change cars," in the language of Principal Haime. Well enough for the fortunate ones who were to continue the academic journey, which implied a postponement of the serious business of life; but month after month of the last term had passed without a hint from my father that I was to change cars. Again and again I almost succeeded in screwing up my courage to the point of mentioning college to him,—never quite; his manner, though kind and calm, somehow strengthened my suspicion that I had been judged and found wanting, and doomed to "business": galley slavery, I deemed it, humdrum, prosaic, degrading! When I thought of it at night I experienced almost a frenzy of self-pity. My father couldn't intend to do that, just because my monthly reports hadn't always been what he thought they ought to be! Gene Hollister's were no better, if as good, and he was going to Princeton. Was I, Hugh Paret, to be denied the distinction of being a college man, the delights of university existence, cruelly separated and set apart from my friends whom I loved! held up to the world and especially to Nancy Willett as good for nothing else! The thought was unbearable. Characteristically, I hoped against hope.

I have mentioned garden parties. One of our annual institutions was Mrs. Willett's children's party in May; for the Willett house had a garden that covered almost a quarter of a block. Mrs. Willett loved children, the greatest regret of her life being that providence had denied her a large family. As far back as my memory goes she had been something of an invalid; she had a sweet, sad face, and delicate hands so thin as to seem almost transparent; and she always sat in a chair under the great tree on the lawn, smiling at us as we soared to dizzy heights in the swing, or played croquet, or scurried through the paths, and in and out of the latticed summer-house with shrieks of laughter and terror. It all ended with a feast at a long table made of sawhorses and boards covered with a white cloth, and when the cake was cut there was wild excitement as to who would get the ring and who the thimble.

We were more decorous, or rather more awkward now, and the party began with a formal period when the boys gathered in a group and pretended indifference to the girls. The girls were cleverer at it, and actually achieved the impression that they were indifferent. We kept an eye on them, uneasily, while we talked. To be in Nancy's presence and not alone with Nancy was agonizing, and I wondered at a sang-froid beyond my power to achieve, accused her of coldness, my sufferings being the greater because she seemed more beautiful, daintier, more irreproachable than I had ever seen her. Even at that early age she gave evidence of the social gift, and it was due to her efforts that we forgot our best clothes and our newly born self-consciousness. When I begged her to slip away with me among the currant bushes she whispered:—"I can't, Hugh. I'm the hostess, you know."

I had gone there in a flutter of anticipation, but nothing went right that day. There was dancing in the big rooms that looked out on the garden; the only girl with whom I cared to dance was Nancy, and she was busy finding partners for the backward members of both sexes; though she was my partner, to be sure, when it all wound up with a Virginia reel on the lawn. Then, at supper, to cap the climax of untoward incidents, an animated discussion was begun as to the relative merits of the various colleges, the girls, too, taking sides. Mac Willett, Nancy's cousin, was going to Yale, Gene Hollister to Princeton, the Ewan boys to our State University, while Perry Blackwood and Ralph Hambleton and Ham Durrett were destined for Harvard; Tom Peters, also, though he was not to graduate from the Academy for another year. I might have known that Ralph would have suspected my misery. He sat triumphantly next to Nancy herself, while I had been told off to entertain the faithful Sophy. Noticing my silence, he demanded wickedly:—"Where are you going, Hugh?"

"Harvard, I think," I answered with as bold a front as I could muster. "I haven't talked it over with my father yet." It was intolerable to admit that I of them all was to be left behind.

Nancy looked at me in surprise. She was always downright.

"Oh, Hugh, doesn't your father mean to put you in business?" she exclaimed.

A hot flush spread over my face. Even to her I had not betrayed my apprehensions on this painful subject. Perhaps it was because of this very reason, knowing me as she did, that she had divined my fate. Could my father have spoken of it to anyone?

"Not that I know of," I said angrily. I wondered if she knew how deeply she had hurt me. The others laughed. The colour rose in Nancy's cheeks, and she gave me an appealing, almost tearful look, but my heart had hardened. As soon as supper was over I left the table to wander, nursing my wrongs, in a far corner of the garden, gay shouts and laughter still echoing in my ears. I was negligible, even my pathetic subterfuge had been detected and cruelly ridiculed by these friends whom I had always loved and sought out, and who now were so absorbed in their own prospects and happiness that they cared nothing for mine. And Nancy! I had been betrayed by Nancy! ... Twilight was coming on. I remember glancing down miserably at the new blue suit I had put on so hopefully for the first time that afternoon.

Separating the garden from the street was a high, smooth board fence with a little gate in it, and I had my hand on the latch when I heard the sound of hurrying steps on the gravel path and a familiar voice calling my name.

"Hugh! Hugh!"

I turned. Nancy stood before me.

"Hugh, you're not going!"

"Yes, I am."

"Why?"

"If you don't know, there's no use telling you."

"Just because I said your father intended to put you in business! Oh, Hugh, why are you so foolish and so proud? Do you suppose that anyone— that I—think any the worse of you?"

Yes, she had read me, she alone had entered into the source of that prevarication, the complex feelings from which it sprang. But at that moment I could not forgive her for humiliating me. I hugged my grievance.

"It was true, what I said," I declared hotly. "My father has not spoken. It is true that I'm going to college, because I'll make it true. I may not go this year."

She stood staring in sheer surprise at sight of my sudden, quivering passion. I think the very intensity of it frightened her. And then, without more ado, I opened the gate and was gone....

That night, though I did not realize it, my journey into a Far Country was begun.

The misery that followed this incident had one compensating factor. Although too late to electrify Densmore and Principal Haime with my scholarship, I was determined to go to college now, somehow, sometime. I would show my father, these companions of mine, and above all Nancy herself the stuff of which I was made, compel them sooner or later to admit that they had misjudged me. I had been possessed by similar resolutions before, though none so strong, and they had a way of sinking below the surface of my consciousness, only to rise again and again until by sheer pressure they achieved realization.

Yet I might have returned to Nancy if something had not occurred which I would have thought unbelievable: she began to show a marked preference for Ralph Hambleton. At first I regarded this affair as the most obvious of retaliations. She, likewise, had pride. Gradually, however, a feeling of uneasiness crept over me: as pretence, her performance was altogether too realistic; she threw her whole soul into it, danced with Ralph as often as she had ever danced with me, took walks with him, deferred to his opinions until, in spite of myself, I became convinced that the preference was genuine. I was a curious mixture of self-confidence and self-depreciation, and never had his superiority seemed more patent than now.

His air of satisfaction was maddening.

How well I remember his triumph on that hot, June morning of our graduation from Densmore, a triumph he had apparently achieved without labour, and which he seemed to despise. A fitful breeze blew through the chapel at the top of the building; we, the graduates, sat in two rows next to the platform, and behind us the wooden benches nicked by many knives— were filled with sisters and mothers and fathers, some anxious, some proud and some sad. So brief a span, like that summer's day, and youth was gone! Would the time come when we, too, should sit by the waters of Babylon and sigh for it? The world was upside down.

We read the one hundred and third psalm. Then Principal Haime, in his long "Prince Albert" and a ridiculously inadequate collar that emphasized his scrawny neck, reminded us of the sacred associations we had formed, of the peculiar responsibilities that rested on us, who were the privileged of the city. "We had crossed to-day," he said, "an invisible threshold. Some were to go on to higher institutions of learning. Others…" I gulped. Quoting the Scriptures, he complimented those who had made the most of their opportunities. And it was then that he called out, impressively, the name of Ralph Forrester Hambleton. Summa cum laude! Suddenly I was seized with passionate, vehement regrets at the sound of the applause. I might have been the prize scholar, instead of Ralph, if I had only worked, if I had only realized what this focussing day of graduation meant! I might have been a marked individual, with people murmuring words of admiration, of speculation concerning the brilliancy of my future!… When at last my name was called and I rose to receive my diploma it seemed as though my incompetency had been proclaimed to the world…

That evening I stood in the narrow gallery of the flag-decked gymnasium and watched Nancy dancing with Ralph.

I let her go without protest or reproach. A mysterious lesion seemed to have taken place, I felt astonished and relieved, yet I was heavy with sadness. My emancipation had been bought at a price. Something hitherto spontaneous, warm and living was withering within me.

# V.

It was true to my father's character that he should have waited until the day after graduation to discuss my future, if discussion be the proper word. The next evening at supper he informed me that he wished to talk to me in the sitting-room, whither I followed him with a sinking heart. He seated himself at his desk, and sat for a moment gazing at me with a curious and benumbing expression, and then the blow fell.

"Hugh, I have spoken to your Cousin Robert Breck about you, and he has kindly consented to give you a trial."

"To give me a trial, sir!" I exclaimed.

"To employ you at a small but reasonable salary."

I could find no words to express my dismay. My dreams had come to this, that I was to be made a clerk in a grocery store! The fact that it was a wholesale grocery store was little consolation.

"But father," I faltered, "I don't want to go into business."

"Ah!" The sharpness of the exclamation might have betrayed to me the pain in which he was, but he recovered himself instantly. And I could see nothing but an inexorable justice closing in on me mechanically; a blind justice, in its inability to read my soul. "The time to have decided that," he declared, "was some years ago, my son. I have given you the best schooling a boy can have, and you have not shown the least appreciation of your advantages. I do not enjoy saying this, Hugh, but in spite of all my efforts and of those of your mother, you have remained undeveloped and irresponsible. My hope, as you know, was to have made you a professional man, a lawyer, and to take you into my office. My father and grandfather were professional men before me. But you are wholly lacking in ambition."

And I had burned with it all my life!

"I have ambition," I cried, the tears forcing themselves to my eyes.

"Ambition—for what, my son?"

I hesitated. How could I tell him that my longings to do something, to be somebody in the world were never more keen than at that moment? Matthew Arnold had not then written his definition of God as the stream of tendency by which we fulfil the laws of our being; and my father, at any rate, would not have acquiesced in the definition. Dimly but passionately I felt then, as I had always felt, that I had a mission to perform, a service to do which ultimately would be revealed to me. But the hopelessness of explaining this took on, now, the proportions of a tragedy. And I could only gaze at him.

"What kind of ambition, Hugh?" he repeated sadly.

"I—I have sometimes thought I could write, sir, if I had a chance. I like it better than anything else. I—I have tried it. And if I could only go to college—"

"Literature!" There was in his voice a scandalized note.

"Why not, father?" I asked weakly.

And now it was he who, for the first time, seemed to be at a loss to express himself. He turned in his chair, and with a sweep of the hand indicated the long rows of musty-backed volumes. "Here," he said, "you have had at your disposal as well-assorted a small library as the city contains, and you have not availed yourself of it. Yet you talk to me of literature as a profession. I am afraid, Hugh, that this is merely another indication of your desire to shun hard work, and I must tell you frankly that I fail to see in you the least qualification for such a career. You have not even inherited my taste for books. I venture to say, for instance, that you have never even read a paragraph of Plutarch, and yet when I was your age I was completely familiar with the Lives. You will not read Scott or Dickens."

The impeachment was not to be denied, for the classics were hateful to me. Naturally I was afraid to make such a damning admission. My father had succeeded in presenting my ambition as the height of absurdity and presumption, and with something of the despair of a shipwrecked mariner my eyes rested on the green expanses of those book-backs, Bohn's Standard Library! Nor did it occur to him or to me that one might be great in literature without having read so much as a gritty page of them....

He finished his argument by reminding me that worthless persons sought to enter the arts in the search for a fool's paradise, and in order to satisfy a reprehensible craving for notoriety. The implication was clear, that imaginative production could not be classed as hard work. And he assured me that literature was a profession in which no one could afford to be second class. A Longfellow, a Harriet Beecher Stowe, or nothing. This was a practical age and a practical country. We had indeed produced Irvings and Hawthornes, but the future of American letters was, to say the least, problematical. We were a utilitarian people who would never create a great literature, and he reminded me that the days of the romantic and the picturesque had passed. He gathered that I desired to be a novelist. Well, novelists, with certain exceptions, were fantastic fellows who blew iridescent soap-bubbles and who had no morals. In the face of such a philosophy as his I was mute. The world appeared a dreary place of musty offices and smoky steel-works, of coal dust, of labour without a spark of inspiration. And that other, the world of my dreams, simply did not exist.

Incidentally my father had condemned Cousin Robert's wholesale grocery business as a refuge of the lesser of intellect that could not achieve the professions,—an inference not calculated to stir my ambition and liking for it at the start.

I began my business career on the following Monday morning. At breakfast, held earlier than usual on my account, my mother's sympathy was the more eloquent for being unspoken, while my father wore an air of unwonted cheerfulness; charging me, when I departed, to give his kindest remembrances to my Cousin Robert Breck. With a sense of martyrdom somehow deepened by this attitude of my parents I boarded a horse-car and went down town. Early though it was, the narrow streets of the wholesale district reverberated with the rattle of trucks and echoed with the shouts of drivers. The day promised to be scorching. At the door of the warehouse of Breck and Company I was greeted by the ineffable smell of groceries in which the suggestion of parched coffee prevailed. This is the sharpest remembrance of all, and even to-day that odour affects me somewhat in the manner that the interior of a ship affects a person prone to seasickness. My Cousin Robert, in his well-worn alpaca coat, was already seated at his desk behind the clouded glass partition next the alley at the back of the store, and as I entered he gazed at me over his steel-rimmed spectacles with that same disturbing look of clairvoyance I have already mentioned as one of his characteristics. The grey eyes were quizzical, and yet seemed to express a little commiseration.

"Well, Hugh, you've decided to honour us, have you?" he asked.

"I'm much obliged for giving me the place, Cousin Robert," I replied.

But he had no use for that sort of politeness, and he saw through me, as always.

"So you're not too tony for the grocery business, eh?"

"Oh, no, sir."

"It was good enough for old Benjamin Breck," he said. "Well, I'll give you a fair trial, my boy, and no favouritism on account of relationship, any more than to Willie."

His strong voice resounded through the store, and presently my cousin Willie appeared in answer to his summons, the same Willie who used to lead me, on mischief bent, through the barns and woods and fields of Claremore. He was barefoot no longer, though freckled still, grown lanky and tall; he wore a coarse blue apron that fell below his knees, and a pencil was stuck behind his ear.

"Get an apron for Hugh," said his father.

Willie's grin grew wider.

"I'll fit him out," he said.

"Start him in the shipping department," directed Cousin Robert, and turned to his letters.

I was forthwith provided with an apron, and introduced to the slim and anaemic but cheerful Johnny Hedges, the shipping clerk, hard at work in the alley. Secretly I looked down on my fellow-clerks, as one destined for a higher mission, made out of better stuff,—finer stuff. Despite my attempt to hide this sense of superiority they were swift to discover it; and perhaps it is to my credit as well as theirs that they did not resent it. Curiously enough, they seemed to acknowledge it. Before the week was out I had earned the nickname of Beau Brummel.

"Say, Beau," Johnny Hedges would ask, when I appeared of a morning, "what happened in the great world last night?"

I had an affection for them, these fellow-clerks, and I often wondered at their contentment with the drab lives they led, at their self-congratulation for "having a job" at Breck and Company's.

"You don't mean to say you like this kind of work?" I exclaimed one day to Johnny Hedges, as we sat on barrels of XXXX flour looking out at the hot sunlight in the alley.

"It ain't a question of liking it, Beau," he rebuked me. "It's all very well for you to talk, since your father's a millionaire" (a fiction so firmly embedded in their heads that no amount of denial affected it), "but what do you think would happen to me if I was fired? I couldn't go home and take it easy—you bet not. I just want to shake hands with myself when I think that I've got a home, and a job like this. I know a feller—a hard worker he was, too who walked the pavements for three months when the Colvers failed, and couldn't get nothing, and took to drink, and the last I heard of him he was sleeping in police stations and walking the ties, and his wife's a waitress at a cheap hotel. Don't you think it's easy to get a job."

I was momentarily sobered by the earnestness with which he brought home to me the relentlessness of our civilization. It seemed incredible. I should have learned a lesson in that store. Barring a few discordant days when the orders came in too fast or when we were short handed because of sickness, it was a veritable hive of happiness; morning after morning clerks and porters arrived, pale, yet smiling, and laboured with cheerfulness from eight o'clock until six, and departed as cheerfully for modest homes in obscure neighbourhoods that seemed to me areas of exile. They were troubled with no visions of better things. When the travelling men came in from the "road" there was great hilarity. Important personages, these, looked up to by the city clerks; jolly, reckless, Elizabethan-like rovers, who had tasted of the wine of liberty—and of other wines with the ineradicable lust for the road in their blood. No more routine for Jimmy Bowles, who was king of them all. I shudder to think how much of my knowledge of life I owe to this Jimmy, whose stories would have filled a quarto volume, but could on no account have been published; for a self-respecting post-office would not have allowed them to pass through the mails. As it was, Jimmy gave them circulation enough. I can still see his round face, with the nose just indicated, his wicked, twinkling little eyes, and I can hear his husky voice fall to a whisper when "the boss" passed through the store. Jimmy, when visiting us, always had a group around him. His audacity with women amazed me, for he never passed one of the "lady clerks" without some form of caress, which they resented but invariably laughed at. One day he imparted to me his code of morality: he never made love to another man's wife, so he assured me, if he knew the man! The secret of life he had discovered in laughter, and by laughter he sold quantities of Cousin Robert's groceries.

Mr. Bowles boasted of a catholic acquaintance in all the cities of his district, but before venturing forth to conquer these he had learned his own city by heart. My Cousin Robert was not aware of the fact that Mr. Bowles "showed" the town to certain customers. He even desired to show it to me, but an epicurean strain in my nature held me back. Johnny Hedges went with him occasionally, and Henry Schneider, the bill clerk, and I listened eagerly to their experiences, afterwards confiding them to Tom....

There were times when, driven by an overwhelming curiosity, I ventured into certain strange streets, alone, shivering with cold and excitement, gripped by a fascination I did not comprehend, my eyes now averted, now irresistibly raised toward the white streaks of light that outlined the windows of dark houses....

One winter evening as I was going home, I encountered at the mailbox a young woman who shot at me a queer, twisted smile. I stood still, as though stunned, looking after her, and when halfway across the slushy street she turned and smiled again. Prodigiously excited, I followed her, fearful that I might be seen by someone who knew me, nor was it until she reached an unfamiliar street that I ventured to overtake her. She confounded me by facing me.

"Get out!" she cried fiercely.

I halted in my tracks, overwhelmed with shame. But she continued to regard me by the light of the street lamp.

"You didn't want to be seen with me on Second Street, did you? You're one of those sneaking swells."

The shock of this sudden onslaught was tremendous. I stood frozen to the spot, trembling, convicted, for I knew that her accusation was just; I had wounded her, and I had a desire to make amends.

"I'm sorry," I faltered. "I didn't mean—to offend you. And you smiled —" I got no farther. She began to laugh, and so loudly that I glanced anxiously about. I would have fled, but something still held me, something that belied the harshness of her laugh.

"You're just a kid," she told me. "Say, you get along home, and tell your mamma I sent you."

Whereupon I departed in a state of humiliation and self-reproach I had never before known, wandering about aimlessly for a long time. When at length I arrived at home, late for supper, my mother's solicitude only served to deepen my pain. She went to the kitchen herself to see if my mince-pie were hot, and served me with her own hands. My father remained at his place at the head of the table while I tried to eat, smiling indulgently at her ministrations.

"Oh, a little hard work won't hurt him, Sarah," he said. "When I was his age I often worked until eleven o'clock and never felt the worse for it. Business must be pretty good, eh, Hugh?"

I had never seen him in a more relaxing mood, a more approving one. My mother sat down beside me…. Words seem useless to express the complicated nature of my suffering at that moment,—my remorse, my sense of deception, of hypocrisy,—yes, and my terror. I tried to talk naturally, to answer my father's questions about affairs at the store, while all the time my eyes rested upon the objects of the room, familiar since childhood. Here were warmth, love, and safety. Why could I not be content with them, thankful for them? What was it in me that drove me from these sheltering walls out into the dark places? I glanced at my father. Had he ever known these wild, destroying desires? Oh, if I only could have confided in him! The very idea of it was preposterous. Such placidity as theirs would never understand the nature of my temptations, and I pictured to myself their horror and despair at my revelation. In imagination I beheld their figures receding while I drifted out to sea, alone. Would the tide—which was somehow within me—carry me out and out, in spite of all I could do?

"Give me that man
That is not passion's slave, and I will wear him
In my heart's core…."

I did not shirk my tasks at the store, although I never got over the feeling that a fine instrument was being employed where a coarser one would have done equally well. There were moments when I was almost overcome by surges of self-commiseration and of impotent anger: for instance, I was once driven out of a shop by an incensed German grocer whom I had asked to settle a long-standing account. Yet the days passed, the daily grind absorbed my energies, and when I was not collecting, or tediously going over the stock in the dim recesses of the store, I was running errands in the wholesale district, treading the burning brick of the pavements, dodging heavy trucks and drays and perspiring clerks who flew about with memorandum pads in their hands, or awaiting the pleasure of bank tellers. Save Harvey, the venerable porter, I was the last to leave the store in the evening, and I always came away with the taste on my palate of Breck and Company's mail, it being my final duty to "lick" the whole of it and deposit it in the box at the corner. The gum on the envelopes tasted of winter-green.

My Cousin Robert was somewhat astonished at my application.

"We'll make a man of you yet, Hugh," he said to me once, when I had performed a commission with unexpected despatch....

Business was his all-in-all, and he had an undisguised contempt for higher education. To send a boy to college was, in his opinion, to run no inconsiderable risk of ruining him. What did they amount to when they came home, strutting like peacocks, full of fads and fancies, and much too good to associate with decent, hard-working citizens? Nevertheless when autumn came and my friends departed with eclat for the East, I was desperate indeed! Even the contemplation of Robert Breck did not console me, and yet here, in truth, was a life which might have served me as a model. His store was his castle; and his reputation for integrity and square dealing as wide as the city. Often I used to watch him with a certain envy as he stood in the doorway, his hands in his pockets, and greeted fellow-merchant and banker with his genuine and dignified directness. This man was his own master. They all called him "Robert," and they made it clear by their manner that they knew they were addressing one who fulfilled his obligations and asked no favours.

Crusty old Nathaniel Durrett once declared that when you bought a bill of goods from Robert Breck you did not have to check up the invoice or employ a chemist. Here was a character to mould upon. If my ambition could but have been bounded by Breck and Company, I, too, might have come to stand in that doorway content with a tribute that was greater than Caesar's.

I had been dreading the Christmas holidays, which were indeed to be no holidays for me. And when at length they arrived they brought with them from the East certain heroes fashionably clad, citizens now of a larger world than mine. These former companions had become superior beings, they could not help showing it, and their presence destroyed the Balance of Things. For alas, I had not wholly abjured the feminine sex after all! And from being a somewhat important factor in the lives of Ruth Hollister and other young women I suddenly became of no account. New interests, new rivalries and loyalties had arisen in which I had no share; I must perforce busy myself with invoices of flour and coffee and canned fruits while sleigh rides and coasting and skating expeditions to Blackstone Lake followed one another day after day,—for the irony of circumstances had decreed a winter uncommonly cold. There were evening parties, too, where I felt like an alien, though my friends were guilty of no conscious neglect; and had I been able to accept the situation simply, I should not have suffered.

The principal event of those holidays was a play given in the old Hambleton house (which later became the Boyne Club), under the direction of the lively and talented Mrs. Watling. I was invited, indeed, to participate; but even if I had had the desire I could not have done so, since the rehearsals were carried on in the daytime. Nancy was the leading lady. I have neglected to mention that she too had been away almost continuously since our misunderstanding, for the summer in the mountains,—a sojourn recommended for her mother's health; and in the autumn she had somewhat abruptly decided to go East to boarding-school at Farmington. During the brief months of her absence she had marvellously acquired maturity and aplomb, a worldliness of manner and a certain frivolity that seemed to put those who surrounded her on a lower plane. She was only seventeen, yet she seemed the woman of thirty whose role she played. First there were murmurs, then sustained applause. I scarcely recognized her: she had taken wings and soared far above me, suggesting a sphere of power and luxury hitherto unimagined and beyond the scope of the world to which I belonged.

Her triumph was genuine. When the play was over she was immediately surrounded by enthusiastic admirers eager to congratulate her, to dance with her. I too would have gone forward, but a sense of inadequacy, of unimportance, of an inability to cope with her, held me back, and from a corner I watched her sweeping around the room, holding up her train, and leaning on the arm of Bob Lansing, a classmate whom Ralph had brought home from Harvard. Then it was Ralph's turn: that affair seemed still to be going on. My feelings were a strange medley of despondency and stimulation....

Our eyes met. Her partner now was Ham Durrett. Capriciously releasing him, she stood before me,

"Hugh, you haven't asked me to dance, or even told me what you thought of the play."

"I thought it was splendid," I said lamely.

Because she refrained from replying I was farther than ever from understanding her. How was I to divine what she felt? or whether any longer she felt at all? Here, in this costume of a woman of the world, with the string of pearls at her neck to give her the final touch of brilliancy, was a strange, new creature who baffled and silenced me.... We had not gone halfway across the room when she halted abruptly.

"I'm tired," she exclaimed. "I don't feel like dancing just now," and led the way to the big, rose punch-bowl, one of the Durretts' most cherished possessions. Glancing up at me over the glass of lemonade I had given her she went on: "Why haven't you been to see me since I came home? I've wanted to talk to you, to hear how you are getting along."

Was she trying to make amends, or reminding me in this subtle way of the cause of our quarrel? What I was aware of as I looked at her was an attitude, a vantage point apparently gained by contact with that mysterious outer world which thus vicariously had laid its spell on me; I was tremendously struck by the thought that to achieve this attitude meant emancipation, invulnerability against the aches and pains which otherwise our fellow-beings had the power to give us; mastery over life,—the ability to choose calmly, as from a height, what were best for one's self, untroubled by loves and hates. Untroubled by loves and hates! At that very moment, paradoxically, I loved her madly, but with a love not of the old quality, a love that demanded a vantage point of its own. Even though she had made an advance—and some elusiveness in her manner led me to doubt it I could not go to her now. I must go as a conqueror,—a conqueror in the lists she herself had chosen, where the prize is power.

"Oh, I'm getting along pretty well," I said. "At any rate, they don't complain of me."

"Somehow," she ventured, "somehow it's hard to think of you as a business man."

I took this for a reference to the boast I had made that I would go to college.

"Business isn't so bad as it might be," I assured her.

"I think a man ought to go away to college," she declared, in what seemed another tone. "He makes friends, learns certain things,—it gives him finish. We are very provincial here."

Provincial! I did not stop to reflect how recently she must have acquired the word; it summed up precisely the self-estimate at which I had arrived. The sting went deep. Before I could think of an effective reply Nancy was being carried off by the young man from the East, who was clearly infatuated. He was not provincial. She smiled back at me brightly over his shoulder.... In that instant were fused in one resolution all the discordant elements within me of aspiration and discontent. It was not so much that I would show Nancy what I intended to do—I would show myself; and I felt a sudden elation, and accession of power that enabled me momentarily to despise the puppets with whom she danced.... From this mood I was awakened with a start to feel a hand on my shoulder, and I turned to confront her father, McAlery Willett; a gregarious, easygoing, pleasure-loving gentleman who made only a pretence of business, having inherited an ample fortune from his father, unique among his generation in our city in that he paid some attention to fashion in his dress; good living was already beginning to affect his figure. His mellow voice had a way of breaking an octave.

"Don't worry, my boy," he said. "You stick to business. These college fellows are cocks of the walk just now, but some day you'll be able to snap your fingers at all of 'em."

The next day was dark, overcast, smoky, damp-the soft, unwholesome dampness that follows a spell of hard frost. I spent the morning and afternoon on the gloomy third floor of Breck and Company, making a list of the stock. I remember the place as though I had just stepped out of it, the freight elevator at the back, the dusty, iron columns, the continuous piles of cases and bags and barrels with narrow aisles between them; the dirty windows, spotted and soot-streaked, that looked down on Second Street. I was determined now to escape from all this, and I had my plan in mind.

No sooner had I swallowed my supper that evening than I set out at a swift pace for a modest residence district ten blocks away, coming to a little frame house set back in a yard,—one of those houses in which the ringing of the front door-bell produces the greatest commotion; children's voices were excitedly raised and then hushed. After a brief silence the door was opened by a pleasant-faced, brown-bearded man, who stood staring at me in surprise. His hair was rumpled, he wore an old house coat with a hole in the elbow, and with one finger he kept his place in the book which he held in his hand.

"Hugh Paret!" he exclaimed.

He ushered me into a little parlour lighted by two lamps, that bore every evidence of having been recently vacated. Its features somehow bespoke a struggle for existence; as though its occupants had worried much and loved much. It was a room best described by the word "home"—home made more precious by a certain precariousness. Toys and school-books strewed the floor, a sewing-bag and apron lay across the sofa, and in one corner was a roll-topped desk of varnished oak. The seats of the chairs were comfortably depressed.

So this was where Mr. Wood lived! Mr. Wood, instructor in Latin and Greek at Densmore Academy. It was now borne in on me for the first time that he did live and have his ties like any other human being, instead of just appearing magically from nowhere on a platform in a chalky room at nine every morning, to vanish again in the afternoon. I had formerly stood in awe of his presence. But now I was suddenly possessed by an embarrassment, and (shall I say it?) by a commiseration bordering on contempt for a man who would consent to live thus for the sake of being a schoolteacher. How strange that civilization should set such a high value on education and treat its functionaries with such neglect!

Mr. Wood's surprise at seeing me was genuine. For I had never shown a particular interest in him, nor in the knowledge which he strove to impart.

"I thought you had forgotten me, Hugh," he said, and added whimsically: "most boys do, when they graduate."

I felt the reproach, which made it the more difficult for me to state my errand.

"I knew you sometimes took pupils in the evening, Mr. Wood."

"Pupils,—yes," he replied, still eyeing me. Suddenly his eyes twinkled. He had indeed no reason to suspect me of thirsting for learning. "But I was under the impression that you had gone into business, Hugh."

"The fact is, sir," I explained somewhat painfully, "that I am not satisfied with business. I feel—as if I ought to know more. And I came to see if you would give me lessons about three nights a week, because I want to take the Harvard examinations next summer."

Thus I made it appear, and so persuaded myself, that my ambition had been prompted by a craving for knowledge. As soon as he could recover himself he reminded me that he had on many occasions declared I had a brain.

"Your father must be very happy over this decision of yours," he said.

That was the point, I told him. It was to be a surprise for my father; I was to take the examinations first, and inform him afterwards.

To my intense relief, Mr. Wood found the scheme wholly laudable, and entered into it with zest. He produced examinations of preceding years from a pigeonhole in his desk, and inside of half an hour the arrangement was made, the price of the lessons settled. They were well within my salary, which recently had been raised....

When I went down town, or collecting bills for Breck and Company, I took a text-book along with me in the street-cars. Now at last I had behind my studies a driving force. Algebra, Latin, Greek and history became worth while, means to an end. I astonished Mr. Wood; and sometimes he would tilt back his chair, take off his spectacles and pull his beard.

"Why in the name of all the sages," he would demand, "couldn't you have done this well at school? You might have led your class, instead of Ralph Hambleton."

I grew very fond of Mr. Wood, and even of his thin little wife, who occasionally flitted into the room after we had finished. I fully intended to keep up with them in after life, but I never did. I forgot them completely....

My parents were not wholly easy in their minds concerning me; they were bewildered by the new aspect I presented. For my lately acquired motive was strong enough to compel me to restrict myself socially, and the evenings I spent at home were given to study, usually in my own room. Once I was caught with a Latin grammar: I was just "looking over it," I said. My mother sighed. I knew what was in her mind; she had always been secretly disappointed that I had not been sent to college. And presently, when my father went out to attend a trustee's meeting, the impulse to confide in her almost overcame me; I loved her with that affection which goes out to those whom we feel understand us, but I was learning to restrain my feelings. She looked at me wistfully.... I knew that she would insist on telling my father, and thus possibly frustrate my plans. That I was not discovered was due to a certain quixotic twist in my father's character. I was working now, and though not actually earning my own living, he no longer felt justified in prying into my affairs.

When June arrived, however, my tutor began to show signs that his conscience was troubling him, and one night he delivered his ultimatum. The joke had gone far enough, he implied. My intentions, indeed, he found praiseworthy, but in his opinion it was high time that my father were informed of them; he was determined to call at my father's office.

The next morning was blue with the presage of showers; blue, too, with the presage of fate. An interminable morning. My tasks had become utterly distasteful. And in the afternoon, so when I sat down to make out invoices, I wrote automatically the names of the familiar customers, my mind now exalted by hope, now depressed by anxiety. The result of an interview perhaps even now going on would determine whether or no I should be immediately released from a slavery I detested. Would Mr. Wood persuade my father? If not, I was prepared to take more desperate measures; remain in the grocery business I would not. In the evening, as I hurried homeward from the corner where the Boyne Street car had dropped me, I halted suddenly in front of the Peters house, absorbing the scene where my childhood had been spent: each of these spreading maples was an old friend, and in these yards I had played and dreamed. An unaccountable sadness passed over me as I walked on toward our gate; I entered it, gained the doorway of the house and went upstairs, glancing into the sitting room. My mother sat by the window, sewing. She looked up at me with an ineffable expression, in which I read a trace of tears.

"Hugh!" she exclaimed.

I felt very uncomfortable, and stood looking down at her.

"Why didn't you tell us, my son?" In her voice was in truth reproach;

yet mingled with that was another note, which I think was pride.

"What has father said?" I asked.

"Oh, my dear, he will tell you himself. I—I don't know—he will talk to you."

Suddenly she seized my hands and drew me down to her, and then held me away, gazing into my face with a passionate questioning, her lips smiling, her eyes wet. What did she see? Was there a subtler relationship between our natures than I guessed? Did she understand by some instinctive power the riddle within me? divine through love the force that was driving me on she knew not whither, nor I? At the sound of my father's step in the hall she released me. He came in as though nothing had happened.

"Well, Hugh, are you home?" he said....

Never had I been more impressed, more bewildered by his self-command than at that time. Save for the fact that my mother talked less than usual, supper passed as though nothing had happened. Whether I had shaken him, disappointed him, or gained his reluctant approval I could not tell. Gradually his outward calmness turned my suspense to irritation....

But when at length we were alone together, I gained a certain reassurance. His manner was not severe. He hesitated a little before beginning.

"I must confess, Hugh; that I scarcely know what to say about this proceeding of yours. The thing that strikes me most forcibly is that you might have confided in your mother and myself."

Hope flashed up within me, like an explosion.

"I—I wanted to surprise you, father. And then, you see, I thought it would be wiser to find out first how well I was likely to do at the examinations."

My father looked at me. Unfortunately he possessed neither a sense of humour nor a sense of tragedy sufficient to meet such a situation. For the first time in my life I beheld him at a disadvantage; for I had, somehow, managed at length to force him out of position, and he was puzzled. I was quick to play my trump card.

"I have been thinking it over carefully," I told him, "and I have made up my mind that I want to go into the law."

"The law!" he exclaimed sharply.

"Why, yes, sir. I know that you were disappointed because I did not do sufficiently well at school to go to college and study for the bar."

I felt indeed a momentary pang, but I remembered that I was fighting for my freedom.

"You seemed satisfied where you were," he said in a puzzled voice, "and your Cousin Robert gives a good account of you."

"I've tried to do the work as well as I could, sir," I replied. "But I don't like the grocery business, or any other business. I have a feeling that I'm not made for it."

"And you think, now, that you are made for the law?" he asked, with the faint hint of a smile.

"Yes, sir, I believe I could succeed at it. I'd like to try," I replied modestly.

"You've given up the idiotic notion of wishing to be an author?"

I implied that he himself had convinced me of the futility of such a wish. I listened to his next words as in a dream.

"I must confess to you, Hugh, that there are times when I fail to understand you. I hope it is as you say, that you have arrived at a settled conviction as to your future, and that this is not another of those caprices to which you have been subject, nor a desire to shirk honest work. Mr. Wood has made out a strong case for you, and I have therefore determined to give you a trial. If you pass the examinations with credit, you may go to college, but if at any time you fail to make good progress, you come home, and go into business again. Is that thoroughly understood?"

I said it was, and thanked him effusively.... I had escaped,—the prison doors had flown open. But it is written that every happiness has its sting; and my joy, intense though it was, had in it a core of remorse....

I went downstairs to my mother, who was sitting in the hall by the open door.

"Father says I may go!" I said.

She got up and took me in her arms.

"My dear, I am so glad, although we shall miss you dreadfully.... Hugh?"

"Yes, mother."

"Oh, Hugh, I so want you to be a good man!"

Her cry was a little incoherent, but fraught with a meaning that came home to me, in spite of myself....

A while later I ran over to announce to the amazed Tom Peters that I was actually going to Harvard with him. He stood in the half-lighted hallway, his hands in his pockets, blinking at me.

"Hugh, you're a wonder!" he cried. "How in Jehoshaphat did you work it?"...

I lay long awake that night thinking over the momentous change so soon to come into my life, wondering exultantly what Nancy Willett would say now. I was not one, at any rate, to be despised or neglected.

# VI.

The following September Tom Peters and I went East together. In the early morning Boston broke on us like a Mecca as we rolled out of the old Albany station, joint lords of a "herdic." How sharply the smell of the salt-laden east wind and its penetrating coolness come back to me! I seek in vain for words to express the exhilarating effect of that briny coolness on my imagination, and of the visions it summoned up of the newer, larger life into which I had marvellously been transported. We alighted at the Parker

House, full-fledged men of the world, and tried to act as though the breakfast of which we partook were merely an incident, not an Event; as though we were Seniors, and not freshmen, assuming an indifference to the beings by whom we were surrounded and who were breakfasting, too,— although the nice-looking ones with fresh faces and trim clothes were all undoubtedly Olympians. The better to proclaim our nonchalance, we seated ourselves on a lounge of the marble-paved lobby and smoked cigarettes. This was liberty indeed! At length we departed for Cambridge, in another herdic.

Boston! Could it be possible? Everything was so different here as to give the place the aspect of a dream: the Bulfinch State House, the decorous shops, the still more decorous dwellings with the purple-paned windows facing the Common; Back Bay, still boarded up, ivy-spread, suggestive of a mysterious and delectable existence. We crossed the Charles River, blue-grey and still that morning; traversed a nondescript district, and at last found ourselves gazing out of the windows at the mellowed, plum-coloured bricks of the University buildings…. All at once our exhilaration evaporated as the herdic rumbled into a side street and backed up before the door of a not-too-inviting, three-storied house with a queer extension on top. Its steps and vestibule were, however, immaculate. The bell was answered by a plainly overworked servant girl, of whom we inquired for Mrs. Bolton, our landlady. There followed a period of waiting in a parlour from which the light had been almost wholly banished, with slippery horsehair furniture and a marble-topped table; and Mrs. Bolton, when she appeared, dressed in rusty black, harmonized perfectly with the funereal gloom. She was a tall, rawboned, severe lady with a peculiar red-mottled complexion that somehow reminded one of the outcropping rocks of her native New England soil.

"You want to see your rooms, I suppose," she remarked impassively when we had introduced ourselves, and as we mounted the stairs behind her Tom, in a whisper, nicknamed her "Granite Face." Presently she left us.

"Hospitable soul!" said Tom, who, with his hands in his pockets, was gazing at the bare walls of our sitting-room. "We'll have to go into the house-furnishing business, Hughie. I vote we don't linger here to-day—we'll get melancholia."

Outside, however, the sun was shining brightly, and we departed immediately to explore Cambridge and announce our important presences to the proper authorities…. We went into Boston to dine…. It was not until nine o'clock in the evening that we returned and the bottom suddenly dropped out of things. He who has tasted that first, acute homesickness of college will know what I mean. It usually comes at the opening of one's trunk. The sight of the top tray gave me a pang I shall never forget. I would not have believed that I loved my mother so much! These articles had been packed by her hands; and in one corner, among the underclothes on which she had neatly sewed my initials, lay the new Bible she had bought. "Hugh Moreton Paret, from his Mother. September, 1881." I took it up (Tom was not looking) and tried to read a passage, but my eyes were blurred. What was it within me that pressed and pressed until I thought I could bear the pain of it no longer? I pictured the sitting-room at home, and my father and mother there, thinking of me. Yes, I must acknowledge it; in the bitterness of that moment I longed to be back once more in the railed-off space on the floor of Breck and Company, writing invoices....

Presently, as we went on silently with our unpacking, we became aware of someone in the doorway.

"Hello, you fellows!" he cried. "We're classmates, I guess."

We turned to behold an ungainly young man in an ill-fitting blue suit. His face was pimply, his eyes a Teutonic blue, his yellow hair rumpled, his naturally large mouth was made larger by a friendly grin.

"I'm Hermann Krebs," he announced simply. "Who are you?"

We replied, I regret to say, with a distinct coolness that did not seem to bother him in the least. He advanced into the room, holding out a large, red, and serviceable hand, evidently it had never dawned on him that there was such a thing in the world as snobbery. But Tom and I had been "coached" by Ralph Hambleton and Perry Blackwood, warned to be careful of our friendships. There was a Reason! In any case Mr. Krebs would not have appealed to us. In answer to a second question he was informed what city we hailed from, and he proclaimed himself likewise a native of our state.

"Why, I'm from Elkington!" he exclaimed, as though the fact sealed our future relationships. He seated himself on Tom's trunk and added: "Welcome to old Harvard!"

We felt that he was scarcely qualified to speak for "old Harvard," but we did not say so.

"You look as if you'd been pall-bearers for somebody," was his next observation.

To this there seemed no possible reply.

"You fellows are pretty well fixed here," he went on, undismayed, gazing about a room which had seemed to us the abomination of desolation. "Your folks must be rich. I'm up under the skylight."

Even this failed to touch us. His father—he told us with undiminished candour—had been a German emigrant who had come over in '49, after the cause of liberty had been lost in the old country, and made eye-glasses and opera glasses. There hadn't been a fortune in it. He, Hermann, had worked at various occupations in the summer time, from peddling to farming, until he had saved enough to start him at Harvard. Tom, who had been bending over his bureau drawer, straightened up.

"What did you want to come here for?" he demanded.

"Say, what did you?" Mr. Krebs retorted genially. "To get an education, of course."

"An education!" echoed Tom.

"Isn't Harvard the oldest and best seat of learning in America?" There was an exaltation in Krebs's voice that arrested my attention, and made me look at him again. A troubled chord had been struck within me.

"Sure," said Tom.

"What did you come for?" Mr. Krebs persisted.

"To sow my wild oats," said Tom. "I expect to have something of a crop, too."

For some reason I could not fathom, it suddenly seemed to dawn on Mr.

Krebs, as a result of this statement, that he wasn't wanted.

"Well, so long," he said, with a new dignity that curiously belied the informality of his farewell.

An interval of silence followed his departure.

"Well, he's got a crust!" said Tom, at last.

My own feeling about Mr. Krebs had become more complicated; but I took my cue from Tom, who dealt with situations simply.

"He'll come in for a few knockouts," he declared. "Here's to old Harvard, the greatest institution of learning in America! Oh, gee!"

Our visitor, at least, made us temporarily forget our homesickness, but it returned with redoubled intensity when we had put out the lights and gone to bed.

Before we had left home it had been mildly hinted to us by Ralph and Perry Blackwood that scholarly eminence was not absolutely necessary to one's welfare and happiness at Cambridge. The hint had been somewhat superfluous; but the question remained, what was necessary? With a view of getting some light on this delicate subject we paid a visit the next evening to our former friends and schoolmates, whose advice was conveyed with a masterly circumlocution that impressed us both. There are some things that may not be discussed directly, and the conduct of life at a modern university —which is a reflection of life in the greater world—is one of these. Perry Blackwood and Ham did most of the talking, while Ralph, characteristically, lay at full length on the window-seat, interrupting with an occasional terse and cynical remark very much to the point. As a sophomore, he in particular seemed lifted immeasurably above us, for he was—as might have been expected already a marked man in his class. The rooms which he shared with his cousin made a tremendous impression on Tom and me, and seemed palatial in comparison to our quarters at Mrs. Bolton's, eloquent of the freedom and luxury of undergraduate existence; their note, perhaps, was struck by the profusion of gay sofa pillows, then something of an innovation. The heavy, expensive furniture was of a pattern new to me; and on the mantel were three or four photographs of ladies in the alluring costume of the musical stage, in which Tom evinced a particular interest.

"Did grandfather send 'em?" he inquired.

"They're Ham's," said Ralph, and he contrived somehow to get into those two words an epitome of his cousin's character. Ham was stouter, and his clothes were more striking, more obviously expensive than ever.... On our way homeward, after we had walked a block or two in silence, Tom exclaimed:—"Don't make friends with the friendless!—eh, Hughie? We knew enough to begin all right, didn't we?"...

Have I made us out a pair of deliberate, calculating snobs? Well, after all it must be remembered that our bringing up had not been of sufficient liberality to include the Krebses of this world. We did not, indeed, spend much time in choosing and weighing those whom we should know and those whom we should avoid; and before the first term of that Freshman year was over Tom had become a favourite. He had the gift of making men feel that he delighted in their society, that he wished for nothing better than to sit for hours in their company, content to listen to the arguments that raged about him. Once in a while he would make a droll observation that was greeted with fits of laughter. He was always referred to as "old Tom," or "good old Tom"; presently, when he began to pick out chords on the banjo, it was discovered that he had a good tenor voice, though he could not always be induced to sing.... Somewhat to the jeopardy of the academic standard that my father expected me to sustain, our rooms became a rendezvous for many clubable souls whose maudlin, midnight attempts at harmony often set the cocks crowing.

"Free from care and despair,
What care we?
'Tis wine, 'tis wine
That makes the jollity."

As a matter of truth, on these occasions it was more often beer; beer transported thither in Tom's new valise,—given him by his mother,—and stuffed with snow to keep the bottles cold. Sometimes Granite Face, adorned in a sky-blue wrapper, would suddenly appear in the doorway to declare that we were a disgrace to her respectable house: the university authorities should be informed, etc., etc. Poor woman, we were outrageously inconsiderate of her.... One evening as we came through the hall we caught a glimpse in the dimly lighted parlour of a young man holding a shy and pale little girl on his lap, Annie, Mrs. Bolton's daughter: on the face of our landlady was an expression I had never seen there, like a light. I should scarcely have known her. Tom and I paused at the foot of the stairs. He clutched my arm.

"Darned if it wasn't our friend Krebs!" he whispered.

While I was by no means so popular as Tom, I got along fairly well. I had escaped from provincialism, from the obscure purgatory of the wholesale grocery business; new vistas, exciting and stimulating, had been opened up; nor did I offend the sensibilities and prejudices of the new friends I made, but gave a hearty consent to a code I found congenial. I recognized in the social system of undergraduate life at Harvard a reflection of that of a greater world where I hoped some day to shine; yet my ambition did not prey upon me. Mere conformity, however, would not have taken me very far in a sphere from which I, in common with many others, desired not to be excluded.... One day, in an idle but inspired moment, I paraphrased a song from "Pinafore," applying it to a college embroglio, and the brief and lively vogue it enjoyed was sufficient to indicate a future usefulness. I had "found myself." This was in the last part of the freshman year, and later on I became a sort of amateur, class poet-laureate. Many were the skits I composed, and Tom sang them....

During that freshman year we often encountered Hermann Krebs, whistling merrily, on the stairs.

"Got your themes done?" he would inquire cheerfully.

And Tom would always mutter, when he was out of earshot: "He has got a crust!"

When I thought about Krebs at all,—and this was seldom indeed,—his manifest happiness puzzled me. Our cool politeness did not seem to bother him in the least; on the contrary, I got the impression that it amused him. He seemed to have made no friends. And after that first evening, memorable for its homesickness, he never ventured to repeat his visit to us.

One windy November day I spied his somewhat ludicrous figure striding ahead of me, his trousers above his ankles. I was bundled up in a new ulster,—of which I was secretly quite proud,—but he wore no overcoat at all.

"Well, how are you getting along?" I asked, as I overtook him.

He made clear, as he turned, his surprise that I should have addressed him at all, but immediately recovered himself.

"Oh, fine," he responded. "I've had better luck than I expected. I'm correspondent for two or three newspapers. I began by washing windows, and doing odd jobs for the professors' wives." He laughed. "I guess that doesn't strike you as good luck."

He showed no resentment at my patronage, but a self-sufficiency that made my sympathy seem superfluous, giving the impression of an inner harmony and content that surprised me.

"I needn't ask how you're getting along," he said....

At the end of the freshman year we abandoned Mrs. Bolton's for more desirable quarters.

I shall not go deeply into my college career, recalling only such incidents as, seen in the retrospect, appear to have had significance. I have mentioned my knack for song-writing; but it was not, I think, until my junior year there was startlingly renewed in me my youthful desire to write, to create something worth while, that had so long been dormant.

The inspiration came from Alonzo Cheyne, instructor in English; a remarkable teacher, in spite of the finicky mannerisms which Tom imitated. And when, in reading aloud certain magnificent passages, he forgot his affectations, he managed to arouse cravings I thought to have deserted me forever. Was it possible, after all, that I had been right and my father wrong? that I might yet be great in literature?

A mere hint from Alonzo Cheyne was more highly prized by the grinds than fulsome praise from another teacher. And to his credit it should be recorded that the grinds were the only ones he treated with any seriousness; he took pains to answer their questions; but towards the rest of us, the Chosen, he showed a thinly veiled contempt. None so quick as he to detect a simulated interest, or a wily effort to make him ridiculous; and few tried this a second time, for he had a rapier-like gift of repartee that transfixed the offender like a moth on a pin. He had a way of eyeing me at times, his glasses in his hand, a queer smile on his lips, as much as to imply that there was one at least among the lost who was made for better things. Not that my work was poor, but I knew that it might have been better. Out of his classes, however, beyond the immediate, disturbing influence of his personality I would relapse into indifference....

Returning one evening to our quarters, which were now in the "Yard," I found Tom seated with a blank sheet before him, thrusting his hand through his hair and biting the end of his penholder to a pulp. In his muttering, which was mixed with the curious, stingless profanity of which he was master, I caught the name of Cheyne, and I knew that he was facing the crisis of a fortnightly theme. The subject assigned was a narrative of some personal experience, and it was to be handed in on the morrow. My own theme was already, written.

"I've been holding down this chair for an hour, and I can't seem to think of a thing." He rose to fling himself down on the lounge. "I wish I was in Canada."

"Why Canada?"

"Trout fishing with Uncle Jake at that club of his where he took me last summer." Tom gazed dreamily at the ceiling. "Whenever I have some darned foolish theme like this to write I want to go fishing, and I want to go like the devil. I'll get Uncle Jake to take you, too, next summer."

"I wish you would."

"Say, that's living all right, Hughie, up there among the tamaracks and balsams!" And he began, for something like the thirtieth time, to relate the adventures of the trip.

As he talked, the idea presented itself to me with sudden fascination to use this incident as the subject of Tom's theme; to write it for him, from his point of view, imitating the droll style he would have had if he had been able to write; for, when he was interested in any matter, his oral narrative did not lack vividness. I began to ask him questions: what were the trees like, for instance? How did the French-Canadian guides talk? He had the gift of mimicry: aided by a partial knowledge of French I wrote down a few sentences as they sounded. The canoe had upset and he had come near drowning. I made him describe his sensations.

"I'll write your theme for you," I exclaimed, when he had finished.

"Gee, not about that!"

"Why not? It's a personal experience."

His gratitude was pathetic.... By this time I was so full of the subject that it fairly clamoured for expression, and as I wrote the hours flew. Once in a while I paused to ask him a question as he sat with his chair tilted back and his feet on the table, reading a detective story. I sketched in the scene with bold strokes; the desolate bois brule on the mountain side, the polished crystal surface of the pool broken here and there with the circles left by rising fish; I pictured Armand, the guide, his pipe between his teeth, holding the canoe against the current; and I seemed to smell the sharp tang of the balsams, to hear the roar of the rapids below. Then came the sudden hooking of the big trout, habitant oaths from Armand, bouleversement, wetness, darkness, confusion; a half-strangled feeling, a brief glimpse of green things and sunlight, and then strangulation, or what seemed like it; strangulation, the sense of being picked up and hurled by a terrific force whither? a blinding whiteness, in which it was impossible to breathe, one sharp, almost unbearable pain, then another, then oblivion.... Finally, awakening, to be confronted by a much worried Uncle Jake.

By this time the detective story had fallen to the floor, and Tom was huddled up in his chair, asleep. He arose obediently and wrapped a wet towel around his head, and began to write. Once he paused long enough to mutter:—"Yes, that's about it,—that's the way I felt!" and set to work again, mechanically,—all the praise I got for what I deemed a literary achievement of the highest order! At three o'clock, a.m., he finished, pulled off his clothes automatically and tumbled into bed. I had no desire for sleep. My brain was racing madly, like an engine without a governor. I could write! I could write! I repeated the words over and over to myself. All the complexities of my present life were blotted out, and I beheld only the long, sweet vista of the career for which I was now convinced that nature had intended me. My immediate fortunes became unimportant, immaterial. No juice of the grape I had ever tasted made me half so drunk.... With the morning, of course, came the reaction, and I suffered the after sensations of an orgie, awaking to a world of necessity, cold and grey and slushy, and necessity alone made me rise from my bed. My experience of the night before might have taught me that happiness lies in the trick of transforming necessity, but it did not. The vision had faded,—temporarily, at least; and such was the distraction of the succeeding days that the subject of the theme passed from my mind....

One morning Tom was later than usual in getting home. I was writing a letter when he came in, and did not notice him, yet I was vaguely aware of his standing over me. When at last I looked up I gathered from his expression that something serious had happened, so mournful was his face, and yet so utterly ludicrous.

"Say, Hugh, I'm in the deuce of a mess," he announced.

"What's the matter?" I inquired.

He sank down on the table with a groan.

"It's Alonzo," he said.

Then I remembered the theme.

"What—what's he done?" I demanded.

"He says I must become a writer. Think of it, me a writer! He says I'm a young Shakespeare, that I've been lazy and hid my light under a bushel! He says he knows now what I can do, and if I don't keep up the quality, he'll know the reason why, and write a personal letter to my father. Oh, hell!"

In spite of his evident anguish, I was seized with a convulsive laughter. Tom stood staring at me moodily.

"You think it's funny,—don't you? I guess it is, but what's going to become of me? That's what I want to know. I've been in trouble before, but never in any like this. And who got me into it? You!"

Here was gratitude!

"You've got to go on writing 'em, now." His voice became desperately pleading. "Say, Hugh, old man, you can temper 'em down—temper 'em down gradually. And by the end of the year, let's say, they'll be about normal again."

He seemed actually shivering.

"The end of the year!" I cried, the predicament striking me for the first time in its fulness. "Say, you've got a crust!"

"You'll do it, if I have to hold a gun over you," he announced grimly.

Mingled with my anxiety, which was real, was an exultation that would not down. Nevertheless, the idea of developing Tom into a Shakespeare,— Tom, who had not the slightest desire to be one I was appalling, besides having in it an element of useless self-sacrifice from which I recoiled. On the other hand, if Alonzo should discover that I had written his theme, there were penalties I did not care to dwell upon .... With such a cloud hanging over me I passed a restless night.

As luck would have it the very next evening in the level light under the elms of the Square I beheld sauntering towards me a dapper figure which I recognized as that of Mr. Cheyne himself. As I saluted him he gave me an amused and most disconcerting glance; and when I was congratulating myself that he had passed me he stopped.

"Fine weather for March, Paret," he observed.

"Yes, sir," I agreed in a strange voice.

"By the way," he remarked, contemplating the bare branches above our heads, "that was an excellent theme your roommate handed in. I had no idea that he possessed such—such genius. Did you, by any chance, happen to read it?"

"Yes, sir,—I read it."

"Weren't you surprised?" inquired Mr. Cheyne.

"Well, yes, sir—that is—I mean to say he talks just like that, sometimes —that is, when it's anything he cares about."

"Indeed!" said Mr. Cheyne. "That's interesting, most interesting. In all my experience, I do not remember a case in which a gift has been developed so rapidly. I don't want to give the impression—ah that there is no room for improvement, but the thing was very well done, for an undergraduate. I must confess I never should have suspected it in Peters, and it's most interesting what you say about his cleverness in conversation." He twirled the head of his stick, apparently lost in reflection. "I may be wrong," he went on presently, "I have an idea it is you—" I must literally have jumped away from him. He paused a moment, without apparently noticing my panic, "that it is you who have influenced Peters."

"Sir?"

"I am wrong, then. Or is this merely commendable modesty on your part?"

"Oh, no, sir."

"Then my hypothesis falls to the ground. I had greatly hoped," he added meaningly, "that you might be able to throw some light on this mystery."

I was dumb.

"Paret," he asked, "have you time to come over to my rooms for a few minutes this evening?"

"Certainly, sir."

He gave me his number in Brattle Street....

Like one running in a nightmare and making no progress I made my way home, only to learn from Hallam,—who lived on the same floor,—that Tom had inconsiderately gone to Boston for the evening, with four other weary spirits in search of relaxation! Avoiding our club table, I took what little nourishment I could at a modest restaurant, and restlessly paced the moonlit streets until eight o'clock, when I found myself in front of one of those low-gabled colonial houses which, on less soul-shaking occasions, had exercised a great charm on my imagination. My hand hung for an instant over the bell.... I must have rung it violently, for there appeared almost immediately an old lady in a lace cap, who greeted me with gentle courtesy, and knocked at a little door with glistening panels. The latch was lifted by Mr. Cheyne himself.

"Come in, Paret," he said, in a tone that was unexpectedly hospitable.

I have rarely seen a more inviting room. A wood fire burned brightly on the brass andirons, flinging its glare on the big, white beam that crossed the ceiling, and reddening the square panes of the windows in their panelled recesses. Between these were rows of books,—attractive books in chased bindings, red and blue; books that appealed to be taken down and read. There was a table covered with reviews and magazines in neat piles, and a lamp so shaded as to throw its light only on the white blotter of the pad. Two easy chairs, covered with flowered chintz, were ranged before the fire, in one of which I sank, much bewildered, upon being urged to do so.

I utterly failed to recognize "Alonzo" in this new atmosphere. And he had, moreover, dropped the subtly sarcastic manner I was wont to associate with him.

"Jolly old house, isn't it?" he observed, as though I had casually dropped in on him for a chat; and he stood, with his hands behind him stretched to the blaze, looking down at me. "It was built by a certain Colonel Draper, who fought at Louisburg, and afterwards fled to England at the time of the Revolution. He couldn't stand the patriots, I'm not so sure that I blame him, either. Are you interested in colonial things, Mr. Paret?"

I said I was. If the question had concerned Aztec relics my answer would undoubtedly have been the same. And I watched him, dazedly, while he took down a silver porringer from the shallow mantel shelf.

"It's not a Revere," he said, in a slightly apologetic tone as though to forestall a comment, "but it's rather good, I think. I picked it up at a sale in Dorchester. But I have never been able to identify the coat of arms."

He showed me a ladle, with the names of "Patience and William Simpson" engraved quaintly thereon, and took down other articles in which I managed to feign an interest. Finally he seated himself in the chair opposite, crossed his feet, putting the tips of his fingers together and gazing into the fire.

"So you thought you could fool me," he said, at length.

I became aware of the ticking of a great clock in the corner. My mouth was dry.

"I am going to forgive you," he went on, more gravely, "for several reasons. I don't flatter, as you know. It's because you carried out the thing so perfectly that I am led to think you have a gift that may be cultivated, Paret. You wrote that theme in the way Peters would have written it if he had not been—what shall I say?—scripturally inarticulate. And I trust it may do you some good if I say it was something of a literary achievement, if not a moral one."

"Thank you, sir," I faltered.

"Have you ever," he inquired, lapsing a little into his lecture-room manner, "seriously thought of literature as a career? Have you ever thought of any career seriously?"

"I once wished to be a writer, sir," I replied tremulously, but refrained from telling him of my father's opinion of the profession. Ambition—a purer ambition than I had known for years—leaped within me at his words. He, Alonzo Cheyne, had detected in me the Promethean fire!

I sat there until ten o'clock talking to the real Mr. Cheyne, a human Mr. Cheyne unknown in the lecture-room. Nor had I suspected one in whom cynicism and distrust of undergraduates (of my sort) seemed so ingrained, of such idealism. He did not pour it out in preaching; delicately, unobtrusively and on the whole rather humorously he managed to present to me in a most disillusionizing light that conception of the university held by me and my intimate associates. After I had left him I walked the quiet streets to behold as through dissolving mists another Harvard, and there trembled in my soul like the birth-struggle of a flame something of the vision later to be immortalized by St. Gaudens, the spirit of Harvard responding to the spirit of the Republic—to the call of Lincoln, who voiced it. The place of that bronze at the corner of Boston Common was as yet empty, but I have since stood before it to gaze in wonder at the light shining in darkness on mute, uplifted faces, black faces! at Harvard's son leading them on that the light might live and prevail.

I, too, longed for a Cause into which I might fling myself, in which I might lose myself... I halted on the sidewalk to find myself staring from the opposite side of the street at a familiar house, my old landlady's, Mrs. Bolton's, and summoned up before me was the tired, smiling face of Hermann Krebs. Was it because when he had once spoken so crudely of the University I had seen the reflection of her spirit in his eyes? A light still burned in the extension roof—Krebs's light; another shone dimly through the ground glass of the front door. Obeying a sudden impulse, I crossed the street.

Mrs. Bolton, in the sky-blue wrapper, and looking more forbidding than ever, answered the bell. Life had taught her to be indifferent to surprises, and it was I who became abruptly embarrassed.

"Oh, it's you, Mr. Paret," she said, as though I had been a frequent caller. I had never once darkened her threshold since I had left her house.

"Yes," I answered, and hesitated.... "Is Mr. Krebs in?"

"Well," she replied in a lifeless tone, which nevertheless had in it a touch of bitterness, "I guess there's no reason why you and your friends should have known he was sick."

"Sick!" I repeated. "Is he very sick?"

"I calculate he'll pull through," she said. "Sunday the doctor gave him up. And no wonder! He hasn't had any proper food since he's be'n here!" She paused, eyeing me. "If you'll excuse me, Mr. Paret, I was just going up to him when you rang."

"Certainly," I replied awkwardly. "Would you be so kind as to tell him —when he's well enough—that I came to see him, and that I'm sorry?"

There was another pause, and she stood with a hand defensively clutching the knob.

"Yes, I'll tell him," she said.

With a sense of having been baffled, I turned away.

Walking back toward the Yard my attention was attracted by a slowly approaching cab whose occupants were disturbing the quiet of the night with song.

"Shollity—'tis wine, 'tis wine, that makesh—shollity."

The vehicle drew up in front of a new and commodious building,—I believe the first of those designed to house undergraduates who were willing to pay for private bathrooms and other modern luxuries; out of one window of the cab protruded a pair of shoeless feet, out of the other a hatless head I recognized as belonging to Tom Peters; hence I surmised that the feet were his also. The driver got down from the box, and a lively argument was begun inside—for there were other occupants—as to how Mr. Peters was to be disembarked; and I gathered from his frequent references to the "Shgyptian obelisk" that the engineering problem presented struck him as similar to the unloading of Cleopatra's Needle.

"Careful, careful!" he cautioned, as certain expelling movements began from within, "Easy, Ham, you jam-fool, keep the door shut, y'll break me."

"Now, Jerry, all heave sh'gether!" exclaimed a voice from the blackness of the interior.

"Will ye wait a minute, Mr. Durrett, sir?" implored the cabdriver. "You'll be after ruining me cab entirely." (Loud roars and vigorous resistance from the obelisk, the cab rocking violently.) "This gintleman" (meaning me) "will have him by the head, and I'll get hold of his feet, sir." Which he did, after a severe kick in the stomach.

"Head'sh all right, Martin."

"To be sure it is, Mr. Peters. Now will ye rest aisy awhile, sir?"

"I'm axphyxiated," cried another voice from the darkness, the mined voice of Jerome Kyme, our classmate.

"Get the tackles under him!" came forth in commanding tones from Conybear.

In the meantime many windows had been raised and much gratuitous advice was being given. The three occupants of the cab's seat who had previously clamoured for Mr. Peters' removal, now inconsistently resisted it; suddenly he came out with a jerk, and we had him fairly upright on the pavement minus a collar and tie and the buttons of his evening waistcoat. Those who remained in the cab engaged in a riotous game of hunt the slipper, while Tom peered into the dark interior, observing gravely the progress of the sport. First flew out an overcoat and a much-battered hat, finally the pumps, all of which in due time were adjusted to his person, and I started home with him, with much parting counsel from the other three.

"Whereinell were you, Hughie?" he inquired. "Hunted all over for you. Had a sousin' good time. Went to Babcock's—had champagne—then to see Babesh in—th'—Woods. Ham knows one of the Babesh had supper with four of 'em. Nice Babesh!"

"For heaven's sake don't step on me again!" I cried.

"Sh'poloshize, old man. But y'know I'm William Shakespheare. C'n do what I damplease." He halted in the middle of the street and recited dramatically:—

"'Not marble, nor th' gilded monuments
Of prinches sh'll outlive m' powerful rhyme.'"

"How's that, Alonzho, b'gosh?"

"Where did you learn it?" I demanded, momentarily forgetting his condition.

"Fr'm Ralph," he replied, "says I wrote it. Can't remember...."

After I had got him to bed,—a service I had learned to perform with more or less proficiency,—I sat down to consider the events of the evening, to attempt to get a proportional view. The intensity of my disgust was not hypocritical as I gazed through the open door into the bedroom and recalled the times when I, too, had been in that condition. Tom Peters drunk, and sleeping it off, was deplorable, without doubt; but Hugh Paret drunk was detestable, and had no excuse whatever. Nor did I mean by this to set myself on a higher ethical plane, for I felt nothing but despair and humility. In my state of clairvoyance I perceived that he was a better man, than I, and that his lapses proceeded from a love of liquor and the transcendent sense of good-fellowship that liquor brings.

# VII.

The crisis through which I passed at Cambridge, inaugurated by the events I have just related, I find very difficult to portray. It was a religious crisis, of course, and my most pathetic memory concerning it is of the vain attempts to connect my yearnings and discontents with the theology I had been taught; I began in secret to read my Bible, yet nothing I hit upon seemed to point a way out of my present predicament, to give any definite clew to the solution of my life. I was not mature enough to reflect that orthodoxy was a Sunday religion unrelated to a world whose wheels were turned by the motives of self-interest; that it consisted of ideals not deemed practical, since no attempt was made to put them into practice in the only logical manner,—by reorganizing civilization to conform with them. The implication was that the Christ who had preached these ideals was not practical.... There were undoubtedly men in the faculty of the University who might have helped me had I known of them; who might have given me, even at that time, a clew to the modern, logical explanation of the Bible as an immortal record of the thoughts and acts of men who had sought to do just what I was seeking to do,—connect the religious impulse to life and make it fruitful in life: an explanation, by the way, a thousand-fold more spiritual than the old. But I was hopelessly entangled in the meshes of the mystic, the miraculous and supernatural. If I had analyzed my yearnings, I might have realized that I wanted to renounce the life I had been leading, not because it was sinful, but because it was aimless. I had not learned that the Greek word for sin is "a missing of the mark." Just aimlessness! I had been stirred with the desire to perform some service for which the world would be grateful: to write great literature, perchance. But it had never been suggested to me that such swellings of the soul are religious, that religion is that kind of feeling, of motive power that drives the writer and the scientist, the statesman and the sculptor as well as the priest and the Prophet to serve mankind for the joy of serving: that religion is creative, or it is nothing: not mechanical, not a force imposed from without, but a driving power within. The "religion" I had learned was salvation from sin by miracle: sin a deliberate rebellion, not a pathetic missing of the mark of life; useful service of man, not the wandering of untutored souls who had not been shown the way. I felt religious. I wanted to go to church, I wanted to maintain, when it was on me, that exaltation I dimly felt as communion with a higher power, with God, and which also was identical with my desire to write, to create....

I bought books, sets of Wordsworth and Keats, of Milton and Shelley and Shakespeare, and hid them away in my bureau drawers lest Tom and my friends should see them. These too I read secretly, making excuses for not joining in the usual amusements. Once I walked to Mrs. Bolton's and inquired rather shamefacedly for Hermann Krebs, only to be informed that he had gone out.... There were lapses, of course, when I went off on the old excursions,—for the most part the usual undergraduate follies, though some were of a more serious nature; on these I do not care to dwell. Sex was still a mystery.... Always I awoke afterwards to bitter self-hatred and despair.... But my work in English improved, and I earned the commendation and friendship of Mr. Cheyne. With a wisdom for which I was grateful he was careful not to give much sign of it in classes, but the fact that he was "getting soft on me" was evident enough to be regarded with suspicion. Indeed the state into which I had fallen became a matter of increasing concern to my companions, who tried every means from ridicule to sympathy, to discover its cause and shake me out of it. The theory most accepted was that I was in love.

"Come on now, Hughie—tell me who she is. I won't give you away," Tom would beg. Once or twice, indeed, I had imagined I was in love with the sisters of Boston classmates whose dances I attended; to these parties Tom, not having overcome his diffidence in respect to what he called "social life," never could be induced to go.

It was Ralph who detected the true cause of my discontent. Typical as no other man I can recall of the code to which we had dedicated ourselves, the code that moulded the important part of the undergraduate world and defied authority, he regarded any defection from it in the light of treason. An instructor, in a fit of impatience, had once referred to him as the Mephistopheles of his class; he had fatal attractions, and a remarkable influence. His favourite pastime was the capricious exercise of his will on weaker characters, such as his cousin, Ham Durrett; if they "swore off," Ralph made it his business to get them drunk again, and having accomplished this would proceed himself to administer a new oath and see that it was kept. Alcohol seemed to have no effect whatever on him. Though he was in the class above me, I met him frequently at a club to which I had the honour to belong, then a suite of rooms over a shop furnished with a pool and a billiard table, easy-chairs and a bar. It has since achieved the dignity of a house of its own.

We were having, one evening, a "religious" argument, Cinibar, Laurens and myself and some others. I can't recall how it began; I think Cinibar had attacked the institution of compulsory chapel, which nobody defended; there was something inherently wrong, he maintained, with a religion to which men had to be driven against their wills. Somewhat to my surprise I found myself defending a Christianity out of which I had been able to extract but little comfort and solace. Neither Laurens nor Conybear, however, were for annihilating it: although they took the other side of the discussion of a subject of which none of us knew anything, their attacks were but half-hearted; like me, they were still under the spell exerted by a youthful training.

We were all of us aware of Ralph, who sat at some distance looking over the pages of an English sporting weekly. Presently he flung it down.

"Haven't you found out yet that man created God, Hughie?" he inquired. "And even if there were a personal God, what reason have you to think that man would be his especial concern, or any concern of his whatever? The discovery of evolution has knocked your Christianity into a cocked hat."

I don't remember how I answered him. In spite of the superficiality of his own arguments, which I was not learned enough to detect, I was ingloriously routed. Darwin had kicked over the bucket, and that was all there was to it.... After we had left the club both Conybear and Laurens admitted they were somewhat disturbed, declaring that Ralph had gone too far. I spent a miserable night, recalling the naturalistic assertions he had made so glibly, asking myself again and again how it was that the religion to which I so vainly clung had no greater effect on my actions and on my will, had not prevented me from lapses into degradation. And I hated myself for having argued upon a subject that was still sacred. I believed in Christ, which is to say that I believed that in some inscrutable manner he existed, continued to dominate the world and had suffered on my account.

To whom should I go now for a confirmation of my wavering beliefs? One of the results—it will be remembered of religion as I was taught it was a pernicious shyness, and even though I had found a mentor and confessor, I might have hesitated to unburden myself. This would be different from arguing with Ralph Hambleton. In my predicament, as I was wandering through the yard, I came across a notice of an evening talk to students in Holder Chapel, by a clergyman named Phillips Brooks. This was before the time, let me say in passing, when his sermons at Harvard were attended by crowds of undergraduates. Well, I stood staring at the notice, debating whether I should go, trying to screw up my courage; for I recognized clearly that such a step, if it were to be of any value, must mean a distinct departure from my present mode of life; and I recall thinking with a certain revulsion that I should have to "turn good." My presence at the meeting would be known the next day to all my friends, for the idea of attending a religious gathering when one was not forced to do so by the authorities was unheard of in our set. I should be classed with the despised "pious ones" who did such things regularly. I shrank from the ridicule. I had, however, heard of

Mr. Brooks from Ned Symonds, who was by no means of the pious type, and whose parents attended Mr. Brooks's church in Boston.... I left my decision in abeyance. But when evening came I stole away from the club table, on the plea of an engagement, and made my way rapidly toward Holder Chapel. I had almost reached it—when I caught a glimpse of Symonds and of some others approaching,—and I went on, to turn again. By this time the meeting, which was in a room on the second floor, had already begun. Palpitating, I climbed the steps; the door of the room was slightly ajar; I looked in; I recall a distinct sensation of surprise,—the atmosphere of that meeting was so different from what I had expected. Not a "pious" atmosphere at all! I saw a very tall and heavy gentleman, dressed in black, who sat, wholly at ease, on the table! One hand was in his pocket, one foot swung clear of the ground; and he was not preaching, but talking in an easy, conversational tone to some forty young men who sat intent on his words. I was too excited to listen to what he was saying, I was making a vain attempt to classify him. But I remember the thought, for it struck me with force,—that if Christianity were so thoroughly discredited by evolution, as Ralph Hambleton and other agnostics would have one believe, why should this remarkably sane and able-looking person be standing up for it as though it were still an established and incontrovertible fact?

He had not, certainly, the air of a dupe or a sentimentalist, but inspired confidence by his very personality. Youthlike, I watched him narrowly for flaws, for oratorical tricks, for all kinds of histrionic symptoms. Again I was near the secret; again it escaped me. The argument for Christianity lay not in assertions about it, but in being it. This man was Christianity.... I must have felt something of this, even though I failed to formulate it. And unconsciously I contrasted his strength, which reinforced the atmosphere of the room, with that of Ralph Hambleton, who was, a greater influence over me than I have recorded, and had come to sway me more and more, as he had swayed others. The strength of each was impressive, yet this Mr. Brooks seemed to me the bodily presentment of a set of values which I would have kept constantly before my eyes.... I felt him drawing me, overcoming my hesitation, belittling my fear of ridicule. I began gently to open the door— when something happened,—one of those little things that may change the course of a life. The door made little noise, yet one of the men sitting in the back of the room chanced to look around, and I recognized Hermann Krebs. His face was still sunken from his recent illness. Into his eyes seemed to leap a sudden appeal, an appeal to which my soul responded yet I hurried down the stairs and into the street. Instantly I regretted my retreat, I would have gone back, but lacked the courage; and I strayed unhappily for hours, now haunted by that look of Krebs, now wondering what the remarkably sane-looking and informal clergyman whose presence dominated the little room had been talking about. I never learned, but I did live to read his biography, to discover what he might have talked about,—for he if any man believed that life and religion are one, and preached consecration to life's task.

Of little use to speculate whether the message, had I learned it then, would have fortified and transformed me!

In spite of the fact that I was unable to relate to a satisfying conception of religion my new-born determination, I made up my mind, at least, to renounce my tortuous ways. I had promised my father to be a lawyer; I would keep my promise, I would give the law a fair trial; later on, perhaps, I might demonstrate an ability to write. All very praiseworthy! The season was Lent, a fitting time for renunciations and resolves. Although I had more than once fallen from grace, I believed myself at last to have settled down on my true course—when something happened. The devil interfered subtly, as usual—now in the person of Jerry Kyme. It should be said in justice to Jerry that he did not look the part. He had sunny-red, curly hair, mischievous blue eyes with long lashes, and he harboured no respect whatever for any individual or institution, sacred or profane; he possessed, however, a shrewd sense of his own value, as many innocent and unsuspecting souls discovered as early as our freshman year, and his method of putting down the presumptuous was both effective and unique. If he liked you, there could be no mistake about it.

One evening when I was engaged in composing a theme for Mr. Cheyne on no less a subject than the interpretation of the work of William Wordsworth, I found myself unexpectedly sprawling on the floor, in my descent kicking the table so vigorously as to send the ink-well a foot or two toward the ceiling. This, be it known, was a typical proof of Jerry's esteem. For he had entered noiselessly, jerking the back of my chair, which chanced to be tilted, and stood with his hands in his pockets, surveying the ruin he had wrought, watching the ink as it trickled on the carpet. Then he picked up the book.

"Poetry, you darned old grind!" he exclaimed disgustedly. "Say, Parry, I don't know what's got into you, but I want you to come home with me for the Easter holidays. It'll do you good. We'll be on the Hudson, you know, and we'll manage to make life bearable somehow."

I forgot my irritation, in sheer surprise.

"Why, that's mighty good of you, Jerry—" I began, struggling to my feet.

"Oh, rot!" he exclaimed. "I shouldn't ask you if I didn't want you."

There was no denying the truth of this, and after he had gone I sat for a long time with my pen in my mouth, reflecting as to whether or not I should go. For I had the instinct that here was another cross-roads, that more depended on my decision than I cared to admit. But even then I knew what I should do. Ridiculous not to—I told myself. How could a week or ten days with Jerry possibly affect my newborn, resolve?

Yet the prospect, now, of a visit to the Kymes' was by no means so glowing as it once would have been. For I had seen visions, I had dreamed dreams, beheld a delectable country of my very own. A year ago—nay, even a month ago—how such an invitation would have glittered!... I returned at length to my theme, over which, before Jerry's arrival, I had been working feverishly. But now the glamour had gone from it.

Presently Tom came in.

"Anyone been here?" he demanded.

"Jerry," I told him.

"What did he want?"

"He wanted me to go home with him at Easter."

"You're going, of course."

"I don't know. I haven't decided."

"You'd be a fool not to," was Tom's comment. It voiced, succinctly, a prevailing opinion.

It was the conclusion I arrived at in my own mind. But just why I had been chosen for the honour, especially at such a time, was a riddle. Jerry's invitations were charily given, and valued accordingly; and more than once, at our table, I had felt a twinge of envy when Conybear or someone else had remarked, with the proper nonchalance, in answer to a question, that they were going to Weathersfield. Such was the name of the Kyme place....

I shall never forget the impression made on me by the decorous luxury of that big house, standing amidst its old trees, halfway up the gentle slope that rose steadily from the historic highway where poor Andre was captured. I can see now the heavy stone pillars of its portico vignetted in a flush of tenderest green, the tulips just beginning to flame forth their Easter colours in the well-kept beds, the stately, well-groomed evergreens, the vivid lawns, the clipped hedges. And like an overwhelming wave of emotion that swept all before it, the impressiveness of wealth took possession of me. For here was a kind of wealth I had never known, that did not exist in the West, nor even in the still Puritan environs of Boston where I had visited. It took itself for granted, proclaimed itself complacently to have solved all problems. By ignoring them, perhaps. But I was too young to guess this. It was order personified, gaining effect at every turn by a multitude of details too trivial to mention were it not for the fact that they entered deeply into my consciousness, until they came to represent, collectively, the very flower of achievement. It was a wealth that accepted tribute calmly, as of inherent right. Law and tradition defended its sanctity more effectively than troops. Literature descended from her high altar to lend it dignity; and the long, silent library displayed row upon row of the masters, appropriately clad in morocco or calf,—Smollett, Macaulay, Gibbon, Richardson, Fielding, Scott, Dickens, Irving and Thackeray, as though each had striven for a tablet here. Art had denied herself that her canvases might be hung on these walls; and even the Church, on that first Sunday of my visit, forgot the blood of her martyrs that she might adorn an appropriate niche in the setting. The clergyman, at one of the dinner parties, gravely asked a blessing as upon an Institution that included and absorbed all other institutions in its being....

The note of that house was a tempered gaiety. Guests arrived from New York, spent the night and departed again without disturbing the even tenor of its ways. Unobtrusive servants ministered to their wants,—and to mine....

Conybear was there, and two classmates from Boston, and we were treated with the amiable tolerance accorded to college youths and intimates of the son of the house. One night there was a dance in our honour. Nor have I forgotten Jerry's sister, Nathalie, whom I had met at Class Days, a slim and willowy, exotic young lady of the Botticelli type, with a crown of burnished hair, yet more suggestive of a hothouse than of spring. She spoke English with a French accent. Capricious, impulsive, she captured my interest because she put a high value on her favour; she drove me over the hills, informing me at length that I was sympathique—different from the rest; in short, she emphasized and intensified what I may call the Weathersfield environment, stirred up in me new and vague aspirations that troubled yet excited me.

Then there was Mrs. Kyme, a pretty, light-hearted lady, still young, who seemed to have no intention of growing older, who romped and played songs for us on the piano. The daughter of an old but now impecunious Westchester family, she had been born to adorn the position she held, she was adapted by nature to wring from it the utmost of the joys it offered. From her, rather than from her husband, both of the children seemed to have inherited. I used to watch Mr. Grosvenor Kyme as he sat at the end of the dinner-table, dark, preoccupied, taciturn, symbolical of a wealth new to my experience, and which had about it a certain fabulous quality. It toiled not, neither did it spin, but grew as if by magic, day and night, until the very conception of it was overpowering. What must it be to have had ancestors who had been clever enough to sit still until a congested and discontented Europe had begun to pour its thousands and hundreds of thousands into the gateway of the western world, until that gateway had become a metropolis? ancestors, of course, possessing what now suddenly appeared to me as the most desirable of gifts—since it reaped so dazzling a harvest-business foresight. From time to time these ancestors had continued to buy desirable corners, which no amount of persuasion had availed to make them relinquish. Lease them, yes; sell them, never! By virtue of such a system wealth was as inevitable as human necessity; and the thought of human necessity did not greatly bother me. Mr. Kyme's problem of life was not one of making money, but of investing it. One became automatically a personage....

It was due to one of those singular coincidences—so interesting a subject for speculation—that the man who revealed to me this golden romance of the Kyme family was none other than a resident of my own city, Mr. Theodore Watling, now become one of our most important and influential citizens; a corporation lawyer, new and stimulating qualification, suggesting as it did, a deus ex machina of great affairs. That he, of all men, should come to Weathersfield astonished me, since I was as yet to make the connection between that finished, decorous, secluded existence and the source of its being. The evening before my departure he arrived in company with two other gentlemen, a Mr. Talbot and a Mr. Saxes, whose names were spoken with respect in a sphere of which I had hitherto taken but little cognizance-Wall Street. Conybear informed me that they were "magnates,"... We were sitting in the drawing-room at tea, when they entered with Mr. Watling, and no sooner had he spoken to Mrs. Kyme than his quick eye singled me out of the group.

"Why, Hugh!" he exclaimed, taking my hand. "I had no idea I should meet you here—I saw your father only last week, the day I left home." And he added, turning to Mrs. Kyme, "Hugh is the son of Mr. Matthew Paret, who has been the leader of our bar for many years."

The recognition and the tribute to my father were so graciously given that I warmed with gratitude and pride, while Mr. Kyme smiled a little, remarking that I was a friend of Jerry's. Theodore Watling, for being here, had suddenly assumed in my eyes a considerable consequence, though the note he struck in that house was a strange one. It was, however, his own note, and had a certain distinction, a ring of independence, of the knowledge of self-worth. Dinner at Weathersfield we youngsters had usually found rather an oppressive ceremony, with its shaded lights and precise ritual over which Mr. Kyme presided like a high priest; conversation had been restrained. That night, as Johnnie Laurens afterwards expressed it, "things loosened up," and Mr. Watling was responsible for the loosening. Taking command of the Kyme dinner table appeared to me to be no mean achievement, but this is just what he did, without being vulgar or noisy or assertive. Suavitar in modo, forbiter in re. If, as I watched him there with a newborn pride and loyalty, I had paused to reconstruct the idea that the mention of his name would formerly have evoked, I suppose I should have found him falling short of my notion of a gentleman; it had been my father's opinion; but Mr. Watling's marriage to Gene Hollister's aunt had given him a standing with us at home. He possessed virility, vitality in a remarkable degree, yet some elusive quality that was neither tact nor delicacy—though related to these differentiated him from the commonplace, self-made man of ability. He was just off the type. To liken him to a clothing store model of a well-built, broad-shouldered man with a firm neck, a handsome, rather square face not lacking in colour and a conventional, drooping moustache would be slanderous; yet he did suggest it. Suggesting it, he redeemed it: and the middle western burr in his voice was rather attractive than otherwise. He had not so much the air of belonging there, as of belonging anywhere—one of those anomalistic American citizens of the world who go abroad and make intimates of princes. Before the meal was over he had inspired me with loyalty and pride, enlisted the admiration of Jerry and Conybear and Johnnie Laurens; we followed him into the smoking-room, sitting down in a row on a leather lounge behind our elders.

Here, now that the gentlemen were alone, there was an inspiring largeness in their talk that fired the imagination. The subject was investments, at first those of coal and iron in my own state, for Mr. Watling, it appeared, was counsel for the Boyne Iron Works.

"It will pay you to keep an eye on that company, Mr. Kyme," he said, knocking the ashes from his cigar. "Now that old Mr. Durrett's gone—"

"You don't mean to say Nathaniel Durrett's dead!" said Mr. Kyme.

The lawyer nodded.

"The old regime passed with him. Adolf Scherer succeeds him, and you may take my word for it, he's a coming man. Mr. Durrett, who was a judge of men, recognized that. Scherer was an emigrant, he had ideas, and rose to be a foreman. For the last few years Mr. Durrett threw everything on his shoulders...."

Little by little the scope of the discussion was enlarged until it ranged over a continent, touching lightly upon lines of railroad, built or projected, across the great west our pioneers had so lately succeeded in wresting from the savages, upon mines of copper and gold hidden away among the mountains, and millions of acres of forest and grazing lands which a complacent government would relinquish provided certain technicalities were met: touching lightly, too, very lightly,—upon senators and congressmen at Washington. And for the first time I learned that not the least of the functions of these representatives of the people was to act as the medium between capital and investment, to facilitate the handing over of the Republic's resources to those in a position to develop them. The emphasis was laid on development, or rather on the resulting prosperity for the country: that was the justification, and it was taken for granted as supreme. Nor was it new to me; this cult of prosperity. I recalled the torch-light processions of the tariff enthusiasts of my childhood days, my father's championship of the Republican Party. He had not idealized politicians, either. For the American, politics and ethics were strangers.

Thus I listened with increasing fascination to these gentlemen in evening clothes calmly treating the United States as a melon patch that existed largely for the purpose of being divided up amongst a limited and favored number of persons. I had a feeling of being among the initiated. Where, it may be asked, were my ideals? Let it not be supposed that I believed myself to have lost them. If so, the impression I have given of myself has been wholly inadequate. No, they had been transmuted, that is all, transmuted by the alchemy of Weathersfield, by the personality of Theodore Watling into brighter visions. My eyes rarely left his face; I hung on his talk, which was interspersed with native humour, though he did not always join in the laughter, sometimes gazing at the fire, as though his keen mind were grappling with a problem suggested. I noted the respect in which his opinions were held, and my imagination was fired by an impression of the power to be achieved by successful men of his profession, by the evidence of their indispensability to capital itself.... At last when the gentlemen rose and were leaving the room, Mr. Watling lingered, with his hand on my arm.

"Of course you're going through the Law School, Hugh," he said.

"Yes, sir," I replied.

"Good!" he exclaimed emphatically. "The law, to-day, is more of a career than ever, especially for a young man with your antecedents and advantages, and I know of no city in the United States where I would rather start practice, if I were a young man, than ours. In the next twenty years we shall see a tremendous growth. Of course you'll be going into your father's office. You couldn't do better. But I'll keep an eye on you, and perhaps I'll be able to help you a little, too."

I thanked him gratefully.

A famous artist, who started out in youth to embrace a military career and who failed to pass an examination at West Point, is said to have remarked that if silicon had been a gas he would have been a soldier. I am afraid I may have given the impression that if I had not gone to Weathersfield and encountered Mr. Watling I might not have been a lawyer. This impression would be misleading. And while it is certain that I have not exaggerated the intensity of the spiritual experience I went through at Cambridge, a somewhat belated consideration for the truth compels me to register my belief that the mood would in any case have been ephemeral. The poison generated by the struggle of my nature with its environment had sunk too deep, and the very education that was supposed to make a practical man of me had turned me into a sentimentalist. I became, as will be seen, anything but a practical man in the true sense, though the world in which I had been brought up and continued to live deemed me such. My father was greatly pleased when I wrote him that I was now more than ever convinced of the wisdom of choosing the law as my profession, and was satisfied that I had come to my senses at last. He had still been prepared to see me "go off at a tangent," as he expressed it. On the other hand, the powerful effect of the appeal made by Weathersfield and Mr. Watling must not be underestimated. Here in one object lesson was emphasized a host of suggestions each of which had made its impression. And when I returned to Cambridge Alonzo Cheyne knew that he had lost me....

I pass over the rest of my college course, and the years I spent at the Harvard Law School, where were instilled into me without difficulty the dictums that the law was the most important of all professions, that those who entered it were a priestly class set aside to guard from profanation that Ark of the Covenant, the Constitution of the United States. In short, I was taught law precisely as I had been taught religion,—scriptural infallibility over again,—a static law and a static theology,—a set of concepts that were supposed to be equal to any problems civilization would have to meet until the millennium. What we are wont to call wisdom is often naively innocent of impending change. It has no barometric properties.

I shall content myself with relating one incident only of this period. In the January of my last year I went with a party of young men and girls to stay over Sunday at Beverly Farms, where Mrs. Fremantle—a young Boston matron had opened her cottage for the occasion. This "cottage," a roomy, gabled structure, stood on a cliff, at the foot of which roared the wintry Atlantic, while we danced and popped corn before the open fires. During the daylight hours we drove about the country in sleighs, or made ridiculous attempts to walk on snow-shoes.

On Sunday afternoon, left temporarily to my own devices, I wandered along the cliff, crossing into the adjoining property. The wind had fallen; the waves, much subdued, broke rhythmically against the rocks; during the night a new mantle of snow had been spread, and the clouds were still low and menacing. As I strolled I became aware of a motionless figure ahead of me, —one that seemed oddly familiar; the set of the shabby overcoat on the stooping shoulders, the unconscious pose contributed to a certain sharpness of individuality; in the act of challenging my memory, I halted. The man was gazing at the seascape, and his very absorption gave me a sudden and unfamiliar thrill. The word absorption precisely expresses my meaning, for he seemed indeed to have become a part of his surroundings,—an harmonious part. Presently he swung about and looked at me as though he had expected to find me there—and greeted me by name.

"Krebs!" I exclaimed.

He smiled, and flung out his arm, indicating the scene. His eyes at that moment seemed to reflect the sea,—they made the gaunt face suddenly beautiful.

"This reminds me of a Japanese print," he said.

The words, or the tone in which he spoke, curiously transformed the picture. It was as if I now beheld it, anew, through his vision: the grey water stretching eastward to melt into the grey sky, the massed, black trees on the hillside, powdered with white, the snow in rounded, fantastic patches on the huge boulders at the foot of the cliff. Krebs did not seem like a stranger, but like one whom I had known always,—one who stood in a peculiar relationship between me and something greater I could not define. The impression was fleeting, but real…. I remember wondering how he could have known anything about Japanese prints.

"I didn't think you were still in this part of the country," I remarked awkwardly.

"I'm a reporter on a Boston newspaper, and I've been sent up here to interview old Mr. Dome, who lives in that house," and he pointed to a roof above the trees. "There is a rumour, which I hope to verify, that he has just given a hundred thousand dollars to the University."

"And—won't he see you?"

"At present he's taking a nap," said Krebs. "He comes here occasionally for a rest."

"Do you like interviewing?" I asked.

He smiled again.

"Well, I see a good many different kinds of people, and that's interesting."

"But—being a reporter?" I persisted.

This continued patronage was not a conscious expression of superiority on my part, but he did not seem to resent it. He had aroused my curiosity.

"I'm going into the law," he said.

The quiet confidence with which he spoke aroused, suddenly, a twinge of antagonism. He had every right to go into the law, of course, and yet!… my query would have made it evident to me, had I been introspective in those days, that the germ of the ideal of the profession, implanted by Mr. Watling, was expanding. Were not influential friends necessary for the proper kind of career? and where were Krebs's? In spite of the history of Daniel Webster and a long line of American tradition, I felt an incongruity in my classmate's aspiration. And as he stood there, gaunt and undoubtedly hungry, his eyes kindling, I must vaguely have classed him with the revolutionaries of all the ages; must have felt in him, instinctively, a menace to the stability of that Order with which I had thrown my fortunes. And yet there were comparatively poor men in the Law School itself who had not made me feel this way! He had impressed me against my will, taken me by surprise, commiseration had been mingled with other feelings that sprang out of the memory of the night I had called on him, when he had been sick. Now I resented something in him which Tom Peters had called "crust."

"The law!" I repeated. "Why?"

"Well," he said, "even when I was a boy, working at odd jobs, I used to think if I could ever be a lawyer I should have reached the top notch of human dignity."

Once more his smile disarmed me.

"And now" I asked curiously.

"You see, it was an ideal with me, I suppose. My father was responsible for that. He had the German temperament of '48, and when he fled to this country, he expected to find Utopia." The smile emerged again, like the sun shining through clouds, while fascination and antagonism again struggled within me. "And then came frightful troubles. For years he could get only enough work to keep him and my mother alive, but he never lost his faith in America. 'It is man,' he would say, 'man has to grow up to it—to liberty.' Without the struggle, liberty would be worth nothing. And he used to tell me that we must all do our part, we who had come here, and not expect everything to be done for us. He had made that mistake. If things were bad, why, put a shoulder to the wheel and help to make them better.

"That helped me," he continued, after a moment's pause. "For I've seen a good many things, especially since I've been working for a newspaper. I've seen, again and again, the power of the law turned against those whom it was intended to protect, I've seen lawyers who care a great deal more about winning cases than they do about justice, who prostitute their profession to profit making,—profit making for themselves and others. And they are often the respectable lawyers, too, men of high standing, whom you would not think would do such things. They are on the side of the powerful, and the best of them are all retained by rich men and corporations. And what is the result? One of the worst evils, I think, that can befall a country. The poor man goes less and less to the courts. He is getting bitter, which is bad, which is dangerous. But men won't see it."

It was on my tongue to refute this, to say that everybody had a chance. I could indeed recall many arguments that had been drilled into me; quotations, even, from court decisions. But something prevented me from doing this,—something in his manner, which was neither argumentative nor combative.

"That's why I am going into the law," he added. "And I intend to stay in it if I can keep alive. It's a great chance for me—for all of us. Aren't you at the Law School?"

I nodded. Once more, as his earnest glance fell upon me, came that suggestion of a subtle, inexplicable link between us; but before I could reply, steps were heard behind us, and an elderly servant, bareheaded, was seen coming down the path.

"Are you the reporter?" he demanded somewhat impatiently of Krebs. "If you want to see Mr. Dome, you'd better come right away. He's going out for a drive."

For a while, after he had shaken my hand and departed, I stood in the snow, looking after him....

# VIII

On the Wednesday of that same week.the news of my father's sudden and serious illness came to me in a telegram, and by the time I arrived at home it was too late to see him again alive. It was my first experience with death, and what perplexed me continually during the following days was an inability to feel the loss more deeply. When a child, I had been easily shaken by the spectacle of sorrow. Had I, during recent years, as a result of a discovery that emotions arising from human relationships lead to discomfort and suffering, deliberately been forming a shell, until now I was incapable of natural feelings? Of late I had seemed closer to my father, and his letters, though formal, had given evidence of his affection; in his repressed fashion he had made it clear that he looked forward to the time when I was to practise with him. Why was it then, as I gazed upon his fine features in death, that I experienced no intensity of sorrow? What was it in me that would not break down? He seemed worn and tired, yet I had never thought of him as weary, never attributed to him any yearning. And now he was released.

I wondered what had been his private thoughts about himself, his private opinions about life; and when I reflect now upon my lack of real knowledge at five and twenty, I am amazed at the futility of an expensive education which had failed to impress upon me the simple, basic fact that life was struggle; that either development or retrogression is the fate of all men, that characters are never completely made, but always in the making. I had merely a disconcerting glimpse of this truth, with no powers of formulation, as I sat beside my mother in the bedroom, where every article evoked some childhood scene. Here was the dent in the walnut foot-board of the bed made, one wintry day, by the impact of my box of blocks; the big arm-chair, covered with I know not what stiff embroidery, which had served on countless occasions as a chariot driven to victory. I even remembered how every Wednesday morning I had been banished from the room, which had been so large a part of my childhood universe, when Ella, the housemaid, had flung open all its windows and crowded its furniture into the hall.

The thought of my wanderings since then became poignant, almost terrifying. The room, with all its memories, was unchanged. How safe I had been within its walls! Why could I not have been, content with what it represented? of tradition, of custom,—of religion? And what was it within me that had lured me away from these?

I was miserable, indeed, but my misery was not of the kind I thought it ought to be. At moments, when my mother relapsed into weeping, I glanced at her almost in wonder. Such sorrow as hers was incomprehensible. Once she surprised and discomfited me by lifting her head and gazing fixedly at me through her tears.

I recall certain impressions of the funeral. There, among the pall-bearers, was my Cousin Robert Breck, tears in the furrows of his cheeks. Had he loved my father more than I? The sight of his grief moved me suddenly and strongly.... It seemed an age since I had worked in his store, and yet here he was still, coming to town every morning and returning every evening to Claremore, loving his friends, and mourning them one by one. Was this, the spectacle presented by my Cousin Robert, the reward of earthly existence? Were there no other prizes save those known as greatness of character and depth of human affections? Cousin Robert looked worn and old. The other pall-bearers, men of weight, of long standing in the community, were aged, too; Mr. Blackwood, and Mr. Jules Hollister; and out of place, somehow, in this new church building. It came to me abruptly that the old order was gone,—had slipped away during my absence. The church I had known in boyhood had been torn down to make room for a business building on Boyne Street; the edifice in which I sat was expensive, gave forth no distinctive note; seemingly transitory with its hybrid interior, its shiny oak and blue and red organ-pipes, betokening a compromised and weakened faith. Nondescript, likewise, seemed the new minister, Mr. Randlett, as he prayed unctuously in front of the flowers massed on the platform. I vaguely resented his laudatory references to my father.

The old church, with its severity, had actually stood for something. It was the Westminster Catechism in wood and stone, and Dr. Pound had been the human incarnation of that catechism, the fit representative of a wrathful God, a militant shepherd who had guarded with vigilance his respectable flock, who had protested vehemently against the sins of the world by which they were surrounded, against the "dogs, and sorcerers, and whoremongers, and murderers and idolaters, and whosoever loveth and maketh a lie." How Dr. Pound would have put the emphasis of the Everlasting into those words!

Against what was Mr. Randlett protesting?

My glance wandered to the pews which held the committees from various organizations, such as the Chamber of Commerce and the Bar Association, which had come to do honour to my father. And there, differentiated from the others, I saw the spruce, alert figure of Theodore Watling. He, too, represented a new type and a new note,—this time a forceful note, a secular note that had not belonged to the old church, and seemed likewise anomalistic in the new....

During the long, slow journey in the carriage to the cemetery my mother did not raise her veil. It was not until she reached out and seized my hand, convulsively, that I realized she was still a part of my existence.

In the days that followed I became aware that my father's death had removed a restrictive element, that I was free now to take without criticism or opposition whatever course in life I might desire. It may be that I had apprehended even then that his professional ideals would not have coincided with my own. Mingled with this sense of emancipation was a curious feeling of regret, of mourning for something I had never valued, something fixed and dependable for which he had stood, a rock and a refuge of which I had never availed myself!... When his will was opened it was found that the property had been left to my mother during her lifetime. It was larger than I had thought, four hundred thousand dollars, shrewdly invested, for the most part, in city real estate. My father had been very secretive as to money matters, and my mother had no interest in them.

Three or four days later I received in the mail a typewritten letter signed by Theodore Watling, expressing sympathy for my bereavement, and asking me to drop in on him, down town, before I should leave the city. In contrast to the somewhat dingy offices where my father had practised in the Blackwood Block, the quarters of Watling, Fowndes and Ripon on the eighth floor of the new Durrett Building were modern to a degree, finished in oak and floored with marble, with a railed-off space where young women with nimble fingers played ceaselessly on typewriters. One of them informed me that Mr. Watling was busy, but on reading my card added that she would take it in. Meanwhile, in company with two others who may have been clients, I waited. This, then, was what it meant to be a lawyer of importance, to have, like a Chesterfield, an ante-room where clients cooled their heels and awaited one's pleasure...

The young woman returned, and led me through a corridor to a door on which was painted Mr. Wailing.

I recall him tilted back in his chair in a debonnair manner beside his polished desk, the hint of a smile on his lips; and leaning close to him was a yellow, owl-like person whose eyes, as they turned to me, gave the impression of having stared for years into hard, artificial lights. Mr. Watling rose briskly.

"How are you, Hugh?" he said, the warmth of his greeting tempered by just the note of condolence suitable to my black clothes. "I'm glad you came. I wanted to see you before you went back to Cambridge. I must introduce you to Judge Bering, of our State Supreme Court. Judge, this is Mr. Paret's boy."

The judge looked me over with a certain slow impressiveness, and gave me a soft and fleshy hand.

"Glad to know you, Mr. Paret. Your father was a great loss to our bar," he declared.

I detected in his tone and manner a slight reservation that could not be called precisely judicial dignity; it was as though, in these few words, he had gone to the limit of self-commitment with a stranger—a striking contrast to the confidential attitude towards Mr. Watling in which I had surprised him.

"Judge," said Mr. Watling, sitting down again, "do you recall that time we all went up to Mr. Paret's house and tried to induce him to run for mayor? That was before you went on the lower bench."

The judge nodded gloomily, caressing his watch chain, and suddenly rose to go.

"That will be all right, then?" Mr. Watling inquired cryptically, with a smile. The other made a barely perceptible inclination of the head and departed. Mr. Watling looked at me. "He's one of the best men we have on the bench to-day," he added. There was a trace of apology in his tone.

He talked a while of my father, to whom, so he said, he had looked up ever since he had been admitted to the bar.

"It would be a pleasure to me, Hugh, as well as a matter of pride," he said cordially, but with dignity, "to have Matthew Paret's son in my office. I suppose you will be wishing to take your mother somewhere this summer, but if you care to come here in the autumn, you will be welcome. You will begin, of course, as other young men begin,—as I began. But I am a believer in blood, and I'll be glad to have you. Mr. Fowndes and Mr. Ripon feel the same way." He escorted me to the door himself.

Everywhere I went during that brief visit home I was struck by change, by the crumbling and decay of institutions that once had held me in thrall, by the superimposition of a new order that as yet had assumed no definite character. Some of the old landmarks had disappeared; there were new and aggressive office buildings, new and aggressive residences, new and aggressive citizens who lived in them, and of whom my mother spoke with gentle deprecation. Even Claremore, that paradise of my childhood, had grown shrivelled and shabby, even tawdry, I thought, when we went out there one Sunday afternoon; all that once represented the magic word "country" had vanished. The old flat piano, made in Philadelphia ages ago, the horsehair chairs and sofa had been replaced by a nondescript furniture of the sort displayed behind plate-glass windows of the city's stores: rocking-chairs on stands, upholstered in clashing colours, their coiled springs only half hidden by tassels, and "ornamental" electric fixtures, instead of the polished coal-oil lamps. Cousin Jenny had grown white, Willie was a staid bachelor, Helen an old maid, while Mary had married a tall, anaemic young man with glasses, Walter Kinley, whom Cousin Robert had taken into the store. As I contemplated the Brecks odd questions suggested themselves: did honesty and warm-heartedness necessarily accompany a lack of artistic taste? and was virtue its own reward, after all? They drew my mother into the house, took off her wraps, set her down in the most comfortable rocker, and insisted on making her a cup of tea.

I was touched. I loved them still, and yet I was conscious of reservations concerning them. They, too, seemed a little on the defensive with me, and once in a while Mary was caustic in her remarks.

"I guess nothing but New York will be good enough for Hugh now. He'll be taking Cousin Sarah away from us."

"Not at all, my dear," said my mother, gently, "he's going into Mr. Watling's office next autumn."

"Theodore Watling?" demanded Cousin Robert, pausing in his carving.

"Yes, Robert. Mr. Watling has been good enough to say that he would like to have Hugh. Is there anything—?"

"Oh, I'm out of date, Sarah," Cousin Robert replied, vigorously severing the leg of the turkey. "These modern lawyers are too smart for me. Watling's no worse than the others, I suppose,—only he's got more ability."

"I've never heard anything against him," said my mother in a pained voice. "Only the other day McAlery Willett congratulated me that Hugh was going to be with him."

"You mustn't mind Robert, Sarah," put in Cousin Jenny,—a remark reminiscent of other days.

"Dad has a notion that his generation is the only honest one," said Helen, laughingly, as she passed a plate.

I had gained a sense of superiority, and I was quite indifferent to Cousin Robert's opinion of Mr. Watling, of modern lawyers in general. More than once a wave of self-congratulation surged through me that I had possessed the foresight and initiative to get out of the wholesale grocery business while there was yet time. I looked at Willie, still freckled, still literal, still a plodder, at Walter Kinley, and I thought of the drabness of their lives; at Cousin Robert himself as he sat smoking his cigar in the bay-window on that dark February day, and suddenly I pitied him. The suspicion struck me that he had not prospered of late, and this deepened to a conviction as he talked.

"The Republican Party is going to the dogs," he asserted.

"It used to be an honourable party, but now it is no better than the other. Politics are only conducted, now, for the purpose of making unscrupulous men rich, sir. For years I furnished this city with good groceries, if I do say it myself. I took a pride in the fact that the inmates of the hospitals, yes, and the dependent poor in the city's institutions, should have honest food. You can get anything out of the city if you are willing to pay the politicians for it. I lost my city contracts. Why? Because I refused to deal with scoundrels. Weill and Company and other unscrupulous upstarts are willing to do so, and poison the poor and the sick with adulterated groceries! The first thing I knew was that the city auditor was holding back my bills for supplies, and paying Weill's. That's what politics and business, yes, sir, and the law, have come to in these days. If a man wants to succeed, he must turn into a rascal."

I was not shocked, but I was silent, uncomfortable, wishing that it were time to take the train back to the city. Cousin Robert's face was more worn than I had thought, and I contrasted him inevitably with the forceful person who used to stand, in his worn alpaca coat, on the pavement in front of his store, greeting with clear-eyed content his fellow merchants of the city. Willie Breck, too, was silent, and Walter Kinley took off his glasses and wiped them. In the meanwhile Helen had left the group in which my mother sat, and, approaching us, laid her hands on her father's shoulders.

"Now, dad," she said, in affectionate remonstrance, "you're excited about politics again, and you know it isn't good for you. And besides, they're not worth it."

"You're right, Helen," he replied. Under the pressure of her hands he made a strong effort to control himself, and turned to address my mother across the room.

"I'm getting to be a crotchety old man," he said. "It's a good thing I have a daughter to remind me of it."

"It is a good thing, Robert," said my mother.

During the rest of our visit he seemed to have recovered something of his former spirits and poise, taking refuge in the past. They talked of their own youth, of families whose houses had been landmarks on the Second Bank.

"I'm worried about your Cousin Robert, Hugh," my mother confided to me, when we were at length seated in the train. "I've heard rumours that things are not so well at the store as they might be." We looked out at the winter landscape, so different from that one which had thrilled every fibre of my being in the days when the railroad on which we travelled had been a winding narrow gauge. The orchards—those that remained—were bare;

stubble pricked the frozen ground where tassels had once waved in the hot, summer wind. We flew by row after row of ginger-bread, suburban houses built on "villa plots," and I read in large letters on a hideous sign-board, "Woodbine Park."

"Hugh, have you ever heard anything against—Mr. Watling?"

"No, mother," I said. "So far as I knew, he is very much looked up to by lawyers and business men. He is counsel, I believe, for Mr. Blackwood's street car line on Boyne Street. And I told you, I believe, that I met him once at Mr. Kyme's."

"Poor Robert!" she sighed. "I suppose business trouble does make one bitter,—I've seen it so often. But I never imagined that it would overtake Robert, and at his time of life! It is an old and respected firm, and we have always had a pride in it." ...

That night, when I was going to bed, it was evident that the subject was still in her mind. She clung to my hand a moment.

"I, too, am afraid of the new, Hugh," she said, a little tremulously. "We all grow so, as age comes on."

"But you are not old, mother," I protested.

"I have a feeling, since your father has gone, that I have lived my life, my dear, though I'd like to stay long enough to see you happily married—to have grandchildren. I was not young when you were born." And she added, after a little while, "I know nothing about business affairs, and now—now that your father is no longer here, sometimes I'm afraid—"

"Afraid of what, mother?"

She tried to smile at me through her tears. We were in the old sitting-room, surrounded by the books.

"I know it's foolish, and it isn't that I don't trust you. I know that the son of your father couldn't do anything that was not honourable. And yet I am afraid of what the world is becoming. The city is growing so fast, and so many new people are coming in. Things are not the same. Robert is right, there. And I have heard your father say the same thing. Hugh, promise me that you will try to remember always what he was, and what he would wish you to be!"

"I will, mother," I answered. "But I think you would find that Cousin Robert exaggerates a little, makes things seem worse than they really are. Customs change, you know. And politics were never well—Sunday schools." I, too, smiled a little. "Father knew that. And he would never take an active part in them."

"He was too fine!" she exclaimed.

"And now," I continued, "Cousin Robert has happened to come in contact with them through business. That is what has made the difference in him. Before, he always knew they were corrupt, but he rarely thought about them."

"Hugh," she said suddenly, after a pause, "you must remember one thing,—that you can afford to be independent. I thank God that your father has provided for that!"

I was duly admitted, the next autumn, to the bar of my own state, and was assigned to a desk in the offices of Watling, Fowndes and Ripon. Larry

Weed was my immediate senior among the apprentices, and Larry was a hero-worshipper. I can see him now. He suggested a bullfrog as he sat in the little room we shared in common, his arms akimbo over a law book, his little legs doubled under him, his round, eyes fixed expectantly on the doorway. And even if I had not been aware of my good fortune in being connected with such a firm as Theodore Watling's, Larry would shortly have brought it home to me. During those weeks when I was making my first desperate attempts at briefing up the law I was sometimes interrupted by his exclamations when certain figures went by in the corridor.

"Say, Hugh, do you know who that was?"

"No."

"Miller Gorse."

"Who's he?"

"Do you mean to say you never heard of Miller Gorse?"

"I've been away a long time," I would answer apologetically. A person of some importance among my contemporaries at Harvard, I had looked forward to a residence in my native city with the complacency of one who has seen something of the world,—only to find that I was the least in the new kingdom. And it was a kingdom. Larry opened up to me something of the significance and extent of it, something of the identity of the men who controlled it.

"Miller Gorse," he said impressively, "is the counsel for the railroad."

"What railroad? You mean the—" I was adding, when he interrupted me pityingly.

"After you've been here a while you'll find out there's only one railroad in this state, so far as politics are concerned. The Ashuela and Northern, the Lake Shore and the others don't count."

I refrained from asking any more questions at that time, but afterwards I always thought of the Railroad as spelled with a capital.

"Miller Gorse isn't forty yet," Larry told me on another occasion. "That's doing pretty well for a man who comes near running this state."

For the sake of acquiring knowledge, I endured Mr. Weed's patronage. I inquired how Mr. Gorse ran the state.

"Oh, you'll find out soon enough," he assured me.

"But Mr. Barbour's president of the Railroad."

"Sure. Once in a while they take something up to him, but as a rule he leaves things to Gorse."

Whereupon I resolved to have a good look at Mr. Gorse at the first opportunity. One day Mr. Watling sent out for some papers.

"He's in there now;" said Larry. "You take 'em."

"In there" meant Mr. Watling's sanctum. And in there he was. I had only a glance at the great man, for, with a kindly but preoccupied "Thank you, Hugh," Mr. Watling took the papers and dismissed me. Heaviness, blackness and impassivity,—these were the impressions of Mr. Gorse which I carried away from that first meeting. The very solidity of his flesh seemed to suggest the solidity of his position. Such, say the psychologists, is the effect of prestige.

I remember well an old-fashioned picture puzzle in one of my boyhood books. The scene depicted was to all appearances a sylvan, peaceful one, with two happy lovers seated on a log beside a brook; but presently, as one gazed at the picture, the head of an animal stood forth among the branches, and then the body; more animals began to appear, bit by bit; a tiger, a bear, a lion, a jackal, a fox, until at last, whenever I looked at the page, I did not see the sylvan scene at all, but only the predatory beasts of the forest. So, one by one, the figures of the real rulers of the city superimposed themselves for me upon the simple and democratic design of Mayor, Council, Board of Aldermen, Police Force, etc., that filled the eye of a naive and trusting electorate which fondly imagined that it had something to say in government. Miller Gorse was one of these rulers behind the screen, and Adolf Scherer, of the Boyne Iron Works, another; there was Leonard Dickinson of the Corn National Bank; Frederick Grierson, becoming wealthy in city real estate; Judah B. Tallant, who, though outlawed socially, was deferred to as the owner of the Morning Era; and even Ralph Hambleton, rapidly superseding the elderly and conservative Mr. Lord, who had hitherto managed the great Hambleton estate. Ralph seemed to have become, in a somewhat gnostic manner, a full-fledged financier. Not having studied law, he had been home for four years when I became a legal fledgling, and during the early days of my apprenticeship I was beholden to him for many "eye openers" concerning the conduct of great affairs. I remember him sauntering into my room one morning when Larry Weed had gone out on an errand.

"Hello, Hughie," he said, with his air of having nothing to do. "Grinding it out? Where's Watling?"

"Isn't he in his office?"

"No."

"Well, what can we do for you?" I asked.

Ralph grinned.

"Perhaps I'll tell you when you're a little older. You're too young." And he sank down into Larry Weed's chair, his long legs protruding on the other side of the table. "It's a matter of taxes. Some time ago I found out that Dickinson and Tallant and others I could mention were paying a good deal less on their city property than we are. We don't propose to do it any more—that's all."

"How can Mr. Watling help you?" I inquired.

"Well, I don't mind giving you a few tips about your profession, Hughie. I'm going to get Watling to fix it up with the City Hall gang. Old Lord doesn't like it, I'll admit, and when I told him we had been contributing to the city long enough, that I proposed swinging into line with other property holders, he began to blubber about disgrace and what my grandfather would say if he were alive. Well, he isn't alive. A good deal of water has flowed under the bridges since his day. It's a mere matter of business, of getting your respectable firm to retain a City Hall attorney to fix it up with the assessor."

"How about the penitentiary?" I ventured, not too seriously.

"I shan't go to the penitentiary, neither will Watling. What I do is to pay a lawyer's fee. There isn't anything criminal in that, is there?"

For some time after Ralph had departed I sat reflecting upon this new knowledge, and there came into my mind the bitterness of Cousin Robert Breck against this City Hall gang, and his remarks about lawyers. I recalled the tone in which he had referred to Mr. Watling. But Ralph's philosophy easily triumphed. Why not be practical, and become master of a situation which one had not made, and could not alter, instead of being overwhelmed by it? Needless to say, I did not mention the conversation to Mr. Watling, nor did he dwindle in my estimation. These necessary transactions did not interfere in any way with his personal relationships, and his days were filled with kindnesses. And was not Mr. Ripon, the junior partner, one of the evangelical lights of the community, conducting advanced Bible classes every week in the Church of the Redemption?... The unfolding of mysteries kept me alert. And I understood that, if I was to succeed, certain esoteric knowledge must be acquired, as it were, unofficially. I kept my eyes and ears open, and applied myself, with all industry, to the routine tasks with which every young man in a large legal firm is familiar. I recall distinctly my pride when, the Board of Aldermen having passed an ordinance lowering the water rates, I was intrusted with the responsibility of going before the court in behalf of Mr. Ogilvy's water company, obtaining a temporary restricting order preventing the ordinance from going at once into effect. Here was an affair in point. Were it not for lawyers of the calibre of Watling, Fowndes and Ripon, hard-earned private property would soon be confiscated by the rapacious horde. Once in a while I was made aware that Mr. Watling had his eye on me.

"Well, Hugh," he would say, "how are you getting along? That's right, stick to it, and after a while we'll hand the drudgery over to somebody else."

He possessed the supreme quality of a leader of men in that he took pains to inform himself concerning the work of the least of his subordinates; and he had the gift of putting fire into a young man by a word or a touch of the hand on the shoulder. It was not difficult for me, therefore, to comprehend Larry Weed's hero-worship, the loyalty of other members of the firm or of those occupants of the office whom I have not mentioned. My first impression of him, which I had got at Jerry Kyme's, deepened as time went on, and I readily shared the belief of those around me that his legal talents easily surpassed those of any of his contemporaries. I can recall, at this time, several noted cases in the city when I sat in court listening to his arguments with thrills of pride. He made us all feel—no matter how humble may have been our contributions to the preparation—that we had a share in his triumphs. We remembered his manner with judges and juries, and strove to emulate it. He spoke as if there could be no question as to his being right as to the law and the facts, and yet, in some subtle way that bated analysis, managed not to antagonize the court. Victory was in the air in that office. I do not mean to say there were not defeats; but frequently these defeats, by resourcefulness, by a never-say-die spirit, by a consummate knowledge, not only of the law, but of other things at which I have hinted, were turned into ultimate victories. We fought cases from one court to another, until our opponents were worn out or the decision was reversed. We won, and that spirit of winning got into the blood. What was most impressed on me in those early years, I think, was the discovery that there was always a path—if one were clever enough to find it—from one terrace to the next higher. Staying power was the most prized of all the virtues. One could always, by adroitness, compel a legal opponent to fight the matter out all over again on new ground, or at least on ground partially new. If the Court of Appeals should fail one, there was the Supreme Court; there was the opportunity, also, to shift from the state to the federal courts; and likewise the much-prized device known as a change of venue, when a judge was supposed to be "prejudiced."

# IX.

As my apprenticeship advanced I grew more and more to the inhabitants of our city into two kinds, the who were served, and the inefficient, who were separate efficient, neglected; but the mental process of which the classification was the result was not so deliberate as may be supposed. Sometimes, when an important client would get into trouble, the affair took me into the police court, where I saw the riff-raff of the city penned up, waiting to have justice doled out to them: weary women who had spent the night in cells, indifferent now as to the front they presented to the world, the finery rued that they had tended so carefully to catch the eyes of men on the darkened streets; brazen young girls, who blazed forth defiance to all order; derelict men, sodden and hopeless, with scrubby beards; shifty looking burglars and pickpockets. All these I beheld, at first with twinges of pity, later to mass them with the ugly and inevitable with whom society had to deal somehow. Lawyers, after all, must be practical men. I came to know the justices of these police courts, as well as other judges. And underlying my acquaintance with all of them was the knowledge —though not on the threshold of my consciousness—that they depended for their living, every man of them, those who were appointed and those who were elected, upon a political organization which derived its sustenance from the element whence came our clients. Thus by degrees the sense of belonging to a special priesthood had grown on me.

I recall an experience with that same Mr. Nathan. Weill, the wholesale grocer of whose commerce with the City Hall my Cousin Robert Breck had so bitterly complained. Late one afternoon Mr. Weill's carriage ran over a child on its way up-town through one of the poorer districts. The parents, naturally, were frantic, and the coachman was arrested. This was late in the afternoon, and I was alone in the office when the telephone rang. Hurrying to the police station, I found Mr. Weill in a state of excitement and abject fear, for an ugly crowd had gathered outside.

"Could not Mr. Watling or Mr. Fowndes come?" demanded the grocer.

With an inner contempt for the layman's state of mind on such occasions I assured him of my competency to handle the case. He was impressed, I think, by the sergeant's deference, who knew what it meant to have such an office as ours interfere with the affair. I called up the prosecuting attorney, who sent to Monahan's saloon, close by, and procured a release for the coachman on his own recognizance, one of many signed in blank and left there by the justice for privileged cases. The coachman was hustled out by a back door, and the crowd dispersed.

The next morning, while a score or more of delinquents sat in the anxious seats, Justice Garry recognized me and gave me precedence. And Mr. Weill, with a sigh of relief, paid his fine.

"Mr. Paret, is it?" he asked, as we stood together for a moment on the sidewalk outside the court. "You have managed this well. I will remember."

He was sued, of course. When he came to the office he insisted on discussing the case with Mr. Watling, who sent for me.

"That is a bright young man," Mr. Weill declared, shaking my hand. "He will get on."

"Some day," said Mr. Watling, "he may save you a lot of money, Weill."

"When my friend Mr. Watling is United States Senator,—eh?"

Mr. Watling laughed. "Before that, I hope. I advise you to compromise this suit, Weill," he added. "How would a thousand dollars strike you? I've had Paret look up the case, and he tells me the little girl has had to have an operation."

"A thousand dollars!" cried the grocer. "What right have these people to let their children play on the streets? It's an outrage."

"Where else have the children to play?" Mr. Watling touched his arm. "Weill," he said gently, "suppose it had been your little girl?" The grocer pulled out his handkerchief and mopped his bald forehead. But he rallied a little.

"You fight these damage cases for the street railroads all through the courts."

"Yes," Mr. Watling agreed, "but there a principle is involved. If the railroads once got into the way of paying damages for every careless employee, they would soon be bankrupt through blackmail. But here you have a child whose father is a poor janitor and can't afford sickness. And your coachman, I imagine, will be more particular in the future."

In the end Mr. Weill made out a cheque and departed in a good humour, convinced that he was well out of the matter. Here was one of many instances I could cite of Mr. Watling's tenderness of heart. I felt, moreover, as if he had done me a personal favour, since it was I who had recommended the compromise. For I had been to the hospital and had seen the child on the cot,—a dark little thing, lying still in her pain, with the bewildered look of a wounded animal....

Not long after this incident of Mr. Weill's damage suit I obtained a more or less definite promotion by the departure of Larry Weed. He had suddenly developed a weakness of the lungs. Mr. Watling got him a place in Denver, and paid his expenses west.

The first six or seven years I spent in the office of Wading, Fowndes and Ripon were of importance to my future career, but there is little to relate of them. I was absorbed not only in learning law, but in acquiring that esoteric knowledge at which I have hinted—not to be had from my seniors and which I was convinced was indispensable to a successful and lucrative practice. My former comparison of the organization of our city to a picture puzzle wherein the dominating figures become visible only after long study is rather inadequate. A better analogy would be the human anatomy: we lawyers, of course, were the brains; the financial and industrial interests the body, helpless without us; the City Hall politicians, the stomach that must continually be fed. All three, law, politics and business, were interdependent, united by a nervous system too complex to be developed here. In these years, though I worked hard and often late, I still found time for convivialities, for social gaieties, yet little by little without realizing the fact, I was losing zest for the companionship of my former intimates. My mind was becoming polarized by the contemplation of one object, success, and to it human ties were unconsciously being sacrificed.

Tom Peters began to feel this, even at a time when I believed myself still to be genuinely fond of him. Considering our respective temperaments in youth, it is curious that he should have been the first to fall in love and marry. One day he astonished me by announcing his engagement to Susan Blackwood.

"That ends the liquor, Hughie," he told me, beamingly. "I promised her
I'd eliminate it."

He did eliminate it, save for mild relapses on festive occasions. A more seemingly incongruous marriage could scarcely be imagined, and yet it was a success from the start. From a slim, silent, self-willed girl Susan had grown up into a tall, rather rawboned and energetic young woman. She was what we called in those days "intellectual," and had gone in for kindergartens, and after her marriage she turned out to be excessively domestic; practising her theories, with entire success, upon a family that showed a tendency to increase at an alarming rate. Tom, needless to say, did not become intellectual. He settled down—prematurely, I thought—into what is known as a family man, curiously content with the income he derived from the commission business and with life in general; and he developed a somewhat critical view of the tendencies of the civilization by which he was surrounded. Susan held it also, but she said less about it. In the comfortable but unpretentious house they rented on Cedar Street we had many discussions, after the babies had been put to bed and the door of the living-room closed, in order that our voices might not reach the nursery. Perry Blackwood, now Tom's brother-in-law, was often there. He, too, had lapsed into what I thought was an odd conservatism. Old Josiah, his father, being dead, he occupied himself mainly with looking after certain family interests, among which was the Boyne Street car line. Among "business men" he was already getting the reputation of being a little difficult to deal with. I was often the subject of their banter, and presently I began to suspect that they regarded my career and beliefs with some concern. This gave me no uneasiness, though at times I lost my temper. I realized their affection for me; but privately I regarded them as lacking in ambition, in force, in the fighting qualities necessary for achievement in this modern age. Perhaps, unconsciously, I pitied them a little.

"How is Judah B. to-day, Hughie?" Tom would inquire. "I hear you've put him up for the Boyne Club, now that Mr. Watling has got him out of that libel suit."

"Carter Ives is dead," Perry would add, sarcastically, "let bygones be bygones."

It was well known that Mr. Tallant, in the early days of his newspaper, had blackmailed Mr. Ives out of some hundred thousand dollars. And that this, more than any other act, stood in the way, with certain recalcitrant gentlemen, of his highest ambition, membership in the Boyne.

"The trouble with you fellows is that you refuse to deal with conditions as you find them," I retorted. "We didn't make them, and we can't change them. Tallant's a factor in the business life of this city, and he has to be counted with."

Tom would shake his head exasperatingly.

"Why don't you get after Ralph?" I demanded. "He doesn't antagonize Tallant, either."

"Ralph's hopeless," said Tom. "He was born a pirate, you weren't, Hughie.
We think there's a chance for his salvation, don't we, Perry?"

I refused to accept the remark as flattering.

Another object of their assaults was Frederick Grierson, who by this time had emerged from obscurity as a small dealer in real estate into a manipulator of blocks and corners.

"I suppose you think it's a lawyer's business to demand an ethical bill of health of every client," I said. "I won't stand up for all of Tallant's career, of course, but Mr. Wading has a clear right to take his cases. As for Grierson, it seems to me that's a matter of giving a dog a bad name. Just because his people weren't known here, and because he has worked up from small beginnings. To get down to hard-pan, you fellows don't believe in democracy,—in giving every man a chance to show what's in him."

"Democracy is good!" exclaimed Perry. "If the kind of thing we're coming to is democracy, God save the state!"…

On the other hand I found myself drawing closer to Ralph Hambleton, sometimes present at these debates, as the only one of my boyhood friends who seemed to be able to "deal with conditions as he found them." Indeed, he gave one the impression that, if he had had the making of them, he would not have changed them.

"What the deuce do you expect?" I once heard him inquire with good-natured contempt. "Business isn't charity, it's war.

"There are certain things," maintained Perry, stoutly, "that gentlemen won't do."

"Gentlemen!" exclaimed Ralph, stretching his slim six feet two: We were sitting in the Boyne Club. "It's ungentlemanly to kill, or burn a town or sink a ship, but we keep armies and navies for the purpose. For a man with a good mind, Perry, you show a surprising inability to think things, out to a logical conclusion. What the deuce is competition, when you come down to it? Christianity? Not by a long shot! If our nations are slaughtering men and starving populations in other countries,—are carried on, in fact, for the sake of business, if our churches are filled with business men and our sky pilots pray for the government, you can't expect heathen individuals like me to do business on a Christian basis,—if there is such a thing. You can make rules for croquet, but not for a game that is based on the natural law of the survival of the fittest. The darned fools in the legislatures try it occasionally, but we all know it's a sop to the 'common people.' Ask Hughie here if there ever was a law put on the statute books that his friend Watling couldn't get 'round'? Why, you've got competition even among the churches. Yours, where I believe you teach in the Sunday school, would go bankrupt if it proclaimed real Christianity. And you'll go bankrupt if you practise it, Perry, my boy. Some early, wide-awake, competitive, red-blooded bird will relieve you of the Boyne Street car line."

It was one of this same new and "fittest" species who had already relieved poor Mr. McAlery Willett of his fortune. Mr. Willett was a trusting soul who had never known how to take care of himself or his money, people said, and now that he had lost it they blamed him. Some had been saved enough for him and Nancy to live on in the old house, with careful economy. It was Nancy who managed the economy, who accomplished remarkable things with a sum they would have deemed poverty in former days. Her mother had died while I was at Cambridge. Reverses did not subdue Mr. Willett's spirits, and the fascination modern "business" had for him seemed to grow in proportion to the misfortunes it had caused him. He moved into a tiny office in the Durrett Building, where he appeared every morning about half-past ten to occupy himself with heaven knows what short cuts to wealth, with prospectuses of companies in Mexico or Central America or some other distant place: once, I remember, it was a tea, company in which he tried to interest his friends, to raise in the South a product he maintained would surpass Orange Pekoe. In the afternoon between three and four he would turn up at the Boyne Club, as well groomed, as spruce as ever, generally with a flower in his buttonhole. He never forgot that he was a gentleman, and he had a gentleman's notions of the fitness of things, and it was against his principles to use, a gentleman's club for the furtherance of his various enterprises.

"Drop into my office some day, Dickinson," he would say. "I think I've got something there that might interest you!"

He reminded me, when I met him, that he had always predicted I would get along in life....

The portrait of Nancy at this period is not so easily drawn. The decline of the family fortunes seemed to have had as little effect upon her as upon her father, although their characters differed sharply. Something of that spontaneity, of that love of life and joy in it she had possessed in youth she must have inherited from McAlery Willett, but these qualities had disappeared in her long before the coming of financial reverses. She was nearing thirty, and in spite of her beauty and the rarer distinction that can best be described as breeding, she had never married. Men admired her, but from a distance; she kept them at arm's length, they said: strangers who visited the city invariably picked her out of an assembly and asked who she was; one man from New York who came to visit Ralph and who had been madly in love with her, she had amazed many people by refusing, spurning all he might have given her. This incident seemed a refutation of the charge that she was calculating. As might have been foretold, she had the social gift in a remarkable degree, and in spite of the limitations of her purse the knack of dressing better than other women, though at that time the organization of our social life still remained comparatively simple, the custom of luxurious and expensive entertainment not having yet set in.

The more I reflect upon those days, the more surprising does it seem that I was not in love with her. It may be that I was, unconsciously, for she troubled my thoughts occasionally, and she represented all the qualities I admired in her sex. The situation that had existed at the time of our first and only quarrel had been reversed, I was on the highroad to the worldly success I had then resolved upon, Nancy was poor, and for that reason, perhaps, prouder than ever. If she was inaccessible to others, she had the air of being peculiarly inaccessible to me—the more so because some of the superficial relics of our intimacy remained, or rather had been restored. Her very manner of camaraderie seemed paradoxically to increase the distance between us. It piqued me. Had she given me the least encouragement, I am sure I should have responded; and I remember that I used occasionally to speculate as to whether she still cared for me, and took this method of hiding her real feelings. Yet, on the whole, I felt a certain complacency about it all; I knew that suffering was disagreeable, I had learned how to avoid it, and I may have had, deep within me, a feeling that I might marry her after all. Meanwhile my life was full, and gave promise of becoming even fuller, more absorbing and exciting in the immediate future.

One of the most fascinating figures, to me, of that Order being woven, like a cloth of gold, out of our hitherto drab civilization,—an Order into which I was ready and eager to be initiated,—was that of Adolf Scherer, the giant German immigrant at the head of the Boyne Iron Works. His life would easily lend itself to riotous romance. In the old country, in a valley below the castle perched on the rack above, he had begun life by tending his father's geese. What a contrast to "Steeltown" with its smells and sickening summer heat, to the shanty where Mrs. Scherer took boarders and bent over the wash-tub! She, too, was an immigrant, but lived to hear her native Wagner from her own box at Covent Garden; and he to explain, on the deck of an imperial yacht, to the man who might have been his sovereign certain processes in the manufacture of steel hitherto untried on that side of the Atlantic. In comparison with Adolf Scherer, citizen of a once despised democracy, the minor prince in whose dominions he had once tended geese was of small account indeed!

The Adolf Scherer of that day—though it is not so long ago as time flies—was even more solid and impressive than the man he afterwards became, when he reached the dizzier heights from which he delivered to an eager press opinions on politics and war, eugenics and woman's suffrage and other subjects that are the despair of specialists. Had he stuck to steel, he would have remained invulnerable. But even then he was beginning to abandon the field of production for that of exploitation: figuratively speaking, he had taken to soap, which with the aid of water may be blown into beautiful, iridescent bubbles to charm the eye. Much good soap, apparently, has gone that way, never to be recovered. Everybody who was anybody began to blow bubbles about that time, and the bigger the bubble the greater its attraction for investors of hard-earned savings. Outside of this love for financial iridescence, let it be called, Mr. Scherer seemed to care little then for glitter of any sort. Shortly after his elevation to the presidency of the Boyne Iron Works he had been elected a member of the Boyne Club, —an honour of which, some thought, he should have been more sensible; but generally, when in town, he preferred to lunch at a little German restaurant annexed to a saloon, where I used often to find him literally towering above the cloth,—for he was a giant with short legs,—his napkin tucked into his shirt front, engaged in lively conversation with the ministering Heinrich. The chef at the club, Mr. Scherer insisted, could produce nothing equal to Heinrich's sauer-kraut and sausage. My earliest relationship with Mr. Scherer was that of an errand boy, of bringing to him for his approval papers which might not be intrusted to a common messenger. His gruffness and brevity disturbed me more than I cared to confess. I was pretty sure that he eyed me with the disposition of the self-made to believe that college educations and good tailors were the heaviest handicaps with which a young man could be burdened: and I suspected him of an inimical attitude toward the older families of the city. Certain men possessed his confidence; and he had built, as it were, a stockade about them, sternly keeping the rest of the world outside. In Theodore Watling he had a childlike faith.

Thus I studied him, with a deliberation which it is the purpose of these chapters to confess, though he little knew that he was being made the subject of analysis. Nor did I ever venture to talk with him, but held strictly to my role of errand boy,—even after the conviction came over me that he was no longer indifferent to my presence. The day arrived, after some years, when he suddenly thrust toward me a big, hairy hand that held the document he was examining.

"Who drew this, Mr. Paret!" he demanded.

Mr. Ripon, I told him.

The Boyne Works were buying up coal-mines, and this was a contract looking to the purchase of one in Putman County, provided, after a certain period of working, the yield and quality should come up to specifications. Mr. Scherer requested me to read one of the sections, which puzzled him. And in explaining it an idea flashed over me.

"Do you mind my making a suggestion, Mr. Scherer?" I ventured.

"What is it?" he asked brusquely.

I showed him how, by the alteration of a few words, the difficulty to which he had referred could not only be eliminated, but that certain possible penalties might be evaded, while the apparent meaning of the section remained unchanged. In other words, it gave the Boyne Iron Works an advantage that was not contemplated. He seized the paper, stared at what I had written in pencil on the margin, and then stared at me. Abruptly, he began to laugh.

"Ask Mr. Wading what he thinks of it?"

"I intended to, provided it had your approval, sir," I replied.

"You have my approval, Mr. Paret," he declared, rather cryptically, and with the slight German hardening of the v's into which he relapsed at times. "Bring it to the Works this afternoon."

Mr. Wading agreed to the alteration. He looked at me amusedly.

"Yes, I think that's an improvement, Hugh," he said. I had a feeling that I had gained ground, and from this time on I thought I detected a change in his attitude toward me; there could be no doubt about the new attitude of Mr. Scherer, who would often greet me now with a smile and a joke, and sometimes went so far as to ask my opinions.... Then, about six months later, came the famous Ribblevale case that aroused the moral indignation of so many persons, among whom was Perry Blackwood.

"You know as well as I do, Hugh, how this thing is being manipulated," he declared at Tom's one Sunday evening; "there was nothing the matter with the Ribblevale Steel Company—it was as right as rain before Leonard Dickinson and Grierson and Scherer and that crowd you train with began to talk it down at the Club. Oh, they're very compassionate. I've heard 'em. Dickinson, privately, doesn't think much of Ribblevale paper, and Pugh" (the president of the Ribblevale) "seems worried and looks badly. It's all very clever, but I'd hate to tell you in plain words what I'd call it."

"Go ahead," I challenged him audaciously. "You haven't any proof that the
Ribblevale wasn't in trouble."

"I heard Mr. Pugh tell my father the other day it was a d—d outrage. He couldn't catch up with these rumours, and some of his stockholders were liquidating."

"You, don't suppose Pugh would want to admit his situation, do you?" I asked.

"Pugh's a straight man," retorted Perry. "That's more than I can say for any of the other gang, saving your presence. The unpleasant truth is that Scherer and the Boyne people want the Ribblevale, and you ought to know it if you don't." He looked at me very hard through the glasses he had lately taken to wearing. Tom, who was lounging by the fire, shifted his position uneasily. I smiled, and took another cigar.

"I believe Ralph is right, Perry, when he calls you a sentimentalist. For you there's a tragedy behind every ordinary business transaction. The Ribblevale people are having a hard time to keep their heads above water, and immediately you smell conspiracy. Dickinson and Scherer have been talking it down. How about it, Tom?"

But Tom, in these debates, was inclined to be noncommittal, although it was clear they troubled him.

"Oh, don't ask me, Hughie," he said.

"I suppose I ought to cultivate the scientific point of view, and look with impartial interest at this industrial cannibalism," returned Perry, sarcastically. "Eat or be eaten that's what enlightened self-interest has come to. After all, Ralph would say, it is nature, the insect world over again, the victim duped and crippled before he is devoured, and the lawyer—how shall I put it?—facilitating the processes of swallowing and digesting...."

There was no use arguing with Perry when he was in this vein....

Since I am not writing a technical treatise, I need not go into the details of the Ribblevale suit. Since it to say that the affair, after a while, came apparently to a deadlock, owing to the impossibility of getting certain definite information from the Ribblevale books, which had been taken out of the state. The treasurer, for reasons of his own, remained out of the state also; the ordinary course of summoning him before a magistrate in another state had naturally been resorted to, but the desired evidence was not forthcoming.

"The trouble is," Mr. Wading explained to Mr. Scherer, "that there is no law in the various states with a sufficient penalty attached that will compel the witness to divulge facts he wishes to conceal."

It was the middle of a February afternoon, and they were seated in deep, leather chairs in one corner of the reading room of the Boyne Club. They had the place to themselves. Fowndes was there also, one leg twisted around the other in familiar fashion, a bored look on his long and sallow face. Mr. Wading had telephoned to the office for me to bring them some papers bearing on the case.

"Sit down, Hugh," he said kindly.

"Now we have present a genuine legal mind," said Mr. Scherer, in the playful manner he had adopted of late, while I grinned appreciatively and took a chair. Mr. Watling presently suggested kidnapping the Ribblevale treasurer until he should promise to produce the books as the only way out of what seemed an impasse. But Mr. Scherer brought down a huge fist on his knee.

"I tell you it is no joke, Watling, we've got to win that suit," he asserted.

"That's all very well," replied Mr. Watling. "But we're a respectable firm, you know. We haven't had to resort to safe-blowing, as yet."

Mr. Scherer shrugged his shoulders, as much as to say it were a matter of indifference to him what methods were resorted to. Mr. Watling's eyes met mine; his glance was amused, yet I thought I read in it a query as to the advisability, in my presence, of going too deeply into the question of ways and means. I may have been wrong. At any rate, its sudden effect was to embolden me to give voice to an idea that had begun to simmer in my mind, that excited me, and yet I had feared to utter it. This look of my chief's, and the lighter tone the conversation had taken decided me.

"Why wouldn't it be possible to draw up a bill to fit the situation?" I inquired.

Mr. Wading started.

"What do you mean?" he asked quickly.

All three looked at me. I felt the blood come into my face, but it was too late to draw back.

"Well—the legislature is in session. And since, as Mr. Watlin says, there is no sufficient penalty in other states to compel the witness to produce the information desired, why not draw up a bill and—and have it passed—" I paused for breath—"imposing a sufficient penalty on home corporations in the event of such evasions. The Ribblevale Steel Company is a home corporation."

I had shot my bolt.... There followed what was for me an anxious silence, while the three of them continued to stare at me. Mr. Watling put the tips of his fingers together, and I became aware that he was not offended, that he was thinking rapidly.

"By George, why not, Fowndes?" he demanded.

"Well," said Fowndes, "there's an element of risk in such a proceeding I need not dwell upon."

"Risk!" cried the senior partner vigorously. "There's risk in everything. They'll howl, of course. But they howl anyway, and nobody ever listens to them. They'll say it's special legislation, and the Pilot will print sensational editorials for a few days. But what of it? All of that has happened before. I tell you, if we can't see those books, we'll lose the suit. That's in black and white. And, as a matter of justice, we're entitled to know what we want to know."

"There might be two opinions as to that," observed Fowndes, with his sardonic smile.

Mr. Watling paid no attention to this remark. He was already deep in thought. It was characteristic of his mind to leap forward, seize a suggestion that often appeared chimerical to a man like Fowndes and turn it into an accomplished Fact. "I believe you've hit it, Hugh," he said. "We needn't bother about the powers of the courts in other states. We'll put into this bill an appeal to our court for an order on the clerk to compel the witness to come before the court and testify, and we'll provide for a special commissioner to take depositions in the state where the witness is. If the officers of a home corporation who are outside of the state refuse to testify, the penalty will be that the ration goes into the hands of a receiver."

Fowndes whistled.

"That's going some!" he said.

"Well, we've got to go some. How about it, Scherer?"

Even Mr. Scherer's brown eyes were snapping.

"We have got to win that suit, Watling."

We were all excited, even Fowndes, I think, though he remained expressionless. Ours was the tense excitement of primitive man in chase: the quarry which had threatened to elude us was again in view, and not unlikely to fall into our hands. Add to this feeling, on my part, the thrill that it was I who had put them on the scent. I had all the sensations of an aspiring young brave who for the first time is admitted to the councils of the tribe!

"It ought to be a popular bill, too," Mr. Schemer was saying, with a smile of ironic appreciation at the thought of demagogues advocating it. "We should have one of Lawler's friends introduce it."

"Oh, we shall have it properly introduced," replied Mr. Wading.

"It may come back at us," suggested Fowndes pessimistically. "The Boyne
Iron Works is a home corporation too, if I am not mistaken."

"The Boyne Iron Works has the firm of Wading, Fowndes and Ripon behind it," asserted Mr. Scherer, with what struck me as a magnificent faith.

"You mustn't forget Paret," Mr. Watling reminded him, with a wink at me.

We had risen. Mr. Scherer laid a hand on my arm.

"No, no, I do not forget him. He will not permit me to forget him."

A remark, I thought, that betrayed some insight into my character... Mr. Watling called for pen and paper and made then and there a draft of the proposed bill, for no time was to be lost. It was dark when we left the Club, and I recall the elation I felt and strove to conceal as I accompanied my chief back to the office. The stenographers and clerks were gone; alone in the library we got down the statutes and set to work. to perfect the bill from the rough draft, on which Mr. Fowndes had written his suggestions. I felt that a complete yet subtle change had come over my relationship with Mr. Watling.

In the midst of our labours he asked me to call up the attorney for the Railroad. Mr. Gorse was still at his office.

"Hello! Is that you, Miller?" Mr. Watling said. "This is Wading. When can
I see you for a few minutes this evening? Yes, I am leaving for
Washington at nine thirty. Eight o'clock. All right, I'll be there."

It was almost eight before he got the draft finished to his satisfaction, and I had picked it out on the typewriter. As I handed it to him, my chief held it a moment, gazing at me with an odd smile.

"You seem to have acquired a good deal of useful knowledge, here and there, Hugh," he observed.

"I've tried to keep my eyes open, Mr. Watling," I said.

"Well," he said, "there are a great many things a young man practising law in these days has to learn for himself. And if I hadn't given you credit for some cleverness, I shouldn't have wanted you here. There's only one way to look at—at these matters we have been discussing, my boy, that's the common-sense way, and if a man doesn't get that point of view by himself, nobody can teach it to him. I needn't enlarge upon it"

"No, sir," I said.

He smiled again, but immediately became serious.

"If Mr. Gorse should approve of this bill, I'm going to send you down to the capital—to-night. Can you go?"

I nodded.

"I want you to look out for the bill in the legislature. Of course there won't be much to do, except to stand by, but you will get a better idea of what goes on down there."

I thanked him, and told him I would do my best.

"I'm sure of that," he replied. "Now it's time to go to see Gorse."

The legal department of the Railroad occupied an entire floor of the Corn Bank building. I had often been there on various errands, having on occasions delivered sealed envelopes to Mr. Gorse himself, approaching him in the ordinary way through a series of offices. But now, following Mr. Watling through the dimly lighted corridor, we came to a door on which no name was painted, and which was presently opened by a stenographer. There was in the proceeding a touch of mystery that revived keenly my boyish love for romance; brought back the days when I had been, in turn, Captain Kidd and Ali Baba.

I have never realized more strongly than in that moment the psychological force of prestige. Little by little, for five years, an estimate of the extent of Miller Gorse's power had been coming home to me, and his features stood in my mind for his particular kind of power. He was a tremendous worker, and often remained in his office until ten and eleven at night. He dismissed the stenographer by the wave of a hand which seemed to thrust her bodily out of the room.

"Hello, Miller," said Mr. Watling.

"Hello, Theodore," replied Mr. Gorse.

"This is Paret, of my office."

"I know," said Mr. Gorse, and nodded toward me. I was impressed by the felicity with which a cartoonist of the Pilot had once caricatured him by the use of curved lines. The circle of the heavy eyebrows ended at the wide nostrils; the mouth was a crescent, but bowed downwards; the heavy shoulders were rounded. Indeed, the only straight line to be discerned about him was that of his hair, black as bitumen, banged across his forehead; even his polished porphyry eyes were constructed on some curvilinear principle, and never seemed to focus. It might be said of Mr. Gorse that he had an overwhelming impersonality. One could never be quite sure that one's words reached the mark.

In spite of the intimacy which I knew existed between them, in my presence at least Mr. Gorse's manner was little different with Mr. Watling than it was with other men. Mr. Wading did not seem to mind. He pulled up a chair close to the desk and began, without any preliminaries, to explain his errand.

"It's about the Ribblevale affair," he said. "You know we have a suit."

Gorse nodded.

"We've got to get at the books, Miller,—that's all there is to it. I told you so the other day. Well, we've found out a way, I think."

He thrust his hand in his pocket, while the railroad attorney remained impassive, and drew out the draft of the bill. Mr. Gorse read it, then read it over again, and laid it down in front of him.

"Well," he said.

"I want to put that through both houses and have the governor's signature to it by the end of the week."

"It seems a little raw, at first sight, Theodore," said Mr. Gorse, with the suspicion of a smile.

My chief laughed a little.

"It's not half so raw as some things I might mention, that went through like greased lightning," he replied. "What can they do? I believe it will hold water. Tallant's, and most of the other newspapers in the state, won't print a line about it, and only Socialists and Populists read the Pilot. They're disgruntled anyway. The point is, there's no other way out for us. Just think a moment, bearing in mind what I've told you about the case, and you'll see it."

Mr. Gorse took up the paper again, and read the draft over.

"You know as well as I do, Miller, how dangerous it is to leave this Ribblevale business at loose ends. The Carlisle steel people and the Lake

Shore road are after the Ribblevale Company, and we can't afford to run any risk of their getting it. It's logically a part of the Boyne interests, as Scherer says, and Dickinson is ready with the money for the reorganization. If the Carlisle people and the Lake Shore get it, the product will be shipped out by the L and G, and the Railroad will lose. What would Barbour say?"

Mr. Barbour, as I have perhaps mentioned, was the president of the Railroad, and had his residence in the other great city of the state. He was then, I knew, in the West.

"We've got to act now," insisted Mr. Watling. "That's open and shut. If you have any other plan, I wish you'd trot it out. If not, I want a letter to Paul Varney and the governor. I'm going to send Paret down with them on the night train."

It was clear to me then, in the discussion following, that Mr. Watling's gift of persuasion, though great, was not the determining factor in Mr. Gorse's decision. He, too, possessed boldness, though he preferred caution. Nor did the friendship between the two enter into the transaction. I was impressed more strongly than ever with the fact that a lawsuit was seldom a mere private affair between two persons or corporations, but involved a chain of relationships and nine times out of ten that chain led up to the Railroad, which nearly always was vitally interested in these legal contests. Half an hour of masterly presentation of the situation was necessary before Mr. Gorse became convinced that the introduction of the bill was the only way out for all concerned.

"Well, I guess you're right, Theodore," he said at length. Whereupon he seized his pen and wrote off two notes with great rapidity. These he showed to Mr. Watling, who nodded and returned them. They were folded and sealed, and handed to me. One was addressed to Colonel Paul Varney, and the other to the Hon. W. W. Trulease, governor of the state.

"You can trust this young man?" demanded Mr. Gorse.

"I think so," replied Mr. Watling, smiling at me. "The bill was his own idea."

The railroad attorney wheeled about in his chair and looked at me; looked around me, would better express it, with his indefinite, encompassing yet inclusive glance. I had riveted his attention. And from henceforth, I knew, I should enter into his calculations. He had made for me a compartment in his mind.

"His own idea!" he repeated.

"I merely suggested it," I was putting in, when he cut me short.

"Aren't you the son of Matthew Paret?"

"Yes," I said.

He gave me a queer glance, the significance of which I left untranslated. My excitement was too great to analyze what he meant by this mention of my father....

When we reached the sidewalk my chief gave me a few parting instructions.

"I need scarcely say, Hugh," he added, "that your presence in the capital should not be advertised as connected with this—legislation. They will probably attribute it to us in the end, but if you're reasonably careful, they'll never be able to prove it. And there's no use in putting our cards on the table at the beginning."

"No indeed, sir!" I agreed.

He took my hand and pressed it.

"Good luck," he said. "I know you'll get along all right."

END OF Ashed Phoenix Library'S A FAR COUNTRY, BOOK 1, BY WINSTON CHURCHILL

Lightning Source UK Ltd.
Milton Keynes UK
UKHW020212230219
337868UK00009B/184/P